I will not live to see you grow to womanhood, so I have written my story for you, my beloved grandchild, so that you can know the truth of what happened here so many years ago. I'm sure that in the course of your life you have wondered about whispered conversations that stop when you are near. Wondered too about the knowing looks cast at you and your family. I am equally sure that your father has never found it in his heart to tell you the truth you are about to read. I beg you not to be angry with him for withholding the truth from you. He has suffered greatly for my sins.

The biggest fact of my life is this. I have been an outcast. I'm kin to just about everybody for miles around McNairy Station, but in the many webbed network of cousins, double cousins and kissing cousins that is the heart beat of every Southerner, you won't find many, even now, who will admit to it. Most have never forgiven the large and ugly blot I cast on that spotless roll call of kinship. They turned their backs to me in moral outrage many years ago. Most never looked me in the eye again, or reached out to help me in the years that followed.

Kate's Pride

by

Reneé Russell

A Wings ePress, Inc.

General Fiction Novel

Wings ePress, Inc.

Edited by: Leslie Hodges
Copy Edited by: Elizabeth Struble
Senior Editor: Dianne Hamilton
Managing Editor: Leslie Hodges
Executive Editor: Lorraine Stephens
Cover Artist: Gerald Jarnagan

All rights reserved

Names, characters and incidents depicted in this book are products of the author's imagination or are used fictitiously. Any resemblance to actual events, locales, organizations, or persons, living or dead, is entirely coincidental and beyond the intent of the author or the publisher.

No part of this book may be reproduced or transmitted in any form or by any means, electronic or mechanical, including photocopying, recording, or by any information storage and retrieval system, without permission in writing from the publisher.

Wings ePress Books
http://www.wings-press.com

Copyright © 2007 by Susan Jarnagan
ISBN 1-59705-918-8
978-1-59705-918-3

Published In the United States Of America

January 2007

Wings ePress Inc.
403 Wallace Court
Richmond, KY 40475

Dedication

For Gerald,

who always knew I could.

Prologue

"Ashes to ashes, dust to dust..."

The hole gaped in the dark red clay like a hungry mouth waiting to be fed. To one side stood a small group of poorly clad people, defying a frigid winter wind, grief etching their wind chapped faces. Pulling coats and scarves tight around them, shifting their frozen feet, they listened in silence broken only by the wind as Reverend Thatcher read the service through chattering teeth. All eyes were fixed on the cheap pine box that sat above the gaping hole. All eyes except for those of one man whose broad shoulders were bowed with sorrow under a threadbare coat.

Sherman Randsome's mind did not focus on the service, though it was his mother being buried here today. The wind blew his black hair awry, chapping his chiseled face to the color of a ripe tomato. His steely blue eyes refused to gaze at the pine box above the hole that waited to receive the mortal remains. His ears did not register the faltering efforts of the Reverend. His body stood here, but his mind drifted back at home. Locked on the manuscript his mother had left with him. Her dying wish, his promise that he would give it to his oldest daughter when she had grown up. Dread twisted his guts. He burned to read those pages, yet feared that he already knew their content. He'd intended to read those pages right away, but attending to the details of his mother's death had kept him too busy.

Her final hour rose in his memory, scalding him despite the cold wind.

The small room lit only by a flickering tallow candle on a packing crate that served as a table. The iron bed on which his mother lay, wasted by illness. Her soft voice reaching out to caress him as she spoke, "You've been a good son, Sherman. I've always been proud of you. I just want you to promise me one last thing."

Reaching out, he had taken his mother's small, cold hands into his large, warm, callused ones. Her too thin face was framed by dark hair, which had lost its fullness and luster. Her bright blue-grey eyes were dimmed now by sickness. Knowing she wouldn't last through the night, he answered gently, "What is it, Mama? What do you want me to do for you?"

Kate had removed her hands from Sherman's and lifted the heavy sheaf of papers that lay beside her on the faded patchwork quilt.

"I want you to give this to Mary Susan when she's grown. It's all I have to leave to her. Promise me you'll do that for me, son."

Her fever bright eyes bored into his own as he hesitated to give her his promise. He feared what might be contained within those pages. Feared that those closely written words were truths he intended to keep from his children.

Reluctantly he said the words he knew she wanted to hear, "I promise, Mama."

Once the words were uttered, she had smiled and nodded her head. His unease increased to a level where he felt she must be able to read it on his face, but she lay back tiredly on her pillow. He reached out and brushed her cheek lightly as he said, "You just rest easy now. I'll stay here right by you."

Kate closed her tired eyes and rested as well as she could. Her breath rattled in her throat as she struggled to take in air. Eventually, she fell into a restless doze. A short while later, the rattling breaths stopped. Sherman knew she was gone. He bent over, kissed her forehead and whispered, "Goodbye, Mama."

Crossing her hands on her chest, he pulled her old quilt gently up over her face.

The shuffling of feet caught Sherman's attention. He realized the service was over and all eyes were on him. He hadn't listened as his mother was laid to rest. A wave of guilt rushed over him. She had loved him fiercely all his life and he hadn't even shown respect for her at her funeral. The curiosity that had eaten at him ever since he had first held those pages his mother had written would not let go of him. He had loved her dearly and now she was lost to him forever.

The mourners moved toward him to share final condolences. Old Mr. McIntosh came first. Bent now from rheumatism, he walked awkwardly over the uneven ground with the aid of a cane. Grasping Sherman by the arm, he mutely shook his head and stumped away, but not before Sherman had seen the shine of tears in the old man's eyes. Other people whom he'd known all his life offered their sympathies. Cousin Emily who had shared a home with them when he was a young boy. His cousin Rufus, who had defied his immediate family to come here. They all spoke kindly of his mother and offered their help if he should need any.

Finally, Sherman stood alone at the side of his mother's grave. The marker for his older brother John had been moved aside temporarily. It would be replaced after his mother's name and dates of birth and death had been engraved on it. Kate had insisted on taking in washing and mending for months in order to earn the money to buy that stone. Now it would serve as her marker also. He could not afford another one. Mother and brother both gone now. Both to lie here in this lonely cemetery for all eternity. He supposed that someday he and his family would lie here also, sleeping through the ages. He was the last of them now. They should have had so many more years together. John had been barely a man when murder had taken him to an early grave. His mother barely sixty.

He dropped to his knees, the impact of the cold hard ground sending jolts of pain up his thighs to his back. Dropping his head, raising his hands to cover his ravaged face, he fought back the urge to howl his grief and denial aloud for all to hear. When he finally raised his head, the setting sun refracted off the tears gathered in his eyes. For one brief moment he saw her standing before him, as she had been when he was a young boy. Always energetic and cheerful, her bright eyes and exuberant laugh making light of their poverty. The sun dropped minutely in the sky and the vision vanished. He shook his head sadly; wiping the weak tears from his eyes and slowly made his way back to the church where his family waited for him.

His wife, Josie, laid her hand softly on his arm as her eyes met his. The sorrow and empathy he saw there were almost more than he could bear. Turning gruffly from her, he motioned his family to follow. His daughters, Mary Susan and Johnnie, looked uncertainly after the stone-faced stranger who was their father, then hid their small faces in their mother's skirts. She pulled them gently back and gave them a reassuring smile while pulling them toward their wagon.

~ * ~

Going home in the wagon drawn by a lop-eared mule, Sherman remained silent. The lowering sun set fire to the western sky and threw the pine forest that edged the road into deep shadows. The wagon lurched drunkenly in and out of frozen ruts in the hardpack dirt track.

When they arrived at the clapboard farmhouse they rented, Josie hustled the girls inside, leaving Sherman to unhitch the mule. The burning curiosity that had consumed him seemed to go out. Now that the moment was here to read what his mother had written, he was afraid. *What ghosts would rise up from those pages?*

He found himself currying the mule slowly, taking his time over the task. Dragging the metal comb slowly across the rough hide, following it with a handful of straw to absorb sweat marks and knock off loose dirt, the simple chore somehow hypnotic in its measured strokes. Soon there was no more to be done, no more excuse for delay. When he left the shed, the fiery evening sky had faded to total darkness. A million stars twinkled like distant beacons in the frosty night calling him to some unknown destination. His breath clouded before his face as he walked toward the house. Entering reluctantly, he saw that Josie had fed the girls an early supper and sent them to the loft where they slept, then undressed and gotten into bed herself, leaving the warm front room vacant for him.

~ * ~

After gently closing the bedroom door, he retrieved the manuscript from its hiding place in the pie safe. Sitting in his favorite worn Windsor chair, he looked more closely at the papers he held. In his heart he knew what the pages contained. Reading slowly, he was unaware of the tears streaming down his face, dropping from his square jaw onto the pages, smudging the ink and soaking into the cheap, coarse paper.

December 1901
To My Granddaughter, Mary Susan,

I will not live to see you grow to womanhood, so I have written my story for you, my beloved grandchild, so that you can know the truth of what happened here so many years ago. I'm sure that in the course of your life you have wondered about whispered conversations that stop when you are near. Wondered too about the knowing looks cast at you and your family. I am equally sure that your father has never found it in his heart to tell you the truth you are about to read. I beg you not to be angry with him for withholding the truth from you. He has suffered greatly for my sins.

The biggest fact of my life is this. I have been an outcast. I'm kin to just about everybody for miles around McNairy Station, but in the many webbed network of cousins, double cousins and kissing cousins that is the heart beat of every Southerner, you won't find many, even now, who will admit to it. Most have never forgiven the large and ugly blot I cast on that spotless roll call of kinship. They turned their backs to me in moral outrage many years ago. Most never looked me in the eye again, or reached out to help me in the years that followed.

The first shattering event in my life was the War Between The States. My brother, George, and I were all that was left on the big Randsome family farm by the time it was all over. We were reduced to scratching a living from the hard red clay that had once been covered in the finest cotton. We scraped by, growing vegetables to eat and managing to plant a few acres of cotton to sell. I saw the rest of my life as one of backbreaking work in return for just enough to remain this side of the grave. From time to time George would talk about selling the farm for whatever we could get and going west to start a new life. When I protested leaving McNairy Station, he told me he would give me part of the money from the sale of the farm and I could move in with some of the family if I was so set against leaving. But, my heart was set on staying here where I was born and had grown up.

It was then that the second, and most pivotal, event occurred in my life. I fell in love with a man who was a charming liar. Michael stopped in McNairy Station on his way home to Middle Tennessee. He struck up a conversation with George at the general store and when he found out that George was trying to run our farm single-handedly, he offered to help work the cotton in exchange for room and board and a small share of the profit when the cotton was sold. He told George that he had no family and would eventually return to his home when he had saved a little money. George hated farming and it was only with the help of our brother-in-law that we had managed to get by for so long. They shook hands on the deal. After George told me about Michael and that he would be staying in the loft of the old barn, I took a few things I thought he might find useful and went to the barn

He was like a breath of fresh air to me. From the moment I first saw his face, I was lost. My gaze traveled from his raven black, curly hair to his beautiful blue eyes and I saw something there that I hadn't seen in a man's eyes in a very long time. It was admiration. All the sermons I had heard in church regarding carnal knowledge came flooding into my mind and my face burned with shame. He took one look at my flaming cheeks and no doubt knew every thought that was passing through my head.

George took to Michael in a way that seemed almost hero worship. They became as close as brothers in no time at all. While Michael's relationship with George grew, so did his relationship with me. Soon he was staying after dinner to sit in the parlor with George and me. I could almost imagine that there had been no war and that the shabby parlor still held the fine rugs and fine porcelain from the old days. That my parents were sitting in the other room and that my mother was happily imagining my wedding and the faces of her future grandchildren. I was busy doing my own imagining. A ceremony at the church where I would become Michael's wife with all our friends and neighbors looking on, then joining us at the farm for a party that would last all night. I could almost hear the fiddles playing and feel the rush of wind stirred up by the dancers.

It wasn't long before Michael started escorting me to church socials and barn dances. I was hoping that when Michael eventually asked me to marry him that we would stay here and George would give us part of the family farm as a wedding gift or even all of it, since I knew he still secretly longed to leave the area. There wasn't a cloud on the horizon as far as I could see. I lived through those days and nights in complete happiness.

As the weeks and months went by Michael gradually persuaded me down the road to carnal knowledge. We met in the barn at night after George had gone to sleep. He took his time seducing me. Finally, I gave myself to him completely. I couldn't seem to say "no" to Michael. It was as if he had taken possession of my will. He swore that he loved me. That we would be married. He persuaded me that when two people loved as deeply as we did that it wasn't a sin to consummate that love. I was so deeply in love with him that I deliberately ignored everything I had been taught about correct behavior. Of course the worst came to pass. I remember the day I told Michael and the disaster that followed. That sweet summer of 1867, the last really happy one I knew for many, many years...

One

Kate Randsome held her emotions in tight control as she searched the farm for Michael. He was not in the house, where a peach pie, cooking for supper, scented the air. Not in the cotton fields where several acres of the fluffy white stuff reached verdant arms to the sky for sustenance. As she searched, apprehension chewed at the bonds holding her emotions in check. Michael had not left the farm. She would find him soon. At last, she found him in the barn mucking out the stall that belonged to the one mule that they managed to keep. Watching him from the doorway, she felt panic welling up. She shook her head to clear away the unwanted feeling, then stepped further into the barn. Michael didn't look up from his task. Her feet had made hardly a sound on the hard packed earthen floor.

Maintaining her outward calm she spoke, "Michael, we have to git married right away". *Knowing* that it was the wrong way to go about this all important conversation, but unable to lead up to it more gracefully.

He looked up, startled, then smiled the beautiful smile that she so loved. His face was red from exertion. Sweat ran in rivers from his hairline. Even on this early spring evening, the temperature inside the barn was stifling. Though he was smiling, there was a look in his eyes that made her throat go dry, but when he spoke his voice was loving and gentle.

"My darling, I thought we agreed to wait until we have some money so we can make the wedding the most special day of our lives.

Cain't you wait a few more months, my greedy girl?"

She tried desperately to hold on to her outwardly calm appearance; though her heart was beating so hard she was surprised he couldn't hear it. She must persuade him. The alternative was too painful to contemplate. Her entire future balanced on the outcome of this conversation.

"Yes, we did, but I'm going to have a baby. We have to git married right away. Everyone will be counting on their fingers as it is because we'll be getting married so sudden. Don't you want our child to be born in wedlock?"

His face went a peculiar shade of white under his tan. He staggered back, his eyes skittering from side to side. His hands convulsed on the handle of the shovel he held and the knuckles turned white.

Seeing his reaction, Kate's knees started shaking under her skirt. Her palms were suddenly sweaty. She rubbed them against her skirt and moistened her dry lips. An edge of panic crept into her voice.

"Michael, you swore you loved me and that we would be married. We have to marry now instead of waiting for the crop to be picked. Tell me you'll go to Reverend Thatcher and arrange for the wedding."

He finally focused his eyes on her. The stranglehold on the shovel loosened and he tossed it aside. His beautiful smile bloomed across his face and he came swiftly forward to hold her tightly in his arms. Relief flooded through her at his next words.

"Of course I will, darling. I was just so startled for a minute there. Go on back to the house now. When I come to dinner tonight we'll tell George our good news. I'll go talk to Reverend Thatcher right now and arrange for the date. I love you, dearest girl."

After planting a swift kiss on her lips, Michael walked out of the barn and Kate went back to the house. The rest of that afternoon her heart brimmed with happiness. Michael would marry her. The relief was enormous. She took special pains with the food for dinner that night because she knew she would remember it always. She hummed little melodies as she went about her work.

When George came in for dinner, he immediately noticed the silver candelabra that she had unearthed from an old trunk and placed on the table to give it a more festive appearance. Sniffing at the fragrant cooking smells, he looked at Kate and laughed.

"Let me guess. Michael has finally asked to marry you and there's a wedding in the future."

Excitement shone from Kate's cornflower blue eyes like the flames of two brightly burning candles. She almost danced around the kitchen. "Oh George! Michael and I are going to be married right away. He's gone to talk to Reverend Thatcher about the date."

"Well, I'll be glad to welcome Michael to the family, he's a fine man and he's really been a big help with the cotton. I'm glad the two of you are getting married, but why the rush? You should wait until the cotton crop is picked. Then we'll have a little money and I can give you away with a little style."

Kate looked out across the field in the direction that Michael should be returning, but saw no sign of him. She didn't want to tell George the news without Michael beside her.

"Kate? Did you hear me? Why the rush?"

"We're just so much in love that we don't want to wait any longer. I'm glad that you approve. I cain't imagine what's keeping him. I reckon we'll have to start eating without him or everything'll get cold." A half-truth sat better on her conscience than a lie. She wanted Michael standing next to her, standing up to George and proclaiming his love for her, when George found out about the baby.

They sat down to eat, George talking on and on about the cotton and how he thought they might get a little more ahead this year because Michael had been around to help plant a larger crop. He made plans for planting even more next year because he knew for sure now that Michael would still be here.

Kate couldn't focus on George's conversation. The delicious food she had prepared with such joy stuck in her throat and tasted like sawdust. Where was Michael? He should have been here long before now. She began worrying that something had happened to him. Imagining that a wild dog had attacked him and he lay bleeding and alone in the woods nearby. Or maybe he had fallen and had a broken leg and was waiting patiently for help to arrive. She shook her head to clear away the unwanted images.

Finally George noticed she wasn't paying attention to him and said, "Where the devil is Michael? He couldn't possibly still be at Reverend Thatcher's. It's after nine!"

"I'm sure he just got held up somewhere," she replied evasively. "He'll be here soon. Why don't you go on to bed? You have to be up with the sun tomorrow morning. We'll just celebrate tomorrow night instead."

She spoke in a positive tone to her brother, but doubt was creeping slowly along the pathways of her mind. What could be keeping Michael so long? *Please, God, let him come home soon.* She would never doubt him again, in all her life, if only he would walk through the door and smile at her right now. She looked hard at the door, as if by concentrating all her thoughts on it would make Michael appear there. George's edgy tone broke into her concentration.

"Well, It just seems awful peculiar to me. Michael's never missed dinner before. And he has to get up just as early as I do. Humph! You just tell him not to be trying to sleep late in the morning. I hope he's not going to expect anything to be different just because he's going to be my brother-in-law."

She knew he meant that last part to be a joke, but, suddenly, she just wanted him out of the room. She felt a chill begin around her heart and knew that George would pry the truth out of her if he had any idea that she was upset. She promised to pass along the message and he finally went to his room.

She went out onto the porch and sat in a rocking chair to wait, keeping her lonely vigil through the long, dark hours of the night. Relentlessly she pushed away the buzzing thoughts that swarmed through her mind, accusing her of being the worst kind of fool. When the sun began to paint the eastern sky a gentle pink, she knew without a doubt that Michael was gone. He had run off so he wouldn't have to marry her.

Running down the porch steps and across the yard, she sought a place to hide from her brother. He would be full of questions that she didn't want to answer and some that she couldn't answer. As she ran, all the hounds of Hell snapped and snarled at her heels and the roar of Hellfire echoed in her head like maniacal laughter.

~ * ~

She stayed hidden until the sun began to kiss the horizon, nursing her pain like an injured animal gone to earth. Hiding while visions of horror paraded across her mind. She had broken the rigid moral code of society. As soon as her shame became known, she would begin to pay for the rest of her life. She would be outcast by everyone. She knew that George was probably already worried about her. If she didn't show up soon he would be frantic. With reluctant steps, she went home to face him.

"Where the Hell have you been?" George shouted as soon as he saw her coming across the yard. "I've been worried sick all day. Michael's not here either. I thought the two of you had run off together! Just took off and left me with the burden of this miserable farm all on my own!"

He was worried about being stuck with the farm. Kate couldn't help it. She burst into hysterical laughter, then began crying at the same time. George was aghast. She could see that he didn't have any idea what to do, but she couldn't seem to control herself. She stumbled into the house, found the sofa and managed to sit down. George came to sit next to her, putting his arm around her, concern in his eyes.

"What's the matter, Kate? Has something happened to Michael? Is that it? Please calm down and talk to me. You're scaring me to death!"

As she continued to laugh and cry hysterically, he lost patience and shook her roughly by the shoulders. Her head snapped back and forth. She lost her breath for a minute, then was finally able to control herself. Drawing air deep into her lungs, she told him, "Michael's gone. I don't know where. I only wish that I did."

"*What?*" George looked shocked. "He's gone?" Then in a bewildered tone, "But I thought the two of you were gittin' married.

She had no choice but to tell him. "No, George. He's gone and he's not coming back. I couldn't tell you last night because I wanted Michael to be with me when you found out. I'm going to have his baby. That's why there was going to be a rushed wedding. I guess he just couldn't face what's happened and that's why he left."

The shocked disbelief on his face weighed on her already raw heart. They'd been through so much together and now he had to handle this. He'd had to become a man overnight when their parents died. Now at nineteen, he was shouldering the burden of trying to bring the once fertile acres of their land back to something that would produce a living for the two of them. She was afraid he would break under the strain of what she had told him.

"You're having a baby! Oh my God, Kate." he bellowed. " What were you thinking? What possessed you to give yourself to a man without being married first? You can't possibly be having a baby. Dear Lord, what have you done to us all?"

"I am going to have a baby, and Michael's gone," she explained again. "He won't be coming back. He lied to me, George. He swore to me that he loved me and that we would be married. He probably would have had some excuse not to marry me then either. Or maybe he would just have disappeared the way he has now. George, I don't know what I'm gonna do." Tears filled her eyes as she gazed helplessly at her brother.

He still looked very shocked, but some color was coming back into his face. He stood up and started pacing the room. At last he turned to her. Surprised by the look of optimism on his face, shocked followed his words.

"I'm sure Michael will come back," George said in a confident voice. "He's a good man. Just look at all the things he did here on the farm. Why, he's been the best friend I ever had. He'll have an explanation for this. If he knows that you're having his child he wouldn't just walk off. He has a responsibility to you and to the baby. I just know that he'll be back."

She could see the dumb hope in his eyes, the refusal to believe his hero had cut and run. She wanted to believe, too, but something within her knew that Michael had left for good. George lived in a fantasy world right now. It would give him time to come to terms with what had happened. Time to think of some kind of solution they both could live with.

George came back to the couch and sat next to her. Holding her hands he said, "That's what will happen, Kate. He'll walk back in here in a day or two and y'all will get married. No man would walk out on a woman carrying his child. Not Michael anyway."

~ * ~

As the days turned into weeks, George became more and more withdrawn. He started looking at Kate with suspicion in his eyes. He was losing his belief in Michael and Kate couldn't blame him. The feeling within her, that told her it was fantasy to hope, had been right. Her thoughts turned and turned in her head, an unending rut from which there could be no escape. She became deeply concerned by George's more and more negative reactions to her. He silently ate the meals she prepared for them, rarely speaking a word to her and then went off to the fields or to bed without ever discussing his feelings. Caught in the cage of her own unhappiness and betrayal, she didn't press him to talk to her. He would come around eventually.

Two

George Randsome cursed his fate, rage boiling in his veins. He walked the acres of the family farm he hated, wondering what he had ever done to deserve this. The acres of red earth, once covered in fine cotton and now going to scrub, meant less than nothing to him. He yearned for new sights and sounds. He slashed furiously at scrub grass and bushes with a piece of deadwood picked up on his solitary trek, the action giving life to his inner anger.

From the time he was a young boy, his eyes had been turned westward. He wanted to see for himself the mighty Mississippi River, to cross it and travel always westward. He would travel on and on, always seeking new sights, new sounds. He would spend his life seeking adventure.

His father had understood his dream. Had even encouraged him in the halcyon days of his early childhood. The farm had been prosperous. His two older brothers ready and willing to take over the farm after their father. He had never understood their enthusiasm for the farm. To him it was just a place of unending work. His father had never pushed him to work the fields from dawn to dusk the way his brothers did. His father had understood his need to travel.

His dream had been destroyed by the War. At first he had thought this was a chance for his lifetime of adventure to begin early. At thirteen he had thought himself a man. His father quickly disabused him of that notion. He had planned to join up as a drummer boy. Planned to see the thrill of battle, hear the roar of cannon and smell the unmistakable scent of gunpowder from hundreds of rifles. With their father's approval, his brothers, John and Andrew, joined up with Fielding Hurst's Sixth Calvary. It was a Union calvary and the Randsomes were staunchly Unionist. That made for hard times for the family in a county that was split in loyalties. It made for hard feelings on George's part. He was needed now to help on the hated farm. If he ran away and joined up, his father would track him down and have him brought back in disgrace. He chaffed at the restriction. The war would be over before he was sixteen! His father made him swear that he would wait and he was bound by that promise. That was the beginning of the end of his dream, though he hadn't known it at the time.

After his older brothers had been killed in battle, he had been uneasy, knowing that his father now expected him to stay and work the farm. To give up his long treasured plans and stay here in the red clay hills of West Tennessee. Never to see the places for which his heart yearned. His only hope now was for his sister to marry. Her husband could take his place on the farm. Then, both his parents had died of grief. He became trapped on the farm with his sister in the hellish aftermath at the end of the war.

After the death of his parents, he had wanted to sell the farm, yet his sister refused to listen to him. She had some strange attachment to the place that he couldn't fathom. He didn't need her permission to sell, but he felt bound by the ties of blood to take care of her. He continued to cling to the hope that she would marry soon so he could turn the farm over to his new brother-in-law and shake the dust of Tennessee from his boots forever.

When he had met Michael by chance in McNairy Station, his wily brain had taken over. Here was a man with no ties, in no hurry to return to his home. A young, good looking man who needed a place to stay for a while. Kate's face flashed across his mind. Her wide blue eyes framed by dark hair. Her slender face with its strong chin. She was a pretty woman who could surely capture this stranger for her husband and free him from the farm. With a wide smile on his face, he had invited Michael to live on the Randsome farm. He could certainly use the help and if things went as planned; he might be free within the year!

All had gone so smoothly from the start that he sometimes thought to pinch himself to see if it was all some crazy dream brought on by his own ever-growing desire to get away. Michael and Kate had taken to each other right off. He could hardly hide his glee. An added bonus had been that Michael really did know an enormous amount about farming and seemed to enjoy every aspect. They had reclaimed an additional five acres of the farm and planted it in cotton to offset the high cost of shipping it north. Since the end of the war, a high shipping fee had been imposed on Southern produce. On his own, he had hardly been able to make a profit from all his hard labor.

Where then had everything gone wrong? All his carefully calculated plans were ashes in his mouth. It all came back to Kate. What had possessed her to give herself outside the bonds of marriage? Why had Michael run off when he learned about the coming child? He had dropped so many hints to Michael about his dreams of leaving the area. Surely Michael realized that the farm would belong to him if he married Kate. Why had the man run off?

Now his sister, his *unmarried* sister, had the gall to tell him that she was having a bastard baby and expecting him to stay around and support her. Every time he thought of it, he wanted to choke the life from her. He had genuinely thought that Michael would return in a matter of time and take responsibility for Kate and the unborn child. With each day that passed, that hope grew dimmer and dimmer, while his rage grew in equal measure. His initial sympathy for Kate dimmed and was replaced with thoughts that she must be a whore after all. Why else would a good man like Michael leave her? Every time she looked at him with her eyes full of questions and need, he felt revulsion grow in his heart. He was now at the point that he could hardly stand to be in the same room with her. She had killed his last hope for escape from the farm. No one would marry her now, with a bastard child attached to her.

He felt as though the walls of a cage had suddenly moved closer. Where there had been a door in the past, just waiting for him to use it, there were now solid bars. The unfairness of his fate stung him like gall. He *deserved* his freedom. This was all Kate's fault! She had taken his dream from him. Taken his chance to go west and see new lands and have new experiences! He gnashed his teeth in impotent rage. The deadwood limb whistled through the air and shattered as he smote the ground with all his strength. No! He would not let her steal his dream. She wasn't worth sacrificing his dream! She had proven herself to be trash and he wouldn't stay around to take care of trash. It was past time for him to leave this place of loss and destruction. Time for him to live his own life and make his long forsaken dream come true. No more sacrifices from George Randsome. Having made his decision, he tossed away the remains of the stick and wiped his hands vigorously together. With a jaunty step and a smile on his face he turned back to the house.

It didn't take him long to pack his belongings. His few shirts, two pairs of pants; socks and longhandles. His shaving blade and a small mirror were the last items he packed. Picking up his bag, he started toward the stairs, then hesitated. He didn't plan to come back, so he better take his winter things, too. It was hot now, but cold weather would come along soon enough. Returning to his room, he pulled the remaining bag from his chifforobe and packed his winter coat, heavy woolen stockings, scarf and gloves. Looking at the worn bags and thinking of the equally worn belongings inside, he deeply regretted his lack of money. He would need new boots soon and his clothing was so worn from many washings that it was thin, the colors faded to hazy grays. Also, he wouldn't be able to travel at a fast rate since he would have to work in every town he visited to make enough money to move on from each one. Almost, he changed his mind about leaving now. He could trick Kate into thinking he would stay with her, stay until the cotton was picked, and take the profits for his traveling money.

A feeling of claustrophobia came over him. He couldn't stay here another day. How could he raise money for traveling? He thought of his mother's silver, saved from plundering soldiers during the war and now stored carefully in trunks in the attic. It was too bulky to carry with him and wouldn't bring much money in a pawn shop. Too many people had treasures saved from the war and had pawned them to the point that the shops were overflowing with valuables acquired for a pittance. A plan occurred to him as he stood there. He couldn't think why it hadn't occurred to him long ago. A just solution it was! Chuckling softly to himself, he carried his bags to the front porch. Leaving the bags, he went around the house to the barn, saddled their mule and brought it to the front of the house. He sat down to wait patiently for Kate to return from one of her interminable walks. He had thought of leaving her a note, but decided that his anger had to have an outlet. He wanted to vent it on the person who had very nearly destroyed his dream.

~ * ~

Kate came slowly across the yard toward him, looking puzzled by the saddled mule and the bags sitting by his side. As she came closer, she opened her lips to speak, but George forestalled anything she might want to say. The need to say his piece was too great to listen to any more of her possible futures. He jumped up, motioned her to silence and felt the pent up rage boil over. If lightning had struck her on the spot, she could not have looked more shocked as the acid of his hate poured over her unsuspecting head in a gushing tide.

"You're a whore, Kate Randsome! That's why Michael left. When you gave yourself to him without being married, he knew you were a whore. Never mind that you're from a respectable family. Any woman who would do what you did is a whore! I cain't stay here and live with what you've done to our family. I'm going west and start a new life. When everyone finds out that you're having a baby I won't be able to hold my head up around here. If I hadn't let you talk me out of leaving here a long time ago, this would never have happened. I need a life of my own. One where I can have some pride and someday find a good wife. No father around here will let me court his daughter after they find out about what you've done."

As she stood frozen in horrified silence, the blood draining from her face, he picked up his bags and brushed by her.

"George, wait," she called.

Her hand caught him by the arm. He was surprised by the strength of her small fingers as she pulled him off balance. He swung around to meet her eyes. Fright stared back at him. She was terrified by his leaving. Feeling his resolve wavering slightly, he turned his face away. He would not allow her to sway him.

"You cain't just go off like this! Stay and think this through," she pleaded. " If we stand together, we can get through anything. Please, George, stay with me. I cain't go through this alone. Come back inside and think this over some more."

He pulled his arm from her grasp and continued to walk slowly away from her.

She screamed at his retreating back, " This isn't just my fault! Michael had some to do with it, too! Don't let your opinion of him turn you against your own sister! I'm begging you, George! Please stay!"

He turned to face her again. With contempt written on his face, he said, "Damn you! I've done nothing but think since you told me you're having a baby. I believe no man would desert the woman carrying his child. You must have done something to make Michael leave. He was my best friend and a good man. I cain't stay here and face this with you. I stayed this long hoping you'd git married and I could travel like I always wanted to. You held me here against my will. You knew I never wanted to work this farm. I let you talk me out of it time and again. Well, now I'm leaving no matter what you say. You've ruined your own life, but I won't let you ruin mine."

Mounting the mule, he started slowly, deliberately away, then turned and said in a cruel voice, "If you're worried about running the farm by yourself, I'm sure you can lure another man to your bed as soon as you have your baby. Maybe you'll get lucky and get one who'll stay. Not that any decent man would have you now."

She was left gaping in disbelief as he rode away. He never once looked back.

Three

"Not that any decent man would have you now. Not that any DECENT MAN would have you now. NOT THAT ANY DECENT MAN WOULD HAVE YOU NOW!" Her brother's final words to her echoed through Kate's head, getting louder with each repetition until she thought she would lose her mind. Grasping her head tightly with both hands, she squeezed with all her strength in an effort to block out the hateful words. Her mind struggled to take in the enormity of her downfall. Her world was crumbling around her again, only this time she knew there would be no end to hostilities. There would be no truce declared. She would spend the rest of her life at war with the class she had been born into, never able to call a cease-fire.

Retreating to the sanctuary of her childhood bedroom, she took refuge in the blessed arms of sleep. In that place there was no struggle, no horror, no shame—only a deep, dark, velvety peace that she longed for with all her soul. Then, this last solace deserted her. She could sleep no more. She cried endlessly. George had turned his back on his own flesh and blood and sided with an outsider. A foreboding filled her. George had been the first to turn on her. Who would be next?

A week passed while Kate tried to sleep as much as possible to escape the unbearable thoughts that occupied her waking mind. Each period of consciousness brought on the portentous feeling of the foundations of her life cracking apart. She tried desperately to outrun the emotions hovering over her like giant storm clouds, just waiting to unleash a maelstrom on her head. No matter how she twisted and turned, tried to outrace the storm, it continued to hover menacingly.

~ * ~

One morning, she heard footsteps on the front porch. Thinking that George had had second thoughts and decided to stand by her after all, Kate flew toward the front door. As she entered the hallway, by some strange alchemy, sunlight splashed onto the large gilt framed mirror hanging there. She froze in shock at what she saw. Her hair hung around her shoulders in a tangled rat's nest. Dark circles punctuated her eyes and accented her sunken cheeks. Her dress, wrinkled and stained with sweat. She had become a stranger to herself.

A persistent knocking drew her attention back to the door. From her place in the shadows, she glanced in that direction, then stared in horror. Not George; her sister, Savannah. What now? Should she tell her sister? Would she turn away as George had done? The questions flew through Kate's head one after the other.

Her sister's voice called, "Kate! Are you home? I brought some preserves I made. The ones that George loves so much."

She continued to stand silent in the dim interior as though her feet had grown into the floor. Uncertainty warred within her. Her tongue felt glued to the roof of her mouth. Indecision swirled through her.

Peering through the door, Savannah saw her cowering in the shadows and said, "Kate, why are you just standing there?"

When Kate didn't answer, Savannah pushed the door further open and came in. Taking one look at Kate's ravaged eyes and tangled hair, she dropped the basket of preserves on the floor, where it made a dull thud on the uncarpeted wood. A jar of preserves rolled free and came to rest against the wall a few feet away. Kate experienced a hysterical desire to giggle.

"Are you all right?" Savannah asked her anxiously. " Has something happened? Why didn't you answer me? Where's George?" The questions fired at her one after another like gunshots across the shadowy hallway.

Kate knew that the time had come for her truth to come out. At least to family. She must know as soon as possible who would stand by her and adjust her life accordingly. Her voice felt rusty, her throat sore, making it difficult to get the words to come, but she squeezed them past the blockage.

"I'm going to have a baby." She said in a strangely wooden voice. "It's Michael's baby. He left so he wouldn't have to marry me. When George found out the truth he left, too. He said he wouldn't be able to hold up his head around here when people found out about the baby. "

Savannah staggered as though from a physical blow. Her eyes grew so wide that a white ring showed all the way around the blue-grey color that matched Kate's own eyes. Her voice, when she spoke came as almost a whisper,

"Oh, my God in heaven. What have you done? How did this happen?"

A little girl in Kate's head began to cry helplessly. Why wouldn't anyone help her? She was so scared and alone and no one would help her. Kate became angry at the sniveling child in her head. She grasped at the anger gratefully and turned it on her sister. "Everyone seems to be calling on God for an answer when I tell them what's happened. I don't care what God thinks. I need my family to help me. Are you going to help, or are you going to cut and run like Michael and George?"

The concern vanished from Savannah's face and she snapped back, "Don't you take that tone with me, Missy! You've obviously been a stupid fool. What I don't understand is why George didn't send you packing instead of running off himself."

Struggling to maintain her anger, Kate snapped back. "It seems that George turned out to be the irresponsible, no-account that your sainted husband always said he would be. This farm is mine now and I'm gonna run it myself. I'm gonna hire freemen to pick the cotton for me this year." Anger and fright battled for possession of her as she tried to appear brave in front of her sister.

Savannah had drawn herself up tall and straight at the remark about her husband, Tom. Then, laughing cruelly she asked, "And just what do you think you're gonna use for money to pay this hired labor?"

Thinking quickly, with the cunning of the desperate, she found an idea. "I'll just get them on as sharecroppers. Lots of people are doing that now. I have to do something to keep this place running so I'll have food on my table and a roof over my head. If nobody's gonna stand by me, then I'll just make do for myself." She flung her false bravado in her sister's face in self-protection. Inside her head the little girl continued to cry forlornly, wondering why no one loved her anymore.

As her sister turned in a huff to leave, Kate regretted her harsh words. The false bravado ran out of her. She held out her hand in entreaty.

"Savannah, I'm sorry for talking to you like that. You just don't know what I've been through these last weeks. George leaving was the last straw. I just couldn't cope. Please, don't turn your back on me, too!"

Savannah turned back to Kate with a hard, flinty look in her eyes, but her tone became softer when she spoke.

"I have to talk to Tom about this. What you've done is horrible to me and you know how religious Tom is. I'm afraid there won't be any forgiveness on his part."

As Savannah turned away and went down the porch steps, the little girl in Kate's head began to scream in fear.

After her sister left, Kate walked tiredly into the kitchen and sat at the table. Leaning her elbows on it she put her heavy head in her hands, tried to think of some kind of solution. Despite her brave words to Savannah, she had no idea how she would get the cotton crop picked. It would be difficult to find any men this close to picking time. Most of the men who were interested in working were already on other farms. There was no other house on the property to offer as a home for sharecroppers. Despair threatened to swallow her. She knew that when she started looking around for help it would mean that everyone would know that George had left. And Michael, too. Kate was determined that she wouldn't tell them the truth. She would keep her secret for as long as possible. Now she must think of some believable reason for George and Michael leaving. What would people believe? It had to be something that wouldn't be questioned. Something that the rest of the family would stand by readily.

The rest of the family. Kate didn't think that she could face them all with her disgrace. She would go to Savannah and beg her to tell no one. She *must* keep this secret as long as possible. Maybe some solution would occur that she hadn't thought of yet and no one would need to know. She sat up straight suddenly. Of course. She might be able to cause a miscarriage! That had happened to other women she knew. She would pick the cotton herself until she became so tired she dropped and maybe strain herself so much that she would lose the baby. Why hadn't she thought of it before? Instead of mooning around, feeling sorry for herself, she should have been concentrating on solving the problem. A surge of energy rushed through her. The first thing to do would be to go to Savannah and persuade her to keep the secret.

~ * ~

Kate covered the short distance through the woods to Savannah's house as though she had wings on her feet. She arrived hot and out of breath. She quickly mopped her forehead with her sleeve to remove that layer of dirt and sweat. She knocked on the old wood door with its peeling paint and scuffed her dusty shoes on the equally weathered boards of the front porch.

Savannah pushed open the door on squeaking hinges and remarked, " I didn't expect to see you again today. I haven't had a chance to talk to Tom. He ain't in from the fields just yet. Come on in and sit a spell. I've got over the bad shock and sassy talk you gave me this morning."

Kate interrupted her quickly, "That's just what I came to see you about. To apologize again for how I acted this morning and to ask you a favor. Don't tell anybody about the baby. Just keep it between us two for a while."

"What?" Savannah asked in surprise. "How do you think you're gonna keep this a secret? People will notice something before long. There's gonna be a lot of talk when everyone hears that George and Michael are gone. What are you planning on telling them?"

Kate shifted uncomfortably on the sagging blue sofa in the parlor. Could she tell her sister what she planned? No, Savannah would never go along with trying to kill a baby. Even one that wasn't born yet.

Deciding on a plan, she looked back at Savannah's confused face and said, "I thought we could say that George was really unhappy here now. That he just wanted to try to find a new life out west and he talked Michael into going with him. We don't have to say anything else just yet. Please, Savannah. I'm begging you to help now. Don't turn away from me like George did. I cain't face this alone. You know what will happen when everybody finds out the truth. Just help me right now. Help me to have a little time before everybody knows. Please, Savannah!"

Kate dropped to her knees and put her head in her sister's lap as she sobbed out all the misery in her heart. If only Michael had stayed and married her, she wouldn't be in this fix now. She felt the tension in Savannah's muscles, but her sister stroked her hair with a gently touch.

Kate had begun to think her sister wouldn't help her when she heard Savannah say in a quiet voice, "What do you mean *we* could say this?"

Relief stopped Kate's tears. She sat back on her heels on the rag rug that covered the uneven floor. "Well, it stands to reason that we all have to have the same story. We cain't all be telling different things to people. Then they'll *know* that something's wrong and keep sniffing around till they find out what it is."

Savannah's continued to use the quiet voice, but Kate could see worry growing in her eyes as she said, "You're asking me to lie to Tom and to let him be telling lies to people without him knowing it's a lie he's telling. I don't think I can do that, Kate."

"Please, Savannah. You can blame it all on me. Tell Tom that I lied to *you* all along and you didn't know any different, just like him."

"I don't see what good this will do," Savannah said in a puzzled tone. "The truth will come out eventually. What do you think will change between now and then?"

Her eyes got suddenly huge in her pale face. She looked at Kate sharply, saying, "You don't aim to harm yourself, do you, Kate? If I thought for a minute that you were planning some kind of harm to yourself I wouldn't go along with you on this."

"Then you'll go along with me for now?" Kate asked eagerly. " I don't plan any harm. I just need some time to think this thing through without everybody wagging their tongues before I get used to the idea. That's all."

It wasn't a real lie. She wasn't planning to harm herself. Just the baby that she wished with all her heart wasn't growing in her. As much as she had loved Michael, she now hated him. She didn't think that doing away with his baby would pain her conscience too much. Her future depended on no one ever knowing what she had done. Kate intended to keep her place and respectability. Murder was a sin before God, but she couldn't live her life as an outcast. Not if it was within her power to change fate.

Relief flooded her when Savannah answered, "I'll go along for a *little* while. I don't like lying to Tom. I never have before and I don't think this is a good time to start. But, I'll give you a little time. I don't approve of what you did nor what you're doing now. I just hope we can work something out. Mama and Daddy would want me to take care of you if I can, so I'm gonna try my best to do what's best."

Kate heaved a sigh of relief. They talked a little longer about Savannah's children, the hot weather, speculated about where George might be and what he might be doing. Later, Kate went home through the lengthening afternoon shadows, her secret plan clutched close to her heart.

~ * ~

Savannah Claiborne's thoughts were in a turmoil after Kate left. Her own sister had become a whore. Just thinking the words to herself caused as deep a sense of shock as hearing them from her sister's lips. She knew that their parents had taught Kate that fornication was a sin. What had possessed the silly fool to give herself outside the bonds of marriage? The big question now was how she would handle the information. All their friends and neighbors would take against Kate as soon as word got out. A shudder went down her spine. Would they take against her, too? Surely not. It wasn't her fault her sister was in this fix. But then again, if she stood in support of her sister, she might see a lot of backs turned to her. It just wasn't fair that after everything else she had survived that this should happen now.

Tom would be dumbfounded, then enraged when he knew.

Savannah found that she wasn't looking forward to facing Tom's ire when he knew. His God was not one of forgiveness. Thank goodness Kate had the family farm to live on. When she talked to Tom she would emphasize that point. They could cut contact with Kate to a minimum. She herself had to maintain some contact. She had promised her mother on her deathbed to look after Kate and George as best she could. George had gone out of her reach now, but Kate would have to be looked after. She had never dreamed when she made that promise to her dying mother that something so horrible would happen. She considered how she and her husband would manage things. Tom would have to help with the farm. She shrugged aside Kate's claim that she would get sharecroppers to help her. That was just a fool notion her sister thought up to save face. A sigh escaped her lips. She couldn't help thinking how much easier it would have been on everyone if Kate had left to bear her bastard in secrecy somewhere far away instead of George leaving.

Four

Still a few weeks until time to pick the cotton. The rows stretched away in their red clay furrows, the bolls open, the shining white cotton gaining strength from the hot sun. Kate waited, her patience running thin. Time dragged by at a snail-like pace, with one exception. There was a close call with Tom. He came over as soon as Savannah told him about George and Michael leaving.

Kate's heart leapt into her throat when she saw Tom crossing the yard late in the afternoon. He must have come straight from his own fields to judge from the dust on his shoes and overalls; his expression dark and disapproving as he approached her. Heart racing in a staccato rhythm she wondered, *Had Savannah betrayed my secret, after all?*

"Sister, my wife tells me that George and Michael have high tailed it west," Tom stated. "I'm having some trouble believing that they just took off so sudden." His dark eyes looked sharply at her face. "Are you holding back something the rest of us should know? I heard some ugly talk over to McNairy Station yesterday that George owes a lot of money. What do you know about it?"

Relaxing just a little, her heart slowing to a more normal rhythm, she eyed Tom trying to see if he knew her secret. But she saw noting else in his eyes. Savannah must have kept the secret. Now she must find some way to convince her brother-in-law that George had left for no other reason than that he had been unhappy here for so long. She replied in a calm voice, "Tom, George was just really unhappy here in the last couple of years. You know he's been itching to go west for a long time. He figured the rest of the family would help me with the farm and he could go west and find a new life. Michael decided to go with him. It struck him as some kind of adventure. George don't owe any money. You know how folks are around here. If there ain't some real gossip floating around, then they'll just make up something to talk about. George took some money we had put by, he knew I'd be all right till the crop gets picked and then I'll have the money from that to live on till next year."

Tom didn't look like he believed the story. He attacked next in a vulnerable area that Kate hadn't thought about. "Well, why did Michael go? He's been sparkin' you for months. We've all been waiting to hear a wedding announcement. What happened betwixt the two of you that he would take off with George instead of staying here and marrying you? He'd have this whole place then."

Dangerous ground. Her heart jumped in fear. She must convince Tom of her story. She let a tone of impatience creep into her voice, "I told you! Michael thought it sounded like a grand adventure. It was never serious with Michael and me. We just enjoyed spending time together. I was here on the farm and it just seemed natural for him to escort me anytime we went out to socials and dances."

Puzzlement crept over Tom's face. He let it go, however, and moved on to what she realized was his main reason for coming by to see her. Concerned about getting the cotton picked.

"You'll need a man to help you run this farm. I cain't hardly spare any time to help you out. I got my own place to see to and so does everybody else. George was just plain loco to think we could all pitch in and help you out over here! How we'll manage to get the cotton picked on this place, I don't know. I just cain't figure out why he didn't at least wait till the crop was picked before he took off. That boy never has had much sense of responsibility. I'll have to figure something out to get the cotton picked before it rots in the field."

Kate didn't want him pursuing the subject of George any further, so she blurted out the first lie that occurred to her. She knew it would distract him from the subject of George.

"I've found some freedmen to pick it on a share. I told Savannah about it the other day."

Tom responded just as she'd known he would—outrage. His jaw worked as his eyes bulged in their sockets. Finally he exploded in wrath.

"Dang it, Sister! What fool plan is this? You're gonna need every penny you can get to get you through the winter. This place don't hardly turn a profit as it is. Now you'll have to be sharing with the Nigras who pick the cotton for you."

Tired of dealing with Tom, she wished he would just leave. There were more important things to worry about just now than how the cotton would get picked. Why wouldn't the man just go away and leave her in peace? She said, "Well, I knew that you and the rest wouldn't hardly have the time to be picking the cotton here and at your own places too, so I made arrangements on my own."

Tom looked away for a moment as though suddenly interested in something coming down the road, but when Kate turned to look, she saw only the dusty red track winding away into the shadow of the trees that bordered it just past the farm. She saw his jaw muscles clinching and unclenching under his sunburned skin. Finally he looked back at her and said, "I reckon it's for the best. I really don't know how we could have managed otherwise." His voice took on a stern note as he continued. "But I don't like you making business decisions on your own. In the future, all of us will decide together what's to be done for you."

She didn't much like his tone, but Tom had always been bossy about matters that she thought were none of his business. She could see his point though. She would need his help when it came time to sell the cotton, so she agreed nicely that next time she would consult him about any business matters. She would have agreed to anything just then to get rid of him.

After a long, stern look at her to make sure she had taken his point, he finally went on home, walking with the long legged gait he had always had although he now had a slight stoop to his shoulders and his dark hair was beginning to show gray mixed into it.

~ * ~

Tom Claiborne puzzled over the situation on the way home. The story told to him by his wife just didn't ring true. Somebody was holding something back. He didn't doubt for a minute that young George would take it into his head to run off. Everybody knew that the boy had always wanted to leave the farm and travel. No, what was the real puzzler here was that Michael would take off with George. Tom had thought Michael a reliable, hardworking man and had been relieved, after he had gotten to know Michael, a reliable man helping out on his wife's family farm. Young George had no head for business and Tom had been hard put to help out on the Randsome farm and take care of his own. That was where the puzzle lay. Why had Michael gone west? By staying, he would have come into the family farm through marriage to Kate. Tom was no fool. Kate might claim that there had been nothing between her and Michael till the skies fell, but Tom didn't believe it. He had eyes in his head. Those two had been moony about each other all right. Something was wrong here.

His long stride had eaten up the distance between the Randsome farm and his own. As he entered his front door he smelled pork frying for dinner. Savannah came to the kitchen doorway with a question in her eyes.

"Well, it appears that your sister has hired some sharecroppers to help with the cotton. Or so she claims," he told his wife. "I told her I don't like her making decisions like that without checking with me first. She didn't like that too well."

Savannah smiled. "I can imagine she didn't. She never did like to be told what to do. Did she say if she'd heard from George?" A look of apprehension appeared in her eyes.

Tom saw the apprehension, but couldn't fathom its cause. It just added to his inner puzzlement. Could his own wife be keeping still about something? He watched her with narrowed eyes as he answered, "No, she didn't mention anything about hearing from him. Don't you think that's just a little bit odd? I'd think he would want to write and brag about his grand adventures."

Savannah's eyes did not meet her husband's as she answered, "Well, you know George is pretty irresponsible. It probably hasn't occurred to him that we might be worried about him. We'll hear something eventually."

The averted eyes told Tom that he was right. His wife was keeping still about something. They had been married too long for him not to know her through and through.

"It still don't strike me just right that Michael took off with George. He seemed a responsible, hard working man. Not the kind that would just take off like that. Has Kate told you something you're not telling me?" he probed.

Alarm flared briefly in his wife's eyes before she turned back into the kitchen. He followed her and stood watching as she became suddenly busy turning pork chops and stirring boiled potatoes. She answered him without looking in his direction.

"I don't know what you mean. Kate told me that George and Michael had left to go west and that the farm was hers now and she intends to stay there and run it herself. She said she and Michael were just friends. That there was nothing between them to keep Michael here. Did she say any different to you?"

"No," Tom admitted. "She didn't say any different to me, but something just ain't right here. She's holding something back. I could see it in her eyes. She was nervous as a cat. Then there's the talk around McNairy Station that George owes somebody a lot of money. Kate said she don't know nothing about George owing any money.

You don't think him and Michael went over to the Purdy race track and lost a lot of money they ain't got and lit out because of that, do you?"

Savannah looked startled for a minute, then got busy dishing up dinner for the two of them. "No," She said quietly. "I don't think anything like that happened."

Tom sat down at the kitchen table and began eating his dinner while Savannah called the children to come and eat. His mind went round and round. He knew something was wrong. His instincts told him that the truth was mixed in somewhere between what his wife and sister-in-law had told him and the rumors flying rampant around McNairy Station. It would only be a matter of time before got to the bottom of it.

Five

Kate could not sit idly and wait for the cotton to be ready in order to try her plan. She must take some action or go mad with the thoughts swirling through her mind. She could not sit calmly and wait. She *must* take action now. Feverishly she wandered through the house searching for inspiration. In her bedroom the heavy oak chifferobe beckoned to her. Pushing and pulling, heaving with all her strength, she sought to shift the ponderous weight. Sweat broke out on her face as her muscles strained. At last, she gave up and collapsed to the floor in a sobbing heap. Her fingers ached from their tight grasp on the unyielding wood, her arms quivered and jerked from strained muscles, her back cried out in agony, but she was not rewarded with the cramps she sought. The cramps that would allow her to continue her life as a member of this community. The cramps that would give her back the future she had once despised.

Eventually, she pushed herself up from the floor and wandered back downstairs. Looking sharply, seeking a new inspiration, desperate for anything to rid herself of her unwanted burden, she went into the yard. Her restless feet carried her across the hardpacked dirt. She moved to the barn. In the dim interior, her eyes went to the loft where bales of hay waited to be thrown to the stall below for the mule that George had taken with him. Climbing as quickly as her skirts would allow, she went to examine the bales. Pushing at one, she realized just how heavy they were. Maybe this would work.

Pushing and straining, she managed to maneuver one to the edge and over to the floor below her. It burst open on impact. With a satisfied nod, she continued to maneuver the bales to the edge and onto the floor below the loft. Within an hour she was drenched with sweat and dust hung heavy in the air making her sneeze over and over. When the last bale had gone over with a muffled thump, she waited. No cramps. Perhaps it would take more work to cause them. Climbing down from the loft, she retrieved a pitchfork from the storage area and began pulling apart the large pile of hay. Soon small pieces of hay had joined the dust hanging in the air. They stuck to her sweaty face and hands and lodged in her hair as she furiously pulled the pile apart and spread it across the entire barn area. Her hair came loose from its pins and swung free as she savagely forked the hay far and wide. A spasm caught her lower back and caused her to gasp in pain, then grin in delight. Was this it? Would her prayer be answered? Had she actually been able to cause the baby to let go?

Another spasm ripped across her back and she dropped the pitchfork where she stood. Pain radiated down her legs. She could barely stand. Moving with slow and careful steps, she managed to cross the yard and get to the porch where she collapsed on the weathered boards. Moaning with pain, she rolled to her side and drew her knees up to her chest. There. The pain was more bearable in that position.

Dear God, she prayed, *Please let this baby die. I know it's wrong to wish for its death, but You are kind and merciful. Please look down on me with compassion and understanding. I won't ever ask for another thing for as long as I live if You'll help me now.* She dozed off there on the porch, her lips still moving in silent prayer.

When morning came, she could barely move from the pain in her back. With agonizing slowness, she straightened her legs and rolled to a sitting position, her legs dangling uselessly over the edge of the porch. She could feel no wetness of her undergarments and there were no bloodstains on her skirt. Her prayer had not been answered. Weeping in helpless rage, she continued to sit there in the early morning sun. She had become excited over nothing. Now she would have to wait for the pain in her back and legs to subside before she could try again.

More than a week passed by before she could move in a normal fashion. Thank goodness no one dropped in on her, so she didn't have to make up some excuse for the state she was in. Looking into the barn one afternoon, she was aghast at the scene that greeted her. Hay, knee deep lay strewn from one end to the other. It looked as though some madman had broken in and laid waste to the supply of hay that had been meant to feed their mule that winter. Little by little, she managed to get it mashed into the stalls and closed the half door on each one. Hopefully she wouldn't have to explain to anyone why it was there. Now that she was able to get around again, her mind went in circles seeking yet another way to rid herself of her unwanted burden.

Scanning the rows of cotton in the nearby field, she knew that it would be another week or two before she could try out that idea. Continuing to look around the immediate area, her eyes fastened on the old tree stump that had always been used when chopping firewood. The woodpile near the house looked to be getting low and she would need a lot of wood for the winter. She could go over to Savannah's and ask her to send Tom to chop the wood for her. She knew he would come by when he could and little by little the woodpile would grow. It might be best to go ahead and ask him to do that. Once he found out about her condition, he might be reluctant to be helpful to her. What a fool she'd be to ask for help when this task might take care of her problem. The pile of two foot long pieces needing only to be split beckoned to her. She had never chopped wood in her life. Forking all that hay hadn't worked, so what made her think that chopping wood would work?

She ignored her doubts and went to the storage area of the barn to retrieve the axe. Dragging it to the stump, she laid it down and positioned a section of wood to be split. The axe was unwieldy in her hands. The heavy iron head made to help force the blade through the wood made it difficult for her to lift high enough to get a good swing. Finally getting the axe raised as high as she could, she swung downward with all her might. The blade missed the piece of wood completely and imbedded itself deeply in the stump. Tugging with all her might Kate struggled to get the axe free. It came loose without warning causing her to lose her balance. Her heel caught in her long skirt and she landed flat on her back in the dirt. Sitting up, she saw that the axe imbedded in the dirt right next to her foot. There was even a scrape mark on her boot where the sharp edge had glanced off. Fright caused her heart to gallop in her chest. She might have severed her own foot! If that had happened she knew she would not have been able to reach help in time to save her life. No, chopping wood was not a good way to get rid of the baby. She must resign herself to wait a little while.

~ * ~

At last — time to pick the cotton. The bolls had turned hard and dry and the cotton puffed just like white clouds from them. With a burlap sack slung over her shoulder, Kate went into the field with high hopes. The rows stretched long in front of her. She had never actually picked cotton until the last couple of years. Before the war, her Daddy and brothers had undertaken that arduous task while she had worked in the house at her mother's side learning how to preserve the food they grew. After Daddy had died, George had done most all the picking. Shaking off those poignant memories, she stepped into the first row to begin her task, picking from sunup to sundown with the strap of the burlap sack digging into her shoulder as it filled with cotton. The hot sun bore down mercilessly on her bare head, causing her to feel faint as she staggered along the rows. Her hands were cut to ribbons by the sharp cotton bolls. She kept on going hoping with all her heart that her troubles would soon be solved.

The sun moved in a hot arc across the sky. Thirst clawed at her throat. Her back screamed in agony to accompany the throbbing in her bleeding hands. The rows seemed to stretch longer and longer in her sweat blurred vision. She refused to stop. She mustn't stop if her plan was to succeed. In a stupor she continued to pull automatically at the fluffy bolls and stuff them into her sack. One row done, then two, then three. Finally, the sun went down in a gory red and orange blaze that threw the cotton field into shadow, forcing her to quit for the day. Dragging the heavy, unwieldy sack into the barn, she left it there, then dragged her weary body across the yard, up the sagging porch steps and into the house where she fell into a deep sleep the instant her head touched the pillow on the hand carved oak bed that had been hers since she was a child.

Far too soon, the sun blazed through the window where she had forgotten to pull the shade, poking insistent fingers into her closed eyes. She woke up aching in every bone and muscle of her body, but without the gut wrenching cramps she had hoped for. The baby just kept on sitting there in her belly. Tears of frustration formed in her eyes. Pushing them back angrily, she climbed from the bed.

Determined to try again, she went back out to the fields with another burlap sack. Exhaustion dragged at her with claw-like fingers as she picked and picked. Again, the rows seemed to get longer and longer to her sun dazzled eyes. The thin scabs that had formed over yesterday's cuts on her hands broke open and the cuts bled freely again. At dark she was still carrying the baby. Tears of weakness formed in her eyes, their salt leaving a fiery path on her sunburned cheeks as she wiped them away with a bloody fist. Once again she dragged a bulging bag of cotton into the barn and staggered into the house to collapse on her bed.

She tried for three more days, each one more backbreaking than the one before, but the baby just wouldn't let go. On the fifth day she collapsed in the field from total exhaustion.

~ * ~

What solace there was in that black nothingness. If only she could stay there forever and ever. Her mind drifted peacefully as she wondered if perhaps she had died there in the cotton field and this might be heaven. Surely if it was, she would be called before God any minute now to answer for her sins. Moaning and struggling, she tried to wake up. She opened her eyes to find a kind black face gazing into her own and a gentle black hand wiping her face with a wet kerchief. The woman smiled when she saw Kate's eyes open and said, "Mah name Mary Stancel. Ah wuz out walkin' in de woods an' saw you fall ovah lak a sack o' potatas. Ah runned ober heah to sees whut Ah could do for you."

When Kate didn't answer, the woman continued in a soothing tone, "Ah lives with my son an' his fambly over on ol' Mist' Mcintosh place. Mah son be sharecroppin' for Mist' Mcintosh. You kin call me Aunt Mary lak evabody else do. You gone ter be alright. Jes' lay still for a few mo minutes an' den we gits you into the house and in baid. You is carryin' a baby an' ain' got no bizness out heah in dis cotton fiel'."

Kate lay in slience, accepting the kind ministrations, feeling like she was going to die inside. The baby was still here. No matter how hard she tried, she just couldn't get rid of it. Her plan had failed. Aunt Mary sat quietly beside her humming a little melody. Wiping her face with the handkerchief. She realized that she hadn't told Aunt Mary her name.

"I'm Kate Randsome, Aunt Mary. Thank you for your help, but I'll be fine. I can git back to the house on my own. I don't know why you think I'm carrying a baby; I reckon I just got too hot out here in the sun."

Aunt Mary smiled and shook her head. Her eyes knew Kate was lying about the baby, but she only said, "Ah knows who you is. I done seen you round heah since you was a lil gal. Ah ain' blind neitha. You cain' fool me chile. You kin deny it all you wants, but Ah knows when a woman is cahyin and when she ain' and you is cahyin. You cain' git back to de house on yo own. Ah's gone ter hep you and stay wif you for little while. Now, see iffen you can stan' up an' we'll go on to de house."

Kate fought the dizziness in her head and struggled to a sitting position, determined to get into the house under her own power. But Aunt Mary had to help her to her feet, as the world whirled and swooped in a sickening circle. Aunt Mary half carried her to the house and put her on the sofa in the parlor. It seemed much cooler in the parlor out of the sun. Aunt Mary put a pillow under her head to make her more comfortable. She turned her head away from the knowing eyes looking into her own and said, "Thank you for your help, Aunt Mary. I'll be just fine on my own now."

"Ah's gone ter de kitchen to fix you some tea," Aunt Mary answered. "You got some tea, Miss Kate?"

Sighing in frustration, Kate told her where to find the tea tin and a pitcher and glasses. As she waited, her mind returned to her predicament. Since she hadn't lost the baby by now she figured she wasn't going to at this point. Her plan hadn't worked. Now it wouldn't be long before everyone who knew her would find out about the baby and the blame would be laid on her alone. This was the end of any respectable future. There would be no husband, no nice home with children now. Just a bastard baby and herself branded as a whore for the rest of her life. The relentless groove went through her mind again— What to do? No way out. What to do? No way out. Aunt Mary bustling in with a tall glass of tea interrupted her thoughts.

"Now you drink dis down and doan argue wif me."

She handed Kate the glass, then stood over her like she would force the drink down her throat if Kate didn't drink it on her own. The tea felt wonderful as it slid down her parched throat. Strong and sweet, just the way she liked it. Aunt Mary sat down in a wing back chair near the sofa watching her silently.

Kate began to feel uncomfortable with this woman who saw too much and accepted it so easily. If Aunt Mary could see that she was carrying a baby, then others would see it, too. Hiding her disturbing thoughts, she smiled calmly at Aunt Mary and said, "You were right about me carrying a baby. I'd be right grateful if you didn't say anything to anybody about it. And you don't have to stay with me. I'll be all right now. I'll just lay here a while till I get my strength back."

"Ah doan have to be nowhere jus' now," Aunt Mary replied. "I'll sit here wif you till you goes to sleep, den Ah'll go on home. Doan you be worrin' yo' haid bout me telling anybody 'bout a baby. It not my secret to tell. But whut you gone ter do? You cain' be stayin' heah by yoself in yo condition. An you sho cain' be out dere pickin dat cotton in de hot sun. Ah knows you gots kinfolks roun heah. Ain' dey gone ter hep you?"

"I don't know. The baby's father ran off when he found out and so did my brother, George. I told my sister, Savannah, but I don't know if she'll help me or not. She said she would, but I just don't know. I'm very tired right now. I'd like to just go to sleep for a little while if you don't mind."

Aunt Mary started to hum and Kate began to feel very sleepy. Physical exhaustion combined with tumultuous emotions proved to be too much. She drifted off to sleep. When she woke up later, Aunt Mary was gone and the house was dark. She moved into her bedroom where she would be more comfortable and went back to sleep.

Six

Walking slowly in the gathering dusk, Mary Stancel's heart was troubled. She knew that for Kate Randsome the road ahead could only be one full of heartbreak and sorrow. Young white women of good family just weren't supposed to have a baby without being married. The poor girl would be shut out by everyone when the news got around. Sighing to herself, she wondered why the girl had been out in the draining heat of the day picking that cotton. Surely some of her family could have come over here and picked it for her. That stubborn girl was just too proud to ask for help. She stopped walking abruptly as a chill crawled down her spine. A picture formed in her mind of the young girl in the cotton field with the merciless hot sun beating down on her uncovered head. She knew then why Kate had been picking her own cotton in the hot sun. She was trying to lose that baby. The foolish girl had thought she could rid herself of the unwanted child by laboring in the hot sun. A shiver shook Mary's body at the thought. Shaking her head sadly, she continued on to the two-room house she shared with her son and grandchildren.

A smile of joy suffused her face as she came in sight of her home. Little Andy and Jane saw her coming and ran to her side with screams of delight. She hugged them close to her and again felt a pang of regret for the passing of her daughter-in-law Lutey, who had died when Jane was born. It was an additional sorrow to her that Lutey hadn't lived to see the end of the war and to be free like the rest of her family.

Releasing the children, she went on into the house where she found her son, Sam. An idea suddenly came to her as she watched him peeling potatoes for their supper. Sam could pick the Randsome cotton for a share, just like he was doing for Angus Mcintosh. It was Mr. Mcintosh's land that they lived on and the house belonged to Mr. Mcintosh, too. By picking Kate Randsome's cotton, Sam would have a small amount of additional cotton that he could sell and have some extra money. She was pleased to have thought of the idea. She could help that poor girl all alone in the big farmhouse and help her own family, too. Looking at her son, she decided to wait until they had all eaten a good, hearty supper and put the children to bed before she broached the subject. He looked up just then and saw her standing in the doorway.

"Where you bin, Mammy? We been gittin' worrit bout you," he said.

"Ah been out an about. We kin talk bout it afta de chilluns be put to baid," she replied.

He looked at her sharply. She thought he might be about to question her, but just then the children came running through the house and he was distracted by them. She set about frying up some pork to go with the potatoes Sam had peeled and the subject was dropped for the time being.

~ * ~

Kate woke up the next morning when sunlight peeked around the of the frayed cotton curtains hanging on the east facing window. She tried to get up, but her body just wouldn't cooperate. Pain lanced through every muscle of her body. She groaned and lay back on her bed. Just as she was wondering how she would get some food for breakfast, she heard a knock on the door. She couldn't have gone to answer it if her life depended on it. Then she heard Aunt Mary's voice calling, "Miss Kate! Wheah you at? Ah done brung you some breakfas'."

"I'm in my bedroom, Aunt Mary," she called. "I cain't seem to get out of the bed this morning."

Aunt Mary came into the room and with her came the smell of fried ham and biscuits. Kate's mouth watered just from the smell, her empty stomach cramped in hunger.

"Ah figured you woodn' be able t'git around dis mawnin', so Ah brung you sumpin to eat so's you can git yo strenth back. You eat all dis up. Ah brought you some hawse liniment, too. Ah figures it work just as good on folks as it do on hawses to git de miseries outta yo body."

Kate took the napkin wrapped ham and biscuits and gobbled them down. They tasted delicious and soothed her stomach. Aunt Mary then proceeded to rub the smelly liniment on Kate's back and legs over her protests that she could do it herself. There was a burning sensation all over her skin, but it was a pleasant one that soothed her aching muscles. She couldn't suppress a groan of relief. Aunt Mary smiled.

"Now you be feelin' betta soon. Ah got sumpin to tell you. Sumpin' t'ease yo min' lak dat liniment be easin' yo' muscles. Ah done tole my boy, Sam, bout you out dere pickin' cotton. He gone come and pick it for you when he finish at Mist' McIntosh fiel'."

Kate sat up fast, causing a sharp pain to shoot up her back. She cried out, and Aunt Mary rushed to help her. She pushed away the helping hands.

"Aunt Mary, I don't need Sam to come pick the cotton. I can pick it myself. My brother-in-law, Tom, will come help me. I just haven't told him I need help. I thought I could take care of it myself."

"Doan argue wif me, chile." Then, with a sly look, she asked, " If yo brudder-in law is so ready to hep you, why ain' he been ovah heah already? He outter know you cain' pick de cotton yosef even if you tole him you could." She paused and when Kate didn't answer, continued, "Sam gone ter come ovah heah and pick dat cotton. He gone ter do it for a share, like he doin' for Mist' McIntosh. It all settled and arguin' bout it woan change nuthin'."

She had a look on her face that told Kate it would be useless to argue with her. Kate considered the situation. After all, the cotton had to be picked. At this rate it would rot in the field and she wouldn't have money for the coming winter. She would have to give someone a share to pick it anyway. After Aunt Mary's kindness to her it might as well be Sam who picked the cotton.

"Okay, Aunt Mary. But only because you bullied me into agreeing with you."

Aunt Mary laughed and said, "Them ham and biscuits you done et is givin' you yo spirit back. Ah lak de soun' of dat. Ah reckon you ain' loss all yo good sense out dere in dat heat. Ah be back dis evenin' to bring you more food. Ah bring Sam wif me so's you two can meet." She turned and went out of the house.

~ * ~

Kate lay back and rested for a while longer, then managed to get out of the bed. She staggered over to the washstand that matched her bed where she clung until she felt strong enough to move again. The muscles in her back and legs screamed in tortured protest. When the pain died to a bearable throb, she moved again. The porcelain bowl and pitcher wobbled dangerously when she pushed herself away from the washstand. Determination etched itself on her face. It was rough going, but she knew she had to move to get her muscles working again. She hobbled around in the house all day, taking frequent rests and, by the time Aunt Mary came back with more food, and Sam in tow, she almost felt like she might get back to normal soon.

It was just starting to get dark when they came up on the porch. The birds had stopped singing for the day and the crickets were beginning their rusty anthem to the night. Frogs hollered for rain in the distance. Aunt Mary put the food she had brought on the small wooden table next to the sofa, then turned to Kate.

Her son was with her. He looked to be some younger than Kate and like he had been dragged here against his will. His dark chocolate eyes did not move to meet Kate's and his mahogany skin stretched taunt across the bones of his face. He shifted from one hobnailed boot to the other as his mother spoke.

"Dis here my boy, Sam."

Kate smiled at him and spoke warmly, "I appreciate you helping with the cotton, Sam. Your mother told me you'll pick it when you finish at Mister McIntosh's place."

Sam still did not meet Kate's eyes and his voice was gruff as he answered, "Ain' no need t'be grateful. Ah'm pickin' it for a share, jes lak Ah would for anybody else."

It wasn't the friendliest reply she'd ever heard, but she really didn't have much choice. Just then Aunt Mary shot Sam a look that would have frozen Kate on the spot, but Sam didn't even bat an eye.

Kate tried to ease the tension between mother and son. "Well, you have my gratitude anyway. And so does your mother. She took care of me yesterday when I was so sick."

"Ah knows all 'bout dat. You shudna been out dere pickin' cotton anyway. Some folks ain' got good sense."

Aunt Mary swelled up like a turkey gobbler and Kate thought she might actually strike Sam. Her voice rolled like thunder as she reprimanded her son. "Sam! You doan be talkin' to Miss Kate lak dat. Ah done taught you betta."

Sam looked calmly back at her as he replied, "We ain' slaves no mo, Mammy. Ah doan got to be p'lite to nobody iffen Ah doan want to."

Aunt Mary's face was still stormy as she answered her son, "Ah ain' talkin' 'bout bein' no slave. Ah's talkin' 'bout bein' nice to people whut is nice to you."

Kate jumped in to calm troubled waters. "Aunt Mary, it's all right. Sam doesn't have to be polite to me if he doesn't want to. Like he said, ya'll ain't slaves anymore." Looking at Sam, she told him, "I'd be grateful for your help. That cotton will rot in the field if it don't get picked soon and I need the money to get through the winter."

Sam looked at Kate in some surprise and she saw a small glimmer of something that might have a grudging respect deep in his eyes.

"My Mammy be right," he said. "Ah shouldna spoke to you lak dat. Ah 'pologize for bein' rude."

"Thank you, Sam. I can see that Aunt Mary raised you right. I don't take any offense at what you said."

"Den Ah guess Ah be gittin' on home now. Mammy, you come on home soon. De lil ones be a wantin' to see you befo' dey goes to bed."

"Ah be on soon, Sam. Ah jes' gone ter make sure Miss Kate eat dis heah suppa' Ah done brought."

Sam went out into the night. They heard him whistling as he walked away.

"Doan you pay no min' to Sam, Miss Kate. He a good boy. He jes' havin' trouble gettin' used to dis here freedom like all de res' of us. De President in Washington, he say we ain' slaves no mo'. But what do dat mean to us heah in Tennessee? We ain' on de plantation no mo, but what is we free to do? We is free to struggle for food and a roof ovah ouah haid, jus' lak de wite folks. A lot of de wite folks ain' wantin' us t' be free. But are we really free, Miss Kate? We still pickin' de cotton for de wite man."

Kate had never considered what the end of the war might have meant to the blacks. She had been too busy these last years worrying over her own troubles to see that the blacks in the county were having the same troubles and probably on a much larger scale. Many of the former slaves remained on the land of their previous owners as sharecroppers. Some drifted off, seeking other homes and ended up sharecropping elsewhere. Some who had mechanical skills went to work for small businessmen and others worked for the railroad. All were seeking a place in this new South.

Kate had heard some ugly rumors of men riding at night, disguised in bed sheets, burning homes of blacks and even killing some of them. She didn't know if any of these "night riders" were here in McNairy County. No one ever spoke of them to her as anything other than something that happened elsewhere. McNairy County itself had seemed to be a microcosm of the entire country. Sympathies had been split over Union and Confederate loyalties. A Union calvary had been raised in Bethel Springs during the War and many men from the area, including her brothers, had fought for the Union cause. Hard feelings still seethed throughout the county between Union and Confederate sympathizers. Even the hard times at the end of the war hadn't drawn them back together.

"I see what you mean," she said quietly to Aunt Mary. "My family didn't own any slaves, and my older brothers died at Parker's Crossroads, fighting for the Union. Our daddy didn't hold with owning another human being. He had friends who did though. When John and Andrew joined up with Fielding Hurst, those friends never spoke to any of us again. It cut Daddy deep, but he never said a word about it. I knew though. Some of those friends were people who had traveled all the way from North Carolina with him and Mama forty years ago."

"Ah knows dat, Miss Kate. Dey all did whut dey thought was de right thing like a whole lotta udder folks in de South. Ah jes' wants you to unnerstand why Sam de way he is."

"That's all right Aunt Mary. I didn't take offense."

Aunt Mary smiled and said, "Now you go on an' finish up dat dinner so's Ah can git home and see my granchillen befo' dey goes to sleep."

Kate did as she was told and finished up the excellent dinner of blackeyed peas, cornbread and fried pork.

She held out the plate and said, "You don't have to bring me any food tomorrow. I think I'll be well enough to fend for myself. I'm very grateful for your help yesterday and today."

"No need for gratitude, chile. Ah's glad to hep." Aunt Mary took her plate and disappeared into the night.

Kate could imagine the delight of her grandchildren when she got back home. It made her feel very lonely to think of it, then she wondered why she felt that way. She had plenty of family of her own to go to if she needed to. George leaving the way he did had shaken her badly and when she remembered the look on Savannah's face when she told her about the baby, she started wondering if she really did have family to go to when she needed help.

Seven

As good as his word, Sam arrived first thing the next morning and worked through the day only pausing for a brief lunch break. He followed the same pattern day after day.

A few weeks later as Kate was sitting on the back porch she saw him come out of the barn with an arm load of burlap sacks and head to the cotton field. She wondered how much pressure his mother had placed on him to pick her cotton and why Aunt Mary had done it, and how she had gotten Sam to agree. After a couple of hours she went to the well, filled the bucket with cold water, put the ladle in it and carried it out to the cotton field.

"Here, Sam. It's a hot evening. I thought you might could do with a cold drink of water." She held out the ladle.

He eyed her with suspicion, took the ladle full of water and drank it. Then he took another ladle of water and poured it over his head.

"Thank you kinly, Miss Kate," he said, then went on about his business. She took the bucket back to the house and sat on the porch again, staying there 'til darkness pulled its curtain across the day. Sam pulled the sacks of cotton to the barn, looking in her direction; he nodded his head and walked across the field back home.

~ * ~

Everything continued in this way until the cotton emptied from the fields and filled the barn. Tom dropped by to check on how much cotton the field had yielded and he and Sam exchanged few words. Their entire conversation consisted of how much cotton was Sam's share. Sam took his portion and Kate figured she probably wouldn't be seeing him again anytime soon.

"Well, Sister, it appears you got a pretty good crop here." Tom stated in his irritating way. "I'll take it with mine to sell and bring back your money. The gin ain't gonna want to be dealing with a woman on the price of cotton."

"That's fine, Tom. I'm going over to McNairy Station and get some things I'll be needing in the next few months. I'm all out of supplies and I've got more vegetables than I know what to do with. They'll make good eating this winter though."

"Maybe your sister should go get your supplies for you." A frown creased Tom's forehead, "You're looking a mite peaked these days. Now that the crop is in, maybe you should rest up a bit. I know it's been hard on you what with George leaving and all. I'm mighty sorry I acted the way I did when I found out about him leaving you here by yourself. Like I always said, that boy never had much sense of responsibility."

Kate thought she would faint when Tom said she was looking peaked. Truth to tell, she had been feeling pretty bad for some time now, but thought no one had noticed. For a minute she thought Savannah had told Tom after all, but realized he wouldn't be acting so friendly and concerned if he knew the truth.

"Don't worry yourself, Tom." She grinned at him. " I got over what you said when George left. I'm looking peaked because it's been so hot here lately. I'll be fine as soon as the weather cools off a little. I can go in and git my own supplies. Thank you for offering to ask Savannah to get them though. When do you think you might be taking the cotton to the gin?"

"I'll be going in a about a week. If you're sure you're feeling all right, I'll be on my way home then. Savannah'll have dinner on the table by now."

"Go on home, Tom. I'm just fine. I'll see you when you come to git my cotton. Give my love to Savannah and the children."

After watching him disappear around the curve into the forest, Kate went in the house to think. If he had noticed she didn't look well, then she might get some sharp looks from neighbors when she went to

McNairy Station to get supplies. She would just have to rest up the next few days and hope it would do the trick and she would be looking and feeling better by then. She couldn't have anyone guessing her secret just yet. She hadn't been able to lose the baby by picking cotton 'til she dropped, so she would have to think about what to do now. It looked like she would be having this baby whether she wanted to or not.

~ * ~

On the morning she decided to go for her supplies, it was a little chilly so she draped her shawl loosely around her. It helped to cover her from any discerning eyes. She didn't think anyone would notice the slight thickening in her waist. Thank Heavens she hadn't ballooned up like some other women she knew.

The way to McNairy Station wound along two miles of country dirt road. She set out at a brisk pace enjoying the morning. The sun had climbed well up in the sky by the time she arrived at Mr. Logan's store. Her eyes took a minute to adjust to the dim interior. She saw that several women were ahead of her shopping. While she waited her turn, she looked at the fabrics available. She would be needing some new dresses soon. Her old dresses could be let out some, but not enough. A lovely taffeta in blue caught her eye. What a beautiful party dress it would make. Sighing, she turned to the more serviceable calicos. She wouldn't be needing a party dress any time soon. Maybe never again. There were a couple of patterns in the calico that she liked well enough. As she stood deciding which one she would rather have, Mr. Logan called to her.

"Well, Kate, haven't seen you in a while," Mr. Logan greeted her. "Come to get dress material, have you?"

"Yes, I have. I was just trying to decide on one of these calicos for a new dress this winter."

"Mighty fine patterns there," he said "You could make yourself a real purty dress outta any of 'em. Saw you looking at that there taffeta. Found that in my attic. Left over from before the war."

"Yes, the taffeta's lovely. But, I don't think I'll be needing a new party dress this winter. Gotta have everyday clothes first."

Turning her thoughts from the taffeta, she picked up the calico in a pretty pink and blue color and carried it to the counter.

"I'll take ten yards of this. I think I've got everything else I need."

Measuring out the yardage for her, Mr. Logan continued casually, "Hear tell your brother George and that there feller that was working for ya'll high tailed it to Texas. That true?"

Kate's heart skipped a beat. The grapevine had already telegraphed that bit of juicy gossip. She replied calmly, "Yes, they left and went west. George just had to get out on his own somewhere else. I think he just couldn't handle things here now that our parents are gone. He talked Michael into going with him. Made it sound like a big adventure for them. He knew I'd be all right here on my own what with all the family we have hereabouts."

"You planning to put this here order on account," Mr. Logan asked.

"Well, yes. Tom will be taking my cotton to the gin day after tomorrow. I'll come in and pay you after that. Is there a problem? I've always bought on account from you and paid when the cotton was in."

"Actually, your brother owes me for the cotton seed this year and a new blade for the plow. He didn't pay before he left, so I reckon you'll have to pay me for that stuff, too."

"George bought a new blade for the plow on credit?" Kate was stunned.

"Yessum, he surely did. Come in here with that Michael feller and ordered a new blade to be put on account. Said he'd pay when the crop was in."

"Of course, I'll pay whatever we owe you, Mr. Logan. I hope you didn't think I would try and get out of it," she replied indignantly.

Mr. Logan waved his hands in the air to calm her. "Now don't be getting all het up. I just wanted to mention it in case you didn't know about it, so's you could bring the money for those things at the same time. No sense in you having to make two trips into town just cause you didn't know about the other."

"Thank you," she replied in a calm voice. "I didn't know about the blade. I'll be sure and bring the money for everything when I come back in. Reckon I'll be walking most everywhere now. George took our old mule when he left, so I had to walk in. I can carry the dress material with me."

"Me or one of my boys'll bring it out to you this afternoon. That'll git a mite heavy walking all the way out to your place. You might want to borrow a mule from some of your kin for a while. Cain't be walking everywhere you go."

"Thank you. I'll think about what you said. I'll go ahead and carry the fabric though. I wouldn't want to put you to any trouble on my account."

"Wouldn't be no trouble, but you go on and do what you want."

Picking up her dress material, she started for home thinking hard.

Why had George bought a new plow blade on credit? Hadn't he told her the blade had been bought with money from last year's cotton? She was almost sure she remembered him telling her that when she had asked him about the new blade. Lord knew they hadn't spent money on anything else this past year. It was a puzzler. She couldn't think of any answer for it. After she got home, she put the dress material away in a drawer and went to lie down. She was queasy after the long walk and shocked about the plow blade, too. It was a lot of money and would have to come out of her cotton money—which was now one third less because Sam had gotten that much as his share for picking it.

~ * ~

Tom Claiborne felt right with his world as he wheeled his wagon into his sister-in law's yard to pick up her cotton. He always felt good this time of year knowing that the sale of his crop would bring money to pay off his account at the store. Of course, prices had been falling the last few years and it took more and more cotton to make the money he needed, but he was confident that he could take care of his family.

The early morning sun had not yet heated up the air, but loading cotton was thirsty work and he gladly accepted the glass of sweet tea Kate offered when he had finished. He swung himself back onto his wagon seat and started to the gin. Whistling as he drove along the dusty road in the sun, he reflected on the odd situation with Kate. Nothing had changed in the last several weeks, but the premonition that something wasn't quite right came back to worry him again. He wasn't sure just why Kate's story didn't set just right with him. On the surface it was believable. He knew that George had hankered to travel ever since he was a young boy. The part that stuck in his craw and refused to go down was the part about Michael leaving, too. That just didn't make sense to him, but he had to admit that he had only known Michael for a little over a year. Maybe after the hardships and horror of war, the man just found it not to his liking to settle down and farm. Tom shook his head over that notion. He had been relieved to come home in one piece and settle back on his place. Flapping the reins against the mule's back, he urged it to a marginally faster pace.

~ * ~

Arriving in Purdy, he pulled his wagon up at the gin and got down to talk to his friends while he waited his turn. Standing in the shade of a big maple tree, they grumbled together about the falling prices of crops and as a group looked forward to the Mason's meeting next month when they could air their concerns with everybody else and maybe come up with a plan that would increase their profits. Tom doubted that the meeting would prove profitable in the area of increasing crop prices, but he looked forward to the monthly meetings as a chance to visit with all the other farmers in the area.

When his turn came he took the money for the cotton, carefully separating Kate's from his own. Looking at the position of the sun, he decided he had enough time to stop in at the saloon and have a glass of wildcat. There was quite a crowd inside. Blue smoke hung near the ceiling like fog. Raucous laughter rang out. Hands slapped tabletops to make a point. All the men coming in today to sell their cotton must have had the same idea he did. Standing at the bar, his foot propped on the boot rail, he was enjoying his drink when Jim Jackson from the Purdy Bank walked up to him. Tom nodded politely to the man and went back to concentrating on his drink.

"Ahem! Mr. Claiborne, sorry to interrupt your drink, but I saw you here and thought you might be able to answer a question for me," Jim said.

Tom adjusted his position to face the banker and said, "I'll do my best, if I know the answer."

"You're George Randsome's brother-in-law." At Tom's puzzled

nod, he continued, "Do you happen to know when he might be bringing his cotton to town?"

"Well now," Tom drawled, "I brought the Randsome's cotton in with me. George took off a few weeks ago and we haven't heard hide nor hair of him since. Kate's on the farm by herself now."

Jim's friendly face took on a look of alarm. "You mean ya'll don't have any idea where he is or when he's coming back?"

Now Tom was confused. *Why was the banker so concerned about George leaving town?* "You seem a mite upset, Mr. Jackson. What does George leaving have to do with you?"

"Well, I guess I can tell you. If George is gone and left no information regarding his whereabouts, then you must be considered head of the family now."

Tom sat quietly, with questions in his eyes as he waited to hear what Mr. Jackson had to say. It couldn't be good judging by the ashen complexion of the man standing next to him.

Jim Jackson swallowed convulsively twice before he spoke. "George Randsome came to see me about a month ago. He wanted to take out a lien on the farm. He said the house needed some repairs and he need to buy a new mule and some feed, along with a few other things that I won't go into right now. The point is, that the bank, with my recommendation, loaned George Randsome three hundred and fifty dollars against the farm. The lien was to be paid off in installments starting with the profit from this years cotton." Looking sharply at Tom he said, "You don't know anything about this, do you?"

Tom's hand jerked convulsively, almost knocking over his drink, as the meaning of the words sank into his mind. In a reflex action, he saved the glass from toppling over and gratefully downed the last swallow of liquid. It burned a fiery path down his throat settling comfortably in his now nervous stomach. He vowed that the itchy questions that had gnawed at him would soon be answered by Kate. With the farm itself hanging in the balance, she would have to tell him the truth. The whole truth, not the whitewashed version she had told up to now. Looking calmly at the banker he said, "No, I reckon I don't know anything about a lien. Kate didn't mention it to me. I don't rightly know how we'll be paying you the money. I'll speak to my sister-in-law this evening and we'll work out some kind of arrangement."

Clearing his throat and looking even more nervous and now pale, Mr. Jackson said, "Well now, Mr. Claiborne, I don't rightly know that the bank will let Miss Randsome pay out the lien in installments instead of her brother. Actually, I can tell you right now that they won't. A woman on her own and all. No husband or grown children to help her run the farm. The only way ya'll can keep the bank from taking the farm is to come up with the whole amount at once." Seeing the thunder gathering on Tom's face, he said quickly, "Why don't I come out to the farm tomorrow morning and explain everything to your sister-in-law? Maybe tonight ya'll can figure a way to raise the money. I'll be out pretty early."

Watching the flow of emotion across the younger man's face, Jim Jackson began feeling vaguely frightened. He quickly hustled out of the saloon.

Tom's anger mounted as he watched the older man scurry away. Damn Kate. She had lied right along about George. Why hadn't she told him about the lien? The woman probably had some fool notion about paying it off herself. Now he wondered just how much his own wife knew about the whole thing. Had she lied, too? She had never kept anything back from him before. Surely she wouldn't lie to him after all these years. No, the root of everything went back to Kate. That young woman was far too headstrong and independent. Her parents had spoiled her abominably. George too, for that matter. Pushing away from the bar, Tom strode urgently out of the saloon and over to his wagon.

Driving slowly through town, he nodded and waved to acquaintances. No use alerting everybody that something was amiss. As soon as he was out of sight, he whipped the mule to a flat out run and drove hell for leather back to the Randsome farm. Kate would give him some answers now!

~ * ~

Kate had spent the afternoon washing linens. A fire under the big black kettle in the back yard heated water for washing. She stripped the sheets off the beds and threw them in the kettle along with some shavings from a bar of lye soap. Using a hickory stick, bleached white from numerous stirrings of washing, she stirred everything till it was wet and soapy and left it to soak for a while. Later she scrubbed everything on a washboard, rinsed them in a tub of clean water and wrung them out.

She had just hung everything to dry when Tom turned the wagon into the yard with a look on his face like a thundercloud. He pulled up the horse and jumped from the wagon.

Striding toward her like the wrath of God, he started shouting, "What's this business 'bout George taking out a lien on the farm at the bank? I ran into Mr. Jackson at Purdy and he was asking 'bout the cotton and when George might be coming in to pay. What do you know about that? Are you holding back on me, Sister?" Stepping menacingly close to her he continued, "I thought we had a understanding 'bout running this farm. You were to tell me 'bout any money that was owed and consult with me before making any business decisions. Now I find out that there's a lien on this here farm that you didn't tell me 'bout. Mr. Jackson was some flustered when he found out the George is gone and you're on the place by yourself. He's acomin' out here tomorrow to see you about the lien and I'm agonna be here when he comes!"

Shocked at his words, frightened half to death at what it might mean to her, she faced him squarely. "I don't know anything about any lien!" she shouted in his face, "I just found out the other day that George owes Mr. Logan for cotton seed and a new plow blade. I'm supposed to take him the money for that when I go to McNairy Station again. I cain't believe George took out a lien at the bank, too. He never said a word to me about it! Did Mr. Jackson say when George took out the lien?"

Tom wasn't going to back down to her now. He would get his answers before he left the farm today if he had to shake them from her lying mouth. "That's mighty peculiar, too. Seems George took out the lien the same day he left. Appears he decided he needed some traveling money. You told me he took some money the two of you saved up." Looking her up and down with angry eyes, he insisted,

"You better be telling me the whole story now!"

"Well, it's true that I lied to you about George taking money that we saved up." She looked at him defensively. "But I figured you'd never believe he left with no money at all. Which is what I thought he did. I didn't know anything 'bout him stopping at the bank on his way out. I swear Tom. I didn't know 'bout the lien or 'bout the money owed for the cottonseed and new plow blade, either. How am I gonna pay for all this?" she wailed.

Tom continued to look grim. "That's exactly what Mr. Jackson wants to talk over tomorrow. The money from the cotton won't be anywhere near enough to pay off Mr. Jackson. You can pay Mr. Logan and still have some left over, but you can't pay Mr. Jackson and George put the farm up in exchange for the money. I don't know if Mr. Jackson is going to let you try to pay the lien or take the farm away from you."

"Take the farm!" Kate was aghast. "He can't do that! This is my home. The land is mine now that George left. Mr. Jackson can't take it. I'll make a deal with him to pay the lien and keep the land."

"That ain't never gonna happen, Sister. Your brother's name is on that lien and with him gone, the bank is gonna take this farm." Grabbing her arm roughly, he shook her till her teeth rattled in her head. "What are you holding back on me? What happened here that caused George to take off now instead of later? Why would he take out that lien, knowing you would lose the farm over it? What happened here?"

Kate struggled for breath, tried to think of something to say to calm him. She couldn't tell him the truth, not yet, and prayed that her sister would keep the secret.

Tom continued to hold her arm in a crushing grip while she remained silent. Finally, in disgust, he shoved her away from him and said, "Get away from me, you lying hussy. I'll find out the truth soon enough. When Mr. Jackson gets here tomorrow morning and you see the situation you're in, you'll tell me then."

~ * ~

As soon as he was out of sight Kate sat down abruptly in the yard. Things were just going from bad to worse. She needed the farm more than ever because of the baby. She had to have a place to live and now, according to Tom, she would probably lose the one thing she had counted on having. How would she survive with no place of her own? She wouldn't be welcome in any home once her secret was revealed. She must persuade Mr. Jackson to let her stay on the farm and pay off the lien herself.

Eight

Kate spent the night tossing and turning. Finally the sun peeked over the trees. She rose tiredly to face whatever was coming. Brushing her long, dark hair, she carefully braided it down her back, then put on the nicest dress she had, wishing she'd had time to make up the new calico dress. Then, smiling grimly to herself, she remembered that she owed for that, too. Well, what's done couldn't be undone, so she would do her best to keep what was hers. Determination glowed in her eyes as she walked into the parlor to wait for Tom.

He got there shortly, dressed in his Sunday clothes, looking uncomfortable. He didn't even speak to her, just walked into the parlor and sat down like he was waiting for a hanging. They sat quietly together until they heard hooves in the yard.

He looked at her and said sternly, "You just let me do all the talking. I'll try and work out some arrangement for you."

"No!" She protested indignantly, "This is my farm and I'll do the talking. Mr. Jackson will have to be dealing with me in the future and I want him to know I can speak for myself!"

Tom gave her a hard look as he said, "You'll do better to let me do the talking. This is man's business and women don't need to be mixing in on it. You just keep still."

"Cousin Tenia has been running her farm since Cousin William died and I haven't noticed you trying to tell her to keep still. I can do my own dealing just like her."

Tom sighed and explained patiently. "Cousin Tenia inherited the farm when William died. That's not the same as a lien. She's a lot older than you and knows a lot more 'bout business and farming. She's got grown children to help her. You let me handle this and learn from it. When you know as much as Tenia, then you can do your own business, too."

Kate wanted to stamp her foot and scream at the stubborn man, but Mr. Jackson was walking up the porch steps. She had to hush up and put on a welcoming smile. She pushed past Tom, ignoring his warning look, and opened the front door, saying sweetly, "Hello, Mr. Jackson. I appreciate you coming all the way out here to talk to me about the farm. Tom explained to me about the lien. I wanted to talk to you about that and see what we could work out. Come on in and sit down in the parlor."

Tom cleared his throat loudly just behind her and extended his hand to Mr. Jackson. "Nice to see you, Mr. Jackson! Come on in here and we'll have some tea while we discuss business. Kate will be glad to get us some glasses of tea. Won't you, Sister?"

He shot Kate a nasty look that said to get out of the mens' business and act like a lady. She smiled demurely at him and spoke to Mr. Jackson.

"I'll be happy to get some tea for you, Mr. Jackson. It won't take a minute and then we can discuss business."

She could tell Mr. Jackson was picking up on the tension in the room, but he smiled and said he would like a glass of tea after the dusty ride. She had already made tea that morning in anticipation of Mr. Jackson's arrival. She smiled to herself, knowing that Tom had hoped to trap her in the kitchen making tea while he and Mr. Jackson discussed business. Hurrying in to the kitchen, she poured the tea, put it on a tray and hurried with it back to the parlor where the men were waiting.

Shooting Tom a look of triumph, she set the tray on the table. Ignoring her brother-in-law, she turned to Mr. Jackson, and said in a calm, but firm voice, "Mr. Jackson, I want you to know that the farm is mine now that George has gone off. That I'll honor the lien and pay it off. We can work out the arrangements today."

Mr. Jackson shifted uncomfortably in his seat. Instead of answering her, he turned to Tom as he said, "As I was telling you, Mr. Claiborne, the bank is in a very bad position here. The lien was signed by George Randsome alone and since he has left, we are in the position of having to take the farm in lieu of payment."

Kate interrupted. "You cain't take my home! I'll work day and night to pay off the lien. This place is mine now. I'm gonna stay right here! My cousin, Tenia, has been running her farm for years. The bank didn't take it away from her! Tom tell him!" Turning to her brother-in-law, she implored him with her eyes.

Tom cleared his throat uneasily and turned his eyes to a point just over her head as he said, "Well now, Sister. Mr. Jackson was just explaining the law to me while you were out of the room. The bank appears to have every right to take the farm. You're a young woman alone with no one to help work the farm. The bank cain't take a risk on you. Like I told you, Tenia is a lot older than you and knows more about farming. She's got grown children living there to help her work the farm. Besides, there hadn't ever been a lien on Tenia's farm."

Mr. Jackson cut in just then. "Miss Kate, I realize this is a shock to you. Mr. Claiborne has told me you knew nothing about the lien. I'm sorry to be the bearer of such bad news, but the fact is that the bank will take possession of this farm. I came out here today to explain that to you so that you can make other living arrangements. We'll be taking possession in two weeks. That should give you time to make other plans and move your personal belongings."

Kate was absolutely furious and turned on Tom. "Are you just going to sit there and let him take this farm? Where am I supposed to go? This is completely unfair. Why do I have to lose my home? I can work hard and pay off the lien myself!"

"Calm yourself, Sister. The law is the law. I've said it before and I'll say it again—George never had much sense of responsibility. I don't know what he was thinking when he took out that lien, but he lost the farm for you in the process."

He turned to Mr. Jackson and said, "Thank you for coming out here and explaining the situation. I'm sorry for my sister-in-law's rude behavior. This is quite a shock for her. We'll make arrangements and have her out of here in two weeks."

Mr. Jackson stood up, shook hands with Tom, then turned to Kate and said, "I'm sorry as I can be, Miss Kate. There's just nothing I can do to let you keep this farm. The blame for losing it belongs with your brother, not with me. Good day to you both."

She watched silently as he walked to the door, picked up his hat from the table and left. Then she turned on Tom in fury.

"Why didn't you stop him? Why didn't you tell him we'd come up with the money? Now I'll have to leave here and go live with somebody else! Why didn't you help me?"

Tom's sigh spoke of his exasperation with her. He spoke as though to a child. "Sister, there was nothing I could do. The man had the law on his side. Where do you think the money would come from? You ain't got enough to pay him."

"We could get the money from somewhere!" Kate insisted. "You said I'd have some left after I paid Mr. Logan. We could git some more from the family! If everybody would just give a little, then I could hold off Mr. Jackson till next year and pay off the rest of the lien out of next year's cotton!"

Tom just looked at her sadly and said, "This is a hard thing to swallow. I know that. I hate to see the old place go to the bank, but there's just no way we could come up with enough money to hold the bank off from taking it. Winter's coming on and everybody will need every penny they've got to get through it. None of us have a dime to spare, Sister. You know that as well as I do. There's nothing we can do. It's like Mr. Jackson said, the fault is your brother's. I still aim to find out exactly what happened to make him and Michael take off like that. You got some tall explaining to do."

Kate sat down on the sofa, tears cascading down her face. She couldn't think what she would do now. With the farm gone, she would be dependent on the charity of family. That would work for a little while, but when they found out she was carrying a baby they would change overnight. She sure couldn't tell him about the baby now, on top of everything else. She continued to weep uncontrollably as Tom stood awkwardly by the sofa.

He bent to pat her shoulder in a consoling manner, "There, there,

Sister. I can wait a while longer to hear what happened. I don't reckon another day or two will change anything now. I know you're feeling mighty lost right now, but we'll work something out. I'll just head on home now and send Savannah over here to comfort you."

He made a hasty exit out the front door. Kate experienced a hysterical desire to giggle. Tom was no good at dealing with women in tears. She sat up, wiped the tears off her face and smoothed her hair. Savannah would be here soon. She was probably just waiting for Tom to come home and confirm what they probably had suspected would be the outcome of this interview. At this thought fresh tears spilled from her eyes and continued to flow.

~ * ~

Savannah arrived a little later. She bustled through the door and straight into the parlor. Handing Kate a handkerchief she said gently, "Crying ain't gonna change anything, Kate. You need to pull yourself together so we can figure out what you're gonna do now."

As Kate continued to sob helplessly into the handkerchief, her sister said sharply, "Stop feeling sorry for yourself and pull yourself together. I hate what's happened as much as you do, but we have to make decisions right now. Tom said you can come live with us if you want to. I could use some help around the place what with the children being too young to be much help yet. But there's the other problem that you've got that's worrying me. Sit up and dry your eyes. We have to talk seriously now."

Kate managed through sheer will power to stop the tears and sit up.

Savannah continued, "Tom will have to be told you're carrying a baby and—"

"*No*, Savannah!" Kate beseeched her sister. "You promised you wouldn't tell anyone. Why does Tom have to be told now?"

Savannah reached over and took Kate's hands in hers as she said," He's offering our home to you. I think he needs to know the situation before you move in with us. It was different before. You weren't living under our roof. I have to tell him now, before you move in with us. He has a right to know and I cain't be lying to him." She saw Kate was about to speak and held up one hand to stop her. "I cain't keep quiet about it anymore either. Don't you realize what you're asking me to do? You want me to keep on holding back information from my husband after he's offered you a refuge in our home in good faith. This is something we both know that he feels very strongly about. He knows there's something you ain't telling him. I cain't pretend I don't know and let you move in with us. I'm not even sure *I* can feel good about you moving in with us now."

Kate was very near a total breakdown at her sister's words and almost shouted, "You cain't have changed your mind! You said you'd stand by me. I need you now, more than ever. Why would it be any different just because I live with you instead of over here? I can understand why you need to tell Tom, but surely you can persuade him to stand by your own sister!"

Savannah sighed before she answered. "The difference is that your being in my home in your condition will make it look like what's happened is okay with Tom and me when it ain't at all. It'll reflect on us personally a lot more than it would if you were still living here. Tom ain't gonna stand for any more lies. I just hope he'll still let you live with us when he knows." Then she shouted at the ceiling, "Why did George have to take out that lien?"

She stood up and started pacing the room. Kate had the strange feeling that this had happened before, then recalled that George had paced this very room in the same way when she had told him she was carrying Michael's child. Goose bumps popped up all over her and she shivered. Savannah stopped pacing and stood looking at Kate.

"Kate, honey, I know you're in a real bad spot, but please try to see things from my side too. This is really hard for me. You're my sister and I love you, but you've done what no respectable woman would ever do. You've disgraced yourself in the eyes of everybody with your actions. That'll reflect on Tom and me if you are living with us. Tom has to know what's going on and we'll make a decision together."

"Oh God," Kate moaned. "What if Tom won't let me live with ya'll when he knows? Please, please don't change your mind. I know you can talk Tom into going along with you if you really try."

Savannah walked over, hugged Kate, then said, "I'll be letting you know as soon as we decide. I know it'll be hard waiting to hear, but it might be day or so before I can get back to you. This ain't a decision to be made in haste. Keep safe little sister. I'll be back soon as I can."

~ * ~

After she left, Kate continued to sit on the sofa completely drained by what had happened today. She stared unseeing at the shadows in the room as they shifted, following the sun across the sky. When a ray from the setting sun struck sparks from the mirror over the fireplace, she came to with a start. She had spent the entire afternoon in a mindless haze. She would have to pull herself together and stop wasting time like this. She needed to be getting her personal belongings ready to move—hopefully to Savannah's home. How could George have brought this on her? Was his anger and hurt so deep that he had relished the thought of her being thrown out of their family home? He must be secretly gloating from the safety of whatever distance he had traveled by now.

She knew she would never be able to just sit here and wait for her sister to come back. She'd never sleep a wink tonight wondering what was happening. She would to sneak on over to Savannah's and see if she could hear anything. The parlor window would probably be up just a little to allow the cool night air to circulate and she could listen from outside. Maybe she could hear their discussion about her.

~ * ~

The country at night held no fears for Kate. A quarter moon cast pale golden radiance onto the earth. Hoot owls asked her their eternal question as she quietly made her way through the woods where tree roots raised gnarled, arthritic fingers in her path. These were easily avoided. She had traveled this path so often that her feet had memorized the location of each one. As she neared her destination, she saw that a dim light reached slender fingers into the night through a partially opened window. She crept closer to the house on silent cat feet lest an inadvertent sound betray her listening presence. A voice in the back of her head kept jibbering that this was wrong. That she should turn and go home before it was too late. She extinguished that prickle of conscience as deftly as she would have put out a candlewick while she stationed herself below the window ledge to listen.

"Savannah, I cain't hardly see how we can have Kate living here now that you've told me 'bout her carrying a bastard baby," Tom was saying.

There was a pleading note to Savannah's voice as she said, "Tom, she's my sister. She has no home now. I don't approve of what she done, but Mama and Daddy would want me to try and help her. I promised Mama on her deathbed that I'd look out for Kate. I'm trying to understand why she done what she did, but it's beyond me. I only know I have to try and help her now. I couldn't live with myself if I didn't try to help."

"When word of this gits around we'll have everybody whispering behind our backs and probably cutting us dead to our faces," Tom warned. "Do you want t'live like that? I don't think your Mama would want you to."

"It won't be forever, Tom." Savannah's voice was gentle. "She can find another place—one of her own—after the baby's born. Maybe she'll even want to move away somewhere that she can pretend she's a widow woman. That would be the best thing for her—and for the rest of us as well. I could keep my promise to Mama and Kate can start over somewhere else where we won't ever have to see her again."

~ * ~

Bright light seemed to explode across Kate's vision at her sister's words. A feeling of vertigo overcame her so quickly that she had to cling to the side of the house and concentrate all her energies to remain silent while her soul screamed and shrieked in anguished betrayal. She managed to breathe slowly in and out, in and out, sucking the cool night air into her lungs. Gradually, the world stopped spinning. Sweat soaked her body in a clammy caul. Her knees ached from kneeling on the cold, hard ground. As she moved away from the house she realized her calves had become cramped while she crouched to listen at her sister's window. She sat down in the shadow of the well to tub out the cramps. As soon as she was able to stand, she fled back the way she had come carrying with her the heavy burden of disillusionment and betrayal.

~ * ~

Once she was safely home, she sat in the old porch swing, pushing it slowly back and forth. A gentle night breeze moved loose wisps of hair around and dried the sweat and tears from her face. It was so peaceful here in the dark. She could hear the distant bark of a dog and the wind whispering in the tops of the trees. An occasional bat fluttered by, intent on some mysterious errand and lightnin' bugs flitted across the yard flashing secret messages in the night. If only she could go on sitting in this peaceful darkness always.

Nine

The next morning dawned bright and clear. Birds called to each in the crisp air. A cow lowed in the distance. Savannah arrived about midmorning, a big smile on her face as she ran lightly up the front steps.

"Everything's fine," she burbled. "I talked to Tom last night. He was mighty shocked when I told him 'bout the baby, but I talked him round to letting you live with us anyway." When Kate continued to remain silent she said, "Aren't you happy 'bout that, Kate? I know you hate losing the farm, but at least you'll still have a home."

Kate forced back the hateful words that rose in her throat. How could this deceitful hussy stand here and say those words? Stand here and pretend to care when Kate knew different. She longed to throw the betrayer's offer back in her face, but where would she go if she said those words? She had no choice now. Pushing away the painful thoughts, she managed a weak smile.

"'Course I'm glad, Savannah. It's just all been so much for me to take in all at once. I started packing up my things last night. I should be ready to move pretty quick. I'd like to bring a few of the things here to your house. If that's all right with you. Tom can bring the wagon to move them."

"Bring whatever you what to. We'll have to find room for it at my place, but I think we can manage, if it's not a whole lot."

"I want to bring my bedroom furniture, the rolltop desk and the sofa and tables in the parlor. I know it's a lot to squeeze into your house, but I don't want to leave those things here. The rest of the furniture I don't mind leaving."

Savannah planned aloud. "We'll move Lydia in with Rufus and you can have her room. You'll have to squeeze the rolltop desk and some of the tables in your bedroom and I think we can squeeze the sofa and a couple of tables into my parlor. After all, you'll be wanting your own place someday and you'll need furniture."

The conversation from the night before flashed quickly through Kate's mind and she wasn't quite as touched by her sister's concern as she might have been. The sly creature. Savannah certainly had things planned out. She probably would have suggested bringing the furniture herself if Kate hadn't mentioned it first. She could hardly throw Kate out in a few months with nothing more than the clothes on her back and a small baby. Kate could use the furniture in a home of her own later or she could sell it and use the money to move somewhere else. No doubt Savannah was hoping for the second possibility.

Kate didn't let on that she knew Savannah was anything but sincere. She must be equally as sly as her sister. Pretend that everything was sweetness and love for now and make alternative plans. A deep weariness lodged itself in her heart. Forcing a false note of gratitude into her voice she replied, "Savannah, you're a wonderful sister. Taking me in and all, like you are. And even making room for some of my things! I don't know how I would manage without you." The grateful words almost made her sick. If only she hadn't listened in on them! But then, it would have been an even greater shock later, when her sister asked her to leave. Maybe it was for the best that she knew now.

Forcing herself to appear normal, she invited, "Come on in the house and have some tea, Savannah. If you have the time, that is."

Savannah smiled and said, "I'd be glad for some tea right now. I cain't stay long though. I left Tom with the babies and he's wanting to do some work this morning."

~ * ~

They went into the kitchen where there was a pitcher of tea already sitting on the wooden dresser. Kate poured two glasses and handed one to her sister, then sat down at the kitchen table to drink her own.

Savannah sat sipping her tea quietly for a few minutes, then said, "It's a good thing I told Tom 'bout the baby. You're starting to show now and he would have guessed pretty quick. Everybody will know soon. They'll be talking 'bout it, too. It's gonna be pretty hard for you from now on, Kate."

Wondering how her sister could sound so sincere, Kate replied defiantly, "Let them talk if that's what they want to do! These people have known me all my life. You'd think they would have a little understanding in their hearts for one of their own. I'm not some loose woman who runs around with any man who gives her a wink. I messed up, I know that, but I'm not a bad woman. They ought to forgive one mistake and let me just get on with my life."

Savannah sighed, then said, "This is not a mistake anyone is likely to ever forgive. Kate, you'll have no place in society now. No man will marry you and all the women won't want you 'round their husbands and sons. You know that as well as I do. You were raised the same as me. It don't matter a hill of beans that some man lied to you, you shouldn't have given in. You'll have to live with the shame for the rest of your life. I just wish I could understand why you did it."

"I loved Michael with all my heart! He swore he loved me and that he would marry me!" Kate insisted.

"Then why didn't you wait 'til you was married? How could you give yourself to him without being married first? I just cain't understand you."

"I keep telling you that he swore he would marry me. I trusted him. I never thought he would run out on me. I thought when I told him about the baby, that we'd just go ahead and get married right away instead of waiting. I never wanted this to happen! It's ruined my life!" Why couldn't her sister understand? Where was the love and support that she so desperately needed now?

"You must have known it could happen all along. You should have waited 'til you were married!" Savannah agonized. When Kate didn't answer her, she thumped her glass down on the table and got up saying, "I got to be getting on home. I'll send Tom over to pick up the furniture and your other things. We'll just get along the best we can."

Kate looked her sister straight in the eye as she said, "Yes, I reckon we will." A cocoon descended protectively around her shattered heart.

~ * ~

After Savannah left, Kate walked through each room in the house. Touching a dusty lace curtain here, some flocked wallpaper there, knowing that tomorrow all this would no longer be hers. She walked up the stairs, deliberately treading on the squeaky spots she knew so well. Standing at the window of her room, looking out across the fields, her fingers trailing along the crewelwork of the curtains, she looked inside herself. What was this odd, distant feeling that had taken possession of her? She could find no answer in her heart to that question. It existed as though it had always been there just waiting for the opportunity to protect her. She accepted that and went on about the final business of getting ready for Tom and the wagon.

Ten

At first, all was well in her sister's home and among the people she came in contact with. Everyone thought George was a scoundrel for taking off the way he did—borrowing money on the farm and leaving Kate with nothing when she couldn't pay. Kate was careful to let no comment pass her lips that might lead them to the truth a minute sooner than they had to know. In spite of her detachment, she meant her condition to remain unknown as long as was humanly possible.

At church and at evening socials, everyone was quick to offer her sympathy. To tell her how lucky she was to have family to turn to in her trouble. Kate agreed that George was a scoundrel. She would never forgive him for the revenge he had taken and never doubted for a minute that it was revenge. How different her life would be now if she had agreed to leave, but something in this land called to her heart. She had to stay here.

When she thought about having family to turn to in her trouble, she could not forget what she had overheard as she crouched outside the window at Tom and Savannah's that night. The betrayal that had seared her soul. It stayed there at the back of her mind, but the cocoon wouldn't let it get very close to the surface. As a result Kate was able to live in her sister's house in relative peace. They seemed to accept her in their home and treated her the same as always, but at the back of her mind, she could hear a clock ticking down the time of her stay with them. She tried to make some kind of plans for her future, but her mind just seemed a total blank. She drifted from one day to the next.

All feeling had died in her. She ate, drank, slept, worked and responded outwardly to those around her, but nothing touched her in any way. Her stomach was expanding now. People were starting to look at her in a knowing way. Whispered conversations took place wherever she went and former friends began to treat her coldly.

The need to wear cloaks and shawls against the cooling weather had concealed her condition for a short time, but eventually everyone realized that she was going to have a baby. The trouble began then.

Eyes didn't meet hers. Friends and neighbors began avoiding her, and by extension, the rest of her immediate family. At church empty spaces surrounded them as the members crowded themselves into other seats to avoid the family. Wives drew their husbands and children close to them when Kate was near them. Their eyes raked her face with contempt as they hustled their loved ones away from her. Reverend Thatcher shouted of hellfire from the pulpit. Invitations to social events dried up. Kate could see that her sister was taking these actions hard. Savannah's face grew thinner and more pinched each week, her lips drawn into a thin bloodless line in her face. Tom spoke less and less at home, but his eyes preached silent volumes to Kate. She turned away from their silent reproaches as she drifted through each day. The children sensed that something was wrong, but stopped asking questions after being rebuked several times.

~ * ~

Soon, the inevitable happened. At church one Sunday, old Miz Hopner approached her. Kate had an idea what the old woman might be about to say, but somehow couldn't summon up the emotion to care. Miz Hopner was known for her sharp tongue and even sharper old eyes.

"Why do you keep coming here?" Miz Hopner asked in a viscous tone. "It should be obvious to you that no one wants you here. Who do you think Reverend Thatcher is preaching about lately? Don't you realize it's you he's talking about? Eternal damnation. That's what's in store for a shameless harlot like you!" Then she turned to Savannah, standing nearby. "How you can tolerate this Jezebel in your home is beyond me! And everybody else, too. They just don't have the gumption to say so to your face. Well, I'm not afraid to speak my mind. I think this whore of Babylon should be put out of your home!"

Savannah's eyes darkened with pain and shame. Her shoulders hunched under her cloak as she turned and hurried from the church.

Kate replied to the old woman in a calm voice, "I was taught that God will forgive all our sins if we repent. That's why I come here. I'm sorry for what I've done and seek God's forgiveness. Where's your Christian charity? I believed the sweet lies of a man who left me to face all of you alone. Cain't you find it in your heart to forgive a young girl's foolishness?"

The old woman snorted her contempt. "There's no forgiveness for the likes of you! Fornication is against the laws of God. You'd do best to stay out of everybody's sight and not parade around like you've been doing. If you don't have any shame for yourself, at least show some decency for your family's sake! Stay home! We don't want you here!"

Kate turned away from the hateful old woman and followed her sister across the fields toward home. She could feel the eyes of everyone in the churchyard boring into her back, so she walked slowly with her back straight and head held high. They would not have the satisfaction of seeing her cowed before their judgment. Her cocoon slipped for a moment. Pain clutched her heart. Why couldn't they understand and forgive?

At home, Savannah said distantly, "I think it's best if you don't go to church with us anymore. Not to any more socials either. If we ever git invited to one again." A nervous tic started in the corner of her eye as she turned away from Kate.

~ * ~

Kate stayed at home after that, rarely venturing off the farm. It suited her perfectly in her current state. Her belly continued to expand and the child moved within her. She knew she would probably give birth in the late spring.

The year wound down toward winter. Trees wore their dying colors of scarlet, orange and gold in glorious display, then released their leaves to whirl on the wind and drop onto the ground. Geese and ducks were seen flying on a southerly course, quacking and squawking across the sky in their curious flight patterns, heading for warmer climates. Squirrels gathered acorns and other nuts for winter storage. Some of them were shot as they went about their business by men seeking food for the family table. So much preparation going on around her, yet Kate remained unmoved. For now, she lived through the approaching winter days and nights wrapped softly in her bubble, helping her sister in the endless rounds of housework, mending and sewing. In the evenings, she made cornhusk dolls for Lydia and carved soldiers from sticks for Rufus. The toys kept the children occupied during the long winter evenings when the whole family huddled close to the fire to keep warm. Frigid drafts penetrated around the windows and up through the floor. It was the coldest winter anyone could remember for years.

Biting winter winds kept them indoors most of the time. Ice had to be broken on the surface of the creek where they drew their water supply. Lugging the full buckets back from the creek usually soaked Kate's skirts with water that slopped over the sides from her clumsy gait. They ate well from the supply of vegetables that Savannah had preserved in the late summer and early fall. Meat was supplied from a hog that had been butchered in the fall and smoked in the little wooden smokehouse that Tom maintained out back. Deer and rabbit, shot and skinned by Tom, rounded out their food supply. The heavy hot suppers served to keep their blood flowing fast in the nights while they slept under numerous quilts and blankets to keep from freezing.

After the open declaration by Miz Hopner, the tension had increased even more in the household. Savannah and Tom hardly spoke to Kate. She often heard the sharp buzz of angry whispering in the night from the bedroom they shared. She knew that it had to be about her, but in her current state she just dreamily let the days flow past her.

~ * ~

"She's got to go *now*, Savannah," Tom whispered angrily to his wife in the privacy of their bedroom. When Savannah just shook her head miserably, Tom was angered even more. "I know you promised your Mama to look after your sister, but this is going too far! I don't believe even your Mama would condone this situation! You cain't keep going like this. You're worried to a frazzle. You'll be sick if you keep going at this rate. I should never have agreed to let her come here in the first place. It's gotten even worse than I imagined it would. She has to go now!"

"Just where would she go in the middle of winter in her condition? I cain't stand the sight of her anymore myself, but there's no choice but to let her stay until her time comes!" Savannah whispered angrily. "I never thought it would get this bad with our friends. I thought surely some of them would understand that I had promised my Mama, but they just call me a fool and turn away from me. I don't know how I'll make it till spring, but I just have to! I thought that you at least understood that! Are you gonna turn cold to me now, too?"

"Oh, Savannah!" Tom groaned as he pulled her into his arms and held her close. "You know better than to think like that about me. I just cain't stand to see you put through all this. Kate's nothing but a whore and I don't care if she is your sister. The first minute she can walk after that baby's born, she leaving this house!"

Savannah burrowed deep into her husband's arms and sobbed her heart out while he stroked her hair gently and whispered loving words of comfort into her ears.

Eleven

Tom needed a new coat. His old coat had worn thin at the collar, cuffs and elbows. A large tear in the back, where it had caught on a nail in the barn let in the winter wind. Savannah would cut the old coat down and make a coat for Rufus from it. They were hard pressed for money, but Tom had to have a warm coat. Savannah was too busy to go to the store herself, yet, because of public sentiment, was reluctant to send Kate. From the safety of her cocoon, Kate told Savannah that she didn't mind going, took the silver dollars from Savannah's hand and left.

The cold, brisk air felt good to Kate as she walked the miles into McNairy Station to Mr. Logan's store. It felt good to get out alone for a little while. Kate loved her sister's children, but never seemed to have any time for herself anymore. There was always someone around in the house that was too small for all of them.

As she walked down the rutted dirt road that was the main street of the small town, she saw many of her former friends standing around in conversation. They all eyed her as she approached. Then from the group of women standing near the post office, she heard a voice say loudly, "She should be ashamed to show her face."

Another voice chimed in, " Thank God her Mama and Daddy didn't live to see this day. The shame would've killed them for sure."

Ian McCormac's voice, over in front of the saloon, cut loudly through the quiet air—"Whore!" shouted her former beau, and spat in her direction.

For the first time in months, something in Kate's heart felt the impact of the hateful voices of people who had once been friends. Her step faltered for a single moment. Shaking off her momentary qualm, she continued to walk to Mr. Logan's store as though she hadn't heard. Silently she wondered why the words should impact on her now, when they hadn't at all in the recent past. She shook her head and let it go.

~ * ~

Inside the general store, she met Mr. Logan's disapproving stare with a level gaze. He didn't order her to leave, but his eyes were icy cold as he observed her walk to the warm winter fabric he had available. Her boot heels made hollow little sounds on the plank floor as she walked. He didn't move from his position in an old wooden chair next to the pot-bellied stove that glowed cherry red on this winter afternoon.

Picking up the fabric, she took it over to the counter and in a clear, calm voice said, "I need three yards of this."

Not saying a word, Mr. Logan rose from his chair, walked to the scarred wooden counter. He measured and cut the fabric, wrapped it in brown paper and tied it up in some string. Glaring at her balefully, he stated, "That's three dollar's worth of wool. Where's your money?"

Without a word, Kate put the silver dollars on the counter, picked up her package and walked out of the store without a backward glance.

The wind had picked up while she was inside. A strong, cold gust struck her in the face as she stepped onto the warped boards of the porch outside the store, temporarily robbing her of breath. Looking around, she saw that it had apparently driven everyone inside, which was just as well. She tightened her shabby, old cloak around her, adjusted the package to a more comfortable position and headed back to her sister's house. The walk back cleared her mind. She felt comfortable and safe once more as she arrived at the house.

~ * ~

"Savannah! I'm back," she called out as she walked through the front door.

"I'm in the kitchen! Please come get Lydia out from under my feet!"

Kate hurried to the kitchen, laid the package on the scrubbed table next to Savannah, swept Lydia into her arms and sat down by the table. Savannah frowned at her and then went back to mixing the bread dough for the week. She always baked enough to last for at least a week, because it saved heating the small kitchen to unbearable temperatures so often. Temperatures that were unbearably hot even in this unusually cold winter.

Savannah turned and looked at Kate again. Kate felt extremely uncomfortable with that expression. It was a mixture of pity and anger. That look had been present since Kate had come to live here. The anger becoming more and more dominant as time passed.

Avoiding her gaze, Kate looked around the kitchen. It had once been cheerful, but now the window sported a crack and the walls were in need of a whitewash. The wood showed through in places, but she knew that Tom could ill afford even such a small repair nowadays. It was a struggle just to have enough food to eat, put clothes on their back and keep the roof and walls repaired.

To get away from Savannah, she took Lydia into the parlor to play while she darned socks from the basket that never seemed to empty. Long ago socks in such bad shape would have simply been used as rags or thrown out. Those days were a long time ago now though. Their father had been a brick mason and he saw to it that they never wanted for money to buy the latest fashion in dresses or shoes. Looking down at the homemade calico dress that covered her bulging belly and at her worn boots, Kate sighed.

~ * ~

"Lord A Mercy, Kate! Sitting here wool gathering! That sock won't fix itself and you've let Lydia play in the wood box!"

Kate jolted back to the present as Savannah swept the child into her arms and away from the wood box. Bark and wood chips littered the floor where the little girl had been throwing them. Looking down, she saw that she had made few stitches in the sock that she held. Blue grey shadows reached long arms across the yard as evening set in. Kate realized she had been drifting in time again.

"Oh Savannah, I'm sorry," she said contritely. "I'll clean up the floor and finish these socks. I promise! I just lost track of time."

Thunderheads gathered on Savannah's brow as her temper snapped with an almost audible twang, "You're always losing track of time. You're a grown woman of twenty-three and about to become a mother! It's past time for you to stop acting like a spoiled child and accept that you have responsibilities. I don't think you even realize how your situation is affecting the family. Especially Tom and me and my children!"

A small crack appeared again in Kate's cocoon. Emotion trickled over her for the second time in a single day as she responded wearily, "What are you saying, Savannah? Do you think I haven't heard the whispers? Haven't seen people cross the street to avoid meeting me? Haven't seen the other women actually turn their backs to me? What do you want from me? I promise to be of more help to you, but this other thing is something I cain't change—No matter how much I wish that I could!"

Kate could see that Savannah wanted very badly to say something, but, biting her dry cracked lips, she turned tiredly back into the kitchen saying, "Just clean up in here and finish the socks. Tom will be in from his meeting directly and expecting his supper."

~ * ~

Tom came home that evening in a fit of temper. He didn't waste any time letting them know the reason.

"That Nigra, Sam Stancel, is sharecropping on the old Randsome home place." He looked hard at Kate as he continued, "Seems he's highly thought of by the Macintosh family and they needed somebody to keep up the house and property after Angus bought it. It just makes my blood boil to think of them Nigras aliving in the house that your father built with his own two hands. Angus Mcintosh must have lost his mind!"

Kate replied hotly, "Now, Tom, what's the matter with you? Our people were never slave owners! Now you're talking like some of the people who were! I had to have help getting that cotton picked and you know it! You admitted yourself you didn't have time to help me. I did the best I could! You cain't hold it against me that the bank took the farm. That was George's doing."

Tom's brows drew down over his eyes as he said, "That was George's way of getting back at you. It's a pity he didn't stop to think the rest of us would have to be responsible for you when the bank took the farm. We never owned slaves, but they had their place and we had ours. Now they're gonna be taking work away from poor white men, cause they'll work cheaper. They're gonna be living in homes, fine solid homes, that white men built for their own families! They ought to have to build their own just like we did! If you hadn't been such a dang fool, that farm would still be in this family and we wouldn't be burdened with you now!"

In a fit of temper she shouted back, "I don't want to be here any more than you want me to be here. If I had another place to go, I'd be outta here tomorrow!"

Savannah jumped in trying to make peace, "Tom! Kate! Please stop shouting over what cain't be helped. You're upsetting the children."

Tom and Kate glared at each other, but didn't say anything else.

~ * ~

Dinner that night was a solemn meal. Even the children were very quiet. Kate couldn't even coax a smile from little Rufus who was so fond of her. They seemed to sense the tension hanging in the air. Kate caught Tom looking at her coldly a few times, but he didn't speak except to offer the prayer and to ask that food be passed to him.

Savannah's pinched face looked skull-like in the flickering candlelight, but by some strange twist that same candlelight diminished the worn appearance of the furnishings. The once thick and colorful Aubusson rug worn to the woof in traffic areas and the bright colors faded to an overall washed out look. The damask curtains at the windows, split in places and hanging unevenly from their rods. Bone china plates and crystal glasses, in a mix of several patterns and cracked from careless handling. All in all it saddened Kate to see everything so worn and tattered. These few remnants were all that was left of the beautiful things their mother had packed and moved so carefully across the entire state of Tennessee from North Carolina, where she was born. A painful lump formed in Kate's throat with the knowledge that soon she would be banished from this house and these things would be lost to her forever.

Finishing her dinner, she took up her plate and went to the kitchen where she scraped the leftovers into the hog bucket and started to heat water in a pot on the stove to wash up the dishes.

~ * ~

Things went back to their same routine after that. Nothing was said about the words that had passed between Kate and Tom. Everyone seemed to be pretending that nothing had happened at all. Kate's cocoon, which had been breached so inexplicably, returned just as before and they all continued with their lives, until a few weeks later.

Twelve

Kate and Savannah were sitting on the porch taking advantage of an unseasonably warm late January afternoon when Rufus came running down the road and into the yard. Tears streamed down his little face. Kate got up from her chair in alarm. Taking several steps forward, she reached for him, but he brushed past her and ran straight to his mother, who said, "Why Rufus. What's the matter, honey? What's happened to you? What happened to your face?" Alarm sprang into her eyes.

Kate noticed the blood running down his cheek mixing with his tears. Fear leapt through her veins. She couldn't imagine how this had happened. Rufus continued to sob in his mother's arms as though his heart were breaking.

Savannah was terribly upset and said sternly, "Rufus! What has happened! Tell me this instant."

He looked up at her with his blue eyes full of tears and asked, "Mama, what's a whore?"

Kate felt her knees give out and sat hard in the chair from which she had risen when Rufus had run into the yard. She felt as though she had been punched very hard in the stomach and thought she might be sick over the porch rail. Savannah looked at her in horrified anger. Her safe cocoon shattered and fell away in the face of her nephew's pain and her part in it.

"Where did you hear that word?" Savannah asked Rufus in an angry voice.

Rufus looked at Kate, then back at his mother in confusion. He wasn't sure what he had done wrong and was afraid of giving the wrong answer. Finally he stuttered into the silence that seemed to have fallen over the entire farm, "The other kids at school said that my Aunt Kate is a whore and that a de-de-decent woman would go away somewhere and not shame her family. I told them that my Aunt Kate is wonderful and is my good friend and they s-s-s-said that I must be bad too, if I love her so mu-mu-much! I told them that they were wrong. That I'm a good boy and I help you and Daddy all the time and that I would fight anybody who said bad things about me or my Aunt Kate! That's when they jumped on me. I hit them and hit them, but there were too many of them. When I tried to run away, they threw rocks at m-m-me and one of the rocks hit me in the f-f-face!" He broke down completely then, sobbing in the safety of his mother's arms.

"Kate, run get a sticking plaster," Savannah said without looking at her sister. "The cut isn't very bad and that should stop the bleeding."

Kate went in the house on the run, but could still hear Savannah talking to Rufus.

"That is a very bad word, Rufus. I don't want to ever hear you saying it again. You were a very brave boy to take up for your Aunt Kate and yourself. You know I don't like for you to get into fights, but this time you couldn't help it. I know it wasn't your fault."

Kate knew who's fault Savannah thought it was. Knew too that her sister was right. Guilt flooded through her. She got the sticking plaster from the kitchen and came back to the porch. Savannah took it from her and applied it gently to Rufus' face.

"There. I think that will fix you right up. You can have an apple from the bowl on the kitchen table and go play in the barn for a little while if you feel like it."

"Oh, Mama, do you really think that I was a brave boy?"

He was all smiles now, squirming with embarrassed pride in himself.

"Yes. I think you were a brave little boy. Go on and play now so Mama can talk to Aunt Kate."

He ran into the house and came back out quickly with an apple in hand, then ran to the barn. When he had disappeared inside, Savannah's voice hissed, "Well, do you see what your stupidity has caused? My child is being tortured in the school yard! My God! I'm so upset I can't even look at you right now! We'll have to talk later. Just go somewhere for a while until I can calm down."

Horrified by what had just happened she tried to calm her sister. "Savannah, you know I love Rufus like he's my own child! And Lydia, too! I wouldn't have had this happen for the world. You know those children didn't know what they were saying. They were just repeating what they heard their parents say."

Savannah's fury flames in the afternoon air. Her eyes shot sparks at Kate. When she spoke, her voice was filled with that fury.

"Kate, Please! I cain't talk to you in a reasonable manner right now. Just go somewhere for a little while."

Kate turned, walked off the porch and across the yard to the field across the road. There was big tree there where she often sat, just daydreaming, a private refuge. She went there now. There was a reckoning at hand and she wasn't ready to face it. She knew Savannah would not prevent Tom from throwing her out of their home now. Her children came before her sister and now they were being threatened. Kate would have to go somewhere else. But where? She could think of no answer. As she sat under the tree, she could feel the wind picking up. Could see thunderheads forming in the distance. There would be a storm tonight, brought on by the unseasonably warm weather. She stayed there for over an hour. Tom came home as the sky began to darken. Kate felt sure that Savannah would be telling him what had happened. She stayed there under the tree until dark and the first large drops of rain began to fall, then she headed back to the house.

~ * ~

"You never wanted me here in the first place!" Kate shouted at her sister. When Savannah opened her mouth to speak, Kate rushed on. "Don't bother to deny it! I heard you with my own ears! I was listening outside the window the night you told Tom I was going to have a baby. You told him I wouldn't be here forever, just till the baby came and then I'd be out. I heard every hurtful word you said, but I couldn't think of anywhere else to go, so I came here anyway hoping I could think of something else while I was here!"

The reckoning was at hand. Kate was terrified of being cast out into the night. Savannah, backed by Tom, had told Kate she had to get out. Just as Kate had suspected she would after the incident with Rufus. Tom stood silently in the shadows of the room, but Kate was aware of his angry presence. It oozed over her like molasses and felt just as heavy. Savannah's eyes were flashing as she defended her decision.

"Damn you to hell, Kate! Why did you have to go and get pregnant and bring all this trouble down on our heads? If you'd only acted the way you were raised, we wouldn't be in all this mess! I tried to understand you, but I just cain't! You're a disgrace to us all! For the first time I'm glad that Mama and Daddy are gone. You would have killed them with this behavior just as sure as if you put a bullet in them! After what happened this afternoon, I cain't tolerate you in my home any longer. Tom and I have put up with you and with the reaction of everybody else for your sake and for the sake of the promise I made to Mama. But NO MORE! Get out of my home and don't ever let me lay eyes on you again!"

Fear of being alone at night in the brewing storm, pounded at Kate. She didn't want to be out there with nowhere to go. She tried to placate her sister.

"Savannah, It's dark out now. There's a bad storm coming up."

Savannah didn't back down an inch from her decision. "It didn't seem to bother you to be out in the dark when you were listening at my window to a private conversation! I don't care where you go as long as it's out of my sight!"

Kate tried another delaying tactic in an effort to postpone leaving in the dark. Her belly was huge now and she had difficulty walking in daylight, let alone in the pitch dark of a brewing storm.

"What about my furniture and my things? When do you plan on letting me get those?"

Savannah appeared to be on the verge of a hysterical fit, the cords in her neck stood out like ropes as she screamed, "THINGS?

THINGS? Is that all you can think about? Your precious SELF and your THINGS? My child is mobbed in the schoolyard. All of our friends have deserted us, our lives are wrecked and you're concerned about your THINGS? Get out of my house before I throw you out myself!"

For the first time, Kate saw herself through her sister's angry eyes. What she saw sickened her. She had drifted in her cocoon for months, never clearly seeing what had become of her and her family. Now she saw clearly and was appalled. She had thought that she could remain here and continue her life somewhat as she always had. She realized now that at the back of her mind had lain some kind of thought that perhaps Savannah would take the baby and raise it as her own. Then she, Kate, would just go on with her life. Now that the secret thought had come forward, she could she see that it was something that would never have happened in the best of circumstances, and, after what had happened this afternoon, was beyond impossible. Kate was sickened to her very soul by the mental picture of herself. Without another word, she grabbed up her cloak and fled into the stormy night.

~ * ~

After the door slammed shut behind her sister, Savannah Claiborne stared at it through eyes hot with anger. "I hope she dies out there," she shouted.

Tom went to his wife and pulled her into his arms. Resting his cheek on top of her head, he gently stroked her hair and murmured, "Hush now! Hush! You don't really mean that!"

"Yes I do," she insisted against his chest. "She ruined her own life with her loose ways! Then she thought we would all just pat her on the head and tell her everything would be all right. Just like a child. She has no more sense than a child, I tell you! No consideration of the trouble she caused for us. No! She just sashayed around here like there wasn't a thing wrong in the world! She's almost destroyed my life along with her own. Rufus may never recover from what happened to him today and it's all been her fault."

A muffled sob caught their attention. Whirling around as one, they saw their son, Rufus, standing in the open door of his bedroom, the tails of his nightshirt dragging the floor. Huge eyes stared out of his pale face; one small fist was shoved into his mouth in an attempt to hold back his sobs. His eyes flicked from his mother to his father and back to his mother. Removing his fist from his mouth, he asked in a quavering voice, "Is my Auntie Kate going to die? Is it my fault that she's gone away? I didn't mean to cause any trouble! Daddy, go get her and tell her I'm sorry and I want her to come back! Please, Daddy!"

Tearing herself from her husband's comforting hold, Savannah rushed to comfort her stricken son.

Thirteen

Thunder boomed and lightning crashed around Kate as though God Himself agreed with her sister. Cowering in the darkness, she tried desperately to think of a place to go for shelter. Every face she could think of was one she knew would be turned against her. She staggered numbly off to the scant shelter offered by the woods near the house. Wandered aimlessly between the dark tree trunks that offered little shelter from the wind and pouring rain.

She couldn't think. She *must* think. She must find shelter. Where in all the world would she find a warm, safe place? There was nowhere. Nowhere. She began to shake with cold as the rain soaked through her cloak, then her dress. Drenched through, she wandered the woods like a mad woman. Muttering to herself. Trying to think clearly in a world gone wild and unearthly in the gathering fury of the storm. Her chattering teeth made strange echoes in her head and she realized the spooky sounds she had been hearing were moans coming from her own trembling lips. The wild wind whipped the tops of the trees into an eerie dance, showering her with remnants of dead branches.

She wandered in the woods, her mind crazed and broken. Sleeping on the cold hard ground, wrapped in the tattered remnants of her cloak, time lost all meaning for her. An unknown time later, as she was again wandering the woods in the dark, a voice in her head whispered soothingly, softly, seductively as a lover's voice.

Death. Death is the way out.

She saw a clearing a short distance through the trees. Wandering closer, she found herself back on the old home place. She remembered then who she was and why she was wandering alone in the countryside. This was where it all had started. Those dreams of love that had turned to betrayal and shame. She would end it all here, too. The voice was right. She dragged her exhausted body into the barn and sat down to rest. Lack of food had left her as weak as a kitten.

The soothing voice whispered softly in her head again. *Yes, yes. Soon it will all be over. Soon you'll be at peace.*

Finally, she got up and found a length of rope in a stall. With trembling fingers she fashioned a noose at one end as her mind continued to churn. Because of her, harm had come to little Rufus. Her sister's life was a living hell. She had brought shame on herself and her family. Her death would rid the family of the shame of seeing her and her bastard baby every day. Put an end to her own pain and sense of shame. Why had she been foolish enough to believe Michael would marry her? Her death was best for everybody.

Climbing up to the loft to loop the rope around one of the rafters, she missed her footing on the ladder and fell to the floor below her. Her head slammed sharply against the ground. A blessed blackness covered her.

~ * ~

The door opened suddenly, letting early morning sunlight pour into the barn. Startled and disoriented, Kate jumped up and staggered back into a shadowy corner. She didn't know where she was or how she had come to be here. She cut her eyes from side to side, saw the ladder to the loft and recognized the barn. The events of the last several days flooded into her mind and she moaned. The child, the unwanted child, moved and kicked in her abdomen. *There is no God*, she thought to herself. The fall from the ladder should have at least started the child being born—and born too early too live. Yet even now she could not get rid of this unwanted burden. The merciful God she had been raised to believe in could not exist.

A voice called sharply from the door, "Who dat? Ah knows yous in heah. Ah done heard you. Now step on out heah!"

There was nowhere to run, nowhere she could hide herself. Miserably she stepped forward and saw the shocked surprise on Aunt Mary's face.

"Miss Kate! Honey chile, whut you doin out heah in dis ole bahn? Come on over heah, now. Why, you is soaked thoo! You is gone ter t'get numoney settin round in dose cloes." When Kate cowered back into the corner, she repeated in a soft, gently voice, "Come heah, chile. Aunt Mary ain' gone ter t'hut you. You knows dat."

Kate saw Aunt Mary look at the rope on the floor by the ladder. Knew Aunt Mary saw the makeshift noose at the end of it, but Aunt Mary didn't say a word. There was only kindness and understanding on her face. As their eyes locked, something older than time leaped and crackled between them. A living bond born of Kate's pain and desperation and the understanding that seemed to emanate in waves from the older woman. Kate's resolve to end her life leaked from her like water through a sieve. Whatever madness had possessed her the night before had gone. All her decisions seemed to end in disaster. She couldn't even try to end her life without making a mistake. She staggered weakly forward and whispered desperately, "Help me, Aunt Mary. Please, help me."

Aunt Mary rushed to catch the broken girl and folded her in her arms. The haunted looked faded from Kate's eyes as Aunt Mary held her close and crooned soothing words over her head. Warmth began to creep into her cold body. Then Aunt Mary led her gently from the barn and into the house.

~ * ~

"You shuck dat dress and unner clos. Ah'm gone ter get you sumpin dry to put on and fix you a hot drink, den you gone ter tell me whut you doin in dat ole bahn looking' lak a drownded rat."

She saw Kate look around apprehensively and smiled.

"Doan you be worrin bout Sam and de res' of em. Deys out in de fiels' for while. You g'wan get outta them clos lak Ah tole you. G'wan now! You lissen to Aunt Mary."

She bustled out of the room. Kate stood in front of the fire and did as she was told. The fire felt wonderful, sending warmth through her freezing flesh. Aunt Mary was back quickly with a dress, under clothes and a shawl over her arm. Handing them to Kate, she smiled reassuringly and left the room. Kate put on the clothes, grateful for something warm and dry to wear. Just as she finished, Aunt Mary bustled back with a cup in her hand.

"You drink dis. It a special recipe Ah got frum my Mammy. It woan hut yo baby none, but might keep you from gettin a cole or wus."

Kate took a cautious sip of the brew. It tasted of honey and warmth. It felt wonderful on her long empty stomach. The cup warmed her cold hands. She swallowed the rest of it quickly and handed the cup back to Aunt Mary, who put it on a table, then pulled two chairs over in front of the fire, gesturing for Kate to sit down. She took the opposite chair and reached for Kate's hands.

"Now. You tell Aunt Mary whuts done happen to you. Doan be 'fraid to truss me. Ah spec Ah knows whut happen, but you tells me yo way. You feel betta when you gets it all out."

Aunt Mary's warm hands held Kate's. Her eyes were kind. Kate felt that she could tell this woman the whole sorry truth and it would go no further. The story poured from her in a torrent of words. Once she began, she couldn't stop the ugly, sordid tale of the last several months. All her pain, anguish and betrayal spewed from her. Michael, George, Savannah and Tom. Even little Rufus. Their spirits paraded around the room before her eyes as she spoke. Aunt Mary's eyes never left Kate's face during the telling and she squeezed Kate's hands in an understanding way whenever she hesitated. When the story was told, she was as limp as if she had run a hundred miles. Aunt Mary nodded her head sadly.

"Jus' lak Ah thought. Yo fambly done gibed in to whut other folks thinks . Dey oughtter be shamed of deyself, but Ah spec dey is tellin' deysefs dey don whut was right. Doan you worry yosef, you kin stays wif us for as long as you needs. When yo time come, Ah kin hep you. You gone ter need a woman when de time come and Ah's de bes' midwife in dese pahts." She stood briskly. " Now you gwan in de udder room an' lay down and get some res'."

In total surprise, Kate replied, "But, Aunt Mary, I can't stay with you! What will all your friends and neighbors think! You can't take in a white woman carrying a bastard baby. My own family threw me out because of it. Why would you take me in when my own flesh and blood has turned their backs?" She felt tears rising in her eyes and firmly changed direction. " What on earth will Sam say? I cain't see him agreeing to this."

"Sam be a man grown, but Ah's still his Mammy. He a respecful son. He woan say nutthin' 'gainst dis. Ah ain' worrin my head bout whut my friens think. Ah's worrit bout a young woman lak you out on de roads, sleepin' in bahns and sech and maybe bringin' dat baby early. Den who gwin hep you? You could die sumwhere and nobody'd know. Dat's whut Ah's thinkin'. Yo fambly is fine folks, but Ah done heard dat de Bible says "if thine eye offend thee, pluck it out." Ah spec dats what dey think dey done. It doan make it right, but Ah spec dey doan see it dat way. You is a woman in need and dats de onlies reason Ah need to gibe you a place to stay."

"Maybe it would be better if I did die. And the baby with me. Then they could stick me in a hole somewhere and pretend I never existed. That would work for everybody."

Aunt Mary was outraged. Her eyes flashed fire and her chest heaved.

"You hesh yo mouf. Ah ain' never heard sech trash. Ah seed dat rope in de bahn. Ah knows whut you was fixin ter do. Dat chile is innocent. He din ask to git made and you is responsible. You gone ter have dat baby and bof of you is gone ter live if Ah haf to tie you to my apron till yo time come." Then continued more gently, " You been thoo a worl' of hu't, honey chile. Ah knows bout hu'ttin. Ah done hu't a lot in my lifetime, but we all got to carry de load we giben. Now you gwan and get some res' lak Ah done tole you. You feel stronga afta you gets some res'."

Kate stood up to do as Aunt Mary said, but had to turn back and hug her as hard as she could. "You have shown me more kindness in the last hour than I have known in these last six months. Even before my sister told me I had to leave, they were never really kind after they found out I was having a baby. They tolerated me for family's sake, took me in for a little while to ease their own minds and in the end even being family wasn't enough. I'll never forget this past hour for as long as I live."

Aunt Mary hugged the shattered girl in return, reached out and brushed the hair off her face, the way Kate's mother had done in another lifetime.

"You go res' now chile," she said gently. " Res' is the bes' medcine for a weary body or a weary spirit and you got bof."

Kate walked into the bedroom and fell onto Aunt Mary's' bed. Why was Aunt Mary so understanding? What was there in her that was missing in everyone Kate knew? Aunt Mary saw only a woman in need and not the shameless whore everyone else saw. That was the difference. But why was that compassion missing in the people who had known and loved her all her life? Here she would be accepted, as least by Aunt Mary, as just another person. She was uncertain about living with a black family for an extended period of time. So many people looked down on blacks as unintelligent and lazy. A lower form of life than the whites. By staying here she would be putting herself on an even lower rung of the ladder in the eyes of many of the whites of the community. Then she berated herself for such ingratitude. Aunt Mary had offered her a home out of a kind heart. Why should she concern herself with the vindictive tongues of the very people who had condemned her as a whore? Pulling the faded quilt up over her shoulders she was suddenly overcome with weariness and fell instantly into a peaceful sleep in that safe, warm place.

~ * ~

She was awakened some time later by a loud, outraged male voice, that she instantly recognized as Sam's.

"Lawd Gawd! Miss Kate's asleep in yo room! Ah cain' believe it! Ah done come home to tell you that word is out all over the place that huh sista done tho'd her outta huh place an woan none a the res' of em take huh in and you gone tell me she sleepin in yo room? That you done tole her she can stay heah for as long as he needs?"

Aunt Mary interrupted him in a quiet, but stern voice. Though she spoke quietly, Kate could still hear the words.

"You hesh up! Ah foun dat chile in de bahn, wet thoo and miserable. She done had a rope and was aimin' to hang huhsef! She done been thoo mo dan mos people can stan'. She a woman in need, and wite or black, Ah gone ter hep huh! An you are too iffin Ah says so, an Ah do! You should'a seen dat girl, cryin' lak a baby. I done raised you betta than ter turn yo back on sumbody dat needs hep. We done took in Permelia an huh baby. One mo ain' gone ter make no difference."

Sam was still outraged and didn't back down from his mother.

"One mo ain' gone ter make no difference, ceptin' that that one mo jes happen ter be Miss Kate Randsome! Whut ah people gone ter say when dey fine out bout dis? You know the wite folks be even harder on Miss Kate wen dey fine out, and de black folks gone ter think we done los' ouah mines. Ah feel sorry for huh, but Ah doan know bout dis staying heah. Whut Mist' McIntosh gone ter say wen he fin' out she heah? Dis his lan' now. We jes be fahmin' on it. He might tho' us off de place for lettin' huh stay heah."

Aunt Mary replied firmly, "She gone ter stay heah! Wen she wake up, Ah doan want ter heah you say nuthin' bout huh not bein welcome. An doan be makin no faces neitha! We deals wif Mist' McIntosh iffen we has, too. Whut he doan know woan hut him."

Kate knew that she had to put a stop to this now. She couldn't be the cause of dissent between the two of them. Sam was right, they could be turned off the farm for harboring her here. She had been too optimistic, thinking she could have a home here. She should have thought of Mr. McIntosh herself. No doubt he would have the Stancel's off his land if they insisted on giving her a home. Rolling to the side of the bed, she got up and smoothed her dress and hair. When she opened the bedroom door, both of them looked startled.

~ * ~

"Aunt Mary, I told you Sam would never agree to this," she said. "I have to leave and find somewhere else I can stay. Surely someone will take me in. I didn't try *all* of my kin. I'll just go to some of my cousins and ask them. I cain't let ya'll get thrown out of this place by Mister McIntosh just because you let me stay with you."

They looked at her quietly, then Sam said, "Miss Kate, Ah sho din mean for you to heah whut Ah said. An Ah'm sorry ter be the one ter haf ter tell you, but ain' none of yo fambly gone ter take you in—not even yo cousins. De talk all aroun' is dat ain' none of em evah gone ter look you in de eye agin. Ah'm sorry as Ah can be bout yo problems. Ah jes doan see how it gone ter work out wif you stayin heah."

"Thank you, Sam, for being honest," Kate replied humbly. "I won't stay here and make things hard for you and your family. I'll just have to think of something else, somewhere else."

"You bof jes hesh," Aunt Mary exploded. "Miss Kate, you ain' goin' no wheah in yo condition. You got to at leas' stay 'til dat baby is born. Den you can be thinkin bout goin somewheah else. An you Sam, worrin bout trouble befo it comes. She Gone ter stay heah! An that's mah final word bout it!"

Sam looked at Kate, and then at his mother.

"Okay, she stay till de baby come. Den she go," he insisted and stomped out of the house without a backward glance.

~ * ~

Aunt Mary took Kate's hand in hers, smiling as she said, "You doan be worrin' bout Sam. He a good man. He know his Mammy be right, but sometimes he got ter be ornery bout it."

Kate refused to put off the track by Aunt Mary's words and her smile. "You're right about me needing to stay somewhere until the baby comes, but as soon as it does and I'm back on my feet, I'll be moving on."

Fourteen

And so began the oddest period of Kate's life. The most arduous and yet most peaceful she had known since before the War. Not cast out alone as she had been, yet no longer holding a place in the world she remembered. The Stancels gave her a place in the world they had created for themselves in the aftermath of War. Could she make a place for herself in this society even as she strained to win back her place in the society to which she had been born? Was there a place here for an outcast and shamed white woman in a community that was growing and exerting its presence in the very shadow of the world to which she longed to return? Or would she find herself an outcast here also, bringing pain to those who sought to help her? Only time would tell. She and Sam declared a silent truce. She was introduced to his children and to Permelia and her daughter who were also staying there, because, like Kate, they had nowhere else to go. Kate helped Aunt Mary with chores around the house and helped to take care of the children. Her shattered emotions began to heal. She began to see that she had been wrong to think of suicide. Aunt Mary had been right that first day, the child was innocent. Admitting that to herself didn't cause her to love the child she carried. Her bulging belly was a constant reminder of the mess she had made of her life. She didn't want the child any more now than she had in the beginning, but didn't see how she could get rid of it. Sometimes she fantasized that it would be stillborn, but knew in her heart that that was unlikely. The baby moved and kicked all the time..

Over time a routine developed and she began to feel that she might survive after all. Her emotions settled. She could do nothing for the time being. She was tied here until her baby was born. After the birth, she would have to decide how to live as the outcast she had become.

Aunt Mary never again mentioned the rope in the barn and seemed to take it for granted that Kate would remain with them sharing their lives. She slept in Aunt Mary's room, which had once been her own, and Permelia and her daughter, along with Sam's children slept in the other bedroom that had once belonged to George and her brothers. Sam slept downstairs in the big back room that had belonged to her parents. Aunt Mary said it seemed huge to them after the two-room shotgun house they had lived in on Mr. McIntosh's place.

It felt strange to her to be in this house where she had been born and lived her entire life and know that it wasn't hers anymore. Some of the old furnishings were still in place and were also no longer hers. Sometimes when she woke at night, she thought everything had been a nightmare and she was awake and safe in her own bed in her own home. Then, the baby would move and she would realize anew that this was no nightmare. Her pillow absorbed a flood of muffled tears on those nights.

She didn't hold a grudge against the Stancel's for living here now. It wasn't their fault that the farm had been taken from her. They didn't own it any more than she did. Mr. Mcintosh had bought it at a sale and allowed them to live in it while they sharecropped his land. Kate couldn't even bring herself to feel anger toward Mr. Mcintosh. He had bought the land legally.

~ * ~

Aunt Mary never, by look or demeanor, let on that the family was doing Kate a favor by giving her a home with them. She treated Kate like one of the family and expected her to do her share of the work of the farm, no more, no less. Sam continued to be distant from her, but the largest sour note in their routine was Permelia, who made it clear that she did not like Kate and thought Aunt Mary must be soft in the head to insist that Sam let Kate live with them. She avoided Kate whenever possible and when forced to be together in front of Aunt Mary she took care to never speak to Kate unless it was unavoidable.

In the spring, on one of many occasions when they were washing laundry together, she showed Kate just how much she resented the situation.

"Well, Miss High and Mighty Kate Randsome, look lak you done come down in de worl'. Everbody done know yo shame now. You ain' so high now, is you?"

Kate ignored her and continued to wring out the wet clothes in preparation for drying on the bushes near the house.

"You be down heah at de bottom wid de Nigras now. Ain' no wite fokes gone ter be seen wid you now, Missy." When Kate still didn't reply she continued, "If Aunt Mary wudden sech a kine person, you probly be daid by now and nobody be a sorrowin' ovah you neitha. You done turned out to be trash ebben tho you be born to betta'. Yas ma'am, you be down heah at de bottom now, awright."

Kate's temper finally boiled over. She lashed out at Permelia, "You just shut up, Permelia. You're living here on charity, too. You wouldn't have a place yourself if Aunt Mary weren't so kind. She's the one who says what's what here and you just have to put up with me."

"Thas right," Permelia replied saucily, hands on her hips. "Ah be libbin heah on charity too, but dese my people. Ah wudden born to quality. Ah be doin betta now dan Ah was befo' de woah', but look like ter me you done come way down in de worl'. Yas ma'am, you be trash now and ain' no goin' back for you neda'. You always be trash frum now on. Yas' ma'am, trash libbin on charity in de house you wuz boan in!"

Permelia began to laugh hysterically at the thought and, enraged, Kate leaped on her and knocked her to the ground. Permelia began to scream and claw at Kate as they rolled on the ground. Suddenly, Kate felt a sharp pain in her swollen belly.

As she hesitated momentarily, Permelia took advantage and slapped Kate hard across the face, and shouted, "You wite trash ho! Doan you evah lay hands on me agin! Ah kill you, do you evah do dat agin!"

Kate screamed in agony as another pain caused her to draw her knees up as close to her body as she could. "Run get Aunt Mary," she panted. "I think the baby's coming."

Permelia continued to stand looking down at Kate with contempt on her face, while Kate moaned and rolled on the ground. Kate heard the slap of the back door and hurrying feet come toward her, then Aunt Mary was kneeling next to her and putting a gentle, knowing hand on Kate's rippling belly.

She turned to Permelia and asked, "Whut you doin' standin' dere lak dat? Cain' you see dis girl fixin ter hab dis baby right heah in de yahd? Git ovah heah and hep me git huh ter de house."

Grudgingly, Permelia moved to Kate's side and helped Aunt Mary raise her to her feet. There was still anger on Permelia's face as they moved Kate to the house and Aunt Mary spoke to that anger.

"Ah doan know whut de two of you was up to out heah in de yahd, but dat be ovah now. We be worrin' bout bringin dis baby now and bof of you jes for'get whut evah it was."

~ * ~

They put Kate on the bed in the room she shared with Aunt Mary. Kate continued to moan and scream in pain. Aunt Mary sent Permelia to look after the children while she helped Kate bring her child into the world.

Pain, the likes of which Kate had never known, took possession of her body. She was trapped in a red and black hell from which there seemed no escape. An incredible pressure formed in her belly as her child struggled to be born. Sweat poured from her body, soaking her dress and the bedding below her. Aunt Mary spoke gently to her from what seemed an enormous distance, wiping her sweating forehead with a rag dipped in cool water. She had never imagined that giving birth would be like this. It was beyond anything she could have imagined even if she had tried. She had been present at the birth of several of her nieces and nephews, had listened to the moans and screams of her sister, but had never known that this kind of pain could be lived through. Surely she would die from sheer pain before the baby was born. With each excruciating contraction, she bit down hard onto the leather strap that Aunt Mary had placed in her mouth. Finally, after hours of red hot, searing, sweating pain, Kate delivered her baby into Aunt Mary's waiting hands. She heard the slap and a newborn infant wail, then Aunt Mary left the room with the baby. She came back after only a few minutes, stripped the sweat soaked dress from her and wiped her sweating body with a cool, wet towel. She put a clean, warm nightdress on Kate who was falling into an exhausted sleep even as a quilt was pulled up over her.

~ * ~

Later, Aunt Mary brought the child into the room for Kate to see him, but Kate had no desire to see her child—the cause of all those hours of unbearable pain, the cause of all her unhappiness and exile. She had tried to kill him before he was born, had hated and resented him the entire time she carried him. She turned her face to the wall, ignoring Aunt Mary and the bundle she held so carefully in her arms.

Aunt Mary sat on the edge of the bed. "Ah brung you yo son, Miss Kate. Doan you be actin' lak you ain' gone ter take care of him. You brung him into dis worl' and you gone ter tek care o' him. Now you turn on aroun' heah and hole yo son."

The child was her responsibility. He would need her for the rest of his life and since she had no life of her own, she might as well take care of the baby. Aunt Mary would sit here until Gabriel blew his trumpet if that's how long it took her to acknowledge her child. It was useless to try and avoid her responsibility. Kate rolled to face Aunt Mary. Her son was placed in her arms. She held the mewling child loosely, not looking at him. Aunt Mary gave her a reproachful stare. Finally, she looked down at the baby in her arms. At the moment she looked into the baby's face, she felt the most overwhelming love she had ever known. Her own blue eyes looked back at her from a perfectly formed little face. Dark hair made damp whorls on the baby's head, a small bubble formed between the tiny, rosy lips. Tears spilled from her eyes. When she looked up at Aunt Mary, there were tears in the old woman's eyes, too.

"Ah knowed as soon as you looked at dat lil boy you wuz gone ter love him, no matter whut his bein' heah done cost you. Now he need a name. Whut you gone ter name dat chile, Miss Kate?"

"I'm going to call him John Wesley. I always liked those two names."

"Dat a fine, strong name for' boy chile. Ah lak it, " Aunt Mary declared.

"He'll have to be strong, Aunt Mary," Kate said sadly. "He's the son of Kate Randsome. He'll spend his whole life trying to overcome that." Kate felt a deep ache come over her at the thought of this beautiful child having to bear such a burden. He was marked from birth as an outsider because she hadn't had the sense to wait until she married before she became pregnant. A crushing sense of guilt shot through her. How could she ever give this child a good life when she was outcast from the very people he should associate with? She must find some way back to that world. The world which this child deserved.

Aunt Mary broke into her thoughts, saying, "You have ter be de one to teach him strength. You cain' be hidin' out on dis here farm all de time no mo'. Iffin you wants dat chile to walk proud, you gots to be de one ter show him how it done. You got to hab de courage ter fine a place for de bof of you."

"I don't know how to go about it, Aunt Mary," Kate replied. "I'll never be accepted again. This beautiful, innocent child is the mark that I'm a fallen woman."

"You has ter do yo bes' by dis chile," Aunt Mary insisted. "Maybe you nevah be accepted again, but you kin have some kind of life for yosef and dat chile. Dat's not de same as bein accepted, but it's betta dan hidin' out all yo life. Cos' you could move some weah else and preten' you a widow. Dat be easier."

Even after all that had happened, Kate still couldn't stand to leave this place, even knowing it would be easier for both of them if she did. Maybe there was already some small amount of steel in her spine that she could build on to create some kind of future for herself and John Wesley. Maybe she was just plain soft in the head. She didn't know why she felt so strongly bound to stay. She tried to explain to Aunt Mary.

"I cain't leave this place, Aunt Mary. I was born here and all my kin are here. They may not acknowledge me, but my son will grow up here and know his kin. This will be his home, too. And maybe the home of his children and grandchildren. You're right that it would be easier to start over somewhere else, but I won't run off like some kind of criminal. The only crime I committed was to love a man who lied to me. I won't run just because I was a fool. Can you understand that or do you think I'm just crazy?"

Aunt Mary looked at her thoughtfully, then replied, "Ah thinks you choosin' the hard road wen you doan haf to, but Ah kin unnerstan' pride, too. Ah think you lettin yo' stubborn pride rule ovah you, but dat be a start of dat life you kin build for' de two of you. Stubborn pride kin take you paht of de way you needs ter go." She continued in a cautious tone, "You knows you is welcome to stay here wif us, but you hafta know dat bein' heah will only make things wus for' you. Livin' wif Nigras is just as big a sin ter de wite fokes roun heah as havin' a baby wifout bein' mahied."

"Aunt Mary, I love you like family. You gave me back my life when I was going to end it. You saved me that morning in the barn. You know what I was gonna do, but you never held it against me. You just took me in and loved me like your own. I feel no shame in living' here with you. I'd like to stay for a while."

Aunt Mary's eyes were very kind as she looked at Kate lying there holding John Wesley. Kate knew Aunt Mary really did understand her. Maybe between the two of them her son would learn to be strong. It was a world torn apart with no one really knowing what the future held or what would be their place in it. Perhaps in years to come, in this new world, John Wesley could overcome the stigma of his birth to have a family and a wonderful life. Kate vowed to make it her life work to see that he had every opportunity she could beg, borrow or steal for him.

Fifteen

As the seasons turned, the little while stretched on and on. Aunt Mary had been right. The white community continued to shun her. Her family and those who had known her all her life closed ranks tightly. What Mister McIntosh thought of the situation, Kate never knew. He never appeared at the farm to demand that she be sent off his land, though the fear that he would do so never quite left her. On the few occasions that she saw him ride by the farm when she was outside, she kept her head down hoping that the brim of her sunbonnet shielded her from his gaze. Her family continued to pretend that she didn't exist and she heard rumors calling her a nigger lover and crude speculation about herself and Sam. It was true that she had come to care deeply about Sam, but the rumors about a sexual relationship were made of wholecloth. Sam's initial hostility had mellowed to grudging respect and then to deep friendship as he realized that she would freely help on the farm and with the family in any way she could. When she looked at him, and at the rest of his family, she no longer saw first black skin. They had become her family. They were just people, trying to get along in the world the best way they could. Like her.

The life of sharecropping was something she had never imagined. When she and George had tried to run the family farm themselves, George had taken care of their cotton crop himself with some sporadic help from friends and family. Later Michael had helped with the crop. Now, as one of the Stancel family, Kate was expected to be out in the fields beside Sam, Aunt Mary and Permelia chopping the never-ending weeds that threatened to choke out the cotton plants. Her hands became blistered from the hoe she wielded from sun up to sun down to stay ahead of the weeds. The blisters broke open and oozed pus and blood. Aunt Mary rubbed bag balm on them to close the blisters and harden Kate's hands to her new task. She had to bite her lips tightly together to keep from screaming in agony at the burning sensation, but eventually her hands became tough and calloused. She longed to have some time to spend with her son, but by the time the scorching sun had set on each demanding day, she had to help with supper and by the time that was eaten and cleared away, she was so filled with mind numbing fatigue that she could only kiss his sleeping face and whisper her love for him before she collapsed into bed. It seemed she had slept only minutes when the sun rose again and she trudge through yet another excruciating day of labor. It seemed that they had no sooner finished chopping the weeds from the fields than that they had sprung up anew in the area where they had begun chopping and so they began again the clear the weeds from the cotton plants.

Finally, there came a time of respite from the chopping. Time when Kate could get to know her son. To sit quietly singing to him as he gazed into her face and to think her own thoughts without the mind numbing fatigue of the last weeks. She realized that during the time she had worked so closely with Sam she had come to respect him more and more. He was a fine young man who wasn't afraid to work. His broad muscular shoulders had gleamed with sweat as he swung his hoe with an ease she could never hope to emulate; yet his large calloused hands were gentle with his children and his mother. He never complained about the amount of work to be done and went about it willingly. On occasion, when her strength seemed to have come to an end and she thought she must lay down right there in the field and die, he had grasped he had gently by the shoulder and nodded approvingly as she labored at his side almost as though he could read her heart and knew she needed something to help her go on. A glow of pride at his approval had given her the energy to go on with the work.

Now that she could think clearly again, she remembered the rumors about Sam and herself and felt a blush heat her cheeks. Neighbors had traveled the road along the cotton fields and had seen those occasional touches. The rumors must be at a high pitch by now. Sometimes there was a look in Sam's eyes that spoke of more than a feeling of friendship, but nothing ever came of those moments. The earlier rumors had driven Permelia to distraction. Permelia was in love with Sam and hoped to marry him. With the instincts of a woman in love, instincts as finely developed as the nose of a bloodhound, she sensed the indefinable thing that now hovered between Kate and Sam. It was more than friendship, yet less than love, a meeting of kindred spirits seeking something beyond what was at hand. A soul deep yearning for something better. Because of that indefinable something, a thing she could not understand or combat, Permelia's dislike of Kate blossomed into outright hatred.

A second and then a third round of chopping weeds followed the first and with each one Kate grew more and more weary. Would the backbreaking work never end? How had she dared to think that her life on the farm with George had been unending drudgery? She was ashamed by the memory of the frivolous girl she had been in those days. What was raising and preserving some vegetables and keeping house compared to the appalling amount of work this family did each day without complaint?

When the time came to pick the cotton, Kate picked up her sack and squared her shoulders, determined to be the best picker in the household. Hadn't she picked a lot of her own cotton last year? With a purposeful stride she went into the fields. By midday she was faltering. How had she forgotten the back pain from bending to pull the cotton from the razor sharp bolls? Shouldn't her back be toughened up by now from all the chopping she had all summer? Stopping for a moment to stretch her aching back, she saw Sam, Aunt Mary and Permelia far ahead of her in their rows. At just that moment, Permelia looked back at Kate and gave her a baleful stare as though to say that she knew that Kate would never be able to keep up. With renewed vigor, Kate began picking as fast as she could an d stuffing the cotton into her sack. Her pace picked up and she was even with Permelia within the hour. Glancing sideways, Permelia looked surprised to see that Kate had caught up with her and began picking at a furious pace, determined to get ahead of Kate again. Sam had reached the end of his row and stood glaring at the two of them as they reached him.

"Dis ain' no contest goin' on out heah." He stated firmly, looking them both in the eye. "De two o' you bes' not weah yosefs' out cause we gots plenty mo' cotton to be pickin' befo' we be done. Ah cain' stan' by an' let ya'll mek yosefs' too sick to hep pick de res' jes' cause you be tryin' to out do each otha'.

The two women glared at each other, neither willing to be the first to back down. Sam made a disgusted noise in his throat and they looked away from each other. Nodding their heads at him that they would do as he said, the three of them started on new rows.

They picked cotton for days on end until Kate dreamed she was picking cotton even as she slept. In her dreams the dry branches of the cotton stalks reached out to choke her as she fought desperately to pull the fluffy white balls from them. The fluffy white balls that would bring them the money to live on until next year. The fluffy white balls that would be traded for money to buy shoes and fabric for clothing to keep them through the coming winter. In her nightmare she struggled valiantly to pull the cotton from the stalks. To make sure she picked her share. To make sure she could justify to herself the place she had been given in this family. To feel that she had earned the food and clothing given to herself and her son. She must pull her weight here, only the prickly stalks were grabbing at her clothing and her hair, tangling her in their fierce grasp until she was struggling wildly to pull away. She had to get free! She <u>must</u> pick more cotton. It was rotting in the field in front of her eyes! She had to get it picked before it was too late!

She was being shaken by what now felt like hands. Jerking her eyes open, she realized that Aunt Mary was shaking her by the shoulder.

"Wake up, chile." she whispered. "You be havin' a nightmare. Hush now befo' you wakes up de hole house."

The whites of Kate's eyes glowed in the faint moonlight penetrating the room. She was shivering and shaking enough to make the bed move. That must have been what had wakened the older woman. But Aunt Mary had said to hush. She must have been crying out in her sleep. Smiling sheepishly she said, "I'm sorry, Aunt Mary. I didn't mean to wake you. It was just a bad dream. I'll be all right now. It was nothing really. You go on back to sleep."

"Din' soun lak nuthin' to me. Soun to me lak you be runnin' for yo' life. You betta tell me 'bout it. Den it woan botha you no mo'."

"It was nothing. Let's just get back to sleep. Tomorrow's another long day for all of us and we need our sleep."

Aunt Mary grasped Kate's chin and gazed into her eyes in the dim light. "You cain' fool me Kate Randsome. Ah knows it wuz sumthin' bad. Now go on ahead an git it out."

Looking into Aunt Mary's gentle brown eyes, Kate felt compelled to speak of her nightmare, just to reassure her friend that she was all right.

"It really wasn't anything. I was just dreaming that I was all tangled up in cotton plants and the harder I tried to get away, the more I got tangled up. That's all it was. I'm just so tired of picking cotton that it's got into my dreams. I keep thinking that I'm not doing enough in return for my place in your home."

Aunt Mary smoothed back Kate's hair thoughtfully. "Soun' ter me lak' it be mo' dan dat. Ah ain' sayin' dat sharecroppin' ain' a hahd life, but seem to me lak dere be sumpin else goin' on in yo' min and it jes all mixed up wif de cotton sum how. Doan you be worrin' dat you ain' doin' nuff round heah to pay for yosef and lil John Wesley. You is doin' yo share and mo. Doan be trubblin' yosef bout dat. Ah thinks dat dream is bout sumpin you got on yo mind dat you doan want ter think about so it come to you when you sleepin.'"

"What do you mean?"

"Ah doan knows, chile. Mebbe iffen Ah did, Ah could hep you, but Ah cain' rightly say. It jes a feelin' Ah got in mah bones dat sumpin' be deep on yo' min'. You done bin thoo a lot 'o bad times and thangs ain' much betta now. Mebbe you is tryin' to work thangs out in yo min' while you be sleepin'. Ah cain' promise you dat thangs gonna get much betta any time soon."

Kate sat up startled. "But you said that if I just keep on trying and being strong that things *will* get better, if not for me, then at least for John Wesley. Were you just making that up? Were you telling me a lie just to keep me going when I was so near to killing myself?"

"Hesh now! You knows dat Ah ain' lied to you bout nuthin. Ah b'lieves dat you can make a betta life for yosef, but it gone ter tek time. It ain' gone ter happen right away and Ah be right heah wif you thoo all of it. Ah jes doan want you thinkin' dat it only tek a few months ter happen. It might could be yeahs and dos yeah you can spend right heah on dis heah fahm with me and mah fambly. It gone ter be hahd yeahs, not jes tryin' ter git back wif de wite fokes, but hahd yeahs of sharecroppin'. Ah jes wants you ter know dat an' not be thinkin' dis is jes for' a few months. It a long hahd road you has started down, but you got us ter hep you along it. Now we bes' be gittin' on back ter sleep or we both gone ter be wuthless termorra."

Aunt Mary lay back on the bed and soon her gentle snores could be heard, but Kate lay wide awake long afterwards. Her mind whirled circles. Could she continue to stay here and live the backbreaking life of a sharecropper? There were no other options open to her right now, but maybe next spring or summer? Could things change by then? It stuck her then that this was exactly what Aunt Mary had warned her against. That wise woman had read Kate's heart and seen the truth before she had seen it herself. There was no going back now. There was only forward and forward meant staying here on her old family farm as a sharecropper. Staying and making slow progress whenever and where ever she could. Fatigue finally closed her eyes and she slept dreamlessly until Aunt Mary shook her awake at dawn.

When the all the cotton was finally picked and stored neatly in the barn, Sam went to see Angus Macintosh to make arrangements to go into Purdy and sell the cotton. When Mr. Macintosh arrived at the farm with his wagons to load the cotton to take to town, Kate made sure to be in the house and out of sight. She still feared that if he saw her up close, Angus Macintosh would demand that she be sent off his land.

Aunt Mary found her in the upstairs bedroom that faced toward the barn. She was peering cautiously through the curtains, watching the cotton being loaded on the wagons.

"Whut you doin' hidin' out up heah, Miss Kate?"

Kate nearly jumped out of her skin at the unexpected voice behind her. For a large woman, Aunt Mary could walk as silently as a cat when she chose.

"Ah thought you wusn't no criminal to be run out of town jes cause you b'lieved whut dat man tole to you."

"I-I just wanted to watch the cotton being loaded and it's so much cooler up here in this room than standing out in the yard," Kate stammered.

Aunt Mary looked unconvinced. She silently stared into Kate's eyes and Kate's were the first to drop.

"Ain' no need for you ter be hidin out up heah. Mis' Macintosh know you is livin' heah. Dis his lan and ain' nuthin' go on on his land whut he doan know 'bout. Ain' he de one dat gibes us new cloes eva yeah? You kin be suah dat he knows you be heah for' no mo' reason dan dat. Iffen he din want you stayin heah, he wooda done said sumpin bout it. Iffen you wuz ter go on out dere in de yahd I doan think lightnin would strike you dead jes cause Mis' Macintosh lay eyes on you. De wus dat could happen would be dat he jes ignore you. Iffen you wuz to take de chance, he might even say sumpin kind ter you. He might could be dat fust pusson Ah tole you would sumday reach out dey had ter you."

Aunt Mary watched and waited silently while Kate stood before her. Still looking away and standing as rigidly as a mouse about to be pounced on by a cat, Kate thought over what Aunt Mary had said. Searching deep within her soul, she could find no shred of courage to make her walk out of that room and into the yard to stand before the man who could away her safe haven with one word of command. Looking into Aunt Mary's faced with haunted eyes she whispered, "I cain't."

Sighing with resignation, Aunt Mary left the room and Kate turned back to the window. A surreptitious observer of the activity taking place in the bright autumn sunshine.

Sixteen

Kate's fears that the Stancel's would be shunned by their friends for keeping her in their home proved to be groundless. Now that the harvest was over, their friends came by in the long dusky evenings to relax and talk over glasses of tea. They accepted Kate's presence there as though she belonged. Chatting amiably with her, urging her to join any invitation issued to the Stancel's, they gave her a sense of belonging. As much as she had come to love the Stancel's, and to like their friends, Kate couldn't stop the sting of hurt that pierced her each time she thought of the rejection of her peers. Then she would feel disloyal to the Stancel's for even thinking such thoughts after the way they had taken her to their hearts. She knew though, that in the end, she must face her own truth. For herself she could stay in this safe haven forever, but for her son, she must claw her way back to his birthright.

There had been more than one argument with Aunt Mary over her refusal to attend church with the family when the circuit rider, Reverend Jones, made his monthly visit to the area. At first, Aunt Mary had been convinced that Kate's refusal was based on not wanting to attend a black church meeting. Kate was cut to the quick by that assumption. Surely Aunt Mary knew her well enough by now to know that it was not the color of the skin of the worshipers that make her refuse to attend the services. When she explained to the older woman that she had no intention of attending a church service, white or black ever again, because she no longer believed in God,

Aunt Mary's wrath broke over her head with a vengeance.

"Doan believe in God," she bellowed. "Wheah'd you git sech a fool idea? Ah knows you wuz raised up in de church, so you jes' tell me wheah you cum up with sech a fool notion!" Breathing heavily she waited for Kate to justify her statement.

"God don't exist. I was raised to believe that God existed and that just ain't so. The God I was taught about was a God of love and tolerance. A God who showed mercy for anyone who believed in him. Well I believed in Him," Kate shouted. "I believed everything I was told in church. But look at me now. I asked him to take away the baby that I didn't want and I did everything I could think of to help Him along. Well, He didn't listen to my prayers. Do you know why He didn't listen to my prayers? Because there is no God! My family turned on me. My brother mortgaged the farm out from under me after cursing me as a whore. My sister threw me out of her home not caring that I had nowhere to go. I was even told by someone that I wasn't welcome in the church I had attended all my life. Where was God while all that was going on? I'll tell you where He was not there because He doesn't exist!"

Aunt Mary was taken aback by the anger and vehemence in Kate's tone. She had suspected Kate was trying to get rid of her baby that long ago afternoon in the cotton field. Only now did she realized just how deep the anger and hurt ran in the young woman facing her so defiantly. Here was something that might be more than she could cure. Something that maybe no one could ever cure. A blot on Kate's soul so dark that no light would ever penetrate its recesses.

"Dey is a God, Miss Kate," she said quietly. "An' he be a God of love and mercy and tolerance jes' lak you wuz taught. It wudden God whut put dat baby in yo' stummick. Dat wuz yo' own doin'. Whut you and dat young man did together is whut put dat baby in you. All de prayin' in de worl' wouldn't mek God tek dat baby out o' you. Whut you done, you done of yo' own free will. God gave us dat free will and you cain' mek a mistake and jes pray to God to mek it go away. Dat ain' how de worl' wuks, chile. As for' yo' fambly, well yo' brudder he jes' be selfish and spiteful. Yo sista' she did try ter hep you, she jes' wudden strong enough to stand up ter whut otha fokes thinks and it mek huh do sumpin' wrong. Whoevah tole you dat you wudden welcome in yo' church jes' plain mean and nasty. Dey's all gone ter hab ter answa' for' dose thangs cum Judgement Day. God do exist, Miss Kate. He be watchin' ovah you dis whole time whether you believes it o' not. He sent me out to de bahn dat mawnin' to fin' you and tek you in and ca'ah for you. It wudden no accident dat Ah be libben in dis heah house jus' at dat time. God wanted for you ter live and for yo' baby ter be bawn. He watching you right now and it mek Him sad ter heah you say He doan exist."

"There ain't nothing you can say to make me change my mind," Kate stated firmly. "You go on to church if you want to, you and all the rest of them, but I ain't going to go back ever and that's my final say on it!"

Aunt Mary only said, "It ain' wise to say you ain' nevah gone ter do sumpin, cause someday you jes might fin' yosef doin' it afta all."

Kate sniffed rudely and turned away, while Aunt Mary looked after her sadly, offering up a fervent prayer to God to forgive that crushed and broken spirited girl.

~ * ~

The Stancel family attended the monthly church meetings without Kate and John Wesley. When Sam questioned his mother about it, she would only say that time would change Kate and they should all be patient.

~ * ~

Sam watched Kate often in the evenings. He had never felt *that way* about a white woman and didn't really feel *that way* about her. It was pleasant to watch the way her slender hands danced in the air when she spoke, as though they helped her to form the words. To quietly observe the way tendrils of hair escaped the braid she wore and curled softly about her face. The way her huge blue eyes looked so helplessly out at the world she occupied now. They spoke to him of the things she never voiced. Spoke of her pain and humiliation, of her deep rooted, burning desire for a better life. It was to those unspoken desires that his heart called. She was the mirror of his own need for a different and better way to live. He knew of the rumors about the two of them. Knew too of the additional burden they added to her already ruined life. Watching her step back from the edge of self-destruction and come to the decision to fight her way back to the world of her birth had given him a deep respect for her. Her eyes might be scared, but her spirit was determined. He had seen that determination grow with every day that passed. The knowledge that she would beat herself bloody against the wall of public opinion cut him to the quick. He had spoken often to his mother about the situation, only to be told to let it alone, that Kate would find her own path, and the courage to follow it, in her own time.

~ * ~

Mary Stancel observed Permelia watching Sam watch Kate. She knew that Permelia had disliked Kate from the start and that Sam's interest in Kate had fanned that dislike into hatred. She took Permelia aside in an effort to calm the storm gathering in the other woman's heart.

"Whut you be doin' actin' so hateful to Miss Kate all de time?" Aunt Mary attacked. "She ain' nevah done you no hahm."

"She be afta Sam." Permelia exclaimed. "She knows she ain' nevah gone ter git no wite man now, and she afta Sam ter tek care o' her."

"Is you gone ter soft in de haid, gal," Aunt Mary asked indignantly. She grunted and shook her head at the younger woman. "You bin payin' too much 'tention to wite fokes gossip an' not enuf to whut's goin' on right in front o' yo face. Miss Kate all fired up to git her sef back wif de wite fokes. She ain' be interested in tekkin' up wif Sam."

Permelia's eyes slid away from Aunt Mary's stare. "How cum Sam be watchin' huh all de time? Ah done seed him doin' it. You knows evah thang, you ansa dat," she stated.

Aunt Mary sighed deeply. "Sam be worrit bout huh. He know she got a hahd row ter hoe and she like paht of de fambly now. He ain' fixin' ter tek up wif huh lak dat. He jes got some respec' for huh gumption, dat's all. He know dat she skeered dat no matta whut she do she ain' nevah gone ter git no respec' frum any o' de wite fokes roun' heah and dat huh boy gone ter pay all his life for sumpin' he din' hab nuthin' ter do wif. Now, you lissen to me good. Ah knows dat you be wantin' ter mahy up wif Sam, but you ain' gone ter be doin' it iffen you keeps up actin' so hateful!"

Permelia refused to look her in the eye, but Aunt Mary heard her grumble something that sounded like agreement and so left the other woman alone to think over what she had said. She felt sure that Permelia wouldn't change her mind about Kate, but would hopefully keep her true feelings better hidden in the future.

Seventeen

When the long winter evenings closed in on them, they gathered around the fire in the parlor. The women knitted and sewed. The children played among themselves. Sam seemed at a loss. Often he would sit quietly staring into the leaping fire, his big hands resting on his knees, seeming in deep thought. Sometimes he would whittle pieces of kindling in small toys for the children. Kate felt restless on those long evenings, yearning for something more stimulating that the endless knitting and sewing. All the books that had been in the house previously were gone now, so she had nothing to read. Her thoughts grew stagnant and lazy. One evening as she sat by the fire stitching together pieces for a quilt, she hit upon the idea of teaching the Stancels to read and write. Why hadn't she thought of it before? It would be something to occupy her mind and would be so helpful to everyone.

They were all delighted and Kate felt it was a small thing after all the Stancel's had done for her. Sam was an eager student. He was a bright man and learned quickly. At first, Aunt Mary protested that she was too old to learn to read, but after much cajoling from Kate and Sam, she was persuaded to join the evening lessons. She practiced her new skills diligently. Permelia refused Kate's offer, but Kate caught her listening from a distance when the reading lessons were taking place and smiled to herself. Permelia was no fool. She wanted to read as much as the others. It was only her hatred of the teacher that kept her from joining openly in the lessons.

It was the children who gave Kate the most joy. Just seeing their faces light up with understanding filled her heart to overflowing with pride in them. It was small joys like these, balanced against her inner heartache, that began to give her back a small feeling of self worth. The only taint to her joy was the warning Aunt Mary gave her. Pulling Kate to the side shortly after the lessons had begun, she warned that if it got out to the general community that Kate was teaching them to read and write, she could damage even further her chances of gaining entry back into the white community. Kate could see the wisdom of Aunt Mary's warning, but she was deriving so much pleasure in giving something of value to the family that she couldn't bring herself to call a halt to the lessons. They decided between them that everyone would be sworn to secrecy about the lessons. The children agreed solemnly not to tell anyone, not even their friends, because they didn't want to bring any trouble on their Miss Kate. The lessons continued.

It had been slow going at first. She had no chalk board or slates and chalk for the children to use. Sam solved that problem by bringing home a few pens, a pot of ink and a sheaf of paper for her to use. He refused to answer her questions about how and where he had gotten them, but they made it much easier for her to teach. She had been using a piece of charred wood to write with and attempting to form the letters of the alphabet on a spare piece of lumber from the barn. Now, with the proper tools, she could teach much more easily.

Once she felt they were ready to try reading printed words from a book, she ran into the problem of not having any printed books available. With a wicked grin, Aunt Mary handed Kate a worn Bible that she had found in the attic. Acknowledging Aunt Mary's unspoken irony, Kate took the Bible with a sardonic smile. Starting with Sam, she had everyone attempt to read one line. When they stumbled, she encouraged, when they were at a total loss, she told them the word and had them repeat is several times, so that the next time they saw that word, they would know how to say it.

In no time at all Christmas arrived. The only gifts they had to give to one another were the scarves, mittens and socks they had been knitting. There was no tree in the parlor decorated with tinsel, no tissue wrapping for the gifts. Sam brought home a ham and some oranges that Mister Macintosh had sent, so they had a feast for Christmas dinner with the ham holding place of honor among the yams, peas, cornbread and apple pie. The oranges they gave to the children as a special treat just for them.

Little John Wesley didn't know what to do with this never before seen object. His little hands could barely encompass it. He watched round-eyed as the older Stancel children peeled and ate their oranges. He tried to emulate them, but his hands couldn't hold the orange and try to peel back the tough skin at the same time. Just as tears of frustration began to well in his eyes, Kate took him onto her lap and peeled the orange for him. He took the first piece in his chubby little hands, turning it over and over, examining every inch before placing it in his mouth. They all laughed to see his lips pucker as the tangy slice burst in his mouth. Reaching up he took the piece out of his mouth and began examining it again, puzzled by the texture and taste. Kate took the piece from his sticky hands and broke it into smaller pieces, feeding them to him one at a time. He managed to eat two more slices and Kate divided the rest of the orange among the other children.

As they all sat quietly by the fire, feeling sleepy from the heat and the large quantity of food they had consumed, Aunt Mary handed Kate the worn Bible she used to teach.

"Oh, Aunt Mary! I've eaten way too much food and feel too lazy to have a reading lesson tonight! We'll take it back up tomorrow. Let's just sit here and enjoy being together tonight."

"Ah doan wants ter hab no lesson ternight. Ah wants you to read de Christmas story ter de chillen. Dis be a Holy Night and de story be in dat book. Ah cain' read good enuff ter read to them mysef', so's Ah wants you ter read it ter them."

"You know how I feel about that," Kate replied.

"Dis doan be 'bout you, Miss Kate. Dis be 'bout mah granchillen. Ah'd tek it as a special favah did you do dis for me."

All eyes were on her. She felt trapped. Aunt Mary knew how she felt about God. Just because she was forced to use the Bible to teach reading didn't mean that she was about to read about the birth of someone she didn't believe had ever existed. Aunt Mary's eyes pleaded with her to do this. She found that she didn't have the heart to refuse her friend the only favor she had ever asked. With a sigh, Kate opened the Bible to the well remembered story. It had been a tradition during her own growing up years to hear the Christmas story on Christmas night. She thought sadly of her parents. Her father had always read the story to his family. The children sat enthralled throughout the reading. When she came to the end of the story, she closed the Bible and sat quietly looking at the cover.

Aunt Mary reached over to squeeze her hand. When she looked up, the other woman nodded her head in silent thanks.

As they all went up to bed that night, Kate felt a great sadness come over her as she remembered past Christmases. This year there had been no music, no dancing, no tree with candles and tinsel, no mysterious tissue wrapped packages. She wondered how her sister's family had spent this night. Had they thought of her at all? Had there seemed to be an empty space at their table on this Holy Night? Kate shook herself for such thoughts. It was most probable that she had never crossed their minds.

Eighteen

By the following Spring, Aunt Mary had become Kate's greatest source of strength. She was a rock to lean on as Kate struggled to make a place for herself and John Wesley. The face of every white person in the area was turned against her. When, at Aunt Mary's urging, Kate took John Wesley into McNairy Station on some errand, she was ignored as if she didn't exist, or worse yet, vilified by former friends and neighbors. The unending repudiation of those people scraped constantly at the small store of courage she had managed to build. By the time her son was a year old, Kate felt she would never be able to fight her way back into the world in which she had been born. Aunt Mary found her crying tears of frustration in the dim, dusty interior of the barn one afternoon after yet another ugly visit to town.

~ * ~

"Whut you cryin' bout, Miss Kate? You hu't yosef out heah?"

"Oh, Aunt Mary," she wept. "I just cain't keep on trying anymore. The hateful way the women look at me when they pull their children close to them just breaks my heart. They act like my sin will rub off on them if they get too close. And the ugly leers of the men! It just makes my stomach churn to see them. Those people are never going to accept me again. I don't know why I even care if they do."

"Ah knows why you ca'ah. And so do you. It be for' dat fine boy you got. Dat why you ca'ah. And you is right. Ah knows it be hahd, chile, but it be wuth it in de end. You jes' got to keep on. Even wen you doan think you can."

"Maybe I should just give up on them. John Wesley can have a good life here with your family and friends. Here we're both accepted. He'll have friends here and be a happy little boy. The way a child should be happy. Maybe if I just stay away from everybody, by the time John Wesley is grown, they'll be able to accept him as his own person and forget about me."

The defeated tone of the young woman beside her hurt Aunt Mary. She sat quietly for a moment, considering the raw pain that exuded like musk from Kate. It would be easy for Kate to do just that, to stay here in the black community and be accepted as a part of them. However, her thoughts that someday John Wesley would be accepted for himself, without any taint of his mother's sin was just not possible. People had long memories. As much as she loved Kate and her son, as much as she would like for them to remain with her in safety, she knew that that was not the road for Kate to take. Not here anyway, not in the very place where her sin was known to all. She was about to speak her thoughts to Kate when they were both startled by the sound of footsteps.

Sam came into the barn just then and caught sight of the two of them. Walking over to them, he saw the tear stains on Kate's face and said, "Gal, whut you be cryin' bout?"

Kate turned her face away in embarrassment as Aunt Mary stood up, putting herself between them. Speaking to her son she said, "Git on outta heah, Sam. We be doin' fine."

Sam stepped around his mother and took Kate's hand in his. She looked numbly at the contrast of his mahogany skin against her own. Felt the gentle strength with which he touched her. Squeezing her hand gently, he said, "You know you kin tell me whut's wrong. If Ah kin fix it Ah will."

Kate sniffled, "I'm just feeling sorry for myself. There ain't anything you can do, Sam."

He looked at her suspiciously. "You bin t'McNairy Station today, hadden you?"

When she didn't answer and wouldn't meet his eyes, he dropped her hand in disgust. "Gal, you is jes' as good or betta dan dose people you cryin' ovah. Iffen Ah thought it'd do you any good, Ah'd go bus' a few a them in de face."

Aunt Mary grabbed him by the arm. "An lan' yosef in a tree at de end ob a rope ober sumpin' you cain' change!"

Sam looked calmly at his mother. "Ah ain' no fool. Ah said if Ah thought it would do any good and Ah knows it woan, so doan be worrin' bout it." He looked back at Kate and said, "Iffen deys sumpin' Ah kin do for you, you jes' say so." His face looked so forlorn, his eyes so ineffably sad for her that her heart squeezed painfully. Who was she to cause this good, good man such sorrow over her? He shouldn't carry her burdens for her. She was no kin of his, no blood of his blood and yet she could see that he ached for her sorrow and shame.

Kate shook her head. He hesitated, looking mournfully at her bowed head, then walked slowly away. Aunt Mary sat next to her again. "Miss Kate, you jes' got to keep on tryin'. You gots to keep on b'lievin. You knows Ah be happy for you and lil John Wesley to stay wif us as long as you wants, but dat ain' de right road for you. You knows ain' nobody gone ter fogit 'bout wheah yo son cum frum. Not tomorra, not nex' yeah and not when he be a growd man. Iffen you be stubbun enuf to stay heah instead ob lebbin' and goin' sumwheah doan nobody know 'bout you, den you gonna hab to mek them people tek you back. An' iffen dey doan, afta you trys yo' hahdest, den you got ter lib wif dat. De choice be youah's to mek, an' oncet you mek it, you gots to stick by it. Ah be heah for you, an' Sam, too. Someday, jes' one pusson gone ter reach out dey han' to you. An afta dat, dey be mo'. You cain' gibe up now. You be feelin' low right now, but you feel betta termorra."

"Is that how you survived being a slave? Just never giving up. Waiting for tomorrow?" Kate asked curiously.

"Dat right. Ah nevah gibbed up and look at me now. Ah's free." Aunt Mary beamed with delight.

Kate's brow wrinkled in puzzlement as she asked, "But what if the war hadn't come? You'd still be a slave. You might have been a slave all your life. What good would have been to have never given up, if you died still a slave? Were you content enough with your life that just hoping and praying for freedom were enough?"

"*Content!*" Aunt Mary spat out. "Doan you talk like a fool gal! Ain' no slave *evah* been content. Dere wasn't nuthin' else I could do, but pray and hope." Seeing the look on Kate's face and knowing what the younger woman was thinking about, she continued, "Sho' I cudda run off and tried to git away on de Unnerground Railroad, but I din't know nuthin' bout how to do it and I had my boy ter be thinkin' bout. No Ma'am! I wusn't content, I jes' did the best I could." Then in a calmer voice she said, "De woah did come and made me free. Iffen it hadden, den Ah'd still be hopin' and nevah gibbed up. If Ah nevah got to be free, Ah wooda been hopin' for Sam an mah granchillen to be free. My mammy and pappy nevah got to be free, but dey hoped for me to be free an' heah Ah am. It be de same for' you. Is you content?" Kate shook her head. "Den you gotta keep trying an' hopin' to mek a place for' you an' yo boy. Iffen it doan happen for' you, den mebbe it still mek a diffrunce for' John Wesley. You jes' think bout whut Ah'm sayin'. You see dat Ah'm right."

Aunt Mary left Kate alone in the barn. She mulled over their conversation. Replaying each word in her mind, rolling them around, tasting the bitter along with the sweet. Aunt Mary was right. She must never give up hope. Maybe it wouldn't happen for her, but if she could just make enough of a difference for John Wesley, then she would consider her life well spent.

He was such a bright little boy. Already he was toddling around the house, making every one of them smile with the sound of his joyous laughter. His bright blue eyes missed nothing and whatever they saw, he reached for with his chubby little hands. They were all kept busy making sure he didn't get hurt during any of his exploring. He was fascinated by the other children, who were nearer to his size than the others in his small world, and toddled after them constantly as fast his little legs would carry him. Yes, any pain she suffered, any slight she put behind her, would be well worth the cost to give him the world he deserved.

The mule in the stall next to her snuffled at her through the boards, startling her. Laughing bitterly, she put her hand through to pet the velvety nose.

"Well, mule", she asked, "do you think I've got a chance to change things?"

~ * ~

Aunt Mary, stood motionless outside the barn, tears forming in her eyes. Walking quietly away, she felt her heart ache for the young woman inside. Kate was fighting so hard to win back a place for herself and her son, her only reward, the cold hearts of those she sought to win. Uselessly she wished she could help change those hearts. Kate deserved so much better. Brushing aside the futile tears, she saw Sam watching her from the back porch. He came down the porch steps and cut diagonally across the yard to meet her.

"Whut we gone ter do 'bout Miz Kate," he begged her. "She cain' go on lak dis, beatin' huhsef 'gainst all dose cole hartted fokes. She gone ter break befo dey do."

Sadly Aunt Mary replied, "Ain' nuthin' we kin do, Son. She boun' an' determined on dis. Huh spirit be down right now, but she woan gib up. She want whut evah mama want for' huh chile—to hab a betta life dan she got. It be de right thang for huh to do, too. Ah jes wish it be easier for huh. All we kin do is jes be heah wen she need us."

Sam looked so helpless. Such a big man with strong hands and a loving heart. Her own heart went out to him. He wanted so badly to be able to help Kate and his hands, those strong hands that wrested a living for his family from the hard red clay of this land, were tied. It was strange how that young woman had come to mean so much to both of them.

Nineteen

Time wheeled on. Spring, Summer, Fall, Winter. All passed on their appointed rounds of the endless drudgery of the life of a sharecropper. Planting the cotton, chopping the cotton, picking the cotton and betwixt and between that work was the work of raising food for themselves, picking and preparing and drying the food for the coming winter. The one set of clothing and shoes provided each year by Mr. Macintosh to his sharecropper families became faded and worn from constant washing and the wear and tear of every day living.

Kate continued her struggle. Sometimes buoyed up with hope, other times ground down in discouragement. Winter became her favorite time of the year. All the hard work of the previous seasons was done and she had time to continue her reading and writing lessons with Permelia now joining them openly. She also began teaching Sam arithmetic so that someday, when he found his own better life, he could manage his own money. She still refused to attend any church services with the family, but read the Christmas story each Christmas day and began to derive a bittersweet happiness from the yearly reading. Here was one family tradition from her own childhood that she could pass on to her own child.

John Wesley grew like a weed, going from a toddler to a small boy who spoke to her using real words instead of the babble she had grown used to hearing. Together, they explored the farm and the woods surrounding it. Occasionally, a former friend would pass by on the road and look the other way when they saw Kate with her small son. Kate worried that soon John Wesley would be old enough to notice that, with the exception of the members of the black community, no one spoke to them. She took her troubled thoughts, once again, to Aunt Mary.

After hearing her out, Aunt Mary advised. "Doan borry trouble, chile. You know whut to do wen de time come dat he ax questions. Jes' keep on lak you been doin'. Evathing come out fine."

Kate wasn't as sure that everything would be fine, but took comfort from having confided in Aunt Mary. She drew her inner strength from the old woman and thanked God that she had such a wise friend.

~ * ~

In the summer of 1870, they heard that a government man was traveling the roads of McNairy County taking a census. Sam was excited. This would be the first time his name and the names of his family would be recorded. He waited eagerly for the census taker to arrive at the farm.

He was confused, then angry when the pale, squinty-eyed man assumed that Kate was head of household. They patiently explained that Sam was head of household, not Kate, and gave the information the man needed for his records. The census taker finally left, his book tucked tightly under his arm, shaking his head as he went. Sam was still angry and turned to Kate and his mother, shouting, "Ain' nuthin' done change! Dat man think coz Miz Kate wite, she run dis place an' Ah's jes' a po' dahky hepin' out roun heah so's mah fambly have a place to stay!" Seeing the hurt look in Kate's eyes, he continued, "Ah doan mean you, Miz Kate. You like one o' de fambly. Ah means de wite fokes whut woan nevah think it right for' black man ter be running' his own place."

Aunt Mary commented, "Jes' be happy you free to run dis place. It doan matta whut dat wormy looking' lil man think."

"It matte ter me," stated Sam as he left to work the fields.

Aunt Mary sighed deeply and shook her head. With a worried expression, her eyes followed her son.

Kate continued to worry about every body and everything. She worried about her son and making a place for him in this world. She worried about Sam and his feelings about his place in the world. She worried that one day she must leave this comfortable place for her son's sake. Aunt Mary knew of her worries and, as always, counseled patience and never giving up. That was all well and good, but so far, she hadn't made any progress at all. And her son was getting older and taking more notice of what went on around him.

Twenty

When John Wesley turned four years old, Kate decided it was past time that he met some of his kin. She would take him to her sister's home to meet his aunt and two cousins. Maybe, after all these years, her sister would speak to her if they met alone. She had to make the effort. Just making trips into town and hoping to see a change in the people there was not changing anything. It was past time to take more direct action. She was nervous as she made the familiar walk through the woods. There were ghosts here. Bright images of happier times walked side by side with dark memories of shame and terror. The seemed to get longer and longer as the memories flew and circled above her head. She banished the ghosts with a shake of her head. Surely, when Savannah saw this beautiful child, she would forgive the past.

~ * ~

As they came in sight of Savannah's home, a young boy came around the corner of the house. He looked startled to see them there. A look of recognition came over his face and he ran forward, calling, "Aunt Kate! What are you doing here? Who's this with you?"

Kate smiled at the young boy as a surge of joyful recognition swept through her. It was Rufus. He had grown so much in the last few years. She could see that he would be a tall man like his father. Now he was all adolescent knees and elbows as he galloped toward her. Oh, it felt wonderful to see him again!

"Hello, Rufus. My you've grown since the last time I saw you! This is your cousin. You remember, when I was living here, I was going to have a baby? His name is John Wesley."

Rufus looked suddenly embarrassed and scuffed the toe of his boot in the dirt. He looked back at Kate, then at John Wesley. She could see that he didn't know what to say to her. What had his mother told him about her? What had he thought all these years since she had been in exile? How strange that she had lived so close by, yet been completely cut off from everyone she had known and loved. Rufus was twisting his hands nervously, looking back over his shoulder toward the house.

The door opened and his mother came out onto the porch with a rug. She shook it over the rail and, glancing up, saw who her son was talking to. She dropped the rug and came off the porch like a ship in full sail calling, "Rufus! Git on out to the field and help your Daddy! You know you're not to be talking to her!"

Rufus took off like a startled deer, heading out to the field where Kate could just make out the figure of Tom. Savannah came to a halt before Kate, staring daggers.

"What are you doing here," she asked in a savage voice. "You're not welcome and that little bastard ain't either! Git on back to them dirty Nigras you done took up with."

An unexpected shaft of pain sliced through Kate at her sister's words and tone of voice. She stepped back, unconsciously tightening her grip on her son, who had begun to whimper at the sound of the angry voice. She shouldn't have come here. Time hadn't changed her sister one whit. Now the best thing would be for her to get out of here as quickly as possible. Refusing to show her pain, she stared her sister down. Savannah's eyes never wavered as she returned the stare. Righteous indignation and contempt were written all over her face.

Kate's head went back, her nostrils flared. "I thought maybe enough time had passed that you might feel different toward me now. I see I was wrong. You attend church regular and think you're such a Christian woman, but I see you still ain't got any Christian charity in you. Nor forgiveness either. This child ain't never sinned, but you cain't see that. All you see is *my* sin. Well, he deserves better than you and you don't have to worry that I'll be showing up here again. I don't want any of your poison spilling over onto him. Making him think he's evil just because of his birth. Them "dirty Nigras" as you call them have got more kind and loving hearts than any of my blood kin. They gave me a home when I had no where else to turn after you threw me outta your fine home! They ain't never asked for nothing in return neither! You, my own *sister*, turned me out in a storm to die!"

She wheeled around and marched back the way she had come, holding John Wesley close to her. When she had gotten into the woods, away from her sister's hateful view, she stopped and let the tears come. She was such a fool and always had been. Believing that her sister would change was the thinking of a fool. She had exposed her son to hatred that he was far too young to understand. Now he was patting her tearstained cheek, murmuring, "Don't cry, Mama." His eyes were frightened as he watched her. Seeing his mother cry was a new experience for him.

Kate sniffled and smiled reassuringly at him as she said, "Don't worry, son. Mama's gonna be all right. Everything will be all right. Mama will see to that."

She knew that Aunt Mary's sharp old eyes would see the evidence of her tears if she didn't wash her face before returning to the farm. She meandered through the woods, calming herself while she looked for an artesian well that was nearby. She found it and washed away the visible signs of her distress, but the inner hurt was another matter. That could only scab over with time. She wondered how long would it be before those scabs were ripped away again to let the blood of her pain flow free once more. Shaking her head sadly, she returned to the safe haven of the Stancel farm.

~ * ~

Rufus had not obeyed his mother. Instead of going out the field where his father labored, he had hidden behind the malodorous outhouse. The hot summer sun caused a stench that made his eyes water. Large green flies, attracted by the smell, swarmed toward his face. He impatiently flapped his hands to scare them away. He was too far away to hear the words exchanged between his mother and Aunt Kate. His mother looked very angry and Aunt Kate looked like she wanted to cry. Watching them acting that way conjured up the old guilt from four years ago. It rose in his throat as though to choke him, caused his hands to shake and his heart to beat erratically.

His mother had told him it was not his fault that Aunt Kate was gone, but somehow he had not been able to believe that. Hadn't Aunt Kate left the same day that he had gotten in a fight with the other children at school? Hadn't his mother screamed at Aunt Kate that her child was being beaten in the schoolyard and that Aunt Kate had to get out of the house now? The memory of that night still had the power to frighten him. He sometimes had nightmares that his Aunt Kate was dead somewhere in the woods. He would wake sweating and shaking with fear for her. Sometimes, in the evenings when he had finished his chores, he had searched the woods, dreading that he would find Aunt Kate dead, but he had to know. To his relief, he never found her.

When his mother had found out what he was doing, she had told him to forget all about Aunt Kate, that she was gone now and would not be coming back here. When he asked if Aunt Kate was dead, his mother had laughed in a way that had sent chills down his childish spine and told him that Aunt Kate was still alive, but dead to them. He hadn't understood what that meant. If Aunt Kate were still alive how could she be dead too, he had wanted to know. His mother had gripped his arm in a painful vise and told him not to question her. His Aunt Kate was gone. He was never to speak her name. The painful grip on his arm and the wild look in his mother's eyes had convinced him that is would be best to do as she said. He never mentioned Aunt Kate again, but he did wonder about her from time to time. Nobody ever mentioned Aunt Kate in front of him, but sometimes, when he would walk into a room unexpectedly, conversation between his parents would stop suddenly. Sometimes his classmates would look at him, whispering and giggling behind their hands, but he could never find out what they were saying. Ever since the incident of rock throwing, the others had been wary around him. There was something they knew that he didn't. Even his best friend Stephen wouldn't tell him what it was all about. Stephen would only say that it was just a lot of gossip and he shouldn't pay any attention to any of it.

Now Aunt Kate had turned up unexpectedly with a little boy that was his cousin. Where had she been all this time? Determined to find out, he sneaked along behind her as she walked into the woods. Walking as quietly as a cat on the soft carpet of pine needles, he crept from tree to tree, watching. He could tell Aunt Kate was crying and that his young cousin was frightened. He followed them to the artesian well, where he continued to observe quietly. He heard the words that Aunt Kate spoke to her son and was puzzled by the vehemence in her tone. As the two moved on, he continued to follow. When Aunt Kate came to the old farm that had once belonged to his mother's family, she went inside.

He sat down well back in the trees and tried to solve this riddle. His parents had told him that the old family farm had been sold because his Uncle George was a scoundrel and had mortgaged the farm away. They told him never to come here because it was a disgrace that it was now farmed by a black family. Did they know that Aunt Kate lived here, too? Why was Aunt Kate living here instead of with her family? His young heart tried mightily to understand the complex mystery surrounding the old farm and Aunt Kate. He knew Aunt Kate didn't have a husband, but some of his friends didn't have fathers. Their fathers had been killed in the war. Had Aunt Kate's husband been killed? Thinking hard, he realized that when Aunt Kate had been living with them, the war had been over for a long time. The friends whose fathers had died in the war were older than Aunt Kate's son. Had her husband died in some horrible way after the war? But he didn't remember anyone ever saying anything about a husband. Why was she living on the old family farm if it didn't belong to them any more? And why was Daddy so angry that black people were living here when he had fought for the Union during the war? He shook his head, confused by so many unanswerable questions. Questions he knew he couldn't ask his parents. Noting the position of the sun in the sky, he realized he had better get back home before his Mama realized he was not helping his father like she had told him to do.

When he crept cautiously out of the woods, onto his parent's property, his mother was waiting for him with a stern look in her eyes. Grabbing his hand, she dragged him across the yard to the porch and pushed him into a rocking chair.

"Where have you been," she asked in a harsh voice. "And don't you be lyin' to me neither. I'll have your Daddy tan your hide if you lie to me."

Squirming uncomfortably under her penetrating gaze he stammered, "I-I followed Aunt Kate. She went to the old family farm. Did you know she's living there?"

Ignoring his question she stated, "I *knew* that's where you were! Haven't you been told not to go there?" When he made no answer, she repeated, "Haven't you?" He nodded miserably, head down. "So you deliberately disobeyed your Daddy and me?" she continued.

"No Mama," he insisted. "I didn't know that's where she was going. I just wanted to see where she lives."

"You still deliberately disobeyed. I told you to go to the field and help your Daddy, but you didn't do that, did you?" Silently he shook his head, "Haven't you also been told that that woman is dead to us and not to ever speak to her?"

"I didn't speak to her, Mama. I just followed her. She didn't even know I was there. I'm sorry I didn't go help Daddy like you told me, but I wanted to know about Aunt Kate. Nobody will tell me anything about her." His eyes beseeched his mother to understand.

"She's no fit woman for you to associate with. That's all you need to know. Don't you ever go back to that farm. Don't you ever say her name in my hearing. Do you understand me?" Her eyes bored into his own, waiting for his answer.

"Yes, Mama, I understand," he whispered, not understanding at all.

"Now go help your Daddy like I told you to an hour ago."

Sliding warily from the rocking chair, he eased past his mother. Fearing a box on the ear, he fled around the corner of the house. At the sound of a stifled sob he stopped. Easing carefully back around the corner, he silently watched his mother. She had sunk down on the steps with her hands across her mouth to quiet the sounds of her crying. Then, to the quiet air around her, his mother said, "Oh my poor little sister. What's to become of you? Why did you do such a disgraceful thing and leave me no choice but to choose against you?"

Why was his mother crying? What did she mean about being forced to choose? Didn't she say that Aunt Kate was no good? Why would she be crying about her now? What were the answers and would he ever know them?

Twenty-one

After the crushing humiliation of her attempt to make peace with her sister, Kate fell back into the pattern of her life with the Stancel's with a grateful heart. Here was love and acceptance. She kept the anguish of that meeting deeply buried in her already profoundly overburdened heart. She would admit to no one, ever, that she had attempted a direct reconciliation with her sister and been so cruelly brushed aside again. Being with Aunt Mary and her family and friends soothed her haggard nerves and brought a small sense of peace to her.

~ * ~

One early Fall evening a timid knocking sounded at the front door. Sam went to see who was calling. Young Jebidiah Lincoln from one of the neighboring farms stood there looking abashed.

"Ah wuz wunderin' could Ah see Miz Kate for' minute. Ah woan tek up much o' huh time," he said.

Sam stepped aside and Jebidiah walked over to Kate who looked at him. Waiting to hear what he wanted. He remained silent for another full minute, then looked at her shyly.

"Ah wuz wunderin'," he said, "Well Ah means Ah wuz hopin', uh, well Ah wanted..." His voice trailed off. He looked away.

Kate could see that something of importance to him was on his mind and he was having trouble getting the words out. "It's all right, Jebidiah," she said softly, "You just go on and say what it is that's on your mind."

Looking back at her face, he stammered, "Ah-Ah-Ah cum heah ternight ter ask iffen you would—if you could fine it in yo' heart—iffen you would teach me ter read and write lak you be doin' for Sam and his folks."

A shocked silence came over the room. Feeling that change in atmosphere, Jebidiah rushed on, "Ah knows it be a lot ter ask for frum you, seein' as how you doan really knows me real well an' all, but Ah got a fierce hankerin' ter learn an' Ah figures you is de onlies one dat might be kine enuff ter teach me. Ah ain' got no money ter pay you, but Ah thought mebbe we could wuk out some kine of agreement. Miz Kate, Ah ain' got nuthin' in dis worl' whut b'longs ter me dat Ah could trade wif you for' de lessons, but mebbe deys *sumpin* Ah could do for' you in return." His earnest face was slicked with embarrassed sweat as he stood waiting for Kate's answer.

Kate was so taken aback by his knowledge of the lessons, that she was at a loss for words.

Aunt Mary asked sharply, "Who tole you dat Miz Kate wuz teachin' us ter read and write?"

Surprise covered Jebidiah's face at Aunt Mary's question. Permelia rose suddenly from her place near the fire, retreating to the kitchen. They had their answer then. Jebidiah confirmed it.

"Permelia done be braggin around dat she kin read and write and givin' huhsef airs 'bout it." Looking back to Kate, he continued, "Ah doan be wantin' ter learn ter be settin' mahsef up as betta dan anybody else. Ah jes wants ter learn so's Ah kin betta mahsef. Ah sho would be proud did you say you'd teach me."

"Jebidiah," Aunt Mary said, "Dis wuz suppose to be a secret. Permelia din hab no bizness goin' roun' braggin' on huhsef. Ah be havin' a serious talk wif dat gal 'bout goin' roun' puttin' on airs. We doan want ter cause any trouble for' Miz Kate. Did de wite folks fine out she be teachin' us ter read and write, den a whole worl' o' trouble come crashing down on huh agin. Ah reckon you know she already been thoo enuff trouble already. Ah sorry, Jeb, but we cain' be tekkin' no chances on gettin' Miz Kate in no mo' trouble."

Tears filled young Jebidiah's eyes as he nodded his head and turned away. His shoulders slumped, his head hung low as he headed for the door. Kate's heart went out to the young man. She knew too well what it was to want something so badly and have it denied through no fault of your own.

"Wait," she called. "I'll teach you to read and write, Jebidiah."

The young man turned to her with shining eyes and raced to where she sat. Squatting down by her chair, he reached out tentatively and touched her hand.

"You will," he asked joyfully. "Ah jes knew iffen Ah came and asked you mahsef dat you wooden turn me away. Evabody seys dat you is so kine and dey is right! You done made me de happiest man in de worl'!"

Kate grasped both his hands tightly in her own and said, "I'll teach you and your family and anyone else who wants to learn. You just let everybody know about it."

Jebidiah jumped up, prepared to race into the night and spread the good news. He halted at Aunt Mary's voice.

"Hold up, Jeb!" He looked back to see Aunt Mary looking deep into Kate's eyes. "You knows dis could lead ter bad trouble fo' you. Does you really want ter tek dat chance? You got yo' boy ter be thinkin' bout. Iffen anythan' happen ter you because of dis, who gone ter raise yo' boy? You knows dat do some of de wite fokes round heah find out 'bout dis, dey mount hu't you bad enough dat you die frum it." Turning to Jebidiah, she continued, "Is you willin' ter put her life in danger for' yo' fierce hankerin' ter be satisfied?"

Jebidiah looked ashamed. "Ah din think dat bout somethin' bad happenin' ter Miz Kate. Ah sho' wooden nevah get ovah it iffen Ah was de cause of sumpin' bad happenin' ter huh."

"Now wait just a minute, Aunt Mary, Jebidiah," Kate said. "Permilia has already been bragging around that she can read and write. We don't know who all may already know about the whole thing. The secret is already out. The harm already done. I want to teach everybody who wants to learn. Trouble may already be on the way whether I teach anybody else or not, so I say let anybody who wants to learn come here during the winter months and learn just like what we've been doing in the family. It cain't be every night though. That's bound to look suspicious if everybody starts traipsing over here every night. Maybe just one family group each week. We could do one family, one night a week . That wouldn't look odd at all." Excitement shone in her eyes, pinked her cheeks. Turning to Jebidiah, who had remained frozen in the middle of the room since Aunt Mary's command, she said, "You go on Jebidiah. Tell everybody the plan and ya'll fix it up amongst yourselves who's to come each week."

"Miz Kate," he said, "you has got de kin'est heart. All ob us will do ouah bes' to mek sho dat sumpin bad doan happen ter you cause of it."

"Well," Aunt Mary exclaimed after Jebidiah had raced out the door. "You is de beatinest chile Ah have evah knowed. You cain' get up de gumption ter go out in de yahd anytime Mist' Angus be round heah, but you is gone ter teach all de coloreds round heah ter read and write! Ah jes cain' figure you out."

"Miz Kate," Sam put in, "dis be dangerous for' you. It foolish for' you ter say you gone ter teach evabody! You say you woan go in de yahd wen Mist' Angus 'round cause you is skeered he mount tell you ter git offen his lan'. Ain' you even mo' skeered dat he fin' out dat you teachin' all de coloreds? Iffen you thinks he wooden want you round heah jes cause you got a baby an' no husband, whut do you think he do when he fin' out bout dis?"

Kate looked from one to the other. She could see that they were both concerned that she was making a big mistake. She knew it wasn't because they wanted to know more than their friends, but because they were truly worried that something bad would happen to her..

"You're right, both of you. I am scared. I've been scared for way too long. The white people of this community have shut me out and the colored people have given me a home. I want to give something back to them. I don't see how it could make things worse with the people who won't associate with me. This is something that will make me happy while I'm toiling on that other road. It makes it easier to take the meanness of those people if I have the love and caring of others to uphold me when those people turn me away time and again. I know white folks won't approve if they find out, but they're already determined never to let me back into their world. I *will* git back someday though. Ya'll just wait and see if I don't."

"Miz Kate", Aunt Mary said, "Ah's glad as Ah kin be dat you is findin' some gumption in yosef, but Ah cain' hep feelin' dat you is choosin' wrong in dis. If you is determined, den we do ouah bes' ter mek sho nuthin' bad come of it, but Ah jes cain' see why you has ter do dis perticular thang."

"Couldn't you see in Jeb's eyes how bad he wanted this? I know all about wanting something that bad. If I turned him away, I'd be just like my family and old friends who turn me away just because they think I did something unforgiveable." In her agitation, Kate began pacing the floor, pounding her fist into her hand, "Don't ya'll see? I cain't be like those people! I cain't be cold and mean like that!"

Sam came to her and took her by the shoulder, shaking her slightly to get her attention. "Miz Kate, we knows how it been for' you. We done seed how it hu't you. We jes doan want you ter cause yosef any mo' hu't. We's proud dat you wants ter do it. Doan thank dat we be 'gainst you. We jes ca'ah too much for' you ter let you tek dis on yosef wifout thanking it thoo. We jes' gone ter have ter be real careful frum now on and keep it quiet as we can. It woan be jes you dat gets in trouble ovah dis. It be mah whole fambly, too."

Throwing her arms around Sams' neck, hugging him to her she said, "Sam, you are the best friend I have next to your Mama. I understand your concern, but things will be all right. I just know that they will! We'll just be very, very careful with this. We'll be so careful and so sneaky that nobody will find out."

Aunt Mary came over, pulled Kate from Sam's arms and hugged her close. With tears in her eyes, she said, "Ah love you lak mah own chile, Miz Kate. Sam be right, we jes be wantin' de bes' for you and whut's bes' for us, too. Come on now, we go on up ter baid. Sam gone ter hab a lil talk wif Permelia 'bout runnin' round and gibbin' huhsef airs and puttin' you in danger wif huh loose tongue."

Sam nodded to his mother and went into the kitchen where Permelia was still hiding. Arm in arm, Kate and Aunt Mary went up to their room and prepared for bed. Long after Aunt Mary's gentle snores were heard, Kate lay wide awake. Thoughts and plans for teaching whirled round and round in her mind.

Late during the night, just as she was finally drifting off to sleep, she heard Permelia walking quietly down the hall to her room, sniffling as she went. Sam must have been very harsh with her. Maybe she should go to her and tell her that she wasn't angry about what had happened.

Twenty-two

The plans for the lessons that winter worked beautifully, despite Sam's almost palpable unease. The families round about had gotten together among themselves and set a schedule for which group would come each week. No one seemed to suspect anything was going on in the Stancel household other than casual visiting around and to keep anyone from becoming suspicious, Kate and the Stancel family would sometimes travel to the homes of her students and conduct lessons there. It would have looked odd if the Stancels never visited at the homes of their friends.

These visits brought home to Kate the kind of lives the other sharecroppers lived. Though she had lost her reputation and the regard of her friends and family, her life was lived on a much better level than most of her students. Though the Stancels and she herself labored long and hard in the fields, they at least had a large, warm, solidly built house in which to live. Not so for her students. Most of them lived in one or two room shacks with an open fireplace to cook over and keep the house warm. They slept four and five to a bed and some on the floor on makeshift mattresses made of sheets sewn together and stuffed with straw. The floor, if there was one, would be warped and rough and often had cracks between the boards large enough to see the ground through them. Yet though their home were little better than hovels and they struggled for every mouthful of food they had, they welcomed Kate wholeheartedly into their lives and tried to find some way to repay her for the lessons she was teaching. Most of them had no money. Indeed, she learned that for the most part they were constantly in debt and the cotton they sharecropped was usually only just enough to pay off their credit owed to the landowner who supplied all their needs throughout the year. They tried to pay Kate with strings of dried fruits and vegetables or some sweet potatoes. The first time Kate refused outright to take anything in return for the lessons, Aunt Mary took her aside.

"Miz Kate," she said, "You gots to be takin' what these folks be offerin' to you. They got they pride jes' like you do. Iffen you woan let 'em pay you somehow, they gonna be hurt."

"But Aunty Mary. They've hardly got anything of their own. I cain't be taking anything from when they have so little to start with."

"You got a big heart, honey chile, but they needs to give you something in return for you teachin' 'em. Just take whatever they offering you and tell 'em thank you. You mind me now, gal! You ain't they onlies one with stiff neck pride 'round here. Whenever they comes to our place, we just cook up what they done give you and feed it to 'em while theys visitin'."

Aunt Mary's face held a sly smile and Kate could see the logic behind the other woman's reasoning. With a sly grin of her own, she nodded her agreement. All future offerings were accepted with denials that it was necessary, but with profuse thanks for their thoughtfulness.

~ * ~

The winter passed all too soon, and the growing season with its backbreaking labor was upon them again. Aunt Mary began again to try and persuade Kate to attend the monthly church services. She argued that Kate now knew and had the respect of everyone in the community. She should know by now there would be no shunning of her by any of the member of their flock. She argued that John Wesley was growing up and should go to church as was proper for a child. Kate turned away from all Aunt Mary's persuasions and continued to refuse to attend the services.

Summer passed and the harvest was in full swing. When it was finally done, the annual harvest hoe down was imminent. As in years past, Aunt Mary asked Kate to accompany them. Always before, Kate had refused to attend, content to be a passive part of the community, content with the casual visiting from house to house. This year Aunt Mary persisted with her arguments until Kate finally gave in and grudgingly agreed to go to the dance.

The whole family walked to the clearing where the hoe down was held, each carrying a cake or pie or jug of tea that was their contribution to the festivities. Some of the men had erected a rough platform for the fiddlers and there was a huge bonfire blazing merrily in the darkness. Children raced around the clearing shouting and laughing as they played together.

The Stancel children raced off to join their friends, but in only a few minutes, Sam's son Andy came back.

"Miz Kate, let John Wesley come play with us. I'll watch out for him real good. You don't need to worry yourself over him. I promise."

John Wesley's big blue eyes looked up at his mother. She could see that he wanted to go and play with the other children, but she was afraid to let him out of her sight. She knew that young Andy would take good care of her son, but still she hesitated.

"Please, Miz Kate? You cain't have no good time yourself holding on to your baby all night. You ain't gonna be able to dance or nothing iffen you're holding him all night."

"Well, I wasn't aimin' to dance tonight, Andy." Kate replied. "It ain't that I don't trust you to take care of him, I was just planning to sit on the side and watch everybody else dance."

Andy looked shocked by this revelation. "Ain't gonna dance? Why, Miz Kate, that ain't gonna be no fun for you!"

"Let him take the boy, Miz Kate," Aunt Mary interjected. "John Wesley wants to play with the other chilluns and he ain't gonna do nothing but drive you to distraction asquirming in your lap all evenin'."

Reluctantly, Kate let go of John Wesley's hand. Andy grabbed it immediately and said solemnly, "Don't you be worryin' none, Miz Kate. I promise I won't let nuthin' happen to him."

Kate watched them go off together hand in hand, her heart thumping painfully in her chest. Andy was carefully shortening his steps to John Wesley's smaller legs and chattering to him a mile a minute. A hand touched her arm and when Kate looked over, she saw that Aunt Mary understood her worry.

"Come on now, we got us some dancing to do. Don't be dragging behind. The fiddlers be fixin' to start up."

They walked on to the trestle table that had been set up to hold the food for the evening. Pleasant greeting were called out to both of them from all sides. Kate turned to watch the fiddlers tuning up and saw the looks of anticipation on every face in the crowd gathered round. Looking from face to face to face, Kate suddenly felt her white skin glowing like a beacon among all the dark faces around her. Everyone was smiling at her and obviously glad she had come, but a feeling of separateness, of otherness, overcame her. As the fiddlers struck up a tune, echoes of the past danced across her mind. Her ears heard the sound of silk and taffeta skirts swirling to music long since gone, played by men long since dead. A chasm opened at her feet and sweat broke out on her upper lip and forehead. Just as she thought she would faint, her hand was grabbed and she was pulled quickly among the dancers. With an effort she pulled herself back to the present and found herself dancing with young Jeb. Grinning rakishly, he said, "Pick up your feet, Miz Kate. This be a celebration." The feeling of faintness passed, the chasm closed. A slight smile creased her lips as her feet found the steps to the dance. They flew around the circle of dancers. "There now," Jeb teased, "I knowed you could dance with the best of 'em! Ain't this a fine evenin?"

When the musicians finally took a break, Jeb brought a breathless Kate back to Aunt Mary's side. With a grin and a slight bow he disappeared in the crowd. Aunt Mary said, "There now. That warn't so bad was it? Nothin' to be skeered about at all!"

"I wasn't scared," Kate protested.

"Oh yes you was. I seed the look on your face befo' young Jeb dragged you off to dance. I knows what you was thinkin' 'bout, too. Doan look back child. That ain't gonna do you no good atall. You gots to go forward from here. You just looks straight ahead and go afta what you wants. You gets it sooner or later."

As the night wound on, the moon rose over the trees with an orange red glow that seemed a reflection of the bonfire below it. The food and tea disappeared from the table, consumed by heavy appetites generated from so much dancing. Occasionally some of the men would wander off into the darkness for a short time. She suspected that they were partaking of something stronger than tea to drink and grinned to herself. Eventually sleepy children were gathered up, the fire put out and everyone headed home in a pleasantly tired state. Kate was glad she had let Aunt Mary persuaded her to come tonight and regretted that she hadn't come last year or the year before. Her stubborn pride and fears of her own making had kept her from joining the joyous event. John Wesley lay heavily against her shoulder, tired out from the evening of rambunctious play. His warm breath against her neck felt wonderful on the walk home.

~ * ~

With the end of the harvest and the onset of cooler weather, Kate's rounds of teaching began again. She was very proud of the progress everyone was making. They were all reading more easily this year and the mathematics that had been so troublesome last year was starting to make sense to everyone. Sam still made ominous pronouncements occasionally like some dark skinned male Cassandra, but Kate ignore his warnings, sure that their secret would continue undiscovered.

Twenty-three

Christmas was coming and Aunt Mary and the whole community were excited. This year Reverend Jones' circuit would bring him to their own church on Christmas Eve. Kate was dismayed. She would be spending Christmas Eve alone with her son. She had come to love Christmas Eve with her adopted family and now they would be gone on that special while she and John Wesley stayed alone in the farmhouse. She knew there would be no plea she could make that would dissuade Aunt Mary from attending the church service. A feeling of loneliness settled in the pit of her stomach.

Aunt Mary approached Kate three days before Christmas with the light of battle in her eyes, but when she spoke her tone was merely conversational. "Whut you gonna be wearin' ter de church service on Christmas Eve, Miz Kate?"

Kate looked at her with astonished eyes. "You know I ain't planning on going to church, Christmas Eve or not. Me and John Wesley will just spend it here at home. I'll read the Christmas Story to him and fix him something special for supper and that'll be it."

Aunt Mary sighed. "Well, I sho thought you'd be goin' wif us ter de service, seein' as how you done been teachin' evabody and got ter know all of 'em and eva thang. Dey sho will be disappointed dat you ain't dere. I reckon I'll jes have ter explain dat it ain' nuthin' you got 'gainst them personal, but I knows dey gonna be disappointed and mebbe even hurt by it." Shaking her head sadly, Aunt Mary turned away.

"Now you just wait a minute, Aunt Mary," Kate blazed. "You ain't gonna git around me talking like that! I know what you're up to and it ain't gonna work! You're just trying to make me feel guilty and shame me into going with ya'll. That ain't fair!"

"Are you bein' fair to yo chile by denyin' him de word of God jes cause you is too proud ter go ter church? I know you tole me you doan b'lieve in God, but you is denyin' yo own flesh and blood de upbringin' he oughter have and you knows you is doin' it."

"I ain't denying my son anything. I only want the best out of life for him and you know that! Why you've been with me every step of the way, telling me to keep on trying, to keep on hoping. Why are you acting so mean to me now? You know what I've been through." Tears began to swim in her eyes and she brushed they away angrily, her voice cracked as she continued, "Why are you talking to me this way?"

Folding her friend in her arms, Aunt Mary stroked the long dark hair that spilled down Kate's back. As Kate sobbed on her shoulder she whispered, "I been patient wif you long enough. It be past time for' yo son ter learn about church and it be past time for you ter remember."

Twenty-four

Wild and eerie howling rent the silent cloak of darkness. Kate's eyes popped open in alarm. A flickering orange light shining through the lace curtains at the window cast bizarre shadows around the room. Heart pounding in a mad rhythm, Kate threw back the numerous quilts that covered her and leapt from the bed. Her feet tangled in the thrown back quilts and she fell to the floor with a loud thud. As she scrambled to her feet, ignoring a sharp stab of pain in her hip, she heard Aunt Mary stumbling from the other side of the bed. They regarded each other with frightened eyes in the flickering light.

Racing to the window side by side, they pulled back the curtains. The sight that met their horrified gaze was one to freeze the blood in their veins. A scene straight from Hell itself was being played out in the front yard. The source of the flickering light was a huge cross that had been erected in the yard and set aflame. Highlighted by the hellish flames rode men on horseback, heads covered by some kind of white sacking with burned out holes where evil glinted in hatred bright eyes reflected from torches held by each rider. *"Night Riders"* thought Kate as her knees trembled beneath her nightgown, *"Dear God! I didn't think there were any of them around here!"* All of Sam's warnings and cautions went rushing through her mind. Here was the trouble he had feared, the trouble from which no one could save them. *"My fault,"* beat the rhythm of her heart. *"My fault! My fault!"*

Another round of howling shattered the night. The children began crying in fear across the hall. As she and Aunt Mary stood frozen in horror, they heard the stairs creak. Someone was moving stealthily up the stairs. As one entity, they lunged to the bedroom door intent on reaching the children. Both of them terrified that one or more of the hate mongers riding in the yard and dared to enter the house.

Kate was only a step ahead of Aunt Mary as she bolted through the bedroom door. She was seized around the waist and a rough, callused palm clamped across her lips tightly, cutting off her scream of terror before it was born. Struggling violently in the crushing grip, she heard a familiar voice speak softly, "Settle down, Miz Kate. It me."

"Sam," whispered Aunt Mary loudly. "Whut you mean sneakin' 'roun de house and grabbin' Miz Kate lak dat and skeering de bof o' us haf to def."

Kate ceased her struggle and Sam released her, answering his mother in a soft voice, "Ah cum up heah ter mek suah nobody shows deysef. Them mens git ti'ad in a while and leab iffen we doan show ouhselves. Ternite be a wahning. Dey woan do us no haam dis time, but we kin be suah dey be back agin for' long. We be discussin' dat soon's dey git on outta heah ternight."

Rushing into the room where the children still whimpered and cried, Kate saw that they were all clinging to Permelia as though their lives depended on it. The young negro woman had pulled all four children into her arms and held them tightly against her heart while she whispered softly to them.

In an excess of gratitude, Kate whispered, "Thank you, Permelia. For keeping them safe."

At the sound of his mother's voice, John Wesley broke free of Permelia and raced to her. His small arms snaked around her legs as he pressed himself tightly against her. She could feel his little heart racing wildly against her legs as her clung to her. Reaching down, she softly pushed his hair back from his frightened face and gave him a reassuring smile. Permelia's voice hissed at her out of the darkness, "Ah ain' comfortin' dese chillen for' *yo'* sake. It be yo' fault we in dis mess. You jes cudden' lissen ter reason. You jes *had* ter go roun' teachin' evabody and showin' off yo' book learnin', givin' yosef airs wen you ain' no betta dan nobody else you been teachin'. Sam tried ter tell you dat dis would happen, but you cudden lissen to him! Now we be in a fine mess and all cuz ob *you*!"

Kate stood mute and hung her head dumbly under the assault. There was no rebuke she could make to the onslaught of words that struck like daggers through the air. Her pride, her damnable stubborn pride had brought them to this. She had endangered not only her own life, but the lives of those she had come to love best in the world because of it.

"You hesh up, Permelia," came Sam's angry voice. "We done talked 'bout dis. Iffen you cain' remembah how Miz Kate cum to be teachin', den Ah haf ter remind you! *You* wuz de one went roun' braggin' an' givin' yosef airs wen you done learn ter read a lil bit. Wudden nobody cum roun' heah askin' Miz Kate ter do no teachin' iffen you had kep' quiet lak you wuz sposed ter do. We all knowed dis could happen and we all agreed ter take de chance. Doan you be thowin' all de blame on huh."

Permelia spit on the floor in Kate's direction saying, "How kin you tek huh side 'gainst me, Sam? Ain' we done agreed we's gone ter git mahied soon? You gone ter tek huh side obah me eben now?"

Sam strode to Permelia's side, but his reply was lost in the howling that rose again from outside the house. Then came a voice out of the night, "Kate Randsome! Whore! Nigger lover! Show your face so we can send your soul to its rightful place in Hell tonight!"

Rage rose white hot in Kate's breast. Without thinking, she reached down and wrested her son away from her. Pushing him toward a surprised Aunt Mary, she turned and ran from the room. Taking the stairs two at a time she reached the first floor before any of the shocked adults could stop her. Yanking open the front door, she stepped out on the front porch to face her accusers. Highlighted by the flames of the still burning cross, she shouted, "Here I am! Why don't ya'll show *your* faces? Are you cowards that you come here in disguise to accuse me?"

Startled by her sudden appearance, no one spoke or moved for a moment. Then, in slow motion, Kate saw a pistol rise and aim itself at her head. Terror held her motionless as she looked down the barrel of the pistol, saw a hand come up to cock it. Just as she heard the snap of the trigger cock into position, a hand reached out the door, grabbed her arm and dragged her physically back into the house. A bullet splintered the wood of the doorjamb just where she had been standing. Sprawled there on the floor, she saw Sam reach out and slam the door shut. Grapping her under the arms, he dragged her to the relative safety of the kitchen. They squatted quietly under the kitchen table listening to the renewed howling outside. Finally the sounds died away. After waiting several minutes to be sure the horsemen were gone, Sam dragged her from under the table. Gripping her shoulders tightly, he shook her until her teeth rattled in her head.

"You damn fool! Whut did you think you wuz doin., runnin' out dere lak dat?! Dey wudda' killed you for' sho' iffen Ah hadden got dere in time ter pull you back in de house! Den dey mightta' cum on in heah an kilt us all afta dat! Whut did you think you wuz doin'?

"I was showing them I ain't scared of them," she replied in a shaky voice.

"Iffen you ain' skeered o' them, den you is crazy. You is jes' plum outta yo haid crazy. Dey wuz ready ter kill you right dere on de poach. Den who gone ter raise yo boy? How would he feel knowin' his Mama done been kilt by wite fokes? Wen you gone ter think befo' you does somethin'? We all gone ter hab ter leave heah now cause o' this. Ah wuz plannin' ter move on in anotha' yeah o' two, but now we gone ter hab ter git outter heah quick befo' dey comes back. Nex' time dey woan stop wif some hoopin' an' hollerin'. Nex' time dey comes back it be ter kill us all and cain' nobody stop 'em frum doin' it neitha."

"But S-Sam," Kate stammered, "you went along with the teaching. I know you didn't really want to, but you did. You wanted your friends to learn as much as I wanted to teach them. You said upstairs, just a little while ago to Permelia, that we knew the risk and took it anyway."

"Yas'm. Ah sholy did say dat, but Ah's regrettin' goin' long wif you mo' evah minute. Ah *knowed* sumpin lak dis wuz gone ter happen and Ah went along wif you anyway. Now Ah doan know whut we gone ter do, but we gone ter hab ter do it quick. Yo stubbornness done put us all in danger. Wen is you gone ter git it thoo yo haid dai dey ain' no goin back ter de way thangs wuz befo'? You ain' *nevah* gone ter git back de life you had. You gots ter staht wif whut you got now and build up a new life! Stop hankering fo whut you has lost and git on wif whut you got."

Tears stood in Kate's eyes, but her voice was forceful as she answered him. "I *am* trying to start with what I've got. Teaching you and all the others is part of it. Teaching is the only gift I have to give! It was my way of thanking everyone for how good they've been to me."

Sam snorted. "It be a *fine* thank you ter bring the night riders down on all of us. You knows dat dey be back and do a lot wuss nex' time!"

Aunt Mary bustled down the stairs just then. "You hesh up ,Sam. Done is done. Miss Kate din mean ter bring no hahm on us. Permelia be puttin' de chillen back ter baid, but you betta go on up dere Miz Kate and see ter lil John Wesley. We all done heard dat gun shot and he wuz in a tizzy ter cum down here and see iffen you wuz alright."

With a sad look at the two of them, Kate walked slowly up the stairs. When she was, Sam turned to his mother.

"Whut we gone ter do now, Mammy? We gone ter hab ter leave right quick an' Ah ain' got hardly twenty dollahs put by. Ah wuz plannin' on stayin' heah for' while longa' and put by some mo' money, but Ah jes doan know how we kin move on wif de little Ah got and Ah knows we cain' be stayin' heah no mo'."

"We is sholy in de fiah now, son," she replied. "We gone ter hab ter move on wif whut we got and hope for' de bes'. We go as fah as we kin git on whut we got, den see 'bout gettin' sum work ter make mo' money to move on frum deah. Dose men ain' gone ter chase afta us. Once dey knows we is gone, dey be satisfied. Go on and git some sleep. We got hahd times cumin'."

"Ah's gone ter stay awake 'til dat fiah go out and git rid ob dat thang in de yahd befo' de chillen sees it. Den ah gets some sleep. You go on back ter baid yosef."

He stood with worry in his eyes and watched his mother go back up the stairs. With a sigh, he sat down to wait for the fire in the yard to die down.

Twenty-five

The next morning brought Angus Mcintosh to the farm. He gazed with dismay at the scorched spot in the yard where the cross had burned so hungrily only hours before. Sam joined him. They both stood silently for several minutes. Angus cleared his throat and said quietly, "Well, Sam. I reckon we're in a bad spot now. "

"Yes, suh, Mist' Angus. I reckon we are."

"Why in the name of God did you let Kate go around teaching everybody? You're a smart man, Sam. I cain't figure out how you could have let this happen."

"Miz Kate be a stubborn woman, suh. Ah told huh something like this wuz gonna happen, but she wouldn't lissen ter reason. And besides dat, we got as much right ter learn as anybody else nowadays. Ain't de Freedman's Bureau goin' aroun' and settin up schools for de Negros ter learn?"

A scowl transformed Angus' normally cheerful face as he looked at Sam. "The Freedman's Bureau has the power of the government to back them up and even so, they're having trouble all over the place. I just cain't get over you letting this happen. I put you and your family in this house because your one of my best workers and one of the smartest bucks around. Then you go and let something like this happen."

"As knows you done me and my family a good turn putting us on this here farm, but Ah tole you—once Miz Kate gets her mind set on somethin, there ain't no changin' it."

"Kate Randsome is a fool," bellowed Angus. "She ruined her own life acting like a tramp and now she's ruined yours by going around teaching all the Negros when she ought to have more sense. I know ya'll have the right to learn now, but that don't change the way people think! Now you're in a fine mess. You cain't stay here anymore. Those Riders will be back here to get Kate and probably kill every one of you in the process! What are you planning to do now?"

"Well, suh, Ah done save up a little bit of money in the last few years. I wuz planning on moving my family West in a few mo' years when Ah had a little more saved up. Ah reckon we'll just have to move on a little sooner dan Ah was planning to. Ah wuz gone ter come over ter yo' place this mornin' and let you know about it. Ah knowed we couldn't stay heah no mo' after whut happened last night."

Angus looked thoughtfully at the young man before him. After a moment he said, "Going West were you? I reckon you could maybe find some land for yourself out there, but then again, you might not be able to buy any good land. You couldn't have saved much over the last few years. What if I had another plan for you? I had something in mind when I came over here this morning. You might be better off if you go along with me instead of heading off west somewhere."

"Whut do you mean—another plan and we'd be better off?"

"I've got some kinfolk in Virginia. Cousins in Richmond. My Cousin Sean wrote to me about a school for Negros in Hampton, Virginia. I don't know exactly where that is, but I could send all of you to Sean and he'd see that you got to Hampton." Reaching into his pocket, he drew out some bills and a piece of paper. "This here paper has my cousin's address in Richmond and here's thirty dollars traveling money. I know it ain't much, but it's all I can spare. Times are hard on me too, you know. Added to the money you've saved and if you take plenty of provisions with you, maybe it'll be enough to get you to Richmond. If it's not, surely a smart man like yourself could find some kind of work to tide ya'll over." Pressing the paper and the bills into Sam's limp hand he continued, "Just make sure you take Kate with you when you go. Her life is worthless here. Surely you know that. Convince her to leave with you and your family."

Sam tried to hand the money and the paper back to Angus. "Ah cain't make you no promises 'bout Miz Kate. Like Ah done told you, she be a stubborn woman. Of course Ah intends for huh to go with us when we leave, but Ah cain't make no promises. We just go on west like Ah done planned."

Angus pushed the money back toward Sam. "Taking Kate with you ain't a condition of accepting this money. I want you to have it even if you cain't get her to leave with you. I'm afraid for your life as much or more than I am for hers. The money is yours to take you and your family to safety. I think it would be better for you to go to Virginia than to go west. In Virginia, you could continue your education and who knows how far you could better youself that way. Think of your children. An education would make their future so much better. If Kate is such a fool that she won't leave with you, then let her go her own way and do the best she can for herself. Don't let her endanger your family any more than she already has!"

"You doan understand, Mist' Angus. Miz Kate *is* one of my family now. We all care whut happen to her."

"Then damn it! Tie her to the wagon if you have to, but don't risk your life for her anymore!" Turning his back, Angus stamped across the yard and into the woods.

~ * ~

Sam watched Angus retreat, then walked to the privacy of the barn to sit and think over the startling turn of events. Angus Macintosh was right of course. The best thing to do, now that they were forced to leave the area, would be to go to this place in Virginia. He and his children would have a chance for a much brighter future with an education. A feeling of exhilaration began to build within him. Yes! They would go to Virginia. They would learn and work and make a wonderful future for themselves. It was more than he had ever dreamed would be possible. They would be safe there and so would Kate. Some of his excitement dissipated at the thought of Kate. She would refuse to go with them. After more than four years in the same house, he knew her through and through. She was a stubborn woman. She was committed to staying here and winning back her place in the community. But surely she would see that that was now more impossible than ever before. By teaching the Negros to read, she had committed yet another unforgivable sin. In the eyes of many it would be an even greater sin than that of having a child out of wedlock. He must make her see reason. She must come with them. There was no life for her here. He would battle with her stubbornness and make her see reason. Racing out of the barn, he went in search of his mother to tell her the news. He knew she would be delighted.

Kate was not in the kitchen where he found his mother. He eagerly told her of the plan Angus Macintosh had laid before him. Excitedly showed her the money and the slip of paper with the Richmond address of Sean Macintosh. Aunt Mary was so thrilled and relieved that she had to sit down at the table and hold the money and paper in her hands. They made excited plans for leaving within the next few days. Time was of the essence now that the Night Riders were after Kate. At the thought of Kate they both became quiet and subdued. Discussing the best way to go about persuading her to come with them took up time, but in the end, it was decided that Aunt Mary would be the one to present the plan to Kate. Kate had relied on her advice so much over the last few years that surely she would listen to reason now from her closest ally. Aunt Mary had a backup plan in place, just in case her friend proved to be as stubborn as they feared she might be. She explained to her son that she had made inquiries among their friends about a place for Kate if she did turn out to be as stubborn as they feared. A man by the name of James Richmond in Purdy was looking for someone to keep house and look after his mother. According to her sources, this Mr. Richmond was a powerful man and would be able to keep Kate safe—if he agreed to hire her. If Kate was too stubborn to agree to leave the area with them, then she would tell her about Mr. Richmond with the understanding that if Mr. Richmond didn't hire her, she would leave for Virginia with them.

~ * ~

Aunt Mary came to her in the evening as she sat rocking slowly on the front porch. "Kate, chile," she said gently, "There's somethin' we got to talk about."

Her heart skipped a beat, then lurched back into motion. She knew something was coming that she wouldn't want to hear and that Aunt

Mary was having a hard time coming out with it. She waited gravely for the next words, which confirmed her fears.

"Sam done heard 'bout a place in Virginia that got a school for Negros. He been savin' a little at a time all dese yeah's and Mist' Angus done give him a little extry money so's we kin all go out there. He think things maybe diffrunt out dere. You knows we cain' be stayin' roun heah. Not after whut done happen last night. De Riders be afta you and we cain' pertect you from them. We got to leave right quick now."

Taking Kate's hand, she continued, "Ah wants you to come wif us, honey. You cain' be stayin' heah now. Not afta whut done happened. Permelia be comin' wif us. Sam plannin' to ask huh to jump de broom wif him befo' we go. Ah knows de two of you ain' nevah got along, but maybe do you come wif us, you kin fine yosef a husband out dere. It'ud make my heart glad could I see you happy wif a place of yo' own and a man ter tek care o' you. You cain' be stayin' roun' heah. You has ter go wif us chile and mek a betta life for yosef an dat young'un. Ain' no need for you to be stayin' heah wheah yo own fambly woan have nuthin' to do wif you or yo chile and men hidin' dey faces be comin' ter kill you."

Kate felt Aunt Mary's hand on her arm and looked into the eyes that pleaded with her to come with them and make a new life for herself. She considered for a moment going with the Stancels, but knew she had struggled here for too long to give up now. She would stay here and continue to fight for a place.

She spoke with love when she answered, "No, Aunt Mary. I have to stay here. This is my place. I know you want what's best for me and you think the best would be to go with ya'll, but I want to stay. I'll miss all of you terribly. I don't know how I would have lived these past four years if it hadn't been for all of ya'll, but I cain't leave now. I've sacrificed too much already to cut and run now. If I was going to leave it would have been years ago. Please understand."

Aunt Mary sighed deeply, remained quiet for a minute, and then said, "You a stubborn fool, Kate Randsome. Ah done been too soft on you all dese yeahs. Ah done watched you cryin' fo de moon an' ain' done nuthin' ter stop you frum it."

"Crying for the moon! What are you talking about?"

"You jes' lak a chile cryin' fo sumthin' it cain' have. Dat's whut Ah'm talkin' bout! You been goin' roun' heah all dese yeahs thinkin' you gone get back whut had befo' John Wesley be born an' dat ain' nevah gone happen!"

"But you told me all this time that I could make a place for me and John Wesley is I just tried hard enough! That's what I've been doing all this time! I took you at your word and tried and tried and I'm not gonna give up now just cause you told me a story all these years!"

"Honey, Ah din lie to you all dis time. Ah thought you could make an *new* kine of life somehow with the wite folks iffen you tried hard enough. Well, you done jes' bout broke yo heart tryin' and ain' nuthin' done changed. It be time fo you ter give up beatin' yosef ter death tryin' ter get back wif de wite fokes roun' heah! You come wif us and mek a new life in a new place! You kin keep on teachin' in Virginny and have a good life fo yosef and yo' son. A life you wheah kin be proud and hold yo' head up. Sides, Mist' Angus say you is to go wif us wen we leave. He say you ain' safe round heah no mo'."

"No, Aunt Mary. I won't go with ya'll. I've got to stay here and keep on trying. I won't leave! I won't leave and you cain't make me leave. Angus Mcintosh cain't make me leave either. He's got no say over how I live my life."

"Stubborn Mule! Ah knowed you wuz gonna be dis way, but Ah had ter try anyway. Ah knowed it wuz gonna be lak tryin' ter talk de wind outta blowin'. You woan lissen ter good sense. You got ter have yo' own way evah time and Ah reckon dat's how you got in de mess you is in. Yo Mama and Daddy shoulda' been harder on you bout gettin' yo own way wen you wuz growin' up, God rest dey souls, but dey done let you have yo' own way wen you wuz little and cain' nuthin' change you now. Since you is set on havin' you own way, and Ah figured you would no matta' whut Ah said bout it, Ah asked round wif fokes Ah knows and I foun' out dat a man by de name of James Richmond, over to Purdy, be looking' for' somebody to keep house for' him and his mamma. She got de rheumatiz and cain' tek care of de house, so dey be needin' somebody to come in and do for' 'em. You go on ovah dere termorra and see will Mist' Richmond hire you for de' job. He a powerful man and can pertect you iffen he hires you."

"Oh, I don't think somebody like Mister Richmond will be hiring me to work in his house." In a bitter tone, Kate continued, "He probably already knows all about me, even though he's only been in Purdy a few years. He'll probably have me thrown off his front porch before I could get a word out about the job. No, I'll just find some place where me and John Wesley can make some kind of living while I keep on trying to make some kind of place for us with our kin."

Aunt Mary's usually serene brow creased. "Now doan you be borryin' trouble," she scolded. "You think you gonna fine somewheah else you gone ter' stay? You knows betta dan dat. You just take yosef ovah dere ter Mr. Richmond and see whut he say. Cain' hut nuthin' ter ask. Ah heared he be a fine gentleman." Rising from her chair she said, " You think on it, cause iffen he doan hire you, you is coming wif us iffen we have ter tie you up and throw you in the wagon!"

Kate remembered her sister's still virulent hate and thought about the situation. It was true that she had nothing to lose by going to Mister Richmond and asking for a job. She would need somewhere else to live now that the Stancels were leaving McNairy Station. The worst that could happen would be for Mister Richmond to tell her to get off his property. Aunt Mary would then try to force her to leave with them, but Kate had no intention of leaving. Aunt Mary and Sam would find that tying up Kate Randsome was more than they had bargained for.

Twenty-six

She set off on the five mile walk to Purdy at an energetic pace. It was a beautiful morning. The sun warmed her head and shoulders as she walked along the dusty road humming the tune of "Dixie". Wild roses scented the air from roadside ditches where they tumbled in profusion.

Fear rose up to choke her at the sound of hooves pounding on the hard pack dirt road. A loud rattling sounded behind her and, before she could take cover in the brush along the roadside, the stage from Jackson rumbled past her kicking up a cloud of dust. She saw the astonished faces of the passengers and the driver, Ian McCormick, gave her a nasty look as they passed. She coughed as the dust settled in her lungs when she inadvertently took a deep breath. Now she had a fine layer of dust on her clothes to match the one on her shoes. She would have to find a stream and try to wash off the worst of it. It wouldn't do to show up at Mister Richmonds' home looking like a waif.

There was the sound of running water off in the distance and when she pushed her way through the undergrowth, she found what she was looking for. A narrow stream mumbled and chuckled to itself as it flowed along its rocky bed. Taking her handkerchief from the sleeve of her dress, she wet it in the creek and wiped the worst of the dust from her dress, face and hands. She would wait until just before she arrived at her destination to wipe her shoes. The water felt cool and refreshing against her hot skin. She would love to take off her shoes and stockings and wade in the cool, clear water for a while, but maybe she could do that on her way home. Turning aside from the temptation, she made her way back to the road and went on toward Purdy.

~ * ~

The town was swarming with people, many who knew her and looked at her in shock that she would show her face here. Pasting a smile on her trembling lips, she continued on her way. Past the hotel, the mason hall, the bank and the boarding school, to the new clapboard house where James Richmond lived with his invalid mother. She walked up the steps into the deep shade of the porch, paused to wipe the dust from her shoes, and knocked on the door. It was opened shortly by a man of about Kate's own age.

He was tall, towering over her by nearly a foot and wore the finest suit of clothes Kate had seen in years. He was a handsome man by any standard. The jacket and pants were of fine dark brown broadcloth and fitted him to perfection. His waistcoat was brown and gold stripes and the shirt under it was snowy white. A black silk cravat was knotted carelessly around his neck and held with a gold stickpin. Jet black hair waved smoothly back from his high forehead. Oddly colored green eyes in a hawklike face stood out in vivid contrast. The color calling to mind the scum that gathered on stagnant water. A primitive shudder crawled delicately down her spine. She realized he was looking at her with a question in those unsettling eyes.

Swallowing over the sudden dryness in her throat, she said, " My name is Kate Randsome. I've come about the job as housekeeper."

A startled look came into those strange eyes followed by pleasure. The look of pleasure confused Kate. Why would he be pleased? He looked past her into the street where several people stared in gape mouthed wonder, then motioned her to come inside.

The foyer was even cooler than the front porch. The dark, satiny wood floor shone like glass and she could see a parlor off to both sides. The man motioned her into the parlor on the left and closed the door behind them. Cut glass lamps sat on highly polished tables and the floor was covered in a thick Aubusson rug. The fireplace mantel was light colored marble with a mirror above and was flanked by large potted plants. A brocade sofa in a lovely muted rose color sat before the empty fireplace. Kate sat on the sofa at his signal and waited for the gentleman to speak. He stood before her studying her in an unnerving way. She began to wish that she hadn't come here.

Finally he said, "So, you've come about the housekeeper position. What experience do you have, Miss Randsome?"

"I... I... I only have the experience of keeping my own home and helping to take care of the home of some friends I've been staying with recently... sir." She stammered.

He continued to study her from head to toe. She grew restive under the intense scrutiny and struggled within herself to quench the desire to squirm uncomfortably on the sofa. Some emotion she couldn't name lurked in the recesses of his eyes. She felt sure that it had been a mistake to come here. He would dismiss her from the house any minute now. She was sure. Finally, he spoke, making her jump slightly.

"I think you'll do." He said. "I think you'll do quite nicely. I assume you can start immediately?"

Determined to have everything understood from the beginning, she explained that she had a young son, who would need a home here with her.

"Surely your son can be boarded with someone where you can visit him in your free time. My mother's illness makes her nervous and she doesn't like children underfoot," James objected.

Looking directly into those unsettling eyes, Kate responded quietly, "If you know anything about me at all, Mr. Richmond, you must know that that's impossible. If I'm to work for you, my son must live here, too. John Wesley is very quiet and well behaved. Your mother will hardly know he's in the house."

The seconds ticked by as she waited for his decision. An array of emotions chased across his face as he observed her sitting before him.

After what seemed an eternity of waiting, he said ungraciously, "All right, your son can stay here with you. You can have room and board for the two of you and a rather small wage. Enough to cover the bare necessities beyond food and a roof over your heads."

Her pride flared in resistance to his tone of voice and against a pitifully small wage, but cool reason took over before she could blurt out her feelings. She definitely needed a place to live and this was the only offer she had. It would be unwise to refuse. She knew there would be no other offers. Reaching our her trembling hand, she said, "Thank you, Mr.

Richmond. I accept your offer and will come back in two days time to start work."

He smiled at her discomfiture as he took her hand in his own. His hand was cold to the touch, causing her to shiver involuntarily. His smile grew wider as he took note of that shiver.

As though he could read her mind he said, "Pride is a fine thing to have, my dear, but in these unfortunate times, so many can't afford it. I'm glad you're a woman who can look at things realistically."

Turning away from her, he walked to the parlor door, opened it and motioned her out of the room. Escorting her to the front door, he said, "I look forward to a long and happy association."

Standing again on the shadowy front porch, she wondered if she had done the right thing. Shaking off the feeling of foreboding, she became determined. This was a chance for her to change her life. She must grasp it gratefully and forget any silly notions of strangeness. Had she seen the avaricious gleam in James Richmond's eyes as he watched her slender figure walk away, she might have remained more suspicious of the man who had just hired her.

Back through the gauntlet of the town she walked, only this time with a lighter heart. Surely this was a good omen. She would have respectable employment in this town very soon. In a sudden burst of optimism, she almost felt like skipping along the street and was only prevented by the callous looks cast her way by the townspeople. Thank goodness she had come to apply for this position. She deliberately ignored a tiny voice that suggested maybe it was *too* good to be true.

~ * ~

When she arrived back at the farm, Aunt Mary was waiting to hear the news. When Kate said that she had gotten the job, Aunt Mary was overjoyed.

"Ah tole you Ah heared he be a fine gentleman. Ah know ah wuz harsh wif you bout leavin' heah. Ah still think you'd do betta fo yosef iffen you came wif us, but since you is bound and determined ter stay heah, mebbe you'll do alright fo yosef now. You see, Ah nevah tole you no lie, sometimes thangs works out good iffen you jes tek yosef in hand and stand up for yosef. Ah be still mighty sorry you not comin' wif us."

Twenty-seven

James Richmond was inordinately pleased by the unexpected turn of events. Watching the slender form of Kate Randsome walk down his steps and stride down the street brought a smile to his face. James couldn't' believe the good fortune that had brought this particular young woman to his home. After interviewing a half dozen women of impeccable background, but penurious circumstances, he had been about to settle for one of them. When Kate had appeared unexpectedly on his doorstep, a plan burst full-grown in his mind. He knew that she had seen the expression in his eyes when the plan occurred to him and had been confused by what she had seen. He would have to be far more careful around her in the future. Her family background was good enough to satisfy his mother, if he could just get her past Kate's current reputation—and Kate's current reputation was something he could turn to his own advantage when the time was ripe for his newly blossomed plan.

"James," called a wavering feminine voice from the back parlor. "Who was that at the door?"

~ * ~

Aligning his features into a suitably respectful expression, he strode toward his mother's voice. Entering the brightly lit room where she sat, he knelt by her side and kissed the misshapen hands of the one person in the world whom he loved more than himself.

"I've found the perfect housekeeper and companion for you, Mother."

Rebecca Richmond snorted as she looked at her son looking so lovingly at her. "I told you, James. I don't need a housekeeper or a companion. I can do just fine on my own. I'm a little slower at it these days, but I still get everything done. Doesn't the house look nice enough for you?" she asked in a piteous tone.

Looking around, James could see that she had been trying very hard to keep the house looking spotless, but her crippled hands just weren't up to doing the dusting and sweeping that was necessary to keep the place the way he knew she *really* wanted it to look. Holding back a sigh, he said, "Of course it looks nice, Mother. It's just that I know that it's too much for you now. I thought we had agreed to get someone in to do the heavy work and cooking for you. You know that we had this conversation already and that you agreed that you could use some help. I found just the right person for you. She's young and lively and as an added bonus, she's also lovely to look at."

Rebecca smiled fondly at her son, the look in her eyes conceding defeat on the subject. Just to get back as him she teased, "And, of course, a lovely face would be of prime importance in a housekeeper and companion?"

Laughing at the sly expression on her face, and in relief that she was giving in so graciously on the subject, he replied with a jaunty air, "Of course not! But it certainly is a bonus to have a lovely looking companion for my beautiful Mother!"

His mother pealed with laughter, as though she were a young girl again. "You don't fool me for a minute, James Richmond," she said. "You've always had an eye for a pretty face. Tell me about this lovely paragon."

"Her name is Kate Randsome," he began. "And—"

"Kate Randsome," his mother exclaimed. "Was that wise my dear? Her reputation is scandalous. What will people *think*?"

"I know she's somewhat disreputable, Mother, but when you meet her you'll understand why I chose her. She has a lot of spirit and that's just the thing to cheer you up these days. She comported herself like a lady during the interview. Her family is above reproach, you must admit!"

"We're not hiring her irreproachable family, who by-the-by won't have anything to do with her themselves!" Rebecca replied with some spirit of her own. "You're much too soft hearted, James. Taking pity on someone of her reputation is just like you. How did she manage to get round you?"

"Come now, Mother! I'm not such a fool as you make out. I wouldn't have hired her if she was totally unsuitable—no matter what her circumstances. I'm sure all the ladies around town have told you all about her from their point of view, but I hear things from the men around town."

Drawing herself up as straight as she could Rebecca said coolly, "I am not interested in hearing any lewd and disgusting comments made by those men!"

Grinning wickedly, he said, "I won't repeat any lewd or disgusting comments, but there is something I think you should hear that maybe your lady friends didn't pass on to you when they were entertaining you with the saga of Kate Randsome. The men say that her child's father just took off when he found out Kate was in the family way. Not very chivalrous of him was it? If he had stayed around and married her, then she would have still held her place in the community. Her child would have just been born a little prematurely." Looking slyly at his mother he continued, "Our own family is not above reproach in that area you know. Didn't Cousin Rose have a premature baby a few years ago?"

His mother flushed and looked annoyed at the reminder of her favorite niece, "All right," she relented, "I suppose you're right about that. If you say this Kate Randsome is a fine young woman, then I'll take you at your word. I know you would want only the best for me, son."

Kissing his mother's hands once again, he rose from his kneeling position. "Of course I want only the best for my perfect mother." He felt a slight twinge of guilt at her radiant smile. He hated to manipulate her this way. Only the gut instinct that Kate would win his mother's affection quickly and easily kept him from aborting his plans.

"I need to go out for a while, Mother. Will you be all right here alone? I could ask Mrs. Winston to come and stay with you for a couple of hours if you like."

"No, No. You go on about your business. I'll be fine." She flopped her hands at him in a shooing motion, "I've still got the use of my legs and I can manage on my own. Would you just make a few sandwiches and a pot of tea before you leave? I would like that very much. Use the old tea pot and cup though." Smiling grimly she said, " Just in case I drop them. I don't want to break the ones that came to me through my grandmother."

She rarely referred to her disabilities, but on the few occasions that she did so, his heart caught in his throat with pain for her. He fixed the tea and sandwiches for her and placed them on a small piecrust table within easy reach. He left her reading one of her favorite novels. Holding the book awkwardly in her poor hands. He consoled himself that Kate would be here in two days and would be able to hold the book easily and read to his mother.

His duties concerning his mother accomplished, he headed to the saloon to drink quietly and work out the details of his plans for Kate.

Entering the saloon, he saw that it was already half full of men laughing, talking and sometimes arguing amongst themselves. Several games of poker were in full swing. Blue smoke from numerous cigars hung in thick clouds just below the ceiling like summer thunderheads hovering over the men. The sawdust on the floor around the brass spittoons was already thick with carelessly aimed expectorations of tobacco juice. This was not the environment he wanted to be in to cement his plans for the future. The raucous noise would distract him from fully enjoying his mental calculations. Just as he was turning away from the door, he heard his name called over the din. Turning, back he saw Whit Sanders waving him over to a corner table. With a sign of resignation, he moved to join the man. Whit was not a close friend, but as the owner of the Orpheum, he often was able to throw business to James by directing business men passing through to see James about new enterprises springing up in the area.

"James Richmond," Whit called again. "Come sit down with an old man and buy me a drink. I'm broke as I can be and dry as a corn husk."

Guffaws of laughter broke out from the men in response. Whit was well known for mooching drinks at every possible opportunity. Smiling broadly, James strode across the room and took a seat. "By all means let me buy you a drink." Signaling to the bartender, he continued, "Can't have the local theater owner dying for want of liquid refreshment!"

Whit's eyes gleamed as a bottle of whiskey and two glasses were placed on the table. James poured two glasses and sat back with his own, watching the amber liquid swirl as he absently fondled the tumbler.

Picking up his own glass and eyeing the whiskey appreciatively, Whit asked, "What's new with you, old friend?"

Watching the man raise his drink to his lips, James calculated his answer to the exact moment that Whit was swallowing, "I've hired Kate Randsome to keep house and take care of my mother." he stated.

Jumping up, his face the picture of solicitous concern, when his friend spewed whiskey across the table and began coughing uncontrollably, he pounded Whit sharply between the shoulder blades. "Are you all right," he asked in apparent concern. "Didn't mean to startle you old friend." An imp of glee laughed merrily in his head at what he had caused as he continued to Minster to his friend with an anxious demeanor.

The commotion at their table had drawn the interested attention of everyone in the place. "What's goin' on over there," yelled one patron. "Never knowed Whit not t'be able t'handle his whiskey!" That statement was greeted by guffaws of laughter throughout the room.

"Gawd, James," Whit choked out in a raw whisper. "What possessed ya t'hire that whore t'take care of yore maw?" With a sly look he continued, "But then maybe you're killin' two birds with one stone. Someone to watch out for yore maw during the day and watch out for you after dark. Are you plannin' on a little late night entertainment for yourself? Wouldn't mind a little of *that* action myself!"

A sliver of anger passed quickly behind James' eyes to be replaced by injured innocence. "Now Whit, I've known you a lot of years now, but I don't appreciate you questioning my motives. I know what's being said about the girl. Personally, I think it was a case of poor judgement on her part to trust a stranger who turned out to be a cad. I feel sorry for her. Besides, her brothers died fighting with my father at Parker's Crossroads, you know. For their sakes, I'd like to give her a chance to have a decent life."

Looking annoyed, Whit said, "Well now. That's all well and good, but are you forgetting she's been living with them nigras for the last few years? I know you musta heard what's been said 'bout her and that good looking young buck whilst she's been livin' out there. Now the talk is that she's been teachin' 'em to read and write!"

Leaning back in his chair, James eyed his friend thoughtfully. "Yes, I'm aware of what's been said, but then, I don't believe everything I hear. Lots of people around here just love a good, juicy piece of gossip, and aren't above making up something to suit them when gossip is scarce on the ground. That old nigra woman in running the show out there and I don't think she'd put up with any shenanigans going on in her house. She's smart enough to know that it would do her—and her family—no good for that kind of thinks to be going on out there. No, I think they took her in and cared for her all these years because the old woman is kindhearted. After all, they knew her family before the war and they know that her brothers died to help free them."

Slightly mollified, Whit leaned back in his own chair. "I'm not one to tell a man how to run his own affairs and I suppose you could be right about her. But danged if I'd take her into *my* house!"

"Then it's fortunate for her that she came to my home looking for work and not to yours!" Raising his glass, he tilted toward Whit and said, "Cheers!"

Somewhat sullenly Whit raised his own glass and they drank together. They were called to a poker game just then and both were grateful for an excuse to forget their previous conversation as they concentrated on the game.

Later, as James walked home through the dark and starry night, he was both pleased and disappointed with the evening. He hadn't been able to concentrate on his plans for Kate, but he had won several hundred dollars at poker. No doubt Whit would spread the word that he had hired the notorious Kate Randsome to work in his home and would also pass on his alleged reasons for doing so. There was plenty of time to work out an intricate plan regarding Miss Kate Randsome. Whistling tunelessly, he walked up his front steps and into his home.

Twenty-eight

The two days before she was to join the Richmond household and the Stancel's were to leave Tennessee passed in a blur. Aunt Mary, Kate and Permelia were kept busy packing up the household for the move to Virginia. Sam and Permelia jumped the broom and Kate packed her own and John Wesley's meager belongings in two small carpetbags to take to the Richmond house. Tension was thick at night as they took turns keeping vigil, each of them praying that the Night Riders would not return before they had gotten away.

When the time came to say good-bye, Kate thought she wouldn't be able to bear it. She cried and clung to Aunt Mary, saying, "Oh, Aunt Mary, I don't know how I'll git along without you. You've been my rock these past years. I cain't bear to think I'll never see you again!"

Aunt Mary held her close and crooned over her head. Then she held Kate away from her and, with tears streaming down her face, said, "Chile, Ah'm gonna miss you mo' dan Ah kin say. You one of my fambly now and it teah me up to leave you heah. You sho you woan come wif us?" Kate shook her head. "Den you remembah," Aunt Mary continued, "you gots to hab de courage to dare, jes' lak Sam be doin. You hab de courage to dare greatly an you get whut you wants in de end. You stan' up to fokes. Hold yo haid high chile. Ain' no need for you to feel shamed. You is a fine woman wif a fine chile. You promise me you tek care o' yosef and dis young'un."

"I promise, Aunt Mary. I won't forget any of you and you'll all be in my prayers every night. I love you with all my heart."

Aunt Mary squatted next to John Wesley and hugged him close to her and wiped his tears with her handkerchief.

"You tek good care of yo mama, John Wesley. Ah be rememberin' you always. You kin be suah o' dat."

Kate and John Wesley watched Aunt Mary walk to the wagon and climb slowly onto the seat where Permelia waited. Permelia had no good-byes for Kate. Even though she had gotten her heart's desire and married Sam, she still hated Kate. Her eyes shot daggers as Sam hugged Kate in good-bye. He carried a small burlap sack in his hands and opened it while Kate waited.

"Ah made a box for' you ter remember us by. You kin use it to keep yo' hair pins frum gettin' lost. Ah carved dis hoss an' wagon for' lil John Wesley. Seemed to me lak a boy ought to have at least one toy ter play wif. It jes lak de one Ah carved for' my boys. Now dey have one jes alak. Maybe it hep' John Wesley ter remember us.'"

Kate took the gifts in her hands. Her heart swelled in her chest, emotion nearly choking her. The small objects seemed more precious than gold. They were made from cedar wood and smelled heavenly. The wood was satiny in her hands and spoke of careful workmanship. Sam had carved an oak leaf onto the top of the box. Kate didn't know when he had found the time to make these for her during the upheaval of moving.

"Oh, Sam. They're beautiful. We'll treasure them forever. Every time we look at them, we'll think of you and your family and how kind you have all been to us."

Sam looked embarrassed, then cleared his throat, "Well, Miz Kate, guess we betta be gettin' on de way. It's a long way ter Virginia. We be thinkin' bout you and the young'un and prayin' ya'll be alright." He squatted next to John Wesley and hugged the little boy close to him, then turned and walked to the wagon, got onto the seat and flapped the reins to get the horse started. The children waved from their seats among the furniture. Aunt Mary turned and watched Kate and John Wesley until the wagon went around a bend in the road and was lost from sight. John Wesley stood by Kate's side gripping her skirts and crying as though his heart would break. He didn't understand why the Stancels were leaving.

~ * ~

They started off on the way to Purdy, walking side by side, with Kate carrying the two small carpetbags that held their belongings. Within a mile, she cursed her decision not to accept Sam's offer to take them into the town. She should have known that the five-mile walk would be too much for a four-year-old child. Even though they had started out early in the cool morning air, John Wesley was complaining of being tired and hot.

They walked into the pine forest at the side of the road and sat down on the soft pine needles that covered the ground. Kate had an old canteen that she had filled with water before they left and John Wesley drank eagerly. Kate sighed. At this rate it would be late afternoon before they arrived in Purdy. If only she didn't have two bags, perhaps she could carry John Wesley part of the distance, letting him walk when her arms tired from his weight.

Kate knew that they shouldn't delay and urged her son to his feet. He complained bitterly. He was tired. He wanted a glass of tea. He was getting hungry, he wanted some blackberry cobbler. In a sharp voice, Kate told him to get up and stop acting like a baby. His eyes filled with tears and his lower lip trembled, but he obeyed her and they started down the road again. Kate felt horrible to have spoken to her son in that tone of voice. She knew that the situation was her own fault for lacking foresight, but there was nothing she could do at this point except to get to Purdy as quickly as possible. John Wesley could rest and have something to eat and drink when they arrived.

As they walked along, the sun rose higher in the heavens and felt as though it was trying to press then into the earth. The dust from the hard packed red clay road rose up to tickle their nostrils and dry their throats. Kate felt as though she had left the earth and was traveling in hell. What was she doing walking along this dusty road carrying all her personal belongings in two bags? How had she come to this? Michael's laughing face flashed across her mind in an instant. Yes, that was it. Loving and trusting a man had set her on this dusty road, afoot with a small child to raise on her own. That had been her mistake—loving and trusting a man. She vowed that from here on out, she would never do that again. Heartache and pain were her rewards for loving and trusting. Was she a fool not to go east with the Stancels? Her pride would not let her leave the area in disgrace. She would stay here, near her kin, and show them they had been wrong about her. Her stubborn pride would allow for nothing less. Pigheaded, her Mama had always said and Daddy had agreed, but there had always been a gleam of pride in his own eyes at the same time. *I reckon I take after my Daddy*, she thought. Sighing, she shifted the bags in her hands and continued down the hot, dusty road to whatever future lay ahead. John Wesley walked doggedly at her side whimpering to himself and finally she told him they could rest again when the came to the area where she knew there was a creek flowing through the woods.

They made their way to the creek and John Wesley immediately took off his shoes and stockings and waked into the creek. Kate followed suit. The water felt delicious flowing over her feet and, pulling her skirts high, she waded deeper into it until it flowed around her calves. John Wesley leaned over and patted his little hands on the surface of the water and laughed as the spray splashed onto his face. It caused runnels in the dust on his face and Kate told him to go ahead and wash his face so he wouldn't look like a ragamuffin. He leaned over and plunged his face into the water and when he stood up the water ran onto his shirt, soaking the front. He said he was sorry for getting his clothes wet and Kate told him it was all right and his shirt would dry before they got to the Richmond's. They finally waded out of the creek and Kate unwrapped some cold cornbread she had brought with them.

They ate in silence for a little while and then John Wesley asked, "Mama, why are we going to live with strangers?" then in an almost inaudible voice he said, " Didn't Aunt Mary and Sam want us to go with them?"

Her heart contracted painfully at his words and she spoke gently to him. "Of course Aunt Mary and Sam wanted us to go with them, son. But I thought it would be best for us to stay here. This is our home and all of our kin are here. "

John Wesley thought for a minute and said, "But, Mama, this is

Aunt Mary and Sam's home, too. Why didn't we go with them? I thought our home was with them. Those people you say are my kin won't even talk to me. My cousins run away when I try to play with them. Why do they do that, Mama? Don't they know we're kin? Don't they like me?"

Anger stirred in Kate's heart as she tried to think of an explanation that would satisfy a small child. Finally, she said, "It's nothing to do with you, son. It something that has to do with grown up things. Someday, when you're older, I'll explain everything to you. Right now, you just make friends with other little boys at our new home. I know you love Aunt Mary and Sam and his children, but our place is here. We couldn't be going to Virginia with them. Someday, you'll understand.. For now, we have to be getting on to Purdy. We have to get there before dark. Get up and lets be going."

Twenty-nine

They finally arrived at the Richmond home and stood on the shady front porch facing James himself. Kate looked him straight in the face and said, " This is my son, John Wesley. If it's not too much trouble, I'd like to see our room now. John Wesley is just wore out and I'd like to get him settled and then go meet your mother."

James looked once at John Wesley, then turned to lead them through the kitchen to a small room behind the fireplace.

"Here's where you'll be staying. There's another smaller room beyond this one that the boy can use."

~ * ~

Kate set her carpetbags on the narrow iron bed after James had left and looked around her. The room was really very small. Besides the bed there was only room for a washstand. Hooks on the wall would hold her few dresses. Looking into the other room that was to be John Wesley's, she saw that it was even smaller than this one. It held a narrow cot and nothing else. It was a depressing arrangement, but she could hardly hope to have a large room for herself and another one for John Wesley. She was here as hired help and not a friend of the family.

Kate hung her few dresses on the hooks in her room and saw that there were enough hooks left over for John Wesley's trousers and shirts, so she hung those also. Her son was looking at her with large frightened eyes from where he sat on the bed and her heart went out to him. Poor child, his whole world had changed suddenly and he seemed lost. She sat next to him and pulled him into her arms.

"Well, John Wesley, here we are in our new home. I hope you'll like it here and be a good boy. The lady who lives here don't like noisy children, so you have to promise me you'll be very quiet in the house. No running and shouting. You can play in here with the horse and wagon that Sam made for you or you can run and shout outside, but not near the windows. Can you do those things for me?"

John Wesley's bright blue eyes looked into hers. A shadow of uncertainty still lingered there as he said, "Yes, Mama. I can be quiet in the house. I'm a big boy now. I know how to be quiet, but who will I play with now that John and Andy are gone? Are there other little boys around here who'll be my friend?"

Kate's mind flashed backward across the years and saw her nephew Rufus with a cut on his face and tears streaming form his eyes as he explained to his mother that the children in the schoolyard had teased him about his Aunt Kate and he had fought them. In her mind she cursed the cruelty of children who parroted what they heard from their parents with no understanding of what they were saying. She prayed that John Wesley would not be made to suffer for her sins the way Rufus had suffered. She tightened her arms around her son, then held him away form her so she could look into his face.

"I'm sure there are other little boys near here. Maybe they'll be your friends. I don't know. But you have to tell me if they say anything to you that you don't understand. You know that you can always tell me anything, don't you?"

He nodded at her, then slid from he bed and retrieved his horse and wagon from the washstand where Kate had left it. Kneeling on the floor, he pushed the toy across the highly polished wood, accompanying it with sounds of rattling wagon wheels. Kate went to stand before the small spotted mirror hanging above the washstand. Her normally pale skin looked ghostly in the dimly lit room and her dark hair stood out in vivid contrast. Removing the pins form her hair, she brushed it briskly, then repinned it in her accustomed bun near the crown of her head. She could do nothing about the frayed collar and cuffs of her dress, but at least it was clean. She washed her hands quickly, then turned to her son who was still playing on the floor.

"John Wesley, I'm gonna to talk to Mr. Richmond and his mama now. You stay in here and play till I come back."

He nodded without looking up and Kate left the room, closing the door behind her. Everything in the kitchen looked brand new and shiny. The dry sink stood under a window through which Kate could see the well pump located only a few feet from the door leading out of the kitchen. Across the room, another door lead to the dining room. The furnishings were beautiful. A dark mahogany dining table was surrounded by chairs in a matching wood that curved to form the shape of a shield. Glancing down, Kate saw that the table legs and the front legs of the chairs had brass balls held by what looked like eagle claws. The floor was covered by a rug that had flowers and strange birds on a black background and there was a silky fringe on each end. A massive sideboard took up most of one wall and the mirrored back reflected two cut glass lamps and an ornate silver tea service. Kate couldn't imagine where James Richmond had acquired the money to own such beautiful and expensive things. His accent was Southern, so he wasn't some carpetbagger come to make money from he South's defeat. She realized that she knew absolutely nothing about her new employer except that he appeared to have a lot of money and he needed someone to keep his house and care for his mother. As though her thoughts had summoned him, James appeared in the doorway leading to the parlor and stood staring at Kate. She felt a blush staining her cheeks as she met his eye.

"I was just admiring the furniture in this room. It's real pretty."

"Yes, we're quite fond of it. I had it made to order on a trip to London last year and had it shipped to Montgomery. We were living there before I bought the stage line and had this house built here. Come and meet my mother. She anxious to speak with you."

He turned into the parlor and Kate followed slowly. Entering the room she saw an older woman seated near the fireplace. Her gray hair was drawn back from a face that was thin and pinched with pain. She was dressed in black from head to toe and her only ornaments were a plain gold wedding band on her left hand and a hair brooch pinned at the neck of her high collared dress. The fingers on the hand she lifted toward Kate were twisted and had shiny knuckles.

Kate walked forward and took the hand in hers and said, "I'm Kate Randsome, Mrs. Richmond. I've come to take care of you and this beautiful house. I hope we'll get along fine."

"You may call me Rebecca, my dear. I'm not one to stand on ceremony. James was right, you are very lovely indeed. He tells me you can read and write. That will be a big help. My hands are so painful now; I can scarce turn the pages of a book and can't hold a quill at all. You will have to write my letters to friends for me."

Kate blushed again at the thought of James Richmond telling his mother he thought her lovely. It was such an odd thing for Mrs. Richmond—no—Rebecca—to pass along to the hired help. Working here would certainly be different from what she had expected. It looked like the Mrs. Richmond was going to treat her with respect and courtesy. With real warmth in her voice she responded to Rebecca.

"I'd be real proud to read to you ma'am. And to write your letters for you. You might have to tell me how to spell some of the words at first. I'm not too good at spelling, but I learn real fast."

"I think we'll get along wonderfully, Kate. James tells me you have a young son who will be staying here with you. I'd like to meet him."

"I told him to wait in my room, ma'am. Mr. Richmond told me you don't like noise and I explained to John Wesley that he'll have to be real quiet here. He understands that. He's really a very smart little boy and I'll be sure he's not any trouble to you."

"Nonsense! James is just over protective of his old mother. It's true that I sometimes get headaches if there is a lot of noise around, but I'm sure your little boy will try very hard to be quiet. Bring him here and let us get to know each other a little."

Kate glanced at James who nodded his head, so she went to her room and found John Wesley sitting quietly with his toy. He looked up when she walked in and smiled.

"I was really quiet, Mama. I didn't make any noise at all just like you said. Can I go outside and play for a while?"

"Yes, you can go play out behind the house, but first you have to go meet Mrs. Richmond. She said she would like to get to know you a little bit this afternoon. Come with me now." She held out her hand

and he rose and took it obediently.

~ * ~

They walked together back into the parlor and up to Rebecca. She looked closely at John Wesley, then held out her hand and said, "Come here, young man. Your name is John Wesley isn't it?"

John Wesley walked timidly to the old woman and took her hand in his own small fingers and said, "Yes, Mrs. Richmond. My name is John Wesley and I'm four years old. My mama says I have to be very quiet so you won't be upset and we can stay here with you and Mr. Richmond."

Rebecca smiled at the child and said, "You may call me Miss Rebecca and call my son Mr. James. Don't you worry if you forget now and then and make noise in the house. I'll know that you didn't mean to and will try even harder after that to be a quiet boy."

John Wesley twisted nervously from side to side, not sure what to say next. Rebecca smiled again and said, "Why don't you run on outside and play. I know little boys don't like to sit around and talk to old folks much."

He grinned in relief and ran across the room toward the kitchen, then realized his shoes were making a loud racket on the polished wood floor. He turned to his mother with a stricken look in his eyes.

Rebecca laughed and said, "See? You realized right away you were making noise and stopped. Now you will remember not to run in the house with your shoes on in the future. Won't you?"

"Yes, Miss Rebecca. I'm real sorry to make noise so soon after I got here. I'll do better, I promise."

Rebecca nodded at him and he turned and walked very quietly out of the room. They heard the back door shut as he went out to play.

"He's a delightful boy, Kate. Very intelligent and well spoken for his age. I'm sure he won't be any trouble at all." She looked over at James and motioned that he should go. When he had gone, she continued, "Now why don't you sit down and we'll decide on a schedule for taking care of me and this house."

Kate sat on a highback brocade chair near Rebecca and waited.

"Now, I would like for you to read to me from three until four every afternoon and on Wednesdays we will take care of my correspondence from two until three. The rest of the time you can set your own schedule. Of course you will be free every evening after the dinner things have been cleared, cleaned and put away. Does that sound reasonable to you?"

Kate was at a loss to understand why this woman was treating her with so much courtesy. Surely she knew Kate's history and that she was unwelcome within her own family and that the entire community had shunned her since the news of John's impending birth had made the rounds. Why then was this total stranger showing her more respect than anyone had shown her in years?

Kate realized that Rebecca was waiting for an answer and said, "That sounds fine, ma'am. I'm used to working hard all day. It'll be a real pleasure to read to you for an hour in the afternoon. I haven't had time to read for myself for years. I can see you have a lot of really nice books in here." Three sides of the room had floor to ceiling built-in bookshelves that were full of leather bound expensive looking books. Kate felt a frisson of pleasure at the thought of being able to read so many books. She had missed reading for the last several years. Naturally, Aunt Mary and Sam hadn't had any books and Kate hadn't been able to bring the books from her parent's home when she had left. By the time she had gone back there to live with Aunt Mary and Sam, the books and been gone and she had assumed that someone from the bank had taken them.

"I can see we'll get along like a house afire, Kate. You may have the rest of the day to get accustomed to things in the house and to help young John Wesley to feel more settled. Tomorrow is soon enough to get started on our routine. James and I will be dining with the Winston's this evening, so you don't need to worry about dinner tonight. We like to breakfast at seven in the morning, so please have eggs, bacon, biscuits, grits and gravy ready by that time in the morning."

"Thank you, ma'am. I'll have everything ready for you in the morning." Kate made her exit from the room still puzzled by Rebecca Richmond. She went out the kitchen door to the back yard area and found John Wesley playing under the large pin oak tree that grew there. He had gotten some sticks together and Kate could hear him talking for them. From his conversation she could tell that he was pretending the sticks were a family and her heart hurt for her small son. Even at four years old, he knew that there was something different about them She dreaded the questions she knew he would ask in only a few years. Perhaps sooner, now that he would have contact with children of the families that shunned her.

She walked over to her son and sat down in the grass next to him.

"I see you're keeping yourself busy. Have you seen any little boys who might be your friends?"

"No, Mama. I stayed right here in the back of the house so you could find me. I haven't seen anybody. Do you think we could go out in the front and maybe I would see some little boys there?"

Kate stood and held out her hand. John Wesley took it and they walked around the house to the front yard. The small patch of grass there was surrounded by a black wrought iron fence. Following a stone path out the gate, they made their way along the road that ran directly in front of the house.

~ * ~

Walking along the main street of Purdy, Kate shortening her stride to match her sons small steps. No one spoke to them as they passed along the street. People moved along the street intent on their own business. Kate heard two men standing in front of the brick courthouse arguing over the M&O railroad which had been laid four miles from Purdy after the town had voted that they didn't want it. One man appeared to be arguing that the decision had been right and the other felt that if the railroad had been laid at Purdy, then they would be in better shape right now. Kate remembered the furor over the route of the railroad back in 1858. It surprised her that people were still arguing over it now after everything that had happened since then.

She and John Wesley continued on past the gates of the Purdy Male and Female Academy where she had heard that young men and women from several states came to study. She might have been a student there herself if the war hadn't come. She sighed and John Wesley looked up at her, but said nothing and they continued on past the office of the Purdy News and the Masonic Hall.

Across the street was the McNairy Independent offices and one of the town's two general stores. Kate knew that she would have to shop there for food for the Richmond table. She hoped that the owner would be kind to her, or at least not openly hostile.

They didn't see any children as they circled back to the Richmond home and Kate told John Wesley that they were probably in school or perhaps inside taking a nap or helping their mother's. John Wesley looked disappointed and Kate soothed him by reminding him that they would be living here a long time and there was plenty of time to meet any little boys who lived nearby.

Thirty

Kate's stay at the Richmond home went smoothly for the first several months. She stopped waking in terror every night at any unusual noise. She accustomed herself to the new routine and gradually stopped cringing each time she went to the general store for supplies. The small vegetable garden out back and the cow in her snug shed provided them with much of their food, but she had to purchase flour, salt, sugar and tea on a regular basis. The daily trip to the butcher shop was more disconcerting. Mr. Ramsey never said anything untoward to her, but his suggestive manner and lewd facial expressions were almost more than Kate's heart could bear, but she never protested against the treatment.

John Wesley had made a friend nearby and spent much of his time playing with Timmy Nickles in the woods just outside of town. Kate worried constantly that he would be hurt or bitten by a snake. Always before he had been in her sight or within the sound of her voice. He was five years old now and chaffed at being tied to her all the time and Kate reluctantly let him go where he wanted as long as he was home before dark. He obeyed this rule and all the rules imposed on him in the house and Kate gradually relaxed her worry. She was pleased that Timmy had never said anything to John Wesley about his birth or his mother. Timmy's family had moved to the area only a couple of years before and Kate assumed that they knew nothing about her. It surprised her that no one had taken it on themselves to inform the Nickles family about Kate when their son had taken up with John Wesley. Or perhaps Timmy's parents did know the truth, but were more broad minded than most and would not punish John Wesley for his mother's sins. Whatever the answer to the puzzle, Kate remained grateful that her son had a playmate.

Just as she was beginning to feel comfortable in her new home, she noticed that James seemed to be near her on numerous occasions. Kate didn't like the look in his eyes when she noticed him. It made her feel very uncomfortable and she avoided looking at James's eyes whenever he was around her and altered her routing slightly to try to avoid meeting him alone. He realized what she was doing and seemed amused by her. He soon discovered her altered routine and again began meeting her as if by accident several times a week. Kate didn't know what to make of his actions. He was always so courteous to her during these meetings and, if Kate hadn't seen the look in his eyes, she would have enjoyed passing the time of day with her employer. After a couple of months of these "accidental" meetings, the short hairs on the nape of her neck felt as though they were rising up each time James came near her. Something inside her continued to cry out an obscure warning that she couldn't quite understand.

He approached her one beautiful evening as she was milking the cow in the shed out back.

"Kate, dear." He said in a silky voice. "I wish to speak to you about a personal arrangement. One just between the two of us." He reached out and put his hand on her hair and let it slide down to her shoulder.

Kate looked up into his eyes from where she sat on the milking stool and what she saw there made her leap to her feet. The milking stool clattered against the wall of the shed, startling the cow. The milk bucket, kicked by the cow, turned over, spilling the rich cream into the straw. James was between Kate and the door. Backing slowly into the corner, she looked wildly around and saw nothing that she could use to defend herself. She had left the pitchfork leaning against the wall outside when she had cleaned the cowshed. She looked back at James and waited silently for whatever would happen next.

He laughed softly and said, "My dear, I don't intend to rape you in the cow shed. I prefer my pleasures to take place in more comfortable surroundings. You will come to my room at night, after Mother is asleep. I wouldn't want her to know what kind of woman you really are. She's so fond of you."

"How dare you speak of your mother in the same breath you use to speak me in such a way? I'm not some cheap tart who'll bed you anytime you want! I'll leave here right away. I won't be forced into your bed or anybody else's!" Kate was shaking from fear and anger. She clasped her hands together so that he wouldn't see them tremble and know her fear.

James continued, still laughing softly, but the laughter now had an edge of cruelty and contempt to it. "Where do you intend to go, Kate dear? We both know your options are, shall we say, limited? I don't think you'll be going anywhere. I know you don't have enough money to buy two tickets to anywhere and who will take *you* into their home? Certainly not any of your family. You'd be there now if that were the case. I'll just leave you to think things over for a few days. No doubt, you'll see that this is the best arrangement."

He turned to leave the shed as Kate said, in a voice she hardly recognized as her own, " I'll die first! I'll take John Wesley and we'll go away somewhere. Living in the woods and sleeping under a bush would be better than staying here!"

James turned back and looked at her with contempt in his eyes, " I had hoped you would see reason, my dear. Since you don't seem to be able to do that, let me give you something else to think over before you make an unfortunate decision. There is a law in Tennessee that will allow me to have John Wesley taken away from you and apprenticed to me. As you know Judge Fielding Hurst is a close friend of mine. He would help me on this."

Kate's mind reeled from shock and she found herself sitting in the straw. Her legs would not hold her up and she couldn't seem to get any air into her lungs. Bright spots danced across her vision and her ears rang as though a bell were tolling loudly in them. When her hearing returned and her vision cleared, she saw that James had righted the milking stool and was sitting on it watching her with a satisfied expression on his face.

"Y-y-you're ly-ly-lying," she stuttered. "you're m-m-making that up to trick me into doing what you want." Her voice became firmer as reason returned. "I don't believe you for a minute. I never heard of any such law. You think I'm some ignorant country girl you can fool with you city ways. Besides, my two brothers died fighting with Fielding Hurst. He would help me for their sakes!"

A sardonic laugh escaped James' lips. "Do you really think Judge Hurst would side with you on this? Yes, your brothers died under his command, but look at the disgrace you've brought on their names by what you've done! No, I don't think the Judge would help you at all. As a matter of fact, I', sure he'd think I am the much better person to raise the nephew of two such brave soldiers. Much better than the harlot who is the child's mother! I'd be happy to take you to Nashville to look at the law book there. It might be quite an enjoyable trip. Once you understand that what I'm saying it true. Of course, the law is rarely enforced, but I have friends in high places who would be delighted to help me out in this matter. They owe me a favor here and there. Judge Hurst isn't the only one or even the most powerful. Would you like to go to Nashville, Kate?" His eyes leered at her as he waited for her answer.

Sickness welled up in her at the look in his eyes. He had only bided his time to take advantage of her lost reputation. Her reply spilled from her lips on a tide of revulsion. "No! I don't' want to go anywhere with you." She stood up and held her head high as she said. "I'm going to pack my things and John Wesley's and we're leaving here."

James picked up a piece of straw and drew it though his fingers casually as he said in a friendly voice, "I don't think you will. If you leave here with the boy, it will only prove my point that you are an unfit mother and the boy should be taken from you. After all, you have steady employment in a nice home here. Who would believe any tale you might tell about an arrangement with me? I would simply deny it and my word would be believed over that of an unchaste woman. I let it be known around town that I felt sorry for you. Anything you say against me will never be believed." He stood dropped the straw and stood up facing Kate. His enjoyment of the situation was written plainly on his face. An evil grin lit up his unusual eyes. "I'll leave you to think things over, my dear. I'm sure you'll see that I'm right and you'll be a good girl and do as I say. I'd hate for you to lose your son just because you're too stubborn to see reason. Good night, my dear."

He walked out of the shed, leaving Kate standing amidst the shattered pieces of her life for the second time. What damnable fate kept putting her in situations like this? It just seemed so unfair that the mistake, which had cost her family, should now come back to haunt her in such a way. In her heart she had no doubt that James would take John Wesley away from her if she refused to go along with his plans. After all that she had been through, she couldn't lose her son now. There must be some other way. Some solution that would keep her from James's grasp.

She walked resolutely into the kitchen, washed her hands, and began removing the supper roast, potatoes and carrots from the warming oven where she had placed them earlier. With the hands of an automaton, she transferred the food to a serving platter, then looked to see that James and Rebecca were at the dinner table waiting to eat. When she saw that they were waiting, she picked up the heavy serving platter, carried it to the dining room and placed it next to James, who would carve the roast for his mother and himself. She couldn't bring herself to look at his loathsome face. She would run screaming from the room if she did. Rage and loathing boiled inside her and she thought she might be sick right there in the dining room.

Rebecca looked sharply at Kate and said, "Why Kate, are you feeling ill? You look very pale." Her tone of voice and her expression conveyed a very real concern to Kate who replied in a distant manner;

"I'm fine, ma'am. Just a little tired this evening. A good nights sleep will set me right."

Rebecca reached out and took Kate's hand in her own and exclaimed, "Why your hands are cold as ice! You go lie down right now. James can put the left over food away and leave the dishes to soak in water tonight. I insist."

Kate started to protest, but Rebecca was firm, "Now you listen to me and go lie down right now. You don't want to get so sick we have to call in Dr. Smith, do you?"

Kate shook her head and Rebecca continued; "Then go on now and don't worry about the supper things."

~ * ~

Kate went off to her room. After checking to make sure John Wesley was already asleep in his little trundle bed, she took down her hair and began brushing the silky dark brown curls. It was such a soothing thing, brushing her hair. Each strand lay smooth and soft across her shoulder and fell to her waist. Meeting her own eyes in her reflection in the mirror, she saw that she did look ill. Her normally pink cheeks were pale and her face looked drawn with pain. Her eyes were twin pools of despair; there was no sparkle or life in them at all. She really did feel tired unto death and was grateful that Rebecca had sent her to her room so early.

She struggled to understand how someone so kind and loving could have such a cruel and callous son. Maybe she could tell Rebecca what James had proposed she do for him. A ray of hope bloomed in her chest like sunlight breaking through the clouds on a cold winter day, but then the clouds closed in again as she realized that Rebecca would probably never believe that her beloved son would do such a thing. She would think that Kate was a liar and might even be persuaded by James to help in getting John Wesley away from her. She couldn't take the risk. No, she would just have to make the best of the situation until some other solution could be found. She put on her soft flannel nightgown and lay down in her narrow bed, sure that she would never sleep with all the turmoil churning in her mind, but she drifted off almost immediately.

Her sleep was disturbed by nightmare images of running through dark woods, searching for her son, calling his name over and over again as she wept in terror that he was lost forever. Maniacal laughter roared in her ears as she desperately searched. A small hand shaking her shoulder woke her from her nightmare. John Wesley was standing next to the bed calling to her to wake up.

"Wake up, Mama! What's wrong? You were calling my name over and over. Were you having a bad dream?"

She grabbed his small body, pulled him into the warm bed with her and held him close to her heart.

"It's all right, son. Mamas awake now. I was having a bad dream that you were lost and I couldn't find you. Thank you for waking me up."

John Wesley smiled his sweet smile at her and said, "I won't ever leave you, Mama. You don't have to worry about me getting lost. I know my way around everywhere. Don't worry," he said as he stroked her cheek with his chubby little hand in the same way she had always stroked his cheek when he was upset or worried.

She pulled him close to her again and snuggled them both under the quilt saying, "I know you're a big boy now, but I still worry about you. Mother's do that you know. No matter how old you get, you'll always be my little boy and I'll always worry about you. Why don't you stay here with me the rest of the night, so I'll feel safe?"

"Yes, Mama"; he replied and put his head on her shoulder and closed his eyes. She could tell by his even breathing that he had fallen back to sleep immediately. She lay awake until dawn broke, cursing fate with every breath.

~ * ~

By the time the sun was fully risen fear was beating at her mind with monstrous wings. She knew that she must make one more effort to win a home for herself and John Wesley somewhere else. Telling her son to spend all morning playing outside with his friend, Timmy, she set off in the direction of McNairy Station as fast as her trembling legs would carry her. Her every breath was a silent prayer for reprieve. She absolutely must persuade someone to open their home to her and John Wesley. The alternative was too horrifying to contemplate. Her quick pace ate up the miles. She was soon at Savannah's home. She stood gasping for breath in the shade of a nearby oak tree, waiting for her pounding heart to slow to a normal rate.

As she stood there in the shade, she remembered the last time she had seen her sister and the almost palpable hate that had permeated the air. Taking her faltering courage in a firm grasp, she walked resolutely to her sister's door. Knocking firmly, she stepped back and waited. The ragged lace curtain of one window twitched briefly aside, fell back and hung limply in place. Kate waited a few more minutes, knowing someone had seen her from behind the curtain. Shifting from one foot to the other in nervous anticipation, she continued to wait as the minutes stretched out. She realized that the door was not going to open to her. Without even hearing her out, her sister was making it obvious that Kate was still unwelcome here. James's words echoed through her mind like a warning bell. She stepped forward to hammer loudly on the door in desperation.

The door was flung open to reveal Savannah with a look of pure hatred on her face. "Cain't you take a hint when a door don't open!?" she yelled. "I told you awhile back you're not welcome here! Get off my porch and don't come back here!"

She stepped back and slammed the door so hard that it popped back open before the latch could catch. Taking advantage of the opportunity, Kate sprang forward and forced her way past her sister, into the house. Whirling around with both hands raised, she prepared to fight physically to remain in the house and plead her case. She was surprised to see Savannah standing quietly by the door, a look of utter weariness and guilt on her face.

"Why do you have to be so stubborn?" Savannah asked quietly, looking at the floor. "You've got a place to live in Purdy now. A good place with respectable work. I done heard about it. Why come back here again and rake up all that pain?"

For a moment, Kate was confused by the abrupt change of mood. She reached out and placed her hand gently on her sister's arm as she said, "You made yourself pretty clear about your feelings the last time I came here, but I'm in desperate need now. I'm not here to stir up pain, but I cain't stay at the Richmond's anymore. Hear me out before you make any more judgments agin me." Tightening her grip on Savannah's arm she demanded, "At least look at me while I'm talking to you!"

Savannah raised her head slowly. Kate almost gasped aloud at what was in her sister's eyes. A world of pain, guilt and shame swirled in their depths. Deep emotions that equaled, or perhaps even exceeded, her own. They were the eyes of a soul in torment.

"I cain't. I just cain't. Please don't ask me again." Savannah said to her in a quavering voice. "I tried before, for your sake. Remember?

I did try. I really did, but when everybody started being cold to me and the other children taunted Rufus, I had to make a choice. I had to choose my husband and children over my sister. It was so hard." Lifting a shaking hand to cover her eyes, she continued, "I though I'd lost my mind that night when I screamed at you and you ran out into the storm. I worried myself sick, thinking you must be dead somewhere and it was my fault. Later, I found out that you were with the Stancel's and I was relieved. Relieved that you were alive, but even more relieved that you were gone and not my responsibility anymore. That I didn't need to have you in my home anymore and could just forget all about you. That's awful isn't it? I was relieved that my own sister was living on the charity of a black family, because it allowed me to go one with my own life just like before and put you out of my mind." She looked at Kate with the eyes of a tormented soul. Kate didn't know how to respond to such pain. She had never known that her sister was so distraught over what had happened. Had been so torn over the events of four years ago.

When Kate made no response, Savannah turned away and fiddled with the curtain hanging behind her. "Please leave now," she whispered. "I cain't let you come back here. Nothing's changed. I made my choice all those years ago. I cain't change back now."

Kate's heart thumped painfully in her chest. It ached for her sister's pain, but she must make Savannah understand that her need was desperate. Surely when she knew the reason, she would be horrified at the fate that awaited Kate and would come to terms with her emotions in a way that would allow both of them some kind of peace of mind.

"Savannah," she said calmly, "listen to me now. This is real important. I can feel your pain. I know that you've paid a hard price for the decision you made, but I know when I tell you this you'll understand why I'm here. It's about James Richmond." She hesitated a minute to see if her sister reacted to her words. The words she had to say were stuck in her throat. She <u>must</u> get the words out. Savannah *must* understand. *"Please God,"* she prayed silently, *"let her see my need is desperate. Help her to reach out to me just one more time."* When there was no response, she continued, her voice not quite steady now. "He wants me to be his mistress! He said he'd take John Wesley away from me if I don't do what he says. I cain't stay there and go along with his plans. Please, please let me come back here. Don't turn me away, knowing what'll happen if I stay at the Richmond house. You cain't hate me as much as all that!"

Savannah continued to fiddle with the curtains. Pleating the panel into a fan shape, straightening out the folds, pleating the panel again. Finally, she said in a distant voice, "I don't see why you cain't go along with Mr. Richmond. He would take care of you if you were his mistress. He'd probably give you money and nice clothes. It's not like you're a young virgin. You've got a reputation for being a loose woman. I'm not surprised he thinks you would be his mistress. It would really be best for you to go along with him."

She looked at Kate and her eyes were the eyes of a stranger. Gone was the tormented woman of a few minutes ago. There was no sympathy for Kate in her. "Besides," she continued in a hard voice, "times are harder now than ever. It's all we can do to keep this farm and feed and clothe ourselves. There's not enough for two more. I bet that's why your friends left the area. Looking to better themselves. You should have gone with them. You said they loved you. I've got chores to do now, so you'll have to be leaving."

"Savannah, you don't understand!" Kate wailed. "It's not like you think. I already told him I don't want to be his mistress. That's when he told me he'd take my son. Does that sound like a kind and caring man to you? James Richmond is evil!"

"You always did have an imagination that would choke a horse, Kate." Savannah was exasperated now. Her voice was harsh as she said, "I don't believe for one minute that Mr. Richmond is evil. I'm sure he didn't mean that about your son, he just wants you to go along with him. I told you we cain't support another person on this farm, so's you might as well go on now and make the best of things." She opened the door and stood waiting for Kate to leave.

"So you would let your own sister whore for a man against her will rather than take her into your home. You know I'm not a whore and you would send me back to Purdy to live like that?" Kate asked in disbelief.

Savannah remained silent by the open door, refusing to look at her sister.

Defeated, Kate left the house and wandered aimlessly down the road. She had really thought for a few minutes that her sister's guilt and shame would make her decide in Kate's favor in this instance, but Savannah's will had held firm in the end. She tried to understand her sister. She too had been raised on the concept that when a woman married, her husband and children came before anyone else, but it was a bitter pill to swallow.

Dejection followed her like a black cloud as she made the rounds of other relatives. At every door she met with rejection before she could even explain here dire circumstances. At her last stop, hope broke through the dark cloud momentarily. Tenia Randsome came to the door of her sturdy farmhouse followed by a lovely blonde haired young woman. Kate was startled to realize that the young woman was her cousin, Emily, who had come to live with Tenia after the end of the war. Emily must be fifteen or sixteen now. She smiled kindly, but Tenia's brown eyes were hard as creek rocks as she looked at Kate.

"What do you want?" Tenia asked in a harsh voice.

"I'm looking to find a home for me and John Wesley." Kate replied. "Things have changed where I'm at now. I need to move somewhere else."

"Well, you've come to the wrong place. We don't want your kind round here." replied Tenia. "You get thrown out of that place in Purdy?"

"No," replied Kate stoutly. "I cain't stay there no more. Mr. Richmond wants me to do something I don't aim to do, so I'm looking for another home. "

Tenia snorted contemptuously and said, "I can imagine what he wants, seeing as you're what you are. The answer is still "no". We've got enough to feed and clothe here without taking in any more."

Emily has stood quietly during the exchanged, but now chimed in, "Oh, Cousin Tenia. We cain't let her go back there if that man wants her to do something bad!"

"You hush your mouth missy! You don't know what you're saying. This brazen hussy has no place with decent people. You know that! We don't take in her kind, family or no."

Emily looked hurt by the verbal attack, but pressed on. "She looks so desperate, Cousin. Surely, after all this time, we can find it in our hearts to forgive her. If she stayed here, we could set a good example for her and help her raise her son right."

Kate drew herself up in outrage at the implication that she couldn't raise her son right without help, but before she could draw breath to protest, Tenia said in a poisonous manner.

"She was raised right herself. She knew what she was doing was wrong, but she did it anyway. Living with niggers! Teaching them to read and write like they was as good as whites! Let her suffer for what she's done."

Kate raised her voice to prevent the two women from continuing to talk about her as though she weren't standing right in front of them. "You're a cold woman, Tenia Randsome. Yes, I did wrong having a baby before I got married. I've paid for it every day for years. No doubt, I'll be paying for it till I die, but my son deserves better. All of you think you're so much better than me and won't reach out to help me, but my son deserves your help." Her voice choked with emotion, she pleaded, "Think of him instead of me. Let us come here for his sake, not mine."

Emily's large, clear gray eyes filled with tears at Kate's words. Looking at Tenia, she said, "Cousin Tenia, cain't you see how desperate she is? Let her bring her son and come here to live with us. We can make room for them. Really we can."

"No," said Tenia. "Not now, not ever. She made her bed, now she has to lay in it." Grasping the young girl by the arm, Tenia pulled her away from the door and shut it in Kate's face. She could hear Emily still protesting behind the closed door, but knew it would do no good to remain standing there. There was no one left to go to for shelter. She must return to Purdy before she was missed by Rebecca.

~ * ~

The knowledge that no one would help her tormented her throughout the long walk back. No matter how she twisted and turned in her mind, she could find no solution to her problem. Finally, she came to the decision that James had known she would make in the end. Kate was prepared to do anything to keep her son by her side. The very thought of bedding with James Richmond made her feel physically sick, but the thought of losing her beloved son made her heart feel shriveled and dead in her chest. She knew she could survive bedding James, but she could never survive the loss of her son. She would never let her son be raised by a man of James's nature.

Thirty-one

James left her alone for almost a week. Kate was beginning the think the scene in the cow shed had been some kind of fever dream, when he approached her in the kitchen one morning as she was scrubbing the breakfast dishes.

"You've had sufficient time to think over my proposition. Since you haven't run off, I assume that you've decided to be reasonable and see things my way. I'll expect you in my room tonight after Mother had gone to sleep. Don't come too early, I wouldn't want her to hear you and wonder what's going on."

He turned and left the kitchen as abruptly as he had entered. Kate was left feeling as though she had been punched in the stomach.. The reckoning was at hand. She would face it with as much courage as she could muster.

The rest of the day passed in a blur as she went about her usual routine. Her feet dragged as she moved around the house and into town to buy meat for supper that night. She hardly noticed Mr. Ramsey's manner as she made her purchase. Returning to the house, she saw Rebecca sitting in the rocking chair on the front porch watching people go about their business in town. She smiled as she saw Kate crossing the yard and said, "I never tire of watching people go about their business. I like to see what they're wearing and who they're with. I can pass endless time imagining conversations between them. It's such an interesting way of passing the time. You should join me, dear. We can make up conversations between us about them." There was a mischievous smile on her face as she said that.

Disconcerted by yet another example of Rebecca's eccentric behavior, Kate replied, "Thank you, ma'am, but it wouldn't be right for me to sit here on the porch with you like I was family. I need to git this meat into the kitchen and get started cooking supper. I'm glad you can pass the time so pleasurably. I know it's hard on you not to be able to get around like you used to do."

"You go ahead and put the meat in the kitchen, then come back out on the porch and sit with me for a little while." Rebecca insisted. "Supper can wait half an hour. I'd like to talk with you for a while."

Kate's pulse began a rapid tattoo in her wrists. Did Rebecca know about what James had said to her? She replied through lips suddenly gone dry; "I'll do that, ma'am. Just give me a few minutes and I'll be right on out."

Kate hurried into the kitchen and put the meat on the table. Then she hurriedly washed her hands with water from the bowl next to the dry sink and went back to the porch, smoothing her hair into place as she went. She sat in the rocking chair next to Rebecca, looking around to see who might be observing them and waited to hear what Rebecca had to say to her.

"Kate, I'm worried about James."

Kate was immediately alarmed. Did she know about the arrangement that James had proposed? Would she stop James before everything was ruined? Or would she tell Kate that she had to leave? Maybe that would be for the best. Rebecca was kind; maybe she would give Kate a little money to start out as a tenant farmer somewhere else in the county. Kate would gladly work night and day to pay back the money. Then she realized that James would never allow his mother to find out about the arrangement, so it must be something else on Rebecca's mind. She said, "Oh, ma'am, I don't think it's right for you to be talking to me about such personal things. I mean, I'm just your housekeeper. You should be talking about these things with some of your friends. People of your class, I mean."

"I think of you as a friend, Kate dear. I know you come from good family and have fallen on hard times. I'm happy that you have found a home here with us. I feel toward you much more than an employer and employee. I would like very much for you to hear what I have to say."

Kate's lips trembled. Her eyes filled with tears at Rebecca's kind words. If only things were really the way Rebecca thought they were, Kate would be completely happy here. She reached over and took Rebecca's hand in hers as she said; "I am very fond of you too, Ma'am. You've given me and John Wesley a good home. You've been so kind to me the whole time I've been here. I enjoy your company very much."

Rebecca patted her hand and smiled. "You're a good girl, Kate. I enjoy your company very much, too. I need to speak to someone about my worries. I just don't want to voice them to anyone I know here in town. Would you listen to an old woman's worries?"

"I'd be happy to do anything I can for you ma'am. If you feel you have to talk to someone and want me to be that person, I'll listen to ease your heart." The thought passed through her mind, *If only I had someone to talk to and ease my own heart!*

Rebecca sighed, looked off into the distance for a few minutes, then began, "I'm worried about James. The stage line business hasn't been good for many years. Since the trains started running passengers, so many people prefer to travel that way because it's faster. I tried to get him to sell of the stage lines years ago, but he couldn't be persuaded. Then he insisted on moving here and having this big house built for me." She glanced quickly at Kate, then said, "Don't misunderstand me. This is a lovely little town, but it's dying like so many of the towns that the railroad doesn't pass though. I can understand that the businessmen want to be near the railroad, but it does seem a shame to see such a lovely place as this getting smaller with each passing year. She sighed, then continued, "I wish James would marry. I would like to have some grandchildren before I die." She laughed at the expression on Kate's face and said, "Not that I intend to die soon, but you never know, do you?"

Kate sat dumbstruck throughout Rebecca's outburst, and now squirmed uncomfortably in her rocking chair. Anger and hatred of James roiled in her stomach. Words rose up into her throat like a poisonous mass that threatened to spill like vomit from her lips. One look at Rebecca's kind and loving face forced the horrible mass back. Though every particle of her being cried out to her to tell the shameful secret, she couldn't spew that horrible mass onto this unsuspecting woman. What if Rebecca thought she had led James to think that she wanted to bed him?

She wanted to end this distasteful personal discussion so she said, "I really don't know what to say to you, ma'am. I don't know of any way to help you with this. I'm not the kind of person who knows anything about business. Maybe you should talk to Miz Winston about it. Her husband is a businessman. Maybe she could help you a lot better than I ever could. I know ya'll are close friends and all."

With a deep sigh Rebecca said, "Yes, Anna Winston is a dear friend, but somehow, I don't feel that she would be very helpful with this. She wants James to marry her daughter, Rachel. If she thought James was going to lose his fortune, then she would steer Rachel away from him. I like Rachel very much and would like to see James married to her. He just doesn't seem to be interested in marrying."

Kate felt that the conversation was turning toward dangerous areas again and rose from her chair. "I'm sorry I'm not any help to you, ma'am. I really need to git started on supper now though."

"That's all right, dear. It's done me good just to talk to someone about it. Sometimes it helps just to put worries into words, even if it doesn't solve anything. You go on and get supper started. I'll just stay out here for a while longer."

~ * ~

The kitchen provided a small sanctuary to Kate's strained emotions. She took a minute to lean against the table feeling as though she had run a hundred miles in the last half hour. How could James have his mother so thoroughly fooled about his true character? Or did Rebecca just refuse to see anything about her beloved son that didn't match up with her notions of what a good son he was to her? Her heart whispered to her to run, run, run fast and far; but her head told her that James would carry out his threat to take John Wesley from her if she tried to go. She could never run far enough or fast enough to escape him.

She went about preparing supper as though everything was just as it had been for months. The food turned out beautifully. For desert, Kate made her special blackberry cobbler that Aunt Mary had taught her in what seemed another world.

She served dinner in her usual way, smiling in genuine delight when Rebecca praised her efforts. She felt James's eyes on her all through the evening, like hot two hot coals. Her skin crawled as though physically attempting to escape. Later she ate her own supper in the kitchen with John Wesley, then tucked him into his small bed with a kiss. She removed her shoes, but felt far too restless to lie down in her own bed.

She paced through the downstairs of the house like a caged animal. Her skin felt odd. She was hot one minute, cold the next. The fine hairs on her arms stood up. She unconsciously smoothed them down as she paced feverishly. The grandfather clock in the parlor quietly ticked off the hours in the still house. When midnight came, Kate knew she could delay no longer. She started up the steps in trepidation. The landing squeaked loudly and started her heart hammering in her chest. She stood silently listening for movement from the direction of Rebecca's room, and, hearing none, continued to James's room at the back corner of the second floor.

He was waiting when she finally forced herself to push open the door. He said nothing as she entered, closed the door and began removing her dress. He drew her to the bed and as his lips suckled her breast and one hand moved up her thigh, her flesh tried to shrink physically away from his touch. During the next two hours he performed on her, and forced her to perform, acts of depravity that she had never dreamed existed this side of hell. Her spirit fled to a dream world. When he had finished, she put her dress back on with trembling fingers. Her body ached in unaccustomed places and a sour, metallic taste lingered on her tongue. An evil smile covered James's face in the flickering candlelight. Knowing that she was about to vomit, she fled back to her own room.

After she had emptied her stomach, she cleaned up the mess, crying softly lest she wake her son. Lying safely in her own bed, attempting to overcome her disgust of the last two hours, she reflected bitterly. A man in James's position could force her to such degradation and she had no recourse but to live with it. This was a man's world. She had no more power than a little child. She did not know how she would endure James's treatment of her on a regular basis, but for her son's sake she had no choice. She felt as though she were balanced on the edge of a cliff with a wild wind blowing.

Thirty-two

The year swung on toward the holidays. The excitement in the air was a direct contrast to Kate's state of mind. All happiness seemed to have sealed itself off in some part of her mind that she couldn't reach. For John Wesley, she put on a smiling face. She laughed gaily and often at his pranks and jokes. She was teaching him in the cold winter evenings when the Richmonds were out attending parties. He was such a bright little boy. He soaked up everything she taught him and hungered for more. It was a shame that she could never send him to the Male Academy here in Purdy. He would have been one of their prize pupils, so bright and eager a student he was. Kate pushed on day after endless day. Always trying to think of a way for herself and John Wesley to go somewhere else. Always reaching the same conclusion. Without money or family support, she had no alternative but to continue to endure her life here.

They spent Thanksgiving Day alone and Kate was thankful for at least that much if nothing else. The Richmonds had gone to have supper at the Winston home. Rebecca was still pursuing her plan to have James married to Rachel Winston. Kate thought that was just fine with her. If James were married, he could hardly demand that she come to his room in the dead of the night.

After Thanksgiving, the paced accelerated, so that it seemed that the Richmonds were out almost every night. Rebecca was often out in the afternoons, having tea with the ladies in town. Rebecca returned the favor of the tea parties and Kate served the tea, small cakes and sandwiches. On these occasions she kept her eyes down and made sure everyone was served with whatever they wanted. Kate could just imagine the gossip that went on after the ladies left. They had their heads together as soon as they cleared the porch. Kate just knew they were saying what a fool Rebecca Richmond was to have the likes of Kate Randsome serving tea and keeping house. Didn't everyone know she was a harlot and no one who wasn't a fool would allow her through their door? They probably were insulted to touch the same china that Kate had touched. She sighed and leaned her head against the frame of the window where she stood watching the ladies' progress down the street.

That evening, James brought home a huge cedar tree to decorated for Christmas. Rebecca told Kate that there were fragile glass ornaments packed in straw in the closet under the stairs. Kate brought them to Rebecca who picked each one out of the straw and held them lovingly in her misshapen hands. She passed them to Kate who hung them carefully on the branches of the tree. Revolving slowly in their places, they shot reflected firelight all around the room. John Wesley was enchanted. He had been allowed to sit quietly and watch while the tree was decorated.

"Oh, Mama!' he breathed in awe, " I've never seen anything so beautiful in my life! Have you?"

Kate remembered the festive Christmas trees from her childhood and thought that they had been just as beautiful, but seeing the look in her young son's eyes, she agreed that this was the most beautiful she had ever seen. Poor child. He had never seen a Christmas tree before now. She couldn't dim his pleasure by letting him know that his grandparents had had trees just as lovely. He would ask many questions that she wasn't prepared to answer yet. Time enough, when he was older, to answer those questions.

Rebecca was pleased by the tree and told John Wesley, "On Christmas morning we'll all gather here and open our presents. Will you like that, young John?" For some reason Rebecca always called him by his first name only.

He looked at her and grinned as he said, "You mean an apple and some walnuts? You gonna wrap those things? We never wrapped them before."

Rebecca looked taken aback by his reply, but motioned Kate to silence, as Kate was about to remonstrate John Wesley for such an impolite answer. "Well, young John, perhaps there will be something other than an apple and some walnuts for Christmas this year. Something that would be nice to open on Christmas morning."

John Wesley looked surprised. The only Christmas gifts he had ever received were apples and walnuts. The concept that there were other Christmas gifts struck him silent. He looked at his mother in a puzzled manner and said, "What other things could there be for Christmas, Mama? Do you know about them?"

Kate's heart hurt for him. They had always been too poor to have store bought Christmas gifts in the past. The apples and walnuts were the only things that could be given by people as poor as they on Christmas. She had saved some of her small wages from working for the Richmonds and had bought second hand boots for John Wesley for Christmas. She was looking forward to seeing his eyes light up at them on Christmas morning. She had also bought yarn and crocheted a warm shawl for Rebecca and a scarf for James. She resented the need to have a gift for James, but could hardly have not given him anything. She smiled cheerfully at her son and explained, "Sometimes there are lots of other things for Christmas gifts, but we don't want to forget that it's really a celebration of the birthday of Jesus. Remember? We always read the Christmas story in the Bible on Christmas Eve."

Rebecca said, "What a splendid idea! You must read the Christmas story to all of us this year."

Kate didn't want to have the special closeness she felt to John Wesley ruined by the unholy presence of James on Christmas Eve as she read the story, so she replied, "I think I'd be too nervous the read the story here in the parlor to everybody."

"Nonsense!" Rebecca cried. "Surely you read the story aloud at your other, um, home on Christmas Eve." It was the first time Rebecca had ever referred to Kate and John Wesley's former home. She appeared flustered at mentioning it. She would assume that the Stancel's couldn't read and Kate would have been the one to read the story aloud.

Kate tried desperately to think of a way out of the situation. "Surely, ya'll will be going to a party on Christmas Eve, ma'am. Didn't I hear you telling James that ya'll had been invited to the Winston's?"

"Yes, yes. We'll be going to their party, but surely you could read the story early. Young John will be going to bed early won't he? I would so enjoy hearing the story again. It's been many years since I heard it myself. Not since James was a child really. Would you read it to all of us this year, Kate dear?"

Kate could see no way out of reading the story without hurting Rebecca's feelings, and looking ungrateful herself, so she reluctantly agreed to read the story aloud early on Christmas Eve. She cursed herself for mentioning it in front of Rebecca in the first place, but how could she have known the eccentric woman would think it proper for the housekeeper to read the story to herself and James?

~ * ~

Christmas drew closer and John Wesley speculated endlessly about what his Christmas present might be. Kate was concerned, but didn't want to spoil his Christmas for him. If future Christmases were back to apples and walnuts, at least he would have this one fancy Christmas to remember. She only hoped it wouldn't make future, less festive, Christmases hard for him. She was determined that someday, somehow, she would win freedom for herself, and him, from James' grasp. When she finally gained that freedom, she would never trust another man again.

The morning of Christmas Eve dawned bright and beautiful, but bone chillingly cold. Kate hurried into the kitchen to light the fire in the fireplace and in the cookstove to take the chill from the kitchen before John Wesley awoke. She would be very busy today getting the turkey and dressing, the side dishes of vegetables and the deserts ready in time for the unusually early supper they planned. She was still very nervous at the thought of reading aloud in front of James. If it had only been Rebecca, John Wesley and herself, she knew she would have enjoyed it immensely. She could hardly stand to be in the same room with James and now he would be watching her closely while she read aloud that beautiful story. She felt soiled just thinking about it. She finally put it out of her mind and concentrated on getting everything started for their supper. The pies could be left for last. They only needed to be heated since she had baked them the day before and put them in the safe with the cake she had also made. She was deeply involved when John Wesley came yawning into the kitchen wanting his breakfast. She sat him at one end of the table with a glass of milk and a cold biscuit, telling him, "You must keep out of my way today. I have a lot of cooking to do for our special supper tonight. Eat your breakfast, then go outside and play."

He looked at her out of sleepy eyes and yawned again. Finishing his breakfast, he headed toward the door saying, "I'll be playing with Timmy by the old cemetery if you want me, Mama. I'll come home before dark."

She hugged him close to her and reminded him to put on his mittens and scarf before he went out. He grimaced at her, but grabbed them off the hook by the door on his way out.

She continued with her preparations and by midafternoon was very pleased with the results. The turkey was golden brown and the dressing light and fluffy. The vegetables were cooked to perfection. Now all that remained was to warm the pies. Everything was ready in good time. Taking some warm water, she went into her room to wash up and put on her only other dress. She was just returning to the kitchen when John Wesley burst through the door carrying some mistletoe.

"Look, Mama!" he said excitedly. "Timmy and me found this in a tree over by the cemetery. Some big boys came by and shot it out of the top of the tree for us. We were drawing straws to see who would climb up and get it when they came by. They laughed at us about climbing the tree and said we would fall and get killed doing that and that it would ruin Christmas for the doctor and for our mama's, so they shot it down." He was fairly dancing around the kitchen in his excitement, but Kate had turned pale at the thought of him climbing to the upper branches of a tree to get mistletoe.

"It's beautiful, but you must never climb that high in a tree. Those big boys were right. You might easily have fallen and been killed and what would I do without my boy?"

He handed the mistletoe to her saying, "I wanted to get it for a Christmas present for you, Mama. You can pin it on your dress and be beautiful for Christmas." He looked down, scuffed his shoe on the floor. "I don't have any money to buy you something nice like you should have. I wanted you to have something special just from me."

Tears formed in Kate's eyes as she rummaged in the dresser drawer for a pin to hold the mistletoe on her dress. When she had it secured, she turned to him and said, "It's the nicest present I ever had. But, John Wesley, you're my greatest gift. I don't need anything else. You go wash up now and put on clean clothes for supper."

He skipped happily from the room. Kate put the turkey on the silver Christmas platter and the vegetables in the fine china serving dishes reserved for special occasions. Just as she finished, John Wesley came in, his cheeks pink from the scrubbing he had given them. She picked up the turkey tray and told him to bring the small bowl of cranberries she had prepared. They went into the dining room where Rebecca and James waited.

"What a lovely turkey!" Rebecca cried as they entered. "And who is this handsome young man assisting you tonight? Why, could it be young John?"

John giggled self-consciously and placed the cranberries on the table saying, "Yes, Miss Rebecca, it's really me. Merry Christmas!"

Kate placed the turkey near James. She and John Wesley returned to the kitchen to bring in the rest of the vegetables. When they had brought in all the food, Kate turned to go back into the kitchen, but Rebecca stopped her, "Kate, I want you and young John to have Christmas dinner with us. Bring him in and the two of you sit and eat with us."

Kate was taken aback by the request. It was unheard of for the servants to have dinner with the family. She looked unwillingly to James for assistance, but he just shrugged his shoulders indifferently. Light glinted off the gold stickpin in his cravat and seemed to die in the black of his suit coat. Kate looked back at Rebecca whose diamond necklace glittered in the candlelight. Her dress of emerald green silk whispered softly as she moved to reach out to Kate. "Come, my dear. Humor an eccentric woman on Christmas Eve. Eat here in the dining room with us, not in that drafty kitchen. I know you won't assume any airs and graces because of it. It would please me very much to have the two of you here. After dinner, we'll go to the parlor and read the Christmas story and exchange gifts before James and I go out for the evening."

Kate gave in to the pleading in Rebecca's eyes and fetched John Wesley from the kitchen. He seemed unnerved at the thought of eating at the big dining table. Kate sat close to him so she could help him with the array of silverware. He sat very straight in his chair and looked nervously at James, then at Rebecca, who smiled in return. He smiled back at her, then looked at his mother for help. She picked up his plate and passed it to James who placed a piece of turkey on it and passed it back. Rebecca had already been served, so after James had served Kate and himself, he began passing the vegetables around the table.

Once everyone was served, Kate began to feel even more uncomfortable. She could think of nothing to say and sat in miserable silence. John Wesley appeared awed to be eating at the big, fancy dining table and remained quiet also. Finally, James began telling then about his trip to Jackson the day before and about all of the fine displays for Christmas in the big stores there. Rebecca joined in, asking questions about mutual friends. Kate felt herself relax slightly.

Rebecca, as thought sensing that Kate was feeling more relaxed, asked, "Where did you get the lovely sprig of mistletoe, Kate dear? It looks so festive for the Christmas season."

"John Wesley brought it to me. It's his Christmas present for me."

Rebecca smiled at the little boy who squirmed uncomfortably in his chair. At the head of table, James looked bored. When his mother turned to look at him, he pasted a hasty smile on his face for her.

They finished their meal and Rebecca told them all to come into the parlor. James would light the candles on their Christmas tree and then they would exchange presents after Kate read the Christmas story. Kate went hastily into her room and retrieved her gifts. When she brought them into the parlor and placed them near the tree, she was embarrassed to see how tawdry and cheap they looked next to the brightly wrapped gifts of the Richmonds. The gifts, wrapped in cheap brown paper, sat like lumps of clay next to the tissue paper and ribbon wrapped gifts already there. She flushed a little, then seeing the bright smile of anticipation on Rebecca's face, she felt a little better. After all, the Richmonds could hardly expect her gifts to be expensively wrapped. She had worked hard on the gifts inside the cheap wrapping. Of those she was proud.

James handed her their family bible so that she could read the Christmas story. Kate's hands trembled as she turned the pages. She found the page she wanted and began reading the ancient story. Her voice shook from nervousness. She stopped, cleared her throat slightly, then began again. Now her voice was strong and clear. She read the story through to the end and closed the Bible. The fire whispered and crackled in the silence that enveloped the room now that Kate had finished reading.

Rebecca broke the silence. "That was lovely, Kate. I haven't heard that story in so long. It took me right back to my girlhood. We used to always read the story on Christmas Eve when I was girl. Let's exchange gifts now. Give Kate her gift first, James. I can't wait to see how she likes it!"

James picked up a large tissue wrapped package and brought it to Kate, handing it to her with an ironic bow. There was an amused expression in his eyes. She hesitantly began removing the ribbons and paper, careful not to rip it. She would put it, along with the ribbons, aside for future use. As the tissue paper parted, she caught a glimpse of blue. Pulling aside the paper, she found a large quantity of blue wool so fine that it felt like a kittens fur under her rough hands. Catching her breath, she looked at Rebecca with radiant eyes.

"It's the most beautiful material I ever saw."

"I'm glad you like it so much. I had James get it for me when he was in Jackson. I told him to get a lovely blue to match your eyes." Rebecca was pleased with the effect of her gift. "Now young John must open his gift."

John Wesley went hesitantly to Rebecca, who held a small package out to him. Taking the gift and looking at his mother for permission, he tore open the tissue paper. Kate thought ruefully that she wouldn't be able to save that piece of paper. Then, when she saw her son's shining eyes, she forgot all about the paper. He held out a beautifully bound book of children's stories. She reminded him to remember his manners. He turned to Rebecca.

Eyes still shining, he said, "Thank you for the book, Miss Rebecca."

"I thought your mother could read the stories to you for now. Later, when you can read better, you can read them for yourself. There's nothing more entertaining on a rainy afternoon than reading a book."

"Yes, ma'am," he replied shyly, looking down at the carpet.

To take attention away from him, Kate suggested the Richmonds open her gifts to them. Rebecca exclaimed over the shawl, declaring it was just the thing to wear with her dresses. James smiled sardonically over his scarf. The look in his eyes told Kate that he expected something much more later. Rebecca announced that they really must be on their way or they would be inexcusably late for the Winston's party.

After they left, Kate tidied the parlor and extinguished the candles on the tree. Going into the kitchen, she found John Wesley looking at his book. She smiled as she realized he was earnestly trying to read out the story for himself.

Ruffling his hair, she asked, "Would you like me to read you one of the stories before you go to bed?"

At his nod, she settled herself on a chair and began the first story.

Thirty-three

After New Year's, winter set in in earnest leaving them all breathless with every trip outdoors. Cold winds whipped down the main street of Purdy freezing water wherever it stood. Often low clouds threatened snow, but it rarely fell. The stage line was all but shut down until better weather arrived. James continued to go about his usual business, to Kate's intense relief. Whenever he was away for a few days it provided her with a respite from his attentions. That dark secret hung over Kate, lurking in the shadows, ready to leap on her unawares at all times.

Rebecca's rheumatism became worse, though she tried valiantly to hide it. Her face became drawn with pain. She hardly ate any of the food put before her. Her dresses began to hang on her from the weight she lost. Kate felt deep pity for the old woman, who struggled through each day pretending that her pain didn't exist, and made frequent trips to the general store for the tonic that Rebecca claimed deadened her pain. Her fondness for Rebecca continued to grow apace with her hatred of James. Twin vines that sprang forth from her soul, twining side by side.

In late February a thaw set in that left the formerly rutted roads a quagmire of slippery, stinking mud that still made travel difficult in it's on way. These inconveniences were greeted with a lighter heart by everyone, because spring was definitely on the way. Swelling buds could be seen on trees and flowering shrubs. Winds blew occasionally from the south now and gave a kiss of warmth to winter pale skin, promising better things to come. Kate began making plans for their small vegetable garden. She could hardly wait to get outside and dig in the warm earth. Preparing the garden spot would provide a rough physical outlet for all the frustrations that were building to the point of explosion within her heart.

With an outer calm that belied those inner frustrations, Kate continued her routine. In the mornings she went from room to room, keeping them spotlessly beautiful. Afternoons were spent in the pleasant company of Rebecca, reading or writing letters to the older woman's numerous friends. Evenings were spent in the even more pleasant company of John Wesley, reading to him from his storybook or teaching him to read better himself. The nights when James was home, she still refused to dwell on. Those sneaking, unpleasant hours were something to be pushed to the dusty back corners of her mind. They were the price she paid for keeping her son and therefore worth every hateful minute.

Change did come into the Richmond home that spring from an unexpected direction. James announced his engagement to Rachel Winston. The whole town was astir with the news. Kate heard people talking about it on the streets and in the store. It was considered the match of the season. The newspaper carried a long column announcing the engagement and forthcoming wedding of the local businessman to the daughter of one of Purdy's most prominent citizens. Kate heart leaped with hope. James could not continue their relationship with a wife in the house. Her chance was coming to make her escape. She began counting off the months until the June wedding that would herald her release from James's grasp.

~ * ~

Rachel Winston and her mother began calling more frequently at the Richmond home, giving Kate disparaging looks as she took their wraps and as she served tea. The haughty Winston's appeared to be insulted to be served by the likes of Kate Randsome. If not for her employer's obvious happiness over the engagement, Kate often thought she might resort to deliberate rudeness in self-defense. Rebecca wanted to know all of the details concerning the wedding. It had grown to such proportions that it resembled a huge pageant that would include every person in every prominent family in the county and beyond. Rachel was to have seven brides' maids. She claimed they were to represent each child she wanted to have with James. Of course, all the children would be boys, she claimed. Every man wanted sons to carry on after he was gone didn't they? There was much giggling in the parlor on these occasions. Kate thought she would be ill just from listening. Too bad Rachel didn't know what kind of man she was marrying. Kate could tell her a thing or too about him. But then, James would never treat his wife the way he treated her. She could see that from the way James acted on the occasions when he was present for afternoon tea or when the Winston's dined with them. James was always the perfect gentleman. He bowed deeply over Rachel's hand and kissed it in a lingering manner. He gazed at her with adoration on his face.

The unfairness of it all burned in Kate's breast like a raging forest fire. She didn't want James for herself, but his actions toward his fiancée made her seethe inwardly. He pretended to be such a gentleman with everyone but Kate. To her, he showed his true self. With ever increasing rage, she continued to appear outwardly calm and happy. She rejoiced with Rebecca over the upcoming wedding and when Rebecca commented on how sweet it was of Kate to be so happy for James, Kate just smiled and kept her reasons for rejoicing to herself.

She became concerned that Rebecca was overextending herself. The rheumatism that had afflicted her for years had been so much worse this past winter than ever before and Rebecca had difficulty bending her knees because of the pain in them. Her hands were even more gnarled than before, but she was determined to participate fully in the wedding of her only son. The tonic Rebecca took to ease the pain wasn't helping the way it had in the past. Remembering the excruciating pain she had felt after picking all that cotton years ago, Kate thought of the horse liniment that Aunt Mary had used on her. It might help Rebecca. If it didn't, at least it wouldn't cause any harm. There wasn't any liniment in the house and she asked John Wesley to see if his friend Timmy had any around their house. When John Wesley brought her the bottle, she took it straight upstairs where Rebecca was resting in bed.

"I've got some liniment to rub on you, Miss Rebecca. It smells kinda bad, but maybe it'll help your pain. I'm gonna rub you down with this, then you're gonna spend the morning in bed letting it work. I know the Winston ladies are coming this afternoon. Don't you worry. We'll have you feeling better by then. You be sure and eat some of those cakes and sandwiches I made. You need to put on some weight so you won't be looking like a scarecrow at the wedding."

Over Rebecca's protests, Kate rubbed the old woman down with the liniment. It smelled very strongly of some kind of mint. Kate could feel a burning sensation in her hands from the stuff, and her eyes started watering from the smell. She told Rebecca to close her eyes and rest until time to get dressed for her afternoon company. She pulled down the window shades to darken the room and left quietly, closing the door behind her.

Later, as she was dusting the baseboard in the hallway, she heard light snores coming from Rebecca's bedroom and was pleased that the old woman was resting. Kate would wake her in a little while and help her get dressed for her afternoon with Anna and Rachel Winston.

Humming as she went about her work, Kate reflected how peaceful the house was when James was away. She breathed more easily, not having to wonder if James were lurking in one of the rooms waiting for her. If only there were no James, this would be the perfect place to raise her son. He already had one friend and would probably make more. She had Rebecca's kindness to bolster her spirits and sense of worth. Friends of her own, she could manage to live without. Noticing the angle of sunlight coming through the window, she realized it was getting late. She should wake Rebecca now, so that she would be ready when her afternoon visitors arrived.

~ * ~

They were not quiet finished when there was a knock at the front door. Kate ran downstairs and found the Winston ladies had arrived early. She took their wraps and asked them to wait in the parlor, explaining that Rebecca was not quit ready to receive them, but would be down soon. Hurrying back upstairs, she told Rebecca that her visitors had arrived and were waiting in the parlor.

"Oh dear. I do so hate it when I'm not ready when visitors arrive. Run down, Kate dear, and give them some tea while they wait and tell them I'll be down in just a few minutes."

Kate hurried down the back staircase into the kitchen where she prepared a tea tray. As she waited for the water to boil, she placed the small cakes and sandwiches she had made earlier on china plates. The teakettle whistled and she poured the boiling water into the teapot, which already contained tealeaves. Dainty napkins went on the tray next. She lifted the heavy silver tray and headed to the parlor. As she approached, her feet silent on the carpets, she could hear Rachel talking.

" Miz Richmond is so eccentric." Rachel was saying. "She seems to be genuinely fond of that Randsome creature, but I don't know how I'll stand being under the same roof. What can I say to my friends about having such a servant?"

Anna Winston replied matter-of-factly, "When you're mistress of this house, you can do as you please. Just throw the creature out. You can tell Rebecca that she ran off. Probably with some man. You have to learn early in a marriage how to wrap your husband and mother-in-law around your finger."

Kate felt a flush of anger rise in her cheeks. Her hands, gripping the tea tray, trembled. The vicious cats! Sitting in there and speaking of her and Rebecca in such a nasty way. Tea splashed over the side of the pot onto the dainty linen napkins she had placed on the tray. Turning around quietly, she returned to the kitchen to replace the napkins and calm herself. It was not her business, she reasoned, if those two wanted to speak that way among themselves. But, Oh! How it hurt her to have heard those words. Should she tell Rebecca what she had heard? No, she decided. It would only wound her unnecessarily. Rebecca was fond of Rachel and wanted her as a daughter-in-law. Besides, if Rachel insisted that Kate leave the house, it would better her chance to escape. Placing new napkins on the tray, she took it into the parlor, informed the haughty twosome that Rebecca would be down soon and retreated back to the kitchen.

Thirty-four

Not long after that afternoon, Kate realized that her monthly course was late. It had never been late before—*except when she was carrying John Wesley*. The horrified realization came to her that she must be carrying James's child! No! It couldn't be happening again! It wasn't supposed to work out this way! She was so close to freedom for herself and her son! She couldn't have another bastard child. She would never be able to have a place for John Wesley if she had another child. Everyone would claim that it proved what they had said about her all along. Her heart pounded in thick, irregular beats. Would she be doomed now to turn to prostitution to support herself and her children?

Catching a glimpse of herself in her bedroom mirror she saw that her eyes were huge in a face that was dead white. Her lips began to tremble as she stared at her reflection. A beaten woman gazed back at her. She set her lips in a firm line. Determination stole into her eyes. She was not a whore. She vowed that she wouldn't let anyone turn her into one with their words and their exile of her.

James was still out of town, so she had a while to decide what she would do now. She knew what James's reaction to this would be and that he would have her out of his house immediately. His marriage to Rachel Winston would be in a few months. He would never allow a breath of scandal to touch him, so what plan of action could she form? She chewed over the problem, trying desperately to think of a solution. She must have a plan in place before James returned.

A few days later she was till trying to form a plan of action. As she swept the front porch, she saw Mr. McIntosh from McNairy Station going into the bank. She froze on the spot, staring at the door through which he had disappeared. A possibility bloomed in her mind. He had allowed her to live with the Stancel's on his property once before, would he allow it again if she asked him personally? She tried to remember his reactions, and those of his wife, from the days when she had still been attending church at Refuge. He and his family were staunch members of the church, but try as she might, she couldn't recall any particular reaction towards her from that time. Thoughtfully, she went back into the house, the seed of a plan forming in her mind.

The more she thought about her plan, the better it sounded. She would tell James that she was carrying his child and ask for money to keep quiet about it. That would enable her to go to the McIntosh's, or someone else, with money in hand and ask to rent a small piece of property on which she would raise her children. Starting with the McIntosh's, she would systematically go around McNairy Station until she found someone willing to rent her a small parcel of land to farm. Asking for money put her on level with prostitutes and just thinking about it made her squirm. Surely he owed her at least that much after the hell he had made of her life. She waited for his return.

He came home a few days later with a bunch of buttercups for his mother and a leer in his eyes for Kate when Rebecca's head was turned. Her rage, which had slowed to a simmer in his absence, roared to life again and she wanted to strike him. Wanted to claw his face to erase that look in his eyes. An almost overwhelming urge came over her to act on her feelings. It gave her a moments pleasure to imagine his shock if she acted on that impulse, to claw his face until his blood ran freely under her fingers, to scar that hawklike face forever as he had irrevocably scarred her soul. She managed to push the urge deep within her. Now was not the time to act. She knew that in reality, she could never physically act on that desire, but her freedom was drawing nearer. That gave her enormous comfort. He told them he had some business matters to discuss in town, would then dine with the Winston's and be home late.

The day passed as usual while Kate counted down the hours until her confrontation with James. Kate cleaned the kitchen, taking her time over the task, then went to the parlor to join her employer. She read a few chapters of Dickens, feeling her tension growing with every hour. Finally, Rebecca sat yawning before the fire and Kate accompanied the older woman upstairs to help her prepare for bed. While she was helping Rebecca get into bed, she heard the door slam downstairs and knew that James had returned. She tucked Rebecca into bed and blew out the lamp, closing the bedroom door on her way out. She returned to her room then, to make sure her son was sleeping peacefully and contemplate what she would say to James. She would tell him about the child before he could grab her and start his filthy games. She would tell him and then demand that he give her money in return for her silence. He would surely be angry and what form would that anger take? Surely he wouldn't strike her. He was much too lordly and arrogant to resort to physical violence. Wasn't he? Her heart quailed for a moment at the thought of his reaction, but she pulled her courage firmly about her and started upstairs when she heard the grandfather clock in the hall strike midnight.

From long experience, she avoided the squeaky spots on the staircase and landing as she crept toward his door. She listened outside for a moment. There was only silence within. Taking a deep breath for courage, she slowly opened the door and slipped inside, closing the door quietly behind her. James was sitting fully dressed before the fireplace, looking over some papers in his hand. She was disconcerted for a moment. He was usually waiting for her in the bed when she arrived in his room. He looked up at her as she stood uncertainly by the door.

"Come closer, my dear," he said. "I've been looking forward to our reunion."

Kate remained standing with her back against the door. She felt as though she had been struck mute. Wondering how to begin, she stared at James.

A frown of irritation creased his brow as he said, "What's the matter with you tonight?" He continued in a callous voice, "Surely haven't suddenly been overcome with modesty. Come here now!"

She jumped slightly at the command. Shook her head mutely.

Standing up, he tossed aside the papers in his hand, walked over to her and grabbed her roughly by the arm saying, "What kind of game do you think you're playing?" When she continued to stand silent, he shook her arm roughly. "Answer me, damn you!"

She looked into his face and blurted, "I'm going to have your baby."

His face blanched, just as Michael's had done so long ago. His hand gripped her arm even tighter, pressing the flesh painfully against the bone. There would be bruises tomorrow, she was sure. He hauled her around and flung her toward the bed. She landed against the side and slid to the floor, rubbing her arm where his fingers had bitten into the tender flesh. The look on his face was murderous. Would he rape her now in his rage, she wondered. He marched over, stood directly in front of her, and reaching down, grabbed both her arms and yanked her to her feet. With his face only inches from her own, he said in a low, menacing voice, "Repeat what you just said."

Bravely she stared into his face and repeated, "I'm going to have your baby."

Her shook her savagely from side to side as he said, "What game are you playing now? You stupid fool! I thought women of your kind knew how to prevent this!"

With a strength she didn't know she possessed, she wrenched herself free of his grasp and hissed, "You bastard! Of course I don't know how to prevent something like this! I was only with one man before you, and I had his child! Where would I learn how to prevent getting pregnant?"

"Don't expect me to believe you were only with one other man. I heard the talk about you before you came here. You lived for four years in the same house as that young black buck and never had his child. I thought you would have learned there how to prevent a pregnancy!" he raged at her.

Kate felt all the air explode from her lungs. There was an oily gleam in his eyes. She realized with a shock that the thought of her and Sam together must have been titillating to someone with his perverse appetites. She remembered Sam's kindness to her through the years she had lived in his home and her raged returned ten fold.

"Sam Stancel is more of a gentleman than you will ever be in your life! He cares about me and loves me, but there was never a sexual relationship between us!" she cried.

James's lips curled cruelly as he sneered, "So everything was pure and sweet between the two of you? I don't believe it for a minute. You had an itch that needed to be scratched and he was there to scratch it for you! Don't lie about it now."

He was vile. She had known all along how cruel he was deep inside, but this surpassed her wildest imaginings. This was more than she could stand. She lashed out at James, thinking to wound him with her words. "You are a disgusting lecher. You cain't imagine that a man would give a stranger a home out of the goodness of his heart, not expecting anything in return! No! To you, every man should take advantage of a helpless woman who comes into his home! You sicken me. I'll tell everyone in town that I'm having your child. Miss snooty Rachel Winston will throw you over in a minute! You won't be able to walk the streets of this town without everybody talking about what a scoundrel you are." Realizing that her words were having no effect on him, she abruptly fell silent. She was disconcerted when he began to laugh softly.

"So, you'll tell everyone in town that you're having my child will you?" he said calmly. "I assure you that if you do so, you'll be run out of town on a rail. I have friends who will claim that they've had the pleasure of knowing you intimately. You forget that I'm a very highly thought of gentleman around here. You also forget that the Winstons are a very old and respectable family. They won't stand for any of your lies either. No, my dear, telling *anyone* that you're carrying my child would be a grave mistake." His voice was silky as he finished.

A wave of dismay washed over Kate as she realized she had gone too far with her threats. She had intended only to lay the groundwork for getting him to give her money to leave. If she was run out of Purdy, the word would spread like wildfire across the county. Any hope she had of finding someone to let her farm on their land would die before the day was out. Frantically, she tried to think of some way to regain the ground she had lost by letting her long restrained temper get the better of her. As he continued to laugh softly, she realized that she had played right into his hands. He wanted her gone and gone quickly. By threatening to have her run out of town, he was maneuvering her to a position where she would leave quietly. She should have known she was no match for him.

Holding herself stiffly before his amused eyes, she tried one last time, "I want you to give me a hundred dollars to leave quietly. Maybe what you say is true, but I think that some people might wonder about it. You don't want to take that chance do you?"

He looked at her in a speculative manner. It was obvious he was considering her words for the moment. She began to think that perhaps she had won back some of the lost ground.

"Will you take the money and leave the area?" he asked.

"No," she stated. "I'm going back McNairy Station. With the money, I can rent a place to farm and raise my children."

He had been reaching for his pocket, but at her words he stopped. With a hard glitter in his eyes he said, "I won't give you a cent unless you agree to leave the area."

They stared at each other like enemies on the field of battle. Kate refused to back down.

"I won't leave the area," she insisted. "McNairy Station is my home and I intend to go back there and raise my children. If I wanted to leave the area, I could have left with the Stancel's over a year ago. Not you or anybody else will change me. I ain't a criminal and I won't sneak off like one. I'm gonna stay right in the area come hell or high water and there's nothing you can do about it!"

"Then you'll get no money from me," he said coldly. "The child is your responsibility. If you won't leave the area, you will have to make do with whatever you can find in the way of accommodations. Now get out of my room. Be out of the house by sunrise. I don't want my mother to see you again. Never forget, my dear, that if I hear one word about your child being fathered by me, I will destroy you." He turned his back to her and ignored her presence.

Speaking to his back, she vented the last of her rage, "You're a low down, sneaking bastard James Richmond! If I never see you again in this life, it'll be too soon! I will curse you every day for as long as I live! I hope all you're future children die at birth and you never have a son to take up your business! I reckon I'll be seeing you in hell, cause that's probably where we're both gonna end up at." She walked resolutely from the room and down the stairs. She would pack up her belongings and those of her son and be out of the house by sunrise.

Thirty-five

They started out just as the sky began to turn a pale pink on the horizon. Back they went, along the dusty road they had traveled scarcely a year and a half ago. All through the long walk from Purdy to the McIntosh place, Kate struggled to think what she could say that would soften the heart of that tough old man. Without money to bargain for a piece of land, she felt at an even greater disadvantage. Her hopes latched firmly onto the memory of the four years shed spent with the Stancel's. Mister McIntosh hadn't insisted that she be thrown off his land then, so maybe he would hear her plea now and allow her to live on his land again. How ironic it would be if she did manage to move the McIntosh's to let her live on their land. Knowing that Angus had requested that she leave with the Stancels, she hadn't thought to go to them when the James had made his filthy proposal. If she had gone to them, and they had let her live on their land at that time, she would have saved herself the hellish existence she had endured at the hands of James Richmond. And the added shame of a second illegitimate child.

John Wesley walked doggedly at her side; not asking any questions though his expression was confused. Her heart hurt for him. Poor child. Shuttled from one place to another. Not understanding why. Someday he would understand and she thought that would be even harder for him to bear. Her sins would follow him all his life.

Arriving at the McIntosh farm, Kate raised a trembling had to knock on the door of the big, old farmhouse that sat in the middle of a clearing. The knock was answered by Sarah McIntosh, who looked taken aback to see Kate there. As the silence stretched between them, Kate heard a crow cawing in the distance and felt sweat trickle slowly between her shoulder blades.

She cleared her throat and asked, "Mrs. McIntosh, I-I wonder could I speak to you and your husband for a minute?"

Sarah looked from Kate to John Wesley, who stood quietly at her side. The woman's gaze traveled to the two worn carpetbags sitting on the porch at their feet. She looked back at Kate and stepped back. For one heart stopping moment, Kate was sure the door was going to slam in their faces, but Sarah silently motioned them inside.

Kate didn't want her son to hear what might be said in that house and told him to wait here on the porch. When he had sat down on the edge of the porch with his legs swinging over the side, she stepped through the door.

The smell of apple pie baking wafted toward her and made Kate's mouth water, reminding her that she hadn't eaten in hours. Sarah led her to a big, comfortable looking room just off the kitchen where Angus McIntosh was reading a newspaper. Their son, Sean and daughter, Eileen, were sitting at a small table in front of the empty fireplace with a game of checkers between them. They all looked up, startled to see Kate enter the room behind Sarah.

Sarah hooked her thumb in Kate's direction. "Says she wants to talk to me and you, Angus. You children skedaddle for a while."

Sean and Eileen left, casting curious looks at Kate. Sarah motioned her to the chair vacated by her son and took the other one herself. Angus put aside his paper and picked up a well-used pipe from the side table, packed it with tobacco and lit it without taking his eyes off Kate. She looked around nervously. A brightly colored rag rug covered the smooth boards of the floor. Cheerful cotton curtains in a floral pattern hung at the two windows looking out across the fields to some woods, setting off the whitewashed walls. A plate rail displayed lovely china plates all around the room. The mantel above the fireplace held a clock surrounded by delicate china cups.

The sound of Angus' voice brought her attention back to him. "Well, young Kate, what brings you here this afternoon?"

Smoke from his pipe curled upward around his face, partially obscuring his eyes from Kate's view. She was at a loss to begin. Sarah watched calmly from across the table, waiting for Kate's answer.

"Well... I came to ask if you might have a small house on some of your land that I could live in, with my son, and sharecrop for you." Rubbing her damp palms across her knees, she continued, "I left the Richmonds, over in Purdy. I wanted to be back over here near my kin, you see, and I was hoping, since you let me stay with the Stancel's all that time, that maybe you could help me out now. I'm young and strong and a hard worker.."

Realizing that she was babbling, Kate fell silent and looked from one to the other, waiting. Waiting. Waiting. The clock on the mantel ticked loudly in the silent room. Angus gazed at her reflectively, his eyes betraying nothing of his thoughts to her.

Taking the pipe from his mouth, Angus pointed it at her. "Young and strong and a hard worker you may be, but farming cotton is hard work for a man. Don't think a woman could farm much cotton on her own."

Kate's heart plunged to her toes. Defeat stared her in the face. She started to rise from the chair, planning to try at the Wheaton farm next.

"Sit down, young Kate!" Angus barked. "I didn't say I wouldn't help you."

Kate sat back again and wondered what help he might be about to offer. Glancing at the quiet face of Sarah gave her no clue. Now she was nervous. Maybe the McIntosh's were playing a game with her. Intended to scorch her soul with words of hate and disgust. But why invite her into the house? That could have just as easily been done on the front porch—and in front of her son! Why send away the McIntosh children? They would have been two more to witness her humiliation. Kate's mind went round and round. Were they going to help? Were they playing some cruel game with her?

Her turmoil was interrupted when Angus spoke again. "Why didn't you come here instead of going to work for James Richmond in Purdy?" His shrewd eyes watched her closely.

"Aunt Mary told me you said you wanted me to go with them to

Virginia. I took that to mean I wasn't welcome on your land anymore. I did what I thought was right at the time. Are you saying you would have taken me in back then?"

Without answering her question, Angus replied gruffly, "There's a small house in the woods over there." He pointed out the window with his pipe. "It's just one room with a couple of small beds and a fireplace for cooking. Can't be used by a family—too small. You and your son can stay there. In return, you'll help Sarah with the garden, the chickens and the cows. I don't give out charity. You'll work hard to earn the house and food to eat.

Kate began to express her gratitude and assure him she would work hard, but he cut her off. With a stern look he continued, "I don't condone women having babies without being married first, but more than that, I can't condone a child doing without food and shelter just because he has a fool for a mother. While you're on my land there'll be no running around with men. If I hear so much as a whisper about you and some man, I'll have you off the place—child or no child! And no teaching the Nigras either! I won't have no more of *that* kind of trouble around here."

Sarah nodded her agreement.

Kate was indignant. How dare these people imply that she would give herself to just any man who took her fancy! Hadn't she learned her lesson already? She didn't need to sit here and be insulted like this! Telling her she couldn't teach her old friends anymore! He was no one to tell her how to live her life! Just as she was about to speak those words aloud, the voice of reason took over. Hadn't she endured worse than this already? She could come here to live and prove them wrong about her. Was this the first hand to reach out to her? The one Aunt Mary had told her to hope for? It wasn't friendly, but it was a start. She would grasp it with both hands and build on it. Then her heart sank when she realized that she still had to tell them that she was carrying another child. Best to get it over now and see if they took back their offer.

"There's one more thing," she began, "I'm going to have another baby in the winter. Sometime in early December."

Sarah gasped. Kate waited for a reply. Would they take back the offer now? Angus' bushy gray brows drew together over his nose as he looked at her. He must be thinking that this was strong evidence that she had been "messing around" with another man recently. The one thing he had told her would get her thrown off his property. Surely the two of them could hear the pounding of her heart. It beat loudly in her ears, nearly drowning out the ticking of the mantle clock, as she continued to wait.

Unexpectedly, Sarah broke the strained silence. "I heard James Richmond was a scoundrel, but I didn't think he would carry on such business under the very roof of his mother!" Her look questioned Kate. Asked for an explanation.

"I never said it was..." Kate said weakly.

"No, you didn't say," she replied in a tart voice, "but you better start talking now if you want us to let you live here." In a kinder tone she added, "Anything you do say will go no further than this room, but we must have the truth from you."

A blush stained her cheeks. She had to tell them the truth. It was the only way they might be persuaded. Hoping that they would believe her she told them.

"I-I-I didn't want to. He threatened to take John Wesley away from me. I didn't know what else to do. I didn't have any money and he said if I tried to leave, he would get John Wesley anyway. He's a powerful man around here. I knew he would do what he said if I didn't go along with him. I went to all my kin, begging them to give me and my boy a home with one of them. I told them what was gonna happen to me iffen they didn't take me in." Her voice hardened as she continued, "They said I made my own bed and had to lay in it. My own kin let me go back to that house knowing what would happen to me. I won't never forgive or forget that."

Sarah snorted, and, thinking that the woman didn't believe her, Kate rushed to say, "I'm telling you the God's honest truth about this. You have to believe me! Do you think I'd be such a fool twice?" She looked back and forth between the two of them, silently willing them to believe her.

Angus said, "James Richmond is a rich man. No matter what Sarah's heard about him. Maybe you thought to trap him into marriage."

"No! I tell you he forced me!" she answered vehemently. "When I told him about the child, he threw me out and said if I ever told anyone the child is his that he would deny it. He said he has friends who would claim that they had been with me. That people would believe them over me. I wouldn't ever be the same fool twice. One man told me he'd marry me, then ran out when I was pregnant with his child. Why would I try to trick a man into marrying me by getting with child?"

Both McIntoshes watched her without speaking. Did they believe her? They had no real way of knowing she spoke the truth. She had laid her shame and humiliation before then in order to gain their help. She would not, could not, tell them the full extent of the horror of the last months. Surely, she had admitted enough without that. Sending up a silent prayer, she waited for their answer. Her hands writhed nervously in her lap. She could feel beads of sweat forming on her forehead as she continued to watch them and wait. The sound of pie sizzling over the sides of its Dutch oven, onto the stove, made her jump as though someone had fired a gun.

Sarah said calmly, "Kate, please go into the kitchen and take that pie off the stove while me and Angus talk this over."

Kate rose and, throwing a pleading look in their direction, went into the kitchen. She could hear the low murmur of their voices as she removed the Dutch oven containing the pie from the stovetop and placed it on a cooling rack. It looked and smelled delicious, reminding her again of her empty stomach. She thought of John Wesley, waiting patiently on the porch. He must be hungry, too.

"Kate!" called Sarah a short time later. "Come on back in here now."

Kate felt her muscles tighten as she walked in to face them. Would she have a home here? They still looked grim as she faced them once more. Too tense to sit down again, she remained standing, like a prisoner in the dock, while she waited for their decision.

"We've decided to take you at your word," began Angus. Kate felt herself relax. "Sarah has heard some unpleasant rumors about James Richmond and thinks you're telling the truth. She's got kin up at

Jackson. Her cousin told her a while back that a man named James Richmond had run up quite a bill at a whorehouse just outside of town and refused to pay. Roughed up some of the girls there, too. Dared the madam to go to the sheriff with it and laughed in her face as he was leaving. Supposedly bragged about it in a saloon later. That's where Sarah's cousin heard the tale. You're son is five years old and there's been no other scandalous tales about you since he was born. I heard the talk about you and Sam, but I knew Sam all his life and I don't put any stock in those tales. Now, what I said earlier about you and men still holds. If you agree, you can move into the little house today. If you don't agree, you best be on your way. Daylight's wasting."

Kate looked him in the eye and agreed. She would prove to him, one day at a time, that she was a better person than he believed her to be. He and Sarah smiled at her and sat back. Kate went out to the front porch and retrieved her bags, telling her son that they had a new home. They walked out to the little house.

~ * ~

Angus hadn't exaggerated when he said it was small. There weren't even two beds really. One narrow iron bedstead stood in the corner and there was a trundle bed underneath it. A small washstand stood next to it. When Kate opened one of the doors, she found a chamber pot inside. A small wooden table with two chairs stood before the fieldstone fireplace that contained a metal swing arm for hanging a cook pot on. It was sparse and bare, but it was her own for the time being. She swung her son up into her arms and danced him around the small place in a strenuous polka. Her heart sang. Free! They were free! No matter how small and mean this place, she could live here and close the door and no one would disturb her. John Wesley was laughing happily at her antics. She circled the room a few more times, then set him on his feet, curtsying deeply before him. A shadow blocked the evening light coming through the door, causing her to look up. Sarah stood there, a cook pot dangling from one hand, some linens and a basket in her arms, and an inscrutable look in her eyes.

"I brought you some supper and some other things you'll need." she said. "I expect you haven't eaten in a while and I know growing boys are always hungry."

She set her burdens on the table and turned to go. Kate stopped her.

"Thank you," she said softly. "I suspect it was you that got Angus to agree to letting us stay here. You won't regret it."

Sarah gave her an enigmatic smile and went out of the cabin.

Kate took the lid off the cook pot. The smell of beef stew rose into the air like the sweetest perfume she had ever smelled. Opening the basket, she found bowls, plates and cutlery, a three-legged skillet and a couple of pots with handles. She quickly spooned out two bowls full of stew. Removing the basket and the linens to the bed, she motioned John Wesley to take one of the chairs. She sat in the other and they both wolfed down the wonderful stew. Their first meal in their own home.

~ * ~

With a start, she realized that this was the first time in her life that she had had her own place. Always before there had been someone else to whom the home belonged. First her parents home, then her sister's home, then the Stancel's home, then the Richmond's home. She quickly turned her thoughts away from the Richmond's. She wouldn't be dealing with them ever again, though she would miss Rebecca and wondered what tale James had told to explain her leaving.

She made up both beds with the linens brought by Sarah and tucked her son into the trundle bed. She kissed him softly on the forehead as his eyes closed. Feeling restless, she wandered outside to look around the garden.

Huge old oak trees, bright green with the first early leaves of spring, formed a natural canopy over the tiny house. Kate was grateful for those. They would keep the house from getting overly hot during the summertime. Wild honeysuckle, that smelled thickly sweet, tumbled over a broken down split log fence nearby. Around back, several feet into the woods, she found an old outhouse. It was practically falling down, but she thought a few nails and maybe a couple of new boards were all that would be needed to make it usable again. She would ask Sarah soon about the nails and a couple of boards to make the repairs. Twilight was falling and with it the crickets began fiddling and the frogs harrumphing. Stars began to wink like tiny diamonds in a black velvet sky. With a sigh of deep contentment, Kate went back into her new home and got into her narrow bed. Tomorrow would be a busy day. Listening to the music of a country night, she fell into a deep, peaceful sleep.

Thirty-six

Her new life suited her just fine. She helped Sarah to milk the cows every morning and evening, along with planting the vegetable garden, making soap and churning butter. It was honest, clean work and her nights and evenings were her own, to be spent in the company of her son and no one else. Kate thanked God on her knees every night for this sanctuary. Some of the bitterness born of James' atrocious behavior began to leave her as she became more and more secure in her new home.

She and Sarah, along with Eileen, worked side by side often with the chores, but the older woman remained reticent with her. When Sarah spoke, it was in a kind tone, but her eyes told Kate that they would not soon be good friends. Kate rarely saw Angus and his son, Sean, and then usually from a distance. Angus had plowed the garden spot while she and Sarah and Eileen were busy with other business, so that when they began planting, he was never around anywhere. As they worked together, sowing the seeds that would provide their food for the next year, Kate sometimes wondered what the future held for her. She was proving, day-by-day, to the McIntoshes that she was not the woman public opinion made her out to be. Gradually, she would make friends with Sarah and the rest of the family, but what then? Would she be able to build on those friendships and make a place for her children here? She sighed, shook her head and went on with the planting.

She asked Sarah about nails and a few boards to repair the old outhouse and Sarah promised to have it taken care of, brushing off her protests that she could make the repairs herself if she just had the tools and materials. She returned to the house one evening to find that the repairs had been made and the outhouse was as good as new. John Wesley spent his days in or near the house and told her that Sean had come and made the repairs. She thanked Sarah profusely the next day, only to be told that it was customary for the property owner to supply a decent home for the workers.

Summer arrived and each day blazed hotter and hotter. Only half way through her pregnancy, but suffering already from swollen hands and ankles, Kate prayed nightly for rain to come and cool the weather. The vegetables in the garden all ripened at once and she spent hours, picking them. More hours were spent shelling peas and beans and shucking corn. Cucumbers were sliced and prepared to make pickles and relishes. Apples and peaches were gathered. These were strung and dried to make apple or peach pies over the coming months. The remainder of the peaches were made into peach jelly. The rest of the apples were stored in the cold darkness of the root cellar. Orderly rows of hanging dried fruits and vegetables slowly filled the earthen shelves of the root cellar under the house. Kate, Sarah and Eileen were all rushing from sun-up to sundown with the need to preserve all the vegetables and fruits and still complete their other chores. Sarah told her that in return for the work she did in the garden and her help with the preserving, she could take a share of the vegetables and fruits they preserved to be used for herself. It was a blessed relief to go to her home each evening, fix a meal for herself and her son and listen quietly to his small adventures of the day.

Sarah became friendlier as the months passed and she came to know Kate for herself. She often sent treats home with her for John Wesley, who loved the gingerbread men and cobblers. Eileen followed her mother's lead. The three of them talked as they worked.

Sometimes comparing recipes for preserving, sometimes just talking about the farm in general. They never discussed Kate's past except for areas that were neutral. She would occasionally volunteer an anecdote from her childhood to match the one's Sarah or Eileen told, but the years from 1867 until now were ignored. Sarah never asked anything about the Richmond's or about Kate's years with the Stancel's. Kate thought Eileen was probably curious, but she never broached any sensitive topic with her. They sometimes talked about upcoming socials or picnics, but since Kate refused to attend any of them as a guest of the McIntoshes, there really wasn't much to say. Eileen was full of talk about one beau or another and Kate sometimes felt a twinge of jealousy toward the younger woman. Not about having young men chasing her, she had decided never to trust another man, but rather that Eileen still had her whole unsullied life ahead of her and was transparently happy with herself. Kate knew that she would never again be so innocent or carefree as the young woman in front of her.

On one subject Kate was adamant and it caused a small amount of friction between the two women. Sarah wanted her to attend church with the family. She refused. Sarah argued that John Wesley was well old enough to be attending. That Kate was doing him a disservice by not taking him to church. That the people of the community might change their opinion of her if she was seen to be raising her son the right way. She agreed with Sarah on principal, but could not forget the unforgiving tongues of those church members when she had been carrying John Wesley. To go there now, obviously with child again, was more than she was willing to chance. She would not give them the opportunity to scorn her again. Sarah relented and Kate continued to stay home while the McIntosh family attended church services, picnics and socials.

The months passed swiftly and soon the evenings grew cooler. Kate was grateful for the fireplace in her home which kept the place warm and snug against the growing cold. She had John Wesley go out into the woods every day gathering deadfall to be used for kindling and Angus brought over a cord of freshly cut wood to stack and cure for her use during the winter months. The trees began showing their fiery fall colors. Sugar maples blazed crimson red next to the golden yellow elms. One afternoon as she was making her way home from the Mcintosh house, smiling at John Wesley's shouts of laughter, she realized that someone else was there with him. Another voice laughed aloud along with her son's. Quickening her pace, wondering who could possibly be playing with her son, she came in sight of the house and saw a young boy with curly dark hair, all elbows and knees, jumping into a huge pile of leaves. He stood up still laughing and caught sight of her. He went silent as he watched her approach.

"Hello, Rufus," she said. "I'm surprised to see you over here."

Rufus looked embarrassed and John Wesley piped up, "He's been coming here a couple of times a week, Mama. He thought you might be upset about it and asked me not to tell you. I told him you wouldn't mind."

"No, I don't mind Rufus coming here to play with you. What I do mind is you keeping secrets from me, John Wesley."

"Don't be mad at him, Aunt Kate. I made him promise not to tell, cause I wanted to get to know him. I thought maybe you wouldn't like it, seeing as how our families don't get along no more."

Kate looked sharply at her young nephew, wondering just how much he might have said to her son on the subject of why their families didn't get along anymore. He looked back at her with all the innocence a young boy could muster. She had to smile. Surely, if he had told anything to John Wesley, her son wouldn't have been able to resist asking her questions. She relaxed her guard and said, "Come on in the house and I'll fix us all something to eat. You're welcome to come over here any time you like Rufus. Just don't get yourself in trouble with your Mama."

John Wesley came to her and hugged her hard, then they all went into the house together. They boys played quietly while Kate fixed a simple dinner for all of them. She watched them as she prepared the meal. They seemed to get along well despite the difference in their ages. Kate knew that John Wesley missed his friend Timmy from Purdy. He needed friends near his own age. She felt a stab of guilt that it was her fault that he didn't have those friends. She only hoped that Savannah didn't find out that her young son was spending time here. It was good to see Rufus again and he was full of talk of the doings of everyone in the community. Soon, Kate sent him on his way, knowing that his mother and father would be wondering where he had gotten to. He hugged her and thanked her for the dinner and went on his way, whistling as he crossed the small yard into he woods. John Wesley was yawning where he sat. Kate told him to get washed up and into bed. The late stages of pregnancy caused her to tire easily, so she got into bed as soon as she had cleared away the supper dishes.

Thirty-seven

Her second son came wailing into the world during the storms of winter. In defiance of the Confederate veterans in the area, she gave him the name Sherman. Sarah shook her head over that decision and said it would do the boy no good to grow up with *that* name and Kate for a mother in the bargain, but Kate was firm. Her second son would be named Sherman. John Wesley was delighted to have a little brother to play with and wanted to know when the new baby would be able to run and play with him like their cousin, Rufus. With a gentle smile, Kate told her excited young son that it would be a few years before little Sherman would be able to run and play, but that John Wesley must always look out for his younger brother and see that no harm came to him.

A week after the birth, Sarah dropped by the little house and told Kate that they should take Sherman to Refuge to have him baptized. Kate just smiled grimly at her friend and said that she doubted that the self-righteous Reverend Thatcher would sully himself to baptize a bastard. Besides, John Wesley had never been baptized and she didn't see that it had done him any harm so far. When the boys were grown men, then they could decide on their own if they wanted to be baptized. If Reverend Thatcher was still around by then and refused them, then they would at least be old enough to understand the bigotry behind the action and not grow up stigmatized by the knowledge that the man would not baptize them as children.

"Kate!" Sarah finally exploded in exasperation. "You should come to church with us. Everyone there knows that you're living here near us and that you have become my friend. There are people there who will speak kindly to you."

"Who?" Kate interrupted loudly. "My loving sister, Savannah? Oh yes, I can see her face now if I was to walk through that hallowed door. Oh my yes," she continued sarcastically, " I can just see it now. Savannah will rush to embrace me and beg my forgiveness for all the years of pain I've lived. And her wonderful husband, Tom will be right behind her with tears in his eyes. Yes, I can see it so clearly now!"

"Kate, Kate. There's no call to be like this. We both know that your sister would not be one of the one's to welcome you. I think you do her a disservice with your contempt. *She* has suffered these years, too."

"She's suffered! *She's* suffered! She had it in her power to save me from what happened with James Richmond. She had it in her power to keep me from living on the charity of Negros. She just didn't have the backbone to stand up to anybody! She could have stood by me all those years ago, she could have made the last seven years of my life different! Well, let me tell you something, Sarah. So many people around here look down on the Negros as stupid and lazy and ignorant, but *they* were the ones who took me in. *They* gave me a home and love and laughter when all I wanted was to die. They saved my miserable life and gave without asking anything in return. I gave them the only thing of value I had left in an attempt to repay a tiny portion of their kindness. That was the ability to read and write and for that they were almost killed and had to leave the area! Those riders who came around and scared the life out of all of us are probably members of the very church you want me to go to. Those people are nothing but a bunch of pious hypocrites and I don't want anything to do with them. Refuge! Hah! That place is no refuge for me! I was told to get out a long time ago and I have no intentions of going back there."

"Kate, I understand your anger. I saw what was happening all those years ago. I felt you deserved a chance to continue your life the way you had always lived, and I did nothing to stop what was happening. By doing nothing, I am just as guilty as those who publicly scorned you. Maybe if *I* had said something then, had spoken to Savannah in kindness, it would have been enough to help her hold up under the strain, but I said nothing. We'll never know if my friendship would have made a difference in what happened, but you should realize that Savannah has suffered. Certainly not on the same level as you have, but you should try to find it in your heart to understand her. You rant on and on that she didn't understand or stand by you and yet *you* refuse to understand *her*.

"I cain't believe your taking up for *Savannah*! How can you stand there and say these things to me and claim to be my friend?"

"Kate, I'm not taking up for Savannah! I'm just trying to get you to see that some people are stronger than others. That sometimes people do the wrong thing for what they think is the right reason. You've already shown yourself to be much stronger than your sister just by surviving everything you've been through. *And* by harping on Savannah you've managed to change the subject. You should come to church and bring your sons with you. Hold your head up girl! I've known Mary Stancel all my life and her son Sam all of his and I know that they tried to tell you the same thing. When are you going to get off this farm and get a life for yourself?

"I don't see what going to church has got to do with getting a life for myself. I'm doing just fine as it is. I've got you and Angus and Eileen and Sean. I don't need any more friends. I'm happy. I'm doing just fine thank you."

"Kate, I don't have to explain to you why it's so important that you start going to church with us. You already know the answer to that. The church is the center of the social lives of this community. You are never going to have a place in this community until you join the church again and you know it. Your boys will have no kind of social life if they aren't part of that community."

"My boys will do just fine with me and your family for social life. They don't need the ugliness that they'll find directed at them by the so-called pillars of this society. Heaven only knows what kind of nastiness John Wesley hears at school. He never says a word about anything that goes on over there." An echo of the past floated across

Kate mind, the tearstained face of her young nephew and the question he had asked, *"What's a whore, Mama?"* Was John Wesley enduring the same torments his older cousin had heard as a small child? If he was enduring those torments, he never let on to his mother. A shudder chased its way down her spine at the thought of the spite of ignorant children mouthing the words they heard from their parents. Little savages that's all they were! Ignorant little savages!

"No, Sarah, I won't be going to church with ya'll. I'm happier now than I've been in a long while. Let's just leave things alone, please."

Sarah searched the younger woman's eyes and sighed with resignation. There was no moving Kate when she was in this state of mind. Maybe in a few months or maybe in a year, Kate would change her mind and follow good advice. For the moment she would let the matter rest.

Thirty-eight

By the time Sherman was five, Kate and her sons had settled firmly into life with the Mcintoshes. Sarah and Kate were fast friends and Angus had softened his attitude toward the young woman who had caused so much trouble on his property those years ago, then come here looking for a home, pregnant with yet another bastard child. Sean and Eileen treated John Wesley and Sherman like younger brothers and often took them out riding in the farm wagon or fishing in nearby creeks. Kate settled peacefully into the life she thought would be hers for the time she had left. With a lot of practice, she had managed to put the ugliness of the past behind her. She would never forgive her family for their betrayal, but she found it in her heart to put all of it out of her mind and look to the future.

One piece of news, brought from Purdy by Angus, stirred olds anger for a short time. Angus reported that all the talk at Purdy that day had been about Judge Fielding Hurst. He had died and the good citizens of Purdy had refused to let him be buried there. He had been buried at Mt. Gilead instead, near the Hurst Nation. "The Nation" as was usually referred to, was the stronghold of the Hurst clan. They kept very much to themselves and were rarely seen outside the boundaries of their property. Once someone married into the clan, they were rarely seen again by outsiders. Angus reported with some disgust that unknown people had ridden their horses over the grave of Judge Hurst, allowing them to urinate and shit on the grave. One soul had gone so far as to dig up the body, set it on fire and leave it burning in the road. The atrocities attributed to him during the War were enough to make anyone's blood run cold. Murder and torture of Confederate soldiers during the years he led the 6th Calvary being the worst of a long list. Later, the man had ruled the county with an iron fist for nearly twenty years, even going so far as to have the sheriff get jurors from "the Nation" so that the outcome of any trial would be the verdict he wanted to get. Kate shivered at the news. Judge Hurst was the name that James Richmond had invoked so many years ago to coerce her into becoming his mistress.

"I never had much use for the man myself." Angus remarked. "He was cold and hard, but folks ought to have some respect for the dead."

Kate thought it had been a fitting epithet for the man, but kept her thoughts to herself. Though her brothers had fought and died under his command, she knew they would never have approved the atrocities he committed in later years regardless of his own sense of justification, or the way he had ruled the county after the War.

~ * ~

John Wesley had left school the year before, claiming he had learned all he ever needed to know during the years he had spent there. Kate still wondered exactly what the other children had said to him over the course of those years, but John Wesley never volunteered any information and she was too afraid to ask him. He had become a quiet withdrawn young boy, thoughtful and kind, but without the open heart he had had as a small child. He had never brought any other children to the farm to play during his free time. His only friends remained his brother, his cousin, Rufus and the Mcintosh children who were so much older. Kate didn't protest his quitting school. He had the rudiments of an education. Anything else he needed to learn she could teach him herself.

He began working with Sean Mcintosh in the fields, learning the life of a farmer. At the age of thirteen, he was a tall little boy with the air of manhood already hanging over him. He worked diligently with Sean to become the best farmer he could learn to be. He almost broke Kate's heart one evening when he told her he was working so hard so that in a few years, when he was a man, he could help her to get a few acres for themselves. Then they wouldn't be so dependent on the

Mcinotoshes for every little thing they had. It was a swift look into the heart of her son. He burned for the acceptance that they still did not have, even though Kate had given in several years ago to Sarah's pleading and began attending church service with the Mcintosh family. Kate's' own circle of friends had grown slightly in the intervening years, but her sons still had no friends of their own age. The prejudice of the neighborhood still held and her kin would not allow their children to associates with Kate's'. Her own new friends were older and had grown children with lives of their own and no time for the two small outsiders standing in the shadows of their mother's shame.

~ * ~

That fall, the weather was strange. Far too warm for that time of year. One afternoon the sky began to darken early. Black clouds blew in from the West, blotting out the afternoon sun. A yellow green light cast odd shadows. Knowing what might be coming, Kate hurried through her tasks and ran back the cabin, pushing against the increasing force of the wind. She found John Wesley and Sherman playing calmly on the floor with some marbles she had gotten for them. They looked up as she rushed through the door.

"What's wrong, Mama?" John Wesley asked.

"There's a bad storm blowing in son. I had to make sure ya'll were here and not out playing somewhere." She sat down at the table and said, "We'll have to stay in here till it blows over. It looks like it'll be a bad un."

Outside, the wind moaned and howled in the treetops. It was now dark as midnight. A particularly harsh gust of wind rattled the door and window of the cabin and made the walls shudder. Taking Sherman by the hand, she motioned John Wesley over to the floor next to the bed. They had been cowering there for nearly an hour when the door burst open on its hinges and slammed against the wall. Angus rushed in and grabbed John Wesley by the hand.

"I don't like the sound of that wind nor the color of those clouds." he shouted over the roar of the wind. "We're gonna set it out in the storm cellar. Ya'll need to be there, too. These big trees around the cabin could crash down on it. Come on now, we're gonna make a run for it. Sarah and the children are already there."

They ran out into the weather and the wind immediately pulled Kate's hair loose from its pins. It streamed in a wild mane across her face and whipped in the wind. Carrying Sherman firmly in both arms, she couldn't reach up to clear her hair from her eyes. Shaking her head vigorously from side to side, she tried unsuccessfully to dislodge the whipping mass. Keeping on her feet was a struggle. The pace set by Angus and the force of the wind combined to nearly pull her to the ground. Thirteen-year-old John Wesley's strong young arm came around her waist. He held her upright and attempted to drag her toward the safety of the storm cellar. A sudden shift in the wind pulled her hair from her face and she froze on the spot at what met her eyes. A funnel shape was easing down from the black mass that covered the sky. It writhed and twisted back and forth, snaking down and down and down from the black clouds as it moved ever closer. Horror struck her to the heart at the sight. If the tornado fought free of its mooring, it would wreak havoc on the surrounding area. Angus was at the door of the storm cellar, furiously motioning them to come. John Wesley tried desperately to drag her forward again. Sherman was screaming in fear and struggling in her arms. Taking a firmer grip on her squirming son, she unglued her feet from the ground and ran for safety. Angus slammed and bolted the cellar door, then turned on her.

"What in the name of God were you doing out there gal?" he hollered over the howling wind. "You could get killed standing around gawking like that."

"Now, Angus," interjected Sarah, "Cain't you see the girl is scared through? The sight of a twister is enough to freeze anyone on the spot for a minute. You just leave her be."

Angus subsided grumpily onto one of the boards that had been fashioned into benches along the walls of the shelter. Sarah put a comforting arm around Kate. They all sat quietly listening to the force of the wind outside. Even Sherman remained quiet, as though the feeling of fear and tension around him had stopped his tears at their source. Kerosene lanterns cast shadowy light around the earthen room creating bizarre phantoms in the corners. The stout wooden door shuddered and heaved like a living thing. Particles of dirt sifted down through the cracks in the board ceiling. Kate found herself praying silently. *Yea tho I walk through the valley of the shadow of death I will feel no evil.* Strange how in times of extreme duress her mind conjured up the half forgotten prayers of her girlhood. Little Sherman trembled in her arms and she could see John Wesley's chin quivering though he tried mightily to appear unafraid. It seemed an eon before daylight began to show through the cracks in the door.

Angus stood up and listened intently. Going to the door, he peered cautiously through a crack, then stood back and unbolted the door. Sunlight poured into the room. They all breathed a sigh of relief that the twister had passed. Emerging from the shelter, they stood blinking in the dazzling light. As their eyes adjusted, they stared horrified at the sight of the destruction around them. The twister had cut a swath across the Mcintosh land that extended out of the line of their vision. Looking behind them, they were relieved to see that the farmhouse still stood although several shingles had been torn from the roof and the shutters sagged drunkenly on their hinges. With a cry of alarm, Kate handed Sherman to Sarah and took off at a run toward her home. The path of destruction ran on a straight line in that direction. She arrived to find that several of the large old trees that she had so loved for their shade on hot summer days, had fallen directly on the little cabin, demolishing it. Splintered wood and broken glass was all that lay beneath the giant trunks. John Wesley came panting behind her. They stood together silently looking at the loss of their home. Picking her way carefully through the rubble, Kate located the washstand that had stood beside her bed. It lay almost completely flat on the ground directly under one of the trees. On the ground beside it, smashed beyond repair lay the carved box that Sam had given her on the day the Stancel's had left the county. Picking up the shards of wood, Kate held them close to her, shedding tears for the loss of a precious gift. John Wesley reached past her and pulled his wooden horse and wagon from the wreckage. It too was crushed beyond repair.

"Why, Mama?" he asked. "Why is it that everything that is precious to us, the only things we own for ourselves had to get destroyed?"

"Son, this was a horrible act of nature. It weren't directed at us personally. It just happened. There's no explanation for it. It just happened. That's all."

"I remember the day that Sam gave me this toy." he mused. "I'm too old for it now, but I wanted to keep it to remember Sam and Aunt Mary. They loved us a lot and I don't ever want to forget how good they were to us when I was a little boy."

"Son, we don't need these things to remember Sam and Aunt Mary. They'll always be in our hearts, wherever we go and however long we live, they'll always be there. You know that don't you?"

"Yes, Mama, I know. But I would have liked to have kept this toy always. Just as something I could touch when I remembered them. You cain't touch memories, Mama. They're just pictures in your head. You cain't show them to somebody the way you can show something that they gave you. This little toy seemed to make the pictures clearer when I was holding it. I was going to let Sherman play with it someday and tell him all about Aunt Mary and Sam and the kids I used to play with when I was little. Now I don't have anything to show to Sherman, just memories to tell him about people he never knew."

"I know, honey. I know just how you feel. This here box was something I treasured because it was a gift of love. Whenever I held it in my hands, I could see Sam and Aunt Mary clear as day, just like they were standing right in front of me. The box is broke now. It cain't be fixed, but I will always remember the love behind the gift. I had to learn a long time ago that you cain't always keep the material things that bring back memories, but you'll always have the memories themselves. Like a picture book in your head that you can take out and look through any time you want to. They're pictures you cain't share with anybody, because they cain't see 'em, but they're worth keeping all the same."

Angus and Sarah came up just then.

"Good Lord!" Angus breathed. "Look at that! Thank God I came and got ya'll out of there. Ya'll woulda' been dead for sure it I hadn't."

"Angus!" Sarah cried, "No need to dwell on what didn't happen.

They're all right and we'll see it through just like it never happened. Kate, I give Sherman to Eileen to take back to the house. You and John Wesley come on and go to the house with us. Ya'll will stay there till we work out something." Seeing the wood shards in Kate's hands and the broken toy in John Wesley's, she said softly, "I'm sorry as I can be that them there things got broke. I know they were treasures to the both of you."

"Ya'll go on back to the house," Kate said. "Me and John Wesley will be there directly."

With a last look at the two of them and a nod of reassurance, Angus and Sarah went slowly away.

"Come on son, let's see if we can find anything worth saving. Clothes cain't get broke, neither can iron cook pots and pans, so maybe we can get them and take em with us to Angus and Sarah's house. We'll be needing 'em wherever we live next.

Water dripped steadily from the trees still standing and everything was soaked through. Leaves ripped from surrounding trees covered the ground in a soggy mass. It was a depressing sight. They stood silently looking, not quite having the heart to plunged into the muck.

"Come on, son. It won't get done any quicker with us just a standing here looking at it."

Thirty-nine

They climbed carefully through the wreckage picking up sodden clothing and cooking utensils, tossing them out to clearer ground.

"Mama?"

"Yes, son?"

"What you were saying before, about learning to let go of things that remind you of good times. Did you mean things that belonged to you when you were a little girl? Things that your Mama and Daddy gave to you?"

"Yes, son, I did."

When she said no more, John Wesley continued in a low voice, "You have never told me anything about them or about my daddy either."

Kate froze in the act of picking up her three-legged frying pan. Her heart skipped a beat. Here it was. The questions she had been fearing for so long. She had known this day would come, but had hoped it would be further down the road when John Wesley was a little older and might better understand some of her answers. She didn't want to talk about Michael, but the boy had a right to know something about his daddy. Shying away from that particular subject, she started with her parents.

"Your Gramma and Grampa would have loved you very much. They were wonderful people. I wish with all my heart that you could have known them."

"What'd they die of, Mama?"

"Grief mostly, son. Grief and not having enough good food to eat. When the war was going on, soldiers come through here all the time. Soldiers from both sides traveling to the next battle site. There was some big battles not far from here. At Shiloh and Pittsburgh Landing and at Corinth in Mississippi. The soldiers were always taking food when they come through. We had to survive on what ever we could hide or grow between their visits. But the grief part was want done em in. You had two Uncles. John and Andrew. They was older than me and signed up with the Union Army back in the spring of '62. They was killed in a battle at a place called Parker's Crossroads up north of here a ways. Both of em on the same day. When Mama and Daddy got word of it, it just seemed to take the life out of both of em. They was never the same after that. They just got weaker and weaker and slower and slower and then they died. It just hurt my heart so bad to see em like that. They didn't want to live no more after their boys were gone. Our whole world had changed. There wasn't no going back to the old ways. They knew that and so did I. I really wished they had lived though, to see you and what a fine young man you're turning into. They would have loved you very, very much."

Silently, John Wesley looked into her eyes, as though probing to see if her words were the truth. "Are you sure about that, Mama?" He challenged. "Are you sure they would have loved a bastard grandson so much?"

"John Wesley! How can you say such a thing?" she gasped.

"Well, it's true ain't it? I'm a bastard ain't I? My daddy din't never marry you, did he?" At her shocked expression, he continued, "I hope you din't think I don't know all about it, Mama. I done heard a lot about it after we come here to live and I went to the school with the other kids from around here. I asked Rufus about it onc't, but he said don't never say anything to you about it cause it would only hurt you, but I gotta know the truth, Mama. I ain't a baby no more. I need to know the truth."

He was right. He did have a right to know, but what could she tell him about his father? That the man had been a liar who ran like his britches were on fire when he found out Kate was pregnant? She just couldn't tell him that. Her own hate for Michael became tangled in her son's need to know something about the man who had fathered him. How could she tell this innocent child that she had been taken in by some slick talk. Been betrayed by her own needs. She <u>must</u> put aside her own feelings and give her son something he could live with that was not a complete lie, yet was not quite the whole truth. What to say? How to begin? John Wesley watched her steadily, waiting. Waiting for whatever truth she could bring herself to tell him. She decided to start with the easy part.

"I *know* that your grandparents would have loved you very much. There's not one doubt in my mind about that. Don't you ever doubt it either. As for your daddy, well, this is hard for me, son. I don't know quite what to say. It was all so long ago and I've pretty near put it out of my mind. Your father was a handsome man." At John Wesley's look of impatience, she stumbled on, "I reckon that don't much matter to you, but it mattered to me at the time. I was lonesome and sad and he came along at just that time. Such a fine handsome man, with a way about him that could charm the birds right out of the trees. All the young women here abouts were crazy about him, but he seemed to want me. I know you ain't a baby no more, son, but you ain't quite growed yet either, when you're a little bit older you'll understand better about that kind of thing. The truth is, I fell in love with him. Just flat dab in love with the man. He said he loved me too and I believed him. We made plans to get married that fall after the cotton was in." Kate fell silent remembering that happy time in her life, before all the betrayals that had led her to this place with this heart hungry young boy for whom she realized there would be no explanation that would not bring him pain.

"Mama?" John Wesley interrupted her thoughts. "What happened then? Why didn't you get married like you planned?"

Looking into her sons' bright blue eyes, Kate would have given anything in that moment not to have to answer that question. Not to have to reveal to her son what a fool she had been and what a rogue his father had been. Swallowing against the sudden dryness in her throat she said, "The fact of the matter is that I loved him so much that I let him talk me into doing something I knew was wrong. I let him talk me into having relations with him that a man and woman shouldn't have until after they're married. Do you understand what I mean?"

He nodded without saying a word. Ears pink with embarrassment.

"Then, when I knew I was going to have a baby, I was plumb scared to death. I knew I was in big trouble, but I thought me and your daddy would just go on ahead and get married and everything would be all right. It didn't turn out that way though. Your daddy said he was going to see the reverend and fix up a wedding date for us. I never saw him again."

John Wesley's face had grown whiter and whiter with each damning word she spoke. His slender young shoulders sagged till he was as slumped as an old man. Finally, eyes blazing, he burst out. "Why did you do something like that when you knew it was wrong? No wonder he just took off! You acted like a whore with him just like everybody has always said about you! You're the reason I'm a bastard and nobody wants to have nothing to do with me! It's all your fault! I'll never forgive you! Never!" Turning his back on her he raced away through the woods.

"John Wesley!" she shouted. "John Wesley, you come back here right this minute!"

The sounds of his mad dash away from her receded further and further until she could not hear them any longer. He had rejected her thoroughly. Her heart swelled in her chest until it felt it would burst, leaving her dead amongst the shattered love of her son.

"JOHN WESLEY!!!!!" she screamed at the top of her lungs. And again, "JOHN WESLEY!!!!" The cords of her throat stood out like oak limbs, pressure built behind her eyes until they felt they would burst from their sockets, her throat became raw and bloody and still she screamed, "JOHN WESLEY!!!"

Angus burst into the clearing like a shot fired from a cannon. His eyes darted from side to side looking for the source of Kate's anguish. There was only Kate. Standing alone and screaming her son's name. Grasping her arms, he shook her hard, but the screaming continued unabated. Finally, regretting the necessity of striking a woman, he hit her sharply across the face with the back of his hand. The screaming stopped immediately to be replaced by sobbing that nearly broke his heart with its harshness. She slumped into his arms, whispering her son's name over and over again.

"Kate!" He shook her once again, trying to break through to her. "Kate! Look at me lass! What's happened? Where's John Wesley?"

The huge cornflower blue eyes stared emptily into his own. What he saw there made his soul quake in fear. "Gone," she whispered. "Run off. Gone, gone, gone, gone."

Angus was no longer a young man, but fright lent strength to his arms as he scooped her off her feet and took off back to his house at a jogging pace. She was dead weight in his arms. Goose bumps pricked his skin as she continued to whisper against his neck, like a madwoman. "Gone, gone, gone, gone, gone, gone."

He was immensely relieved when the house came into view. "Sarah!" he called. "Git on out here and help me!"

Sarah came to the porch. When she saw her husband carrying the limp form across the yard, she shouted for Sean to come help his daddy. Sean appeared from the house and ran to take the limp burden from his father's arms. Angus staggered to the porch steps and gratefully sank down, breathing hard from the run with his heavy burden. Sean carefully laid Kate on the porch and stepped back. "Gone, gone, gone, gone," Kate continued to whisper brokenly.

"My God, Angus," breathed Sarah, looking with horror on the

pitiful state of the younger woman. "What's happened? Why is she saying "gone" over and over like that?"

"Don't rightly know exactly what happened. I heard her a screaming in the woods. When I got there she was staring off into the woods and screaming for John Wesley at the top of her voice. I'm sorry to say I had to slap her to get her to stop screaming. Then she just started saying "gone" over and over again. I figured I better get her back her where you could look out for her. John Wesley must've took off for some reason and she's gone off her head. You look after her Sarah. Me and Sean will look through the woods for the boy. He couldn't have gone far. I'll tan his hide when I git my hands on him. Sure as he was born, I'm gonna tan his hide for this."

"Angus, we don't know what happened out there. He must've had some kind of reason to just run off. He's a good boy. Let's hold off on the tanning and harsh talk till we find out exactly what happened."

"Humph!" muttered Angus. Rising from the porch, he motioned Sean to follow.

Forty

Sarah watched her husband and son until they disappeared into the trees, then knelt by the limp form lying on the porch. Eileen came to see what all the ruckus was about and gasped in dismay to see Kate lying nearly comatose on the porch. Sarah looked up and said, "Go one back in the house, Eileen. Keep Sherman busy playing. I don't want him seeing him Mama in this state." As her daughter hesitated, obviously wanting to help, Sarah repeated, "Go on in now. The best help you can be to me right now is to keep Sherman busy." Eileen retreated into the house without a word.

"Kate, honey, listen to me now. Angus and Sean have gone to find John Wesley. We can work out what ever has happened. Come on now, look at me Kate. Stop that whimpering. You're a stronger woman than that. Stop that whimpering and tell me what happened."

A moan escaped from Kate's parched lips. Her tongue came out and licked at them tentatively. Rising to her feet, Sarah went to the water bucket on the porch and scooped up a dipper full of water. Kneeling beside Kate again, she raised the younger woman's shoulders and held the dipper to her lips. Kate drank greedily. Finally the eyes began to focus. Sarah breathed a sigh of relief.

"Sit up now. That's right, sit on up. You cain't be solving any problems a laying down and moaning about em. Now, you tell me what happened out there in the woods."

Kate's sad eyes met the loving concern in Sarah's. She began to weep tiredly. "Oh, Sarah", she wept. "He's run off. My boy has run off. Help me get him back, please."

"Angus and Sean are out combing the woods to find him. They'll bring him back, don't you worry none about that. Tell me why he run off like that."

"He asked me about his daddy, Sarah. What was I supposed to tell him? He has a right to know what happened. I couldn't bring myself to tell him a pack of lies. So, I told him the truth, as soft and easy as I could. He just went to pieces right in front of me. Told me he'd never forgive me for his being born a bastard. Oh, Sarah, what am I gonna do?"

Sarah stiffened in shock at the explanation. Of course the boy would want to know about his daddy, had probably heard all kinds of horrors from others already, but to hear that awful truth from his mother's lips must have been more than his young heart could bear. She knew that when John Wesley was brought back home there would be hard times ahead between him and his mother.

"Come on," she said to Kate. "Let's get you in the house and in a comfortable chair. It won't bring John Wesley back any quicker for us to sit out here on this hard old porch. We'll just have to wait till they bring him home, then we can start to straighten this out. I don't reckon you could have done any different than to tell him the truth, but I imagine it was hard for him to hear. He'll be back. You mark my words. Come on now, up with you and into the house. All we can do right now is to wait."

~ * ~

Angus and Sean tramped through the wet woods, stepping over fallen tree limbs ripped loose earlier by the twister, slipping on fallen leaves, pausing occasionally to call John Wesley's name and listen for any response.

"Damn it to hell!" cried Angus. "What do you figure go into the boy to make him run off like this?"

"Daddy, I reckon he finally got around to asking his Mama about his Daddy. I seen it coming for a while now. I knew it was only a matter of time. I was hoping he would take it better than this."

Angus looked at his son, aghast. "You don't mean to tell me you think she told him the truth do you?"

"I reckon she didn't have no other choice. The boy has probably heard all kinds of shit from the other kids around here over the years. What was she gonna tell him that he would believe?"

"Damnation!" Angus stomped ahead of his son, looking closely for signs of a young boys' flight through the woods, but the mess caused by the twister hid any tracks that might have been left. What a sorry mess <u>this</u> was, but Sean was probably right in his guess as to what had happened. They had to find the boy and begin to mend the breech with his mother as soon as possible. The longer John Wesley brooded over this, the harder it would be to put it behind him.

Passing near the Claiborne place, they saw Rufus outside surveying the storm damage. It was not much. The farm had not been in the direct path of the twister. Seeing the two men walking along the fringe of the woods, he came to join them.

"Rufus, you ain't seen any sign of John Wesley have you?" asked Angus.

"Why do you think he might be over this way?" Rufus asked in concern.

"We figure He got to talking to his Mama about his daddy. It looks like she told him the truth of the matter and he's done took off somewheres. Kate's just about our of her mind over it."

"Hell!" Rufus replied. "I *told* him a long time ago to leave it be and not ever ask his Mama about it. I knew something like this was gonna happen if he ever asked her me, if he won't answer either one of ya'll. It's getting late though. I hope we can find him before it gets dark. Won't be no moon tonight, so we'll have to stop looking at dark. Might do him some good to sit out by hisself all night though. Give him plenty of time to realize he ain't solving anything acting like this."

The three of them set off, continuing the search.

~ * ~

John Wesley sat huddled in the corner of the corncrib on the edge of the property where Jebidiah Lincoln sharecropped. Wet and miserable. His clothes muddy from a fall in his headlong dash away from his mother. He had run off wildly without any thought of where he would go. Knowing only that he had to get away from his mother and the awful truth she had confirmed. In his heart, he had known for a long time that the gossip must be true, but had hoped against all reason that his mother would have some other explanation. When she repeated to him the same story he had heard for years, he had thought he would die. How could his mother have behaved like that? She was so loving and kind. So careful that they learn right from wrong. How could she have insisted all these years that certain behavior was not acceptable when she had done the very things she had taught him were wrong? How could she be the whore that so many thought her to be and at the same time be the woman who instilled such stringent moral values in her sons? It just didn't make sense to him. He could not reconcile the two images in his mind and so, crouched miserably in the corncrib, alone and wretched. Very faintly, in the distance, he could hear male voices shouting his name. Angus and Sean and— Rufus? Rufus who had warned him to leave well enough alone. Rufus who had told him he would only cause trouble by asking such questions. He crouched even smaller into the corner, determined not to answer. He could not face the woman who was his mother and yet had revealed herself to be someone he didn't know this afternoon.

~ * ~

Cold, wet and tired, confused by the darkness after sunset, Angus told the others they were heading home. It would do no good to wander aimlessly in the dark. They would start out again at first light if John Wesley didn't show up at home before then. The three men trudged disconsolately back through the woods toward home. When they came in sight of the Claiborne farm, Rufus asked them to let him know as soon as John Wesley was found. His family had no use for the boy, but he was fond of his young cousin and concerned that he might come to harm alone in the woods at night. The Mcintoshes agreed to get word to him secretly as soon as John Wesley was located and continued back the their farmhouse.

As they came through the door Kate leapt to her feet, looking eagerly past them for her son.

"I'm sorry, Kate." said Angus. "We didn't find him. Rufus helped us to look, but it got too dark for us to see our hands in front of our faces. We'll have to wait till morning to start looking again. He can't have gone far. He's hiding out somewhere and not answering us, I'm sure. We'll get him back home. Don't you worry."

"He cain't stay out all night by himself. He's just a little boy! I shouldn't have ever told him the truth. I should have lied and lied and lied to keep him safe. " Kate rushed past them to the door. Angus caught her by the arm and gently led her back to her chair.

"There ain't no lie you could have told him that he would have believed in his heart. In the long run, it would have done more harm than good to have lied to him now. He'll come back. He just needs some time to get over what he's heard."

"Angus, you didn't hear what he said to me out there. He said he'd never forgive me for his being born a bastard. I've lost him, I just know I have."

"Kate," Sarah interjected softly, "young boys say things in anger and hurt that they don't really mean and regret later. You'll see. Everything will be just fine if you give him time to get over the shock. " Looking at her husband she said, "Did you say Rufus Claiborne was out there with you looking for him?"

"Sure was. He seemed mighty upset about the whole thing. He's fond of John Wesley. Said he told the boy to leave it alone, not ask questions."

"Good advice falling on deaf ears. It's a pity John Wesley didn't listen."

"Sarah!" Kate exclaimed. "He had the right to ask. Any boy would want to know about his daddy. I just wish he was older." Sighing wistfully, she added, "He might understand better if he was older."

"Well, let's all get to bed. We'll be up early in the morning to look for him again. He might even come back tonight. It's wet and cold out there. He'll be getting hungry, too. Might bring him to his senses."

Kate looked at them hopelessly, her eyes saying that she didn't believe a word of it. Turning slowly, she trudged upstairs to the room Sarah had set aside for her and lay fully dressed and wide-eyed on the bed.

Forty-one

At daybreak the next morning, Jebidiah Lincoln went to his corncrib to get feed for the chickens he kept. He found John Wesley curled in a tight ball in the corner and was so startled, he let out a yell. John Wesley woke with a start and stood defiantly before his old friend.

"John Wesley! Whut you doin' in dis here corn crib? Does yo Mama know you is gone?"

"I reckon she does," he replied in an unconcerned voice.

He knew immediately that something was not right here. Kate had raised this boy with better manners than this. Something must be sorely amiss for him to act so rudely. John Wesley continued to stand in silent defiance before him.

"Ah reckon yo Mama done plumb out o' huh mind wif worry if you been hiding out in heah all night. Come on in de house wif me. We'll hab some breakfus' and den ah'll tek you home."

"I ain't got a home no more. I'm on my own now. I ain't never going back there."

"Ah ain' got time fo sech foolishness." Jeb pulled the boy into the house, where his wife exclaimed with astonishment.

"De boy done runned away. Ah foun' him hidin' in de cawn crib. Ah'm gonna hitch up de mule and tek him back ter de Macintosh place right now. His Mama is prob'ly done out o huh mine wif worry."

"I ain't going back there, Jebidiah."

"Oh yes you is! Now, you jes' set yosef down here and my wife dish you up some grits. Soon's Ah git de mule hitched we is goin'."

Sula Lincoln placed a tin plate with grits on it and a fork in front of John Wesley. He ignored it and her, as if neither were there. When Jebidiah returned to the house, he took in the situation at a glance. Pulling the boy from his chair he shook him and said, "Wheah's yo manna's? Ah know yo Mama done taught you betta dan dis. Sula done dished up some breakfas' fo you. You sit down dere lak a young gentlman and eats it!"

John Wesley plopped rudely into the chair and began pushing the grits around the plate with the fork, not taking a single bite.

Cuffing the boy on the ear, Jebidiah said, "Ah tole you ter eat dem grits, boy!"

Sula stepped back, putting her hands to her mouth, eyes wide, as John Wesley sprang to his feet. He stood aggressively in front of Jebdidiah, rage hot in his eyes.

"Don't you be hittin' me and don't you call me 'boy'!" he spat.

Taken aback by the reaction, Jebidiah reached toward John Wesley, but the boy stepped back. Squaring his shoulders, Jebidiah said, "Awright then! Some devil done got into you and Ah ain' puttin' up wif dis kind of rudeness. You git on outside and on dat wagon or Ah sweah Ah'll tek a strap to yo backside."

John Wesley marched out of the cabin and climbed onto the seat of the wagon where he sat straight, looking neither left nor right.

Jebidiah climbed up beside him and they set off for the Mcintosh farm. They rode in complete silence. The young black man and the white boy. Neither offered to make any kind of conversation. The only sound was that of the wagon wheels on the rutted trail. The silence prevailed the entire two miles to the Mcintosh farm. When they pulled into the yard, Angus rushed outside to meet them.

"Jebidiah!" he cried. "Where did you find the little rascal? We were out half the night looking for him. John Wesley, you git on down from that wagon and go into the house and apologize to your Mama for taking off like that and worrying her out of her mind!"

John Wesley didn't move or speak. Angus looked to Jebidiah for an answer.

"Ah reckon de devil done got inter dis boy, Mist' Angus. He been surly lak dis evah since Ah foun' him in my cawn crib dis mawnin. Ah threathened ter tek a strap ter his backside iffen he didn't git on dis wagon and come on back heah wif me."

At that moment, Kate rushed from the house, straight to the wagon. Leaping up onto it, she threw her arm around her son, weeping on his shoulder. John Wesley didn't respond to his mother, continuing to sit like a wax dummy on the wagon seat. Tension hovered in the air, an almost palpable miasma. In distress and at a loss, Jebidiah looked past Kate to Angus. Angus reached up and gently removed Kate from the wagon. John Wesley continued to sit woodenly, as though nothing here concerned him. Reaching up again, Angus grabbed the boy by the arm and yanked him from the wagon seat. John Wesley sprawled in the dirt next to the wagon.

Jebidiah half rose from his seat, but Angus waved him back down. "Thank you for bringing the boy home," he said. "We'll take care of him. It was a misunderstanding between him and his Mama."

"Weren't no trouble bringing him back, Mist' Angus. Miz Kate was allus kind to me in de past. It weren't no trouble ter bring the boy home."

"He'll be all right now. You go on home, Jeb. I'm sure you got plenty to do this morning. And don't worry about the boy and his Mama. We'll make sure everything gets worked out betwixt them."

Nodding his head, Jebidiah turned the wagon and left the yard.

Kate was sprawled in the dirt next to her son, trying to get him to speak to her and getting no response. Angus strode over to them. "John Wesley, you get on up out of the dirt and speak to your Mama or I'll take a strap to you myself. You ain't doing nothing but causing more trouble acting like this."

Getting no response, Angus reached for the boy, but Kate reared up and pushed his hand away. "No, Angus. This is something me and John Wesley have to work out for ourselves. Just leave us here and we'll get started on it."

Marching angrily back into the house, Angus ruminated on the merits of a good thrashing for the boy. In his opinion, it would go far to get rid of the sullen attitude that John Wesley seemed to have adopted.

~ * ~

Kate continued to sit in the dirt next to her son. He still sprawled where he had fallen when Angus yanked him from the wagon and kept his face turned away from her. She reached out and stroked his hair. His already tense body turned rigid at her touch. She ached for the hurt she could feel vibrating throughout him. Spending the night alone hadn't soften his feelings toward her. If anything, it seemed to have made the situation even worse. She continued to stroke his hair lightly, saying nothing, hoping that eventually he would speak. When he finally did speak she was shocked to the core, his voice was so devoid of any emotion.

"Why didn't we go to Virginia with Sam and Aunt Mary?"

"It wasn't for us to go there." She replied in a careful voice.

"If we hadda' gone with them, everything would have been so different," came the hollow voice of her son.

"How do you think it would have been different in Virginia?" she asked softly.

"Nobody there would have known about me. Nobody would have known I'm a bastard like they do here. I coulda' had friends there. I coulda' been proud there. Here, nobody wants to be my friend because of you. Because they know all about you. Why did you make me stay here?"

"All of our people are here, John Wesley. I had a right to stay here and you don't have anything to be ashamed of."

"All of our *people* don't give a damn about us. If we died tomorrow they would care a bit. And I do have something to be ashamed of. I have to be ashamed of who I am because they remind me of it every day of my life. We should have gone to Virginia."

Sarah's words from the past came back to haunt Kate then. *Sometime people do the wrong thing for what they think is the right reason.* Was that what she had done? Condemned her child to a life of shame simply because she was too proud to leave? What about Sherman when he grew older? Would he feel the same as his brother? Would he feel like an unwelcome stranger in the midst of his kinfolk? How could she find the words to mend this child's broken self esteem.

Were there any words in the world that could take away what he had already endured because of her? Were there any words that could make him take pride in himself for himself? She must find some way that he could take hold of, that he could bring himself to live a life that she now realized he did not want to live at all. Has she truly done the wrong thing in staying here when her history was known to all and sundry? A feeling of conviction grew deep within her, one she tried now to express.

"Son, we cain't run away from who we are. You wouldn't have been any less illegitimate in Virginia than you are here. It's true nobody woulda' known as much about you there as they do here, but you would still have been who you are. When I knew I was gonna have you, I thought my life was over. I knew my reputation was ruined forever, but I stuck it out here because I was young enough to believe that people would forgive me for making a mistake if I just tried hard enough to show them that I was the same person they always knew. It didn't work out like that, and I learned some hard lessons along the way. The hardest one was that I cain't never be anybody but myself. I learned to hold my head up and let the rest of em go their own way if that's what they wanted, and it was what most of em wanted. John Wesley, I want you to hold your head up and don't never judge yourself by what other people say about you when you know it ain't true. "

John Wesley turned his head to look at his mother. A universe of pain whirled in the depths of his eyes, accusation still lingering at the edges. Then, slowly, slowly, he pushed himself up from the ground, standing as tall as his height would allow, his head held high.

"Where we gonna live now, Mama?" He said.

With that one sentence he accepted his life, past, present and future. With that one sentence he took his first step toward acceptance of his mother for who she was and who she had been. With that one sentence he expressed his love and respect for his mother.

Forty-two

It was decided that, for the time being, Kate and her sons would stay in the Macintosh farmhouse. Kate shared Eileen's room and the boys shared Sean's room. Kate protested that they were crowding the family, but Sarah insisted. Sean was to marry in the fall and that would leave his room free for the boys. Eileen didn't mind sharing her room with Kate. Kate would continue helping as she had for years to earn her keep and John Wesley would continue to help Angus and Sean with the crops. Sarah would brook no further discussion on the subject. There was no other unoccupied house on the Macintosh property in which Kate could live. In time, if Kate insisted, something else might be worked out.

The relationship between Kate and John Wesley appeared to remain a loving one, but, down deep, Kate knew that there was a rift that would never completely be healed. She grieved secretly, her mother's heart adding yet another indictment against her for her past sins. If only, if only, was the plaintive rhythm of her pulse. She might tell her son she had learned hard lessons, had accepted her life and didn't run away from who she was, but locked away in her psyche still breathed the young, anguished girl who so desperately longed for the approbation of family and friends. Outwardly she lived the invention she had created to preserve her sanity and to create a world for her children.

When the time for Sean's wedding drew near, Sarah took her aside one day to tell her that Angus was giving her old home to Sean and his new bride. The place had stood empty since the Stancel family had left. It had never been an option for Kate because she could not farm it herself. Sarah expressed her hope that Kate wouldn't take against Sean for living in her old home. Kate assured Sarah that she had no such feelings toward Sean. The farm was no longer hers and hadn't been in a very long time. She would not hold it against Sean for living there since it was her own brother's fault that the farm had been lost. She went to Sean and told him she was happy that he would be starting his new life in her old home and expressed her hope that he and his bride would be very happy there. Sean looked relieved and hugged Kate in thanks for her expression of hope for him.

Kate and her sons attended the wedding and the party afterwards as friends of the family. Sean even danced with Kate to the dismay of the many who still considered her beneath knowing. A sibilant hum of hissing whispers, sounding like a pit of snakes, arose as they moved around the dance floor. Sean grinned wickedly and winked at Kate as they danced. His bride smiled from the sidelines. It was a happy day for all concerned. Kate was amused that Sherman was fascinated by the fiddle players. He stood silent and big eyed watching them energetically saw out the music for the dancing. He hardly blinked, he was so fascinated. When they took a break, Sherman came straight to his mother and told her he wanted a fiddle so he could play. He wanted to make people happy the way those other men were doing. Kate smiled fondly at the little boy and explained that a fiddle was much too expensive. She couldn't afford to buy him one. Maybe when he got old enough he could get odd jobs for other farmers and save up his money to buy himself a fiddle. He looked crestfallen and Kate felt sad that she could not afford the gift of a fiddle for the little boy. As soon as the fiddlers struck up the next tune, he was off to stand hypnotized before them until the end of the dance.

As the party ended, the young men and women friends of Sean and his new wife, escorted them to their home while the older people and the children went back to their own homes. Sherman murmured and sighed about his desire for a fiddle until John Wesley finally told him to hush up and forget about getting one. Kate looked at her older son in mild surprise; he was usually so supportive and generous with his little brother. He looked back at her a little sheepishly; muttering quietly that the boy was driving him crazy. They couldn't afford to buy him a fiddle anyway.

~ * ~

They had been living nearly three years in the Macintosh home when Kate was surprised one afternoon by a visit from her cousin, Emily Randsome. She hadn't spoken to her younger cousin since that long ago day when she had asked her cousin Tenia for a home for herself and John Wesley to avoid the fate that awaited her at the hands of James Richmond. She remembered that the younger girl had tried to persuade Tenia to let Kate live with them and been harshly reprimanded.

"Cousin Emily! What are you doing over here?"

"I've come to see you, Cousin Kate. I have a proposition to make to you."

"A proposition? Now you've got my attention!" Kate laughed.

"It's not a laughing matter, Kate. I'm dead serious. I heard that there's a cabin on Robert Smith's property that's available. The folks that was sharecropping there has left and he's looking for someone to take over."

"And you think he'd let me sharecrop over there? You wasted your time coming over here to tell me that. Rob Smith wouldn't dream of letting the likes of me sharecrop on his place."

"Kate! You're not taking me serious! I mean that I want you and me and your boys to sharecrop over there. I've had enough of Cousin Tenia's mean ways and want a place to myself. I cain't farm by myself, so I thought of you and your boys and thought we could share the house and the work."

"If you're so set on a place of your own, why ain't you got married. That's the surest way of getting a place of your own."

"I ain't met a man I'd care to cook and clean and mend for, not to mention wait on him hand and foot and have a passel of babies to take care of in the bargain."

"So," Kate mused. "You've decided to be an old maid and to ad spice to your life you wanna take up with your no count cousin Kate in the bargain. That's a for sure guarantee that no man will want to marry you!"

Emily stamped her foot and cried, "Kate! Will you listen to me? I've come here with a wonderful idea and you won't even consider it. Surely you want a place of your own. A way to make some money. Well, I'm telling you how you can do it."

Kate looked thoughtfully at Emily. At the artfully arranged blonde curls, the large green eyes in the smooth face. Though less than ten years separated them in age, her cousin looked much younger. She knew her own face was finely lined like a county road map that told the story of the hard years of living she had endured to those who could read it. "Hold out your hands," she said to Emily.

"What?"

"You heard me. Hold out your hands."

Mystified, Emily held her hands out to Kate. The nails were neatly filed, the skin soft and unmarred. Kate held out her own hands. The contrast was a statement in itself. Kate's nails were chipped and broken; her palms and fingers callused by years of hard work.

"You mean to tell me," Kate said, "that you want to work in cotton fields? Your hands are telling me something else. You've never worked in a cotton field in your life. Just look at *my* hands. These are the hands of a woman who's labored long and hard in a cotton field. You don't have the beginning of an idea of how hard that work is. You come here because you're unhappy with your life and want me to uproot mine so you can live in some made up world you've imagined for yourself. Go on home, Emily."

"I'm not leaving here until we come to an agreement, Kate. You're right when you say I've never worked in a cotton field. But you're wrong in everything else you're thinking. This is a chance for both of us to get something we want. Between me and you and your two boys, we could make something for ourselves. I stood up for you back then, when you wanted to move in with Cousin Tenia. I've never changed my feelings about that."

"That's real interesting, Emily. I cain't recall that you've said one word to me or my boys at church these years we've been going there. Now all of a sudden you want me to believe that you always cared about me and thought the rest of em were treating me wrong?"

"Kate, if I'da spoke to you at church or anywhere else, Cousin Tenia would have beat me within an inch of my life."

"Won't she beat you within an inch of your life for coming over here today?"

"She don't know where I am. I snuck out when she was upstairs."

"So, in all these years you never had the opportunity to sneak away before? Just to stop in for a friendly chat or something? Now that you want to get away from there and you need me to make your plan work, all of a sudden you found a chance to sneak off?"

"I know how it looks and I'm ashamed I never came over here before, but don't you see that you're doing the same thing now that they did to you in the past? I'm asking your for help and you're turning me away just because you think I'm up to no good."

"How dare you compare your situation to mine!" snarled Kate. "So you're tired of Tenia's nasty ways! So you haven't seen a man you would care to do for the rest of your life! I don't know how you can stand there and think your problem is *anything* like what happened to me!"

"Kate! Please! I'm sorry! I *know* it's not nuthing like what happened to you. I'm just trying to make you see that this would be a good thing for both of us and I went about it the wrong way! Please think over my idea. Forget about what I said about you being like the others."

Emily turned away and walked quickly back the way she had come, leaving Kate to ponder the situation. The idea appealed to her, but she was doubtful about Emily's ability to stick out the situation once she found out just how hard sharecropping would be. Then again, if she was established on the property and showed that she could work the property for profit, she and her sons could continue to sharecrop without Emily. She would think it over for a few days. In the past, hasty decisions had proven devastating.

The idea still appealed to her two days later, so she consulted John Wesley. At sixteen he considered himself a man. He heard her out, then wanted to know why they needed Emily in the first place. If she was so unsure that Emily would last in the long run, why not just approach Rob Smith on their own and ask to sharecrop the land? Kate felt that they needed Emily's respectability on their side in order to persuade Rob to let them take over the piece of land. John Wesley thought that over for a few minutes, then agreed that she was probably right. They decided together to make the move. The question now was how to let Emily know their answer. Neither of them would be allowed to speak to her if they showed up on Tenia's property. John Wesley suggested they wait another few days to see if Emily would come back here. If she didn't, then he would get Rufus to speak to Emily and send her to the Macintosh farm.

John Wesley was proven right when, two days later, Emily again appeared at the Macintosh farm. She said she had felt that Kate should have a week to think over the idea and she had kept tabs on the Smith property. No one had yet offered to take over the sharecropping there. Kate told her that she had decided to accept Emily's offer and she should go to Rob Smith with the proposal. Kate felt it would be better if she were not present at the time, just in case Rob decided to get nasty about her. Emily agreed to go to Rob Smith alone and come back with his decision. Kate decided to wait until Emily returned with the news before she said anything to Sarah about moving out. It would be a wrench to both of them. Their friendship had grown so close over the years that Sarah considered Kate almost a younger sister and Kate's children a part of her own family.

Emily returned the next day, eyes dancing with joy. Rob Smith had agreed to let them sharecrop the property. He had be some taken aback at the thought of Kate Randsome on his property, but Emily had been determined that her plan would succeed. She had pointed out that Kate was now a close friend of the Mcintoshes and had been attending church regularly for many years. She had pointed out that Kate had proven herself to be a strong woman and had two sons who were old enough to work the fields with the two women. Kate thought that there was probably a lot more said about her than Emily was letting on, but kept quiet. The outcome had been in her favor. She would let go of any bad thoughts about Rob Smith.

The wrench of telling Sarah that they were leaving was as bad as Kate had foreseen. Sarah wept and begged her to stay with them, but Kate was firm. She could not live on their charity forever. It was past time for her to move on. The boys were old enough now to work the cotton and they needed a home of their own. Angus' eyes were moist also, but he sided with Kate. She needed to move on now. He told her how much he hated for her and the boys to leave, but he understood her reasons. He wiped his eyes and hugged her, telling her how glad he was that he had given her a home all those years ago and how he had come to respect her in the years since then. She was never to forget, he said, that she and her family were always welcome in his home. Just drop by anytime the urge struck.

Angus insisted on driving them to their new home. Once they had loaded their belongings and all the things Sarah insisted on sending with them, the back of the wagon was full to the brim. The boys tucked themselves in spaces in the back while Kate road on the seat with Angus.

Arriving at their destination, they found Emily already there with her own belongings, along with Rob Smith. Angus jumped down from the wagon and helped Kate down. Walking forward, Kate felt her knees weaken at the speculative look on Rob's face. Angus must have seen it also. He walked straight to Rob and told him how hard it was on the Mcintosh family to lose Kate and her boys, but he knew they would be happy and safe here in their new home. Rob's expression changed to one of hearty welcome. He helped Angus unload the wagon. Once everything had been placed to Kate's satisfaction, Angus took his leave.

"Well, Emily," Kate said, turning to her cousin, "How did you manage to escape from Tenia? Didn't she kick up an almighty fuss about you leaving? Especially to live me!"

"Actually, she doesn't know I'm gone. I just packed up my things and came on over here before sun up."

"What! I cain't believe you just packed up and left without telling her anything! She be on us like a duck on a June bug when she finds out where you are. I don't want my children exposed to her vicious tongue! You get right on back over there and tell her where you are and what you're gonna be doin' and who you're gonna be doing it with!"

"Kate, I ain't gonna go back over there and tell her anything. She can find out on her own, then do whatever she wants to do about it. I ain't gonna go back and live there."

"God Almighty! You're starting off on the wrong foot with me, Emily. I won't let you put my boys in the way of hearing things that have already hurt them enough. You git on over to Tenia's and tell her the truth and tell her I said to keep away from here."

The sound of a wagon coming down the road distracted Kate from her argument. Turning, she saw that the wagon was turning into the yard. Tenia sat on the seat with rage on her face. Kate looked around to see where her boys were, knowing that the coming confrontation would be more than unpleasant. She was relieved to see them inspecting the already planted cotton in a field distant enough from the house that conversation could not be heard.

Tenia pulled the wagon to a halt next to the two women. She dismissed Kate with a withering glance, directing all her attention toward Emily.

"You git your things and git on this wagon immediately, missy! I don't know what you were thinking to take off like this and take up with this piece of trash standing here next to you."

"Damn you to hell, Tenia!" Kate spat. "You turn that wagon around and git off this property right now. I won't have you coming around here with your nasty ways and talking that way about me. You have no rights here, so git on your way."

Ignoring the blazing eyes of Kate, Tenia directed her words to Emily. "You heard me. Git you things and git on this wagon right now. We don't associate with her kind."

Much to Kate's surprised, Emily was not cowed by the harsh words. She stood her ground and said, "You just do like Kate said Tenia. I ain't going home with you. I'm tired of the way you treat me and tired of the way you've always treated Kate. She's family same as you. I'm gonna stay here with her and farm this property and have a life of my own without you telling me what to do every minute of every day of my life. I don't want to git married and I'm tired of you harping at me on that subject, too. I'm here and I'm gonna stay here. You just turn on around and leave."

Tenia glared balefully at Emily. "Is this the thanks I git for raising you from a child after your Mama and Daddy died? Is this how you repay my kindness? Taking up with the trashiest piece of goods in this part of the county after I've been so good to you?"

"You've been good to me all right." Emily responded. "And you've never let me forget for a single day how good you were to take me in when I was orphaned. I've paid you back for that goodness over and over and over, by doing all the chores you didn't want to do. The ones you didn't want your precious daughters to do. You gave me all the hardest, nastiest jobs on the farm and I did them because I thought I owed it to you. I don't feel like I owe you anything else. I gonna have my own life here with my *cousins* and you cain't do nothing about it. I'm a grown woman now, not a scared child."

Tenia clucked to the mule and wheeled the wagon around. "You'll rue this day girl. You mark my words." Looking toward Kate, she said slyly, "I hear James Richmond's wife just gave birth to their sixth daughter. I hear he's wantin' a son real bad." Tenia looked out to the cotton field where John Wesley and Sherman were still inspecting the plants, then looked back at Kate.

"I ain't concerned with what James Richmond wants. He can have as many children as he wants. It ain't none of my business what goes on at his place." Kate replied calmly.

"Is that so?" asked Tenia. "The day may come when you'll be real concerned about James Richmond and what he wants."

"I don't know what you're talking about and don't care. Just git on off this property and leave us to live our own lives without your interference."

Emily was looking in confusion at the two women. "Why would Kate care about James Richmond, Tenia?" Emily asked. "She ain't worked for him in years. You're just trying to stir up trouble like you always do. It's your favorite occupation."

"I ain't the one whose been stirring up trouble. Your cousin here is the one who's always been real good at that. Ask her why she might be concerned with what James Richmond wants; see if she tells you the truth. Now that ya'll are such close friends and everything." Clucking to the mule, Tenia rode out of the yard with a pleased smile on her face.

Turning to Kate, Emily asked, "What was that all about?"

"It was about a bunch of nothing. Just like everything that old woman says. She just ain't happy unless she's stirring up some kind of trouble." Changing the subject, she added, "I have to admit I didn't think you'd stand up to her like that though. I figured as soon as she showed up here, you'd give in and go home with her."

"I told you I'm tired of her nasty ways and cain't stand to live under the same roof with her anymore."

"Well, we'll see how long that lasts when you start chopping that cotton out there." Kate replied enigmatically.

Forty-three

Kate was surprised and pleased by her younger cousin's fortitude in the cotton fields. In the weeks between the departure of the former residents and the arrival of the new ones, the weeds had grown freely among the rows of cotton. It made it that much more difficult to chop them out. Kate and John Wesley were used to working hard. Even Sherman was able to contribute in his own small way, though he was just ten years old. Emily was another matter. Her hands became blistered, the blisters breaking open and oozing blood and pus, as Kate's own hands had done long years ago. Just as Aunt Mary had done for her, she rubbed horse liniment on her cousins' hands to toughen them for the work to be done. Emily bit her lips to silence any sounds of pain and Kate's admiration rose just a little more.

After several weeks in their new home, Kate began to notice that John Wesley was disappearing for an hour or two in the evenings. She let him be for a time, then her curiosity overcame her desire to let her son have as much freedom as possible. She questioned him as to his whereabouts on those evenings. He merely replied that they went to the creek about a mile away to cool off and to think his own thoughts in peace without his little brother bothering him every minute. She didn't think that was the entire truth, but they no longer shared the closeness they had had when he was younger. Since the day that she had admitted to him the truth of his background, he had always held back from her slightly. It was nothing anyone else would notice, but she felt it. Knew that they would never again share that closeness. It was part of the reason she let him go his own way so much. Still she was suspicious of his activities. Nearly seventeen years old, she knew he needed a certain amount of privacy, but spending so much time at a creek struck her as odd.

A month later, she broached the subject with him again.

"You still spending all your free time down by that crick, son?"

"Yes, Mama," he replied.

"What do you find to do down there so much?"

"Actually, I been meeting someone there. I made a new friend. We meet there to talk about things."

"A new friend? Who is it? What's his name?"

"It's a girl. Her name is Sally Spender. We just sit and talk sometimes. She cain't come there all the time, so sometimes I just sit there by myself and think about things."

"Sally Spender! Lord a mercy, John Wesley. You don't want to be taking up with one of the Spender's. They stay to themselves and don't have anything to do with other folks. Why they even marry their own cousins. That girl will get in a world of trouble if her family finds out she's been meeting you. They don't cotton to the idea of other folks knowing their business. They're an odd lot."

"I reckon I can take up with anybody I want to, Mama. She ain't but fourteen years old anyway. What harm could come of her meeting with me?"

"A lot of harm could come to her and maybe to you. I told you they don't cotton to other folks. I cain't imagine how you came to meet her. Don't hardly none of em ever leave their property."

"I was down by the crick one day, just cooling off by the water, soaking my feet and she came out of the woods on the other side, just a crying her eyes out. She didn't even see me at first. When she did see me, she turned around to run off, but I ran over and caught up with her. I just wanted to know why she was crying so hard and did she need some help. She said it wasn't something I could help with. It had to do with becoming a woman and that her daddy said she had to learn. I talked her into sitting with me by the crick till she felt better. Ever since then, we been meeting sometimes just to talk about things."

Kate felt herself go cold at her son's explanation of his first meeting with Sally Spender. Closely acquainted with the evil, twisted ways of the minds of some men, she had immediately jumped to a certain conclusion about the cause of Sally's tears. No, she must be wrong. Surely a father wouldn't do such a thing! She shivered involuntarily. Surely she was wrong.

Seeing his mother shiver in the hot evening air, John Wesley asked, "What are you shivering about, Mama? It hot out tonight."

"Just somebody walking over my grave, son." At his puzzled expression, she explained, "When a person shivers all of a sudden for no reason, they say someone is walking over their grave. It means that somebody is walking on the spot where you'll be buried someday."

"What an awful thought! Where did you hear something like that, Mama?"

"My Mama used to say it. I guess she heard it from her Mama. Lots of older folks say that. It's just an old superstitious explanation for shivering for no reason."

"It sure sounds strange to me. Maybe I'll tell Sally about it next time I see her. She might find it interesting."

"Son, I really wish you wouldn't meet up with her anymore."

"I know you do, Mama, but I'm going to anyway. It's harmless and I like her. She's very nice and easy to talk to. I know you'd like her, too, if you ever met her."

"It would be for the best if I didn't. Somebody might see her over here and tell it around. It would get back to her family and they'd be mighty upset about it."

"Someday, I'd like for you to meet her."

Sighing with resignation, Kate commented, "Maybe I will one of these days."

~ * ~

Time passed, filled with hard work and Kate put her son's meetings out of her mind. The four of them worked too hard for her to be worrying about a harmless friendship. She was more concerned about Sherman. He still begged for a fiddle of his own. At the few barn dances they attended, he continued to stand in fascination before the fiddlers, watching their every move. She had to explain to him, yet again, that they could not afford to buy a fiddle for him. His downcast expression distressed her deeply. She noticed too, that at those dances, Emily was never lacking for partners. Several of the young men had eyes for her cousin. She discussed it once with Emily.

"I noticed several of the young men cutting their eyes at you tonight. I'm surprised they still do, since you're living with the harlot of the county. Ain't you interested in any of them?"

Emily tossed her head, looking exasperated. "They're just looking for someone to do all those things I told you I ain't interested in spending the rest of my life doing. I ain't interested enough in any of em."

"It'd be a easier life for you than chopping and picking cotton and raising all our own food and doing all the housework here. If you got married, your man would do all the chopping and picking. You'd just have to do the gardening and housework."

"I ain't seen a man I'd care to live with. I don't mind the hard work here. At least I ain't waiting hand and foot on nobody. When the works done, my time is my own. I don't have to spend it paying attention to nobody if I don't want to."

"Well, you're right about that much of it anyway. If you're set on living like this I won't try to change your mind. I just hope you don't regret it some day."

"I ain't never gonna regret it, Kate. I ain't ever gonna get married. I'm happy here with ya'll. You don't need to worry on my account."

"Somebody told me once that you shouldn't say you ain't ever gonna do something, because that's surely the one thing you *will* end up doing."

"Who told you that? Sarah?"

"No. It was Aunt Mary. She was right to, so you better take heed to what I'm telling you."

"Aunt Mary? You mean the old woman in that black family that took you in years ago?"

"Yes. She turned out to be a good friend. As good a friend as Sarah is now. I still miss her and wonder what's she's doing these days. I miss her and all the rest of em, too. They were very kind to me when I had nowhere else to go. After a while I never even noticed they were black anymore. They were just my family."

"Your family! How did you ever bring yourself to think of them as your family? I know they took you in and all, but how could you feel that black people were family?"

"You don't want to take that tone with me, Emily. You didn't know them. They treated me better than any of my blood kin. You know that yourself. Just look at the way Tenia acted when I asked her for a home. I know you've heard about Savannah throwing me out of her house. Aunt Mary and Sam took me into their home and treated me just like I belonged there. They gave me love and friendship freely, without asking for one thing in return. I won't listen to you talking like that and looking down on them just because they're black. Color didn't matter to them and it didn't matter to me either. Don't you never say anything bad about them!"

"I didn't mean to get you riled up, Kate. I just never understood before how you felt about them. I'm glad they gave you a good home. You deserved to have one. I'm right sorry about the way the family have treated you, but I cain't change that. I can only speak for myself and tell you that I never thought bad about you. I know that man lied to you and made you think he would marry you before he run off. Sometimes I think that's why I took against men like I have. After what happened to you, I don't know if I could ever trust one of em."

"Don't be thinking they're all like Michael. He was a bad one, but there *are* some good one's out there. Like I said before, don't be saying you won't ever git married. You might just change your mind one of these days."

~ * ~

A year flew by, then two, then three. Kate was happy in the even tenor of their lives. She was even able to put aside just a little each year, hoping to save enough money to buy Sherman his coveted fiddle some day. Randall Rhodes, one of the best fiddlers in the county, had seen the little boy's longing and took to giving Sherman lessons during the winter on his own fiddle. Sherman paid for the lessons by doing odd jobs around the farm for Randall. Kate was pleased that at least the boy was learning to play the instrument he so longed to possess. She did worry from time to time about John Wesley. She knew in her heart he was still meeting the Spender girl secretly. He had never mentioned the girl's name after the one conversation they had, but somehow she knew her son was still seeing her.

Her suspicions were confirmed one warm spring evening when John Wesley brought Sally home with him. Her heart dropped to her feet. Bringing Sally here could only mean one thing and she feared a storm of trouble would come of it. The girl looked like a frightened doe in her faded cotton dress. Kate reckoned that she must be about seventeen now, pretty enough in a slightly too thin way. Sally looked at the floor as John Wesley introduced them. She must have thought Kate would not want to know her. When the girl finally looked at her, there was embarrassment in the lovely hazel eyes gazing at her. Kate reached out here hand.

"Sit down, Sally. Let's have a little talk and git to know each other. I suspicioned John Wesley was still meeting with you all this time."

"Oh! Don't be mad at Johnny. I know I ain't near good enough for him, but he makes me feel like somebody special." She turned an adoring gaze on John Wesley.

She was unnerved by the look on the girl's face. Unnerved too that John Wesley was returning it. This was not good. She felt it in her bones. After all the mistakes of her own life, she had developed a sixth sense for trouble, had learned to listen to the inner voice of warning she had ignored in the past. Trouble would come of this. She prayed it wouldn't be her son who would do the suffering. A selfish thought, but she could not concern herself with Sally's troubles. John Wesley came first. Could she stop this before trouble came to roost in her home? She had nothing against Sally herself, just the reputation of the Spencer clan. She would try to buy enough time to dissuade John Wesley from this path.

"Johnny?" she questioned calmly.

"That's my special name for him. I hope you don't mind."

She realized that she minded very much. A special name meant that the situation had progressed much farther than she was prepared for. John Wesley was watching her closely.

"Sit on down here, Sally. I won't bite you."

John Wesley relaxed and motioned Sally to the chair next to Kate. He sat comfortably across from them. "Where's Emily?" he asked.

"She gone on to bed early. Her back was paining her this evening, so she went on to bed hoping it'll be better in the morning. Sherman's gone over to Randall's to have a fiddle lesson. He's doing so good with it that Randall's gonna teach him all year round when there's a little time to spare."

"I think it's wonderful how Mister Rhodes is teaching Johnny's little brother like that." Sally interjected. "Johnny told me all about it."

"Yes, it's good of Randall to take the time. Tell me more about yourself, Sally. Do your Mama and Daddy know about you and my son?"

Again, the girl's eyes would not meet Kate's. She fiddled with the skirt of her dress. It was answer enough for Kate, but she waited to hear what Sally would say.

"No ma'am. They don't. I reckon you know how my family is about associating with other folks. I don't reckon they need to know anything about it just yet."

"Just yet?" Kate asked.

John Wesley jumped up. "Mama, why are you acting like this? I love Sally. I think you should know that I want to marry her soon. You're treating her like some kind of criminal and you're the judge. I want ya'll to be friends."

"Johnny!" Sally exclaimed. "You shouldn't be talking to your Mama like that! I told you she wouldn't cotton to the idea of us gitting married." Turning to Kate, she continued. "I know you think I ain't good enough for your son, Miz Randsome, but I love him with all my heart and I want to marry him. I was hoping you could find it in your heart to accept me as a wife for Johnny. It's been too much for you to take in all at once. I reckon I'll just go on home now so's the two of you can talk this out."

John Wesley cast a look of disgust at his mother as he escorted Sally out the door. When he didn't return immediately, Kate knew he was walking Sally most of the way home. How to make her son understand that she wasn't against him marrying? It was just one of the Spender clan that she couldn't accept. She knew they would never accept John Wesley either. They probably already had plans for Sally to marry one of her numerous cousins. She waited patiently for John Wesley's return. She would try to explain to him that it was unreasonable to want to marry a Spender.

~ * ~

He returned hours later, walking quietly into the room where Kate waited. He gave her a defiant look and said, "I'm gonna marry Sally, Mama. I'm a grown man and you cain't stop me from doing it. I just hoped you'd be happy for me that I've found someone to love and who loves me back. She don't care that I'm a bastard."

Kate winced. The old wound still ran deep within this fine, handsome young man standing so stubbornly before her. Still, Sally Spender was not someone he should be courting. How to explain what he surely must realize as clearly as she did?

"You cain't be courting Sally Spender, John Wesley. You know that as well as I do. They're not our kind, son."

Nostrils flaring, John Wesley shot back at her. "Who are you to say she's not our kind. After the things you've done, how can you look down on her like that? After the way people have acted toward you, how came you sit in judgment like that? You're acting just like the people who've been against you for all these years for what you claim was an innocent mistake. Don't take against Sally for no reason other than her family. She's a decent, loving girl."

"I'm glad that you've found someone to love. Someone who loves you back. It's just that the Spenders will never allow her to marry you. You know what I'm saying. They won't let her marry outside the family. I just know there's gonna be trouble. I don't want you to get hurt and I don't want her to get hurt either."

"You just don't understand, Mama. I couldn't ever love anyone else. Not the way I love Sally. We *will* be married, even if we have to run off together to do it."

"Son, I beg you to think on this some more before it goes any further. If not for your own sake, then for hers. I don't believe they'll ever let her go. Ya'll cain't live your lives always on the run. Always looking over your shoulders for one of her family coming after you."

"They won't chase after us, Mama. She's old enough to git married if she wants to and they cain't stop her from it. I 'preciate you worrying about what might happen, but nothing bad will happen. She'll make me the happiest man in the world on the day she marries me."

Kate knew there was no turning him back from his decision. He wanted Sally Spender and he would have her. Remembering her own youth, the strong urges of those days, she wept inwardly. Her own impetuous nature had brought her shame. Now she saw that same nature in her son, and feared that, in the end, it would bring him only heartache.

"Mama, for my sake, just get to know her a little, " begged her son. "I know you'll come to love her if you do."

She tried mightily to push aside her own fears. Her son was only asking her to do what was right. Why was she so set against Sally? There was nothing wrong with the girl herself. It was just that she was a Spender and everybody knew the Spenders were trouble. She would have to make John Wesley understand, but when she looked into the light of joy in his eyes, she found she couldn't deny him. "All right," she sighed. "If you're bound and determined on this. I'll get to know her. For your sake."

Forty-four

Being a woman of her word, Kate began getting to know Sally. The girl would come by the house once or twice a week for an hour or so, usually with John Wesley sitting nearby like a lioness protecting her cub. That was how Kate saw the situation. Sally was so quiet and shy; she just drew protection to her like a moth to a flame. Her large doe eyes begged silently for something Kate didn't think anyone, even her son, could give this poor child.

After a few weeks of this, Kate told her son she wanted to talk with Sally alone sometimes. At John Wesley's look of alarm, she reminded him tartly that she had agreed to get to know the girl and wouldn't eat her alive if he left them alone. There were things she wanted to question Sally about, without her son listening. Things she didn't think her son realized and hoped he need never know.

Acceding to her wishes, John Wesley left them alone the next time Sally came by for a visit. Sally sat nervously on the edge of her chair, faded skirt spread demurely around her, feet tucked close together. She looked ready to run at the slightest provocation. Those large, scared, needy eyes trained on Kate made her want to shout at the girl to show a little gumption. Nobody got anywhere in this world without a little gumption. She should know. It was a hard learned lesson. Her heart softened a little then, remembering how scared and needy she had once been. How the intervention of Aunty Mary and her family had been the one thing that had saved her all those years ago. Remembering that kindness made her a little less annoyed with the girl.

In a soft voice she said, "No need to look so scared of me, Sally. I ain't gonna do you no harm. I just wanted to have a little talk with you alone. Woman to woman, so to speak."

At this, Sally gulped audibly, her position becoming even more tense. Kate thought the girl resembled a mouse that has been cornered by a cat and isn't sure which way to run, but run it would.

"What did you wanta talk to me about?" Sally squeaked in a timid voice.

She even sounded like a scared mouse, Kate thought with contempt.

"There's been something on my mind for a long time, Sally. Something you said to my son the first time ya'll met. I don't think he quite took in what you meant, but *I* knew what it was. I knew exactly what it was."

The pale girl before her turned even paler. Kate thought the girl knew exactly what that something was, but didn't look like she intended to talk about it.

"Come on now, Sally. You know what I'm talking about. You don't need to be afraid of me. I'm only concerned about my son. I know that sounds a little harsh, like I don't care a lick about you, but with a mother, her children always come first in her heart. I don't want my son hurt by something he don't know anything about. I don't want you using him as a means of getting away from your family. You know your folks ain't gonna cotton to the idea of you marrying somebody outside your own family. It's time for you to tell the truth here. Ain't nobody but us here. You can tell me the truth."

"I-I don't know what you're talking about, Miz Randsome."

"Oh yes you do, missy! I want some straight answers out of you. You told my boy that you're daddy had done something to you. That it had to do with becoming a woman. Now, John Wesley ain't been around the kind of men that ain't got no respect for woman or their own blood kin, so he didn't know what you meant by that, but *I* knew right off what you meant when he told me about it."

"Miz Randsome, please don't turn Johnny away from me! He's the only good thing I got in my life. You're right about my Daddy, but please don't say anything to Johnny about it. He thinks I'm such a good person. I couldn't bear for him to know what my Daddy done to me! I'm so ashamed! How could he do that to his own daughter? Please don't tell! Please!"

Tears streaked down the girl's face as she begged Kate to keep her secret. Her hands reached out beseechingly. Those eyes. Those large, scared, needy eyes looked into Kate's, pleading for compassion. Again Kate was reminded of herself, pleading with own family for understanding and remembered their cold, hard responses. It was those memories that tipped the scales in Sally's favor. She would not do to this child what had been done to her.

"Hush, child. Dry your eyes. I won't tell John Wesley about something that wasn't your fault. I just want you to tell me truthfully that you love my son. That you're not using him to git away from your folks. If you can convince me that you truly love him, then I will give the two of you my blessing."

"Miz Randsome, I do truly love Johnny. He is the most wonderful man I've ever known. He treats me like I'm a queen or something. I ain't never knowed a man could care about a woman like Johnny cares about me. I love him with all my heart. I know you're some concerned that my family won't let us git married. We're gonna run away together and settle somewheres else. I know it'll hurt you for him to go away, but it's the only way we can be together and we do truly love each other."

Kate could see the truth in the girl. Her eyes were shining now, her slender face lit with an inner joy. Kate knew then that it was inevitable that her son would marry this girl and leave the county. If he could find happiness that way, she would not stand in his way.

"You're right, Sally. It will be just like losing a piece of myself for John Wesley to go away, but he ain't never been happy here. If he can be happy some wheres else with you, then I won't stand in the way. My dream for him has always been for him to be happy. I hoped it would be here, but I reckon that ain't gonna happen. There's too many bad memories for him here. I thought over the years, people would git over him being who he is, but it don't look like that's gonna happen. I tried all his life to make a good life for him here. I reckon I failed him in that."

"No, Miz Randsome, you ain't failed Johnny. Don't never think that. You raised him up to be a fine man. Somebody any woman should be happy to marry. It's my good fortune that it's me he loves."

"You're a good girl, Sally. If you make him happy, then you'll have my gratitude always."

"That's just what I intend on doing, Miz Randsome. Making Johnny the happiest man in the world."

John Wesley came home a little later to escort Sally back to the edge of the Spender property. He was relived to find them chatting like old friends.

"Well, Mama," he said. "Didn't I tell you she's a fine girl?"

"Yes, son, you surely did."

Her heart was still slightly troubled as she watched the two of them disappear toward the Spender land.

~ * ~

John Wesley was much warmer to her after that than he had been in years. They managed to recover some of the closeness they had had when he was a young child, before she had confirmed for the horrible rumors of his childhood. That closeness made Kate happy. The sharecropping was as hard as ever, but she had her two boys and Emily with her to work the fields. They were able to put just a little bit aside from their share of the cotton. Kate was very stringent with all of them. They made do with what they had or did without. That was the only was to stay out of debt. So many of the other sharecroppers were endlessly in debt with the landowners. It wasn't that they were extravagant. In fact, they just bought the necessities on credit, but were never quite able to make enough money from the sharecropping to completely pay off that debt. Kate had no growing children who constantly need larger clothing. Her own clothes and those of her family had been constantly patched and mended, patched and mended until there was no telling the original patterns. She worked diligently in their small garden patch raising root crops that could be preserved in the root cellar that her sons had dug beneath the house. She grew corn that could be dried and ground into cornmeal for cracklin bread or hoecakes. There were apple and peach trees nearby where she got fruit and dried in on strings hung from the kitchen rafters. The dried fruit was boiled in the winter, then used to make deserts for the family. Sarah Mcintosh insisted on seeing that they were supplied with chicken on a regular basis and pork when they had their hog killing. Kate and John Wesley always insisted on helping out with the hog killing as payment for the meat they received. Kate didn't enjoy the hog killing, but she, and her family, loved pork.

Hog killing occurred when the weather dropped toward freezing so the meat wouldn't spoil as it hung. The hog was knock in the head with a mallet to kill it. The thud of the mallet accompanied by the dying squeal of the hog always brought a sickening jolt to Kate's heart. Next the hog was gutted and the entrails given to those helpers who wanted to cook them into chitterlings. The hog was then hung by the heels from a strong tree branch and allowed to bleed out. After that, it was placed in a huge vat of boiling water to make the hair come off. The fire under the vat had to be stoked constantly to keep the water boiling long enough to do the job of softening the hair. Kate didn't relish using the stiff brush that removed the remaining hair from the hog, but it had to be done. The hog was then cut into pieces that were placed in a saltbox or hung in a smoke house to preserve the meat for use throughout the winter. Once all this hard work was done, Kate was grateful for the portions allotted to her by the Mcintoshes in return for her help.

After the hog killing that year, as she and John Wesley were walking home in the gathering dusk, John Wesley commented, "Well, Mama, I reckon Sherman will have to take over for me next year. He's thirteen now. Well old enough to take my place."

Kate's heart skipped a beat. John Wesley was planning to leave soon. Her heart wept, but her face remained calm.

"Does that mean that you and Sally are fixin to take off?"

"Not till Spring, Mama. I just wanted to let you know it would be soon, so you could get used to the idea. I know you already knew that we would go away and git married, but now it's definite. We'll be taking off in the Spring. I hate to leave you short a man on the farm, but I reckon ya'll can handle it without me."

"You're a growed man, John Wesley. I knowed you'd be gitting married and making your own life someday. We can manage the farm without you, but I will surely miss you something awful."

John Wesley put his arm around her shoulders as they made their way home in silence.

Forty-five

All through that long winter, Kate's heart counted off the days. Not with the glad thoughts that the coming of Spring usually brought to her, but with the secret knowledge that her oldest son would soon be gone for her life. More than likely forever.

It was at this point, when her heart was aching with the knowledge of her eldest sons' looming departure, that a face from the past came back to haunt her. Sherman had been attending local dances with his brother and his cousin Emily. Kate rarely attended dances anymore, she was usually left standing at the sides all night since most of her friends were older and did not care to dance. She enjoyed conversing with them, but stopped going to the dances. Randall Rhodes sometimes let Sherman play a set of songs on his fiddle to give himself a rest and to give the boy some experience playing at dances. Sherman's face shone with pride on those occasions and Kate was proud to see him play. One evening, Sherman returned from the dance alone—and with a fiddle in his hands. It was not a new fiddle, but was a very nice one. Kate was surprised to see it. Randall had never let Sherman take the fiddle home with him before. When Kate questioned Sherman, the past blew up in her face.

"What's Randall doing letting you bring his fiddle home with you?"

"It ain't Randall's fiddle, Mama. It's mine."

"Yours! Why you ain't saved up enough money to be buying no fiddle. You tell me where you got that fiddle, and you tell me now!"

"A man at the dance tonight brung it to me. He said it was a gift cause he could see how much I like to fiddle and that I ain't got a fiddle of my own. He said I'm so good, I should have my own fiddle to play and not have to borry one from nobody."

"Some stranger just up and give you a fiddle? That don't sound just right to me. Who was this man?"

"He's been coming to the dances round here lately. He's been real nice and friendly to me. Always wanting to talk about how I'm doing and what kind of things I like to do. He said I should just call him James."

Kate felt her heart stop at the name. James! It *couldn't* be James Richmond. There were lots of men named James. She was over reacting to the situation. What interest could he have in coming to this part of the county? Still, it would be best to find out as much as she could about this beneficent stranger. She had not forgotten her cousin Tenia's sarcastic words regarding the six daughters of James Richmond and his wife.

"Do I know him? What'd this man look like?"

"No, I don't reckon you know him, Mama. He don't live right around here. I think he lives over around Purdy maybe. He's a tall man with dark hair going gray at the sides and he's got the strangest eyes I ever saw. I ain't never seen nobody with eyes that color green."

She knew for sure then. It *was* James Richmond. There could be no other man fitting that description who would take such an intense interest in Sherman. James had come looking for the only son he had fathered. A man of his temperament would hunger for a son. Since his wife had not provided him with one, he had apparently decided to make contact with the son he had denounced before his birth. This was no time to panic. She must remain calm. She must convince Sherman to cut off contact with this man without causing alarm. She did not want Sherman asking certain questions regarding this man. He would someday have to be told that James Richmond was his father, but she wanted to do the telling on her own terms. Not be forced to tell him under duress. Who knew what things James might tell the boy, once he had his affection. Sherman must be protected from the evil taint of his father. Even if it meant telling him an ugly truth—in her own time.

"Now, Sherman," she said. "I cain't believe you'd accept a gift like this from a stranger. You know we work hard for what we got. We don't take no gifts like this from nobody. You just take that fiddle back to the next dance and give it back to that man. You just keep on saving up money from odd jobs and you'll be able to buy your own one of these days. It'll mean a whole lot more to you cause you'll have worked hard to earn the money to pay for it. Put the fiddle away for right now."

"But, Mama, I tried to tell James that I couldn't take the fiddle. I told him I couldn't accept such a expensive gift, but he insisted that I take it. He said it ain't new. It's a second hand one he found in a shop in Jackson when he was there. I told him my mama wouldn't let me keep it, but he just smiled and said he thought you would let me after I explained to you."

"Well, I *ain't* gonna let you keep it. You just go on and put it up for right now, then take it back to him at the next dance, like I told you."

Sherman sighed. He brushed the finely burnished wood of the fiddle with longing fingers. After another look at his mother's face, knowing she meant business by her expression, he placed the fiddle on the mantle and went off to bed.

Kate watched him go. Her blood was boiling. James had sent a veiled threat to her through her son. The mans' arrogance knew no bounds. He had drawn a clear line of battle. He intended to get to know his son, and would stoop to give Sherman his heart's desire to gain the boys' trust. She knew he was counting on her past submissiveness to gain control over the situation. He was counting on his past knowledge of Kate's personality. He was counting on her being afraid to tell Sherman the truth. He thought he held all the winning cards. She smiled a wicked smile to herself. James didn't realize that she had grown up and gotten stronger since he last had seen her. She had friends and protectors now who would stand up with her to stop him if she asked for their help. Yes, James was in for quite a surprise. Kate didn't want Sherman to ever have to know the details of the events leading up to his conception, but she was strong enough now to tell him that sordid story if she had to do it. To keep him from the malevolent influence of the man who had fathered him. The battle for Sherman's soul had begun. Not with the loud boom of cannon fire, but with the thick, dark silence of one woman's' determination.

Emily returned home just then. Her cheeks were becomingly flushed, as though she had been running. Looking closely at her cousin's face, Kate thought she saw something there and pounced.

"You got the look of a woman in love, Emily! Now ain't that a fine how-do-you-do for a woman who swore solemn she'd never git married?"

Emily's cheeks flushed even darker. "I don't reckon there's no call for you to git so nasty about it, Kate," she said tartly. "I reckon a woman can change her mind about things iffen she wants to."

"Course she can. I'm just a little taken aback that it's you doing it. Who's the lucky man?"

"Well, if you must know, it's Randall Rhodes. We been gitting to know each other at the dances when Sherman sits in playing. We just talked about Sherman at first, then we got to know each other a little better and it went on from there. He ain't asked me to marry him or anything."

"But you sure would like for him to ask. Wouldn't you?"

"Yes, I would. He's a fine man. Just look at how kind he's been to Sherman. Taught him to play the fiddle and all, knowing how bad Sherman wanted to learn. He's a good man, Kate. I couldn't care for anybody I didn't think was a good man."

"Well, I told you back when you was swearing you wouldn't never git married that there was some good ones still around. Looks like you found one of em. I'm happy for you Emily, if that's what you want."

"It is what I want, Kate. One of these days he'll ask me to marry him and I'll say "yes" so fast his head will spin!"

~ * ~

Sherman dutifully, if not happily, took the fiddle with him to the next dance. When he returned home that night, he still had the fiddle with him. Kate was upset that he hadn't done as she had told him.

Sherman explained that James absolutely refused to take back the fiddle. He had tried his hardest, he told her, but his new friend wouldn't take back the gift. Kate hid her raged from her son. She told him that at the next dance, he was to find out which wagon belonged to James and put the fiddle under the seat. If James found it and tried to give it back, Sherman was to refuse to take it. Sherman looked depressed, but promised to do as she said.

A few weeks later, he took the fiddle with him to the next local dance and came home empty handed and despondent. He told Kate that he had done as she said and put it under the seat of the wagon belonging to James. The next morning, the fiddle was lying on the front porch. Kate gave in and told a jubilant Sherman that he could keep the fiddle, but was to have nothing else to do with his new friend. Sherman couldn't understand why she was so adamant. She told him that she knew some things about the man who was Sherman's new friend and didn't think James was a suitable friend for him. If James continued to speak to him at the dances, she would have to stop him from going to the dances for a while. She absolutely did not want Sherman to continue his friendship with this particular man. She could see that Sherman was puzzled by her attitude. Should she tell him the truth now? No. She would wait and see how the situation developed.

~ * ~

Into the midst of all her worry over Sherman and her knowledge that John Wesley would be leaving come spring, rode another face from the past. This one a face of happy memories.

She had just stepped out of the chicken coop, where she kept two hens and a rooster she had recently acquired, when she saw the silhouette of a man coming across the yard. The evening sun was in her eyes, but there was something familiar about the breadth of shoulders and swinging stride. Squinting into the sun, she thought she recognized the man. Was it? Could it be?

"Sam?" she called out in question.

"Doan you reckernize me, Miss Kate? Ah ain' changed dat much has Ah?"

"Sam!" she shouted in joy, running across the distance to through her arms around her old friend.

Sam's arms closed around her waist, he swung her high off the ground, around and around, making her faded skirt swirl. Setting her on her feet, he laughed at her dazed expression.

"Miss Kate, you be looking fine. How's lil John Wesley doin?"

"John Wesley's not so little now, Sam. He's grown man. Fixin' to git married and leave the county." A small sob broke from her. The time was very near when her son would leave her. She looked quickly at the ground to hide her wet eyes from Sam.

Sam reached out and caught her chin between his thumb and forefinger, forcing her to look up at him.

"Ain' no need ter hide yo tears frum me. Ain' Ah done seed you in jes' about evah state o' being dat a person can be in? My chilluns, John and Jane, be growed up, too. Dey's still back in Virginia. John be mahied and Jane fixin' ter be mahied. Who John Wesley done fixin' ter mahy?"

"Sally Spender," Kate responded.

Sam's fingers tightened slightly on her chin. It was the only sign of agitation he showed at the Spender name. His voice was happy when he spoke.

"Ah be glad dat de boy foun sumbody ter love and dat love's him back. Ah done worrit bout him all dese yeahs and he tuhned out fine look like. Since it be a Spender gal, Ah reckon dat be why he leavin' de county. Ah knows it be hahd fo you, but yo dream come true. De boy is growed and foun him sumbody ter git mahied ter." He released her chin and stroked her cheek lightly for a fleeting moment.

"My dream," Kate said with a laugh. "I reckon I got my dream in a way, but it ain't quite what I wanted. He took up with a Spender cause wouldn't none of the other girls have him. He's a fine man, Sam, but ain't nobody forgot about the past. You're Mama told me a long time ago that they wouldn't forget. She was right. Where is she anyway? Ain't she with you?"

A look of pain crossed Sam's face. "No, Miss Kate, she ain' wif me. She died back las' yeah. In de summer it wuz. She wuz out in de gahden and just dropped ovah. By de time we got dere, she wuz gone." Seeing the tears streaking Kate's face, he continued, "Doan be grieving too much, Miss Kate. She got huh dream befo' she died. She was free and so wuz huh fambly. She died a happy woman."

"Oh, Sam," Kate wept. "I cain't believe she's gone. She was such a good friend to me. I loved her so much. I always hoped that I'd see her again one day. To thank her again for all that she did for me."

Reaching into the worn haversack slung across his shoulder, Sam pulled out an equally worn book. He handed to Kate. She took it with shaking hands. Looking closely, she realized it was Aunt Mary's old Bible. The one shee had used to teach the family to read. She tried to hand it back to Sam, but he wouldn't take it.

"Dat be one ob de reasons Ah cum back heah. Ah know my mammy would want you ter hab dat ter remember her by. You keep it, Miss Kate."

Folding her arms around the book, holding it close to her chest, Kate questioned, "One of the reasons you came back?"

"Yas'm. Ah cum back ter give back de money Mist' Angus gibed ter me ter take my fambly ter Virginia. He jes broke down and cried wen Ah gibed it to him. He say Ah din' hab ter pay him back. Dat de money wuz a gift, but Ah din' see it dat way. Ah allus planned ter come back wen Ah could and gibe de money back. He be de one tole me wheah ter fine you. "

"Come on in the house and sit a spell, Sam. No need to stand around here in the yard. Maybe John Wesley will come home in a little bit and you can see him. I know he'll be sorry if you leave before he gits to see you."

Forty-six

They were sitting companionably in the front room when Emily came through the door. She looked taken aback to see a strange black man sitting in their home. Her eyes shot a question at Kate.

"Emily, this here is Sam Stancel. Him and his mama gave me a home some years ago. They left the county, but he's back visiting for a day or two and stopped in. Sam, this here is my cousin, Emily. She's been living here with me and my boys. We're all sharecropping together."

Sam's dark liquid eyes looked over Emily silently. Smiling, he said, "Please t'meet ya, ma'am. Any friend o Miss Kate is a friend o mine."

Stiffly Emily replied, "It's nice to meet you to. I reckon I'll just go on out and do some work in the garden and let ya'll catch up on old times." She backed out the door without ever taking her eyes off Sam.

"Don't mind Emily, Sam." Kate said. "It ain't nothing personal. She just don't know how to act around black folks. Jeb and Sula come around ever now and then and she acts just the same with them."

"Ah ain' worrit bout whut she be thinkin'. Ah came by ter gib you dat Bible and ter see wif my own eyes dat you is doin' fine. Mist' Angus tole me you got yosef another boy since Ah last seen you."

"Yes I do. He was born a little over a year after ya'll left. He ain't got no daddy, just like John Wesley. It don't seem to bother him as much as it always did his brother. I reckon they're just different kinds. Tell me about what all ya'll been doing all these years."

"Well, Miss Kate. Ah be on my way ter Alabama."

"Alabama! Why in the world would you be going there?"

"Wen we wuz livin' at de school at Hampton in Virginia, dere wuz a man by de name of Booker T. Washington dere. We got to be real good friends and den a few yeahs ago, he went ter a place called Tuscaloosa, Alabama ter start a school fo' blacks dere. It be call Tuskegee. He wanted me an' my fambly ter come wif him wen he lef', but Ah wudden ready ter leave jes yet. Den a few months ago, he wrote ter me and asked would Ah come ter Alabama now and hep him wif dis school. It a real good school, he say, and Ah wuz ready ter move on ter somewhere's else. Ah wrote him back dat Ah'd be glad ter come down dere and hep out. Anudder friend o mine wuz goin' down dere too, so Permelia and our three young uns went wif him and Ah come back this away so's Ah could pay back Mist' Angus and see you."

"I don't reckon Permelia cared nothing about seeing me again!" Kate laughed. "We never did git along. Always fighting like cats and dogs. I don't know how you and Aunt Mary stood it all the time. I sure am glad that everything worked out so fine for you and your family, Sam. I don't know anybody whos deserves it more."

"Whut about you, Miss Kate. Ain' you doin' all right? How come you ain' nevah foun' yosef some man ter marry up wif and tek care of you?"

"Sam, you know me better than most people. You know my story. Did you really think for one minute that any man would forget about my past and ask me to marry him? A woman who's own family still don't speak to her and has two bastard boys in the bargain? No, Sam. I didn't ever think that would happen and it didn't. I've done just fine without a man. I don't need nobody to take care of me. I can do for myself now. Specially since I got two growed boys to help. Course, John Wesley will be leaving soon, but Sherman will still be here to help me out."

"Sherman!" exclaimed Sam. "Lawd God, Miss Kate, you ain' changed one little bit. Naming a boy Sherman in dis paht o de country is like waving a red flag at a bull. You shoulda' known betta dan ter do sumpin lak dat."

"You know my family were Union supporters. You know about my brothers dying in battle. Why shouldn't I name my son after a Union general?"

Sam shook his head and laughed. "Miss Kate, you is smaht enough ter know de answa ter dat. No wonder ain' no man evah asked you ter marry him. You is too stubborn and foolish fo' any man ter live with fo' a lifetime."

Kate bit back the hurt reply that sprang to her lips. There was nothing she could say anyway. Sam knew her far too well. She was stubborn and foolish. It surprised her just a little that it hurt to hear those words from her old and valued friend.

Just then John Wesley and Sherman came through the door. John Wesley stood in amazed silence at the sight of his old friend. Sam rose from his chair exclaiming over how the little boy he had know had become such a fine man. John Wesley enveloped Sam in a bear hug, then introduced his younger brother. He explained that this was the Sam he remembered so fondly from his childhood. Sherman extended his hand to Sam in greeting.

They all sat down and began to talk over old times. Kate was amazed when John Wesley related to Sam what had happened when he demanded to know the truth of his origins from his mother. He laughed loudly when he related how Jebidiah had found him in the corncrib, then, when John Wesley had acted in a surly manner, threatened to take a strap to him if he didn't do as he was told. His imitation of the mild mannered Jeb in his fit of temper with the recalcitrant young boy he had been brought tears of laughter to all their eyes. Sam listened to the story, laughing in the right places, but Kate could see the sorrow in his eyes. Sam had known John Wesley well as a child and must surely realized how much pain had been involved in the incident now being related so lightly. Kate knew that her son had come a long way from that wounded boy to be able to laugh about the incident so easily now.

Sherman sat big-eyed through the tale, laughing with them, but also looking both puzzled and slightly troubled. Kate was uneasy about that look. Sherman had never inquired about his own father. Looking at him now, she wondered if he had thought all these years that he and his brother shared the same father. She shook off the foreboding that filled her. Though the worst of the local gossip had died down by the time Sherman was old enough to truly understand what it was about, surely he must have heard some version of the story over the years. Kate had never told anyone who had fathered her second son, had let them speculate all they wished, but never given them a clue as to his identity. Perhaps Sherman had heard some garbled version of the two tales and thought they were one and the same. She put the thought out of her mind for the time being. Sam visit was too precious to waste it in speculation of what was going through her younger son's mind just now. There would be plenty of time to work that out later.

All too soon, Sam said he must be on his way. He was staying with Jeb and Sula and they would be wondering what was keeping him. He would stay the night with them, then be on his way to Alabama at first light.

John Wesley was disappointed that Sam couldn't stay longer. He was obviously overjoyed to see his old friend and crestfallen that the visit was such a short one. Hugging Sam in good-bye, he said perhaps he would see him again in the near future. Sam nodded knowingly at the young man, letting him know that his mother had explained the plans for the immediate future.

Sherman shook hands formally with the man whom he had heard about only from his mother and brother, but Kate hugged Sam fiercely and wished him a safe journey and a happy future.

Sam held her hands tightly in his own for a moment, gazing into her face as though to memorize every feature, then turned and was gone.

Emily came into the house, having seen Sam leave. "Well, that surely was a long visit. I reckon ya'll did a heap of talking in all that time."

"Emily," Kate said. "You were welcome to stay in the house and talk with us. We wasn't talking about anything you couldn't know about. Just laughing about old times and Sam was telling us about where he's headed."

"Randall don't believe in mixing with the blacks," Emily replied calmly. "He ain't got nothing against em personal. He just don't think we should mix with em socially."

Kate saw the outraged look on John Wesley's face and the confused one on Sherman's. Before either of them could speak, she said, "I won't say nothing against Randall. He's been good to Sherman. He's a good and fine man. He can believe whatever he wants to, even if I don't agree with his reasoning. I reckon that's why you always take off when Jeb and Sula come around, too. You should have told me before. I won't hold it against you. I'm just glad to have an explanation for the way you been acting. They're my friends and they're gonna stay my friends. I hope Randall understands that." Significantly she added, "I hope you understand that, too. I ain't gonna tell no body how to live their lives."

"I didn't mean nothing against *you*, Kate! If you want to be friends with them, it's fine with me. It's just that Randall don't want me getting mixed up with them, too. Randall ain't got nothing against you personal, it just don't set right with him for you to be socializing with the Nigras. I tried to explain to him, but he still won't see things the way you do. I love him Kate and I hate being torn betwixt the two of you like this. I reckon I'm a coward at heart. I cain't turn away from you for love of him, and I cain't turn away from him for love of you and your boys. "

"I said I understand, Emily. Don't worry none about it. I ain't gonna change the way I live for nobody and I don't expect you to feel like I do about everything either. Like I said, at heart he's a good man, we just don't see eye to eye on this particular subject."

"Well I got a problem with it, Mama!" John Wesley turned angry eyes on his cousin. "You are being a fool, Cousin Emily. You're trying to tippy toe along a fence so's you don't have to take any sides! Well that just ain't right. I know Randall's a good man, but his thinking is dead wrong on this subject. There ain't no harm in being friendly with the blacks. They're fine people! Why if it weren't for Sam and his mama, me and my mama might not be alive today!"

"John Wesley! That's enough. If Emily wants to abide by what Randall Rhodes thinks and says, that's her business. I've had to deal with a lot worse than this in my life. This ain't nothing to be wasting anger and tears over. Some people ain't never gonna agree with us on this, but it only means they're blind, not that they're all bad people."

John Wesley stomped from the room as Emily fled to her bedroom in tears. Sherman looked at her with haunted eyes. "Mama, I need to ask you about something."

Remembering her earlier speculations, Kate was afraid of what he might want to ask about, so she told him she had a headache and didn't feel like answering any questions right now. He went away with head hanging. What an ending for a day that had begun in such joy, she thought to herself.

Forty-seven

    Kate knew she would not be able to put off Sherman's questions for very long. How was she going to handle this problem? Should she come right out and tell Sherman that James was his father and how that came to be? She shivered with the memory of how John Wesley had reacted all those years ago. This situation would be even more difficult to explain. Yet, she would have to tell him eventually. But first she would confront James and let him know in no uncertain terms that she would not allow her son to be manipulated in this way. Should she go to Purdy to confront him at his own home? No, it would be difficult to explain her absence from home for the several hours she would need to make the trip. Also, her presence at the Richmond home would stir up a hornet's nest of gossip. Where could she confront James? After a good deal of thought, she decided that the best place would be at the next dance. Surely he would be there to continue his manipulation of her son. She managed to avoid being alone with Sherman for the next week. When Saturday night came around, she put her plan into motion.

    After Sherman and Emily had left with Randall to go to the dance that evening and John Wesley had gone to meet with Sally, she set out on foot. She planned to accost James outside the barn where the dance was being held. Tired by the time she arrived, she sat in the shadows to watch for James. He had been a drinking man in the past and she was counting on that still being true. If it was, he would come outside to add a little nip of something to his punch out of sight of the others.

That would be her chance.

Sure enough by the time she felt rested and had gathered her anger about her, James emerged from the barn. She breathed a silent prayer of relief that he was alone. She waited until he paused at a wagon she assumed belonged to him, then approached him with silent steps. When he turned away from the wagon and saw her standing silently behind him, he jumped slightly. The reaction please her. He was not prepared for her.

"You keep away from my son!" she hissed in a low voice. "I won't let you manipulate him the way you done me. I won't let you buy him neither."

"Kate!" he replied smoothly. "What a surprise to see you here. But then, perhaps I should have expected it, once you found out about me. I never took you for a fool, even all those years ago."

"I wasn't a fool then, and I ain't one now. I mean it! You keep away from my son!"

"He's my son too, or have you forgotten that?"

"He *ain't* your son. You might have planted the seed that started him, but he ain't your son no more than the kittens born to the first female cat to cross a tom's path."

"Now, Kate, you told me yourself that the child you were carrying was mine. Why deny it now?"

"Ain't I just told you that you planted the seed that started him? But you ain't his daddy."

"I am his Daddy, and I intend to get to know him and to let him know soon that he's my son."

"You ain't his daddy! Where were you when he was born? Where were you when he was growing up on the charity of others and wearing the hand-me-downs from his brother? Where you been for the last fifteen years *Daddy*?" she spat at him. "I'll tell you where you been. You been in your fine house in Purdy with your high class wife. You been trying to get a legitimate son on her. Since that ain't happened, you think you can come out here and upset Sherman's life by claiming him now. Buying him an expensive gift! Trying to sneak your way into his life. He ain't for sale."

"Kate, he's my son. I have every right to get to know him."

"*Rights*! You gave up your rights the day you threw me and John Wesley out of your house with nowhere to go! You ain't got one single right under the sun to be doing what you're doing. You just git on out of here and don't never come back. If Sherman comes looking for you, you just tell him you ain't got time for him. That shouldn't be too hard for you. You ain't never had time before."

A twig snapped off to the side. Both of them turned in that direction. Kate felt the blood drain from her face. Sherman stood in the shadows, not six feet away. They had been so absorbed in their argument that they hadn't been aware of his approach. How much of the argument had he heard? Kate could tell from his ragged breathing that he had heard far more than she would have wanted him to hear. He stepped closer to them and faced James.

"Is it true? Are you my Daddy? Is it true that you threw my Mama and brother out of your house with nowhere to go?" he demanded.

James reached out to the boy, who stepped back just enough to avoid contact. James' hand fell back to his side. "Yes," he said quietly, "I'm your daddy. I would have preferred for you to find out in a gentler way, but your Mama is a headstrong woman. She just had to come here and confront me. Just look at the mess she's made of the situation."

"Don't you say a word against my Mama! She's raised me the best way she could. Maybe we ain't had much, but what we do have, we earned."

Kate saw his arm draw back, as it swung forward; she saw the fiddle in it. Sherman was going to smash it against the wagon and break it forever. Leaping forward, she grabbed his wrist, halting the forward motion.

"Don't!" she cried.

He looked at her in surprise, struggling to pull his arm free. "Why not?" he asked. "You didn't never want me to keep it before. Why keep it now, when I know he was just trying to buy me with it?"

"Keep it, son. Keep it and make beautiful music on it. Make something good come from this. If that ain't enough reason, then keep it to remind you what an evil man tried to do to you."

"Now wait just a minute here!" James exclaimed. "I'm not an evil man. I'm this boy's daddy and I just wanted to get to know him and for him to know me before I told him who I am."

"You ain't never done anything for anybody unless there was something in it for you. I know that from experience." Kate said.

"Kate, I'm a changed man. I know I was cruel to you all those years ago, but I've changed. All these years everything has been falling down around me. My Mama is dead. I've lost a lot of my money. My home is in a town that's more than half dead since most of the businesses moved to the railroad. I know I was an arrogant ass before, but time has changed me. I just want a chance to get to know my son. Can't you grant me that one small wish?"

"No! It ain't no small thing you're asking. He's *my* boy, not yours. Not ever!"

Sherman reached out and grasped her hand. "Come on, Mama," he said. "Let's go home. There ain't nothing for us here."

As they walked away, James called after them, "Sherman, you are my son. Let me get to know you. Let yourself get to know me. You'll see that I'm a good man at heart!"

Neither of them turned to look back at the man standing forlornly by the wagon. They continued home in silence. Once there, they sat in the front room facing each other.

"Tell me, Mama," Sherman said. "Tell me all of it. I want to know the whole story, not just the bits and pieces I heard back there."

Sherman sat quietly as she told him the story of his conception. Her voice was so low that he had to strain at times to hear the awful words. When the telling was done, he felt a deep ache within him for all she had suffered at the hands of the man whom he had thought of as a friend until this night. Moving to sit by her side, he embraced her and cried for her pain and his own loss. She held him close to her the whole while. When his tears had passed, he looked at her with new eyes. Here was a woman who had endured more than he had ever imagined. She was not just his mother; she was much, much more. He only hoped that someday he might find another woman with her strength. The day he found that woman, he would ask her to marry him. For now, he held his mother close to his heart and said, "Don't worry, Mama. I won't ever speak another word to that man. As far as

I'm concerned, they only family I have is you and John Wesley."

It was then that she told him about his brother and Sally Spender. That John Wesley would soon be leaving the county. He would probably never return, but perhaps they would be able to visit him wherever he finally settled.

Sherman was shocked at the news. He had seen Sally with his brother a few times, but not thought anything of it. Everyone knew the Spenders married their own kin. Now he was frightened for his brother. Could he really pull off this plan to run away? Was there any place that the Spenders' would not hunt them down? His mother seemed convinced that it could be done, so he let well enough alone.

Forty-eight

It was a fine early March morning. Jebidiah and Sula rode down the dirt track toward McNairy Station, enjoying the crisp morning air, chatting about nothing in particular. Robins, just recently returned from their winter further south, sang in nearby trees. Wisps of clouds floated high up in a cerulean blue sky. They were totally unprepared to see the body.

Rounding a bend in the road, they saw the legs of a man sticking out from some newly green wild blackberry bushes. Jeb pulled up the mules in surprise. Husband and wife looked quietly at each other for an endless moment, then Jeb climbed slowly down from the wagon to see whos' legs were protruding from the bushes.

He squatted next to the body, reached out a hand and shook it. There was no movement. It was not someone who had imbibed too much the night before and fallen drunk into the bushes. Reaching further into the bushes, Jeb grabbed the arm of the man and pulled him free of the briars. The back of the mans' head was caved in. Dried blood clung in clots to black hair. Jeb turned the man over—and looked straight into the unseeing blue eyes of John Wesley Randsome.

He rocked back on his heels in shock. A loud high pitched keen issued from his mouth followed by another and another.

Sula jumped down from the wagon in shock. When she saw the face of the man lying on the ground next to her husband, tears came to her eyes as she whispered, "Sweet Jesus preserve us!"

Jeb continued to keen as though his heart were breaking. She knelt next to him, putting her arms tight around him, turning his face away from the horror that lay before them. She rocked him against her breast like he was one of their children, muffling the sounds still issuing from his throat. "Jeb?" she said.

When he continued to keen against her breast, she pushed him away from her. Ignoring the pain in his eyes, she shook him by the shoulders, shouting in his face, "Jeb! You gotta pull yosef togetha! Stop that right now! We gotta think whut ter do!"

The hair-raising sounds coming from her husband died away. He leaned away from her and said, "Sweet Jesus, why did it hab ter be me dat foun' dis boy? Ah cain' tek him home ter his Mama lak dis. Ah cain' be de one ter do dat!"

"Hesh now," Sula said softly. "It wuz de Lawd's will dat we be de one's ter fine de boy. At least we be huh friens'. She woan be heahing de news frum no strangers."

"You be right." Jeb sniffled. "We kin break it ter huh mo' gentle dan some would."

"Do you reckon we oughter leab him heah an' go fo' de sherrif fust?" Sula asked fearfully.

"Let's look aroun' and see iffen we kin fin' whut he wuz hit wif. Iffen we fine it, den we'll tek it wif us, but Ah ain' gone ter leab dis boy a layin' out heah no mo'."

They searched the surrounding area, but found nothing that looked like it had been used to crush the skull of John Wesley. Jeb returned to the body, lifted it gently from the ground and placed it in the back of the wagon. Sula climbed in next to him and laid her shawl over John Wesleys faced after Jeb closed the unseeing eyes.

They started slowly in the direction of Kate's home. Both of them silent. Neither in a hurry to arrive with their dire news. Jeb thought back over the years to the night he had had the audacity to ask Kate to teach him to read and she had agreed. It had been a gift beyond his ability to repay. Next he remembered a young, defiant John Wesley hiding out in his corncrib after learning that the rumors about his birth were true. He remembered taking the young boy back to his mother that morning and her relief to see that he was all right. Now he was once again returning John Wesley to his mother. If he could have any wish in the world at this moment, it would be for God to breathe life back into the young man lying in the back of this wagon. He didn't know how he would bear the pain of returning a dead John Wesley to his mother. After all that Kate had born in her life, she did not deserve this. Who could have done it? Why had it been done?

The wagon rattled slowly into the yard of Kate's home. She was on the porch instantly. Jeb found that he could not meet her eyes. He suddenly became very occupied with drawing the mules to a halt and setting the brake on the wagon.

"Jeb!" called Kate in surprise. "What brings ya'll out here so early in the morning?"

Jeb turned anguished eyes to his wife. Sula climbed slowly down from the wagon and went to Kate. Putting her arm around her friend, she said, "Miz Kate, Ah reckon Ah don't know how to tell you this. You allus been so kine ter Jeb and me."

"What is it, Sula? What's happened?" Kate asked in alarm.

Sula led Kate to the back of the wagon. Jeb reached down and slowly drew away the shawl.

Kate's screams brought Sherman and Emily on the run. Sula struggled to hold onto her screaming friend.

"What's going on?" Emily shouted in alarm. "Why's Kate screaming like that?"

As she came even with the back of the wagon, Emily saw what was making Kate scream so loudly. Sherman was walking toward them with a bewildered look on his face. He joined the group at the back of the wagon. Seeing his dead brother's face, he turned instantly to his mother, putting aside for the moment his own grief.

"Nooooo!" the word ripped from Kate's throat like the sound of a dying animal. She climbed into the wagon, throwing herself across the body of her dead son. Her agony seemed to permeate the very air they breathe. Emily and Sherman stood by in dumfounded silence, tears streaking down their faced, unable to move to assist the stricken woman before them.

Jeb climbed into the wagon bed, attempting to gently pull Kate away form her son. Kate clung more fiercely, shaking her head in denial. With tears in his eyes, he said quietly, "Miss Kate, come on now. Ain't nuthin' you ken be doin' fo dis boy now." Kate continued to cling to her son's body. Pulling harder, Jeb spoke more sharply, "Now, Miss Kate, you has got ter let go! We needs ter take him in de house and git him ready ter be buried!"

A deep throated moan was his only answer. "Sherman!" he said. "Git on up heah and hep yo mama!"

Sherman seemed to shake himself free of the spell that held him motionless. Quickly he climbed into the wagon. Pulling at his mother's arm, he attempted to get her to stand up. "Come on, Mama. Jeb's right. We need to take him in the house now."

His voice seemed to penetrate Kate's shock. Slowly, slowly she relaxed her hold on her firstborn and allowed Sherman to assist her from the wagon. When her feet touched the ground, her knees gave way. Sherman quickly caught her before she could fall. His strong young arms holding her erect, he helped her into the house. Jeb gently lifted the lifeless body from his wagon and followed slowly, Emily and Sula trailing numbly behind him.

Sherman gently lay his mother on the settee in the front room, then seemed at a loss as to what he should do. The sound of footsteps on the porch drew his attention. Jeb stood in the doorway, John Wesley cradled tenderly in his arms. Sherman motioned him into the house and pointed the way to John Wesley's room, indicating that Jeb should place his brother there on the bed.

Jeb carried his sad burden into the bedroom Sherman indicated and laid the body on the bed. He arranged John Wesley's body into what he felt was a comfortable position, the laughed silently at himself. The boy was beyond being comfortable in this world. He was in God's hands now. The living would be the ones needing comfort. Accordingly, he went into the front room where Sula, Emily and Sherman stood silently watching Kate. Her keening voice raised the hair on his arms and the back of his neck. Why wasn't anyone comforting her? Why were they all just standing and staring like the? "Whut's wrong wif ya'll?" he demanded indignantly., "Jes standing round lak sat, staring at a woman in pain. Why ain't ya'll comfoting huh."

Sula answered, "Wen we trys to comfot hus, she staht talkin' crazy. She done spooked Sherman good."

Jeb realized the dazed look in Sherman's eyes went beyond the loss of his brother and his mother's pain. There was a confused shock on his face.

"Whut you be talkin' bout, Sula? Whut crazy talk? She be crazy wif grief, she probly jes talkin' out o' huh head."

"Watch," Sula said mysteriously. She went to Kate. Putting her arm around the grieving mother., Sula began to make hushing, comforting sounds. At that point, Kate began to laugh. An eerie, high-pitched sound. There was nothing of joy or happiness in it. It was the laugh of a mad woman. The whites of her eyes stood out around the blue pupil, giving her a look of insanity. Then, Kate began to speak.

"I tried to kill him before he was born." A little giggle escaped her lips. "I tried to kill him before he was born and this is my punishment. The sins of the father. It says so in the Bible. Only he's paid for the sins of his mother!" She began to giggle hysterically again.

Sula looked at Job. *See there?* her look said. *I told you she was acting crazy.* The crazy giggling unnerved Jeb even more than the keening. At least that was normal. The giggling and talking of punishment made his skin creep along his bones, a shiver twitched his body. What in the world was Kate talking about?

Finally, Emily rose to her feet. She went into her bedroom, returning almost immediately with one hand behind her back. She turned sideways to show Jeb a smoky bottle hidden in her hand. Understanding at once, Jeb distracted Kate immediately. Emily slipped two drops from the bottle into a cup of tea. She took the cup to Kate. Standing over her cousin, Emily said, "Here, Kate. Drink this here cup of tea. You need to calm down just a little. Everybody knows that a cup of tea is just the thing to strengthen a body."

Kate looked at her cousin with blank eyes. With a sigh, Emily held the cup to Kate's lips. Obedient as a child, Kate took several gulps of the liquid. They all sat silently watching. Finally Kate's eyelids began to droop. As her posture relaxed, Jeb scooped her up in his arms and carried her to her bedroom where he laid her gently on the bed, pulling a quilt over her. Returning to the front room, he eyed Emily suspiciously.

"Dat wuz laudanum you put in huh tea, wuddn't it?"

"Yes, it was," Emily replied.

"Wheah you be gittin' dat stuff?"

"Don't you be worrying where I got it." She snapped back. "You just be glad I had it. I don't know what we would have done with her without it. She'll sleep for a while now and maybe be in better shape when she wakes up."

Sherman coughed suddenly. All eyes pivoted to the corner where he sat quietly. In the upset over Kate, no one had realized he was in the room.

"Sherman!" exclaimed Emily. "We didn't know you were over there. That stuff I gave your Mama won't hurt her. It'll just make her sleep for a while. It'll help her to git over the shock. We need you to go over to Angus and Sarah's and borrow a mule. Tell them what's happened and that your Mama is sleeping right now. Then you ride into Purdy and bring back the Sheriff. We need to git him to look into this and find out who murdered your brother."

Without a word, Sherman jumped up from his chair, raced across the room and out the door. Emily started after him, but was stopped by Jeb.

"Let de boy go. He needs ter be alone right now. I reckon he be alright by de time he git ter de Macintosh place. Dey's things dat need ter be done heah befo' he git back."

Knowing what he meant, the two women rose. They entered John Wesley's room and stood silently looking at the slain young man. Without a word, the two of them began stripping his clothing from his body. There was no need for them to converse. The ritual was one well known to both of them. The readying of the dead for viewing and burial. Sula went out of the room, leaving Emily quietly gazing at her young cousin. His handsome features were composed and at peace. There was no expression of terror on his still face. *Why, Lord? Emily thought. Why did you see fit to take him now? Now when he had happiness in his grasp? After all he's been through, why did you have to let this happen to him?*

Presently Sula returned with a pan of water and two soft cloths.

Handing them to Emily, she said, "Ah seed Mist' Angus ride into de yahd wif a wagon of wood. Reckon he's gone ter hep Jeb wif de coffin."

    Tenderly they began washing John Wesley's body, their tears mingling with the water. In this way, their sorrow was ingrained on the body before them. Soon, they heard the sound of hammers outside. Jeb and Angus were beginning the construction of John Wesley's last resting place. Knowing what was taking place, they flinched each time a hammer blow was struck. When they had done with the washing, they gently dressed him in the best of his clothes. Even these were worn and faded, but he had no finer ones to wear. Emily lovingly combed his hair, careful to cover the awful gash in his skull. When they had done, John Wesley looked as though he had only lain down for a moment to take a nap. They had done all they could do for him. Retreating from the room, they closed the door quietly. Sitting in the front room they listened to the continuing sound of hammers from outside, each blow striking at their hearts.

    Jeb returned to the house to tell them that the coffin was finished. Angus had gone back home for the time being. He would return with his family this evening.

Forty-nine

Sorrow hung over the house like a suffocating fog as they waited for Sherman to return. In her bedroom, Kate slept in a laudanum-induced haze to make sure she missed the interview with the sheriff. They all held fast to the hope that Kate would be more herself when she wakened. Sula and Jeb sat miserably on the porch, arms entwined, comforting each other silently. Emily, keeping a distance between herself and the sorrowing couple, sat in contemplative silence. Her heart was breaking for her cousin, but how had she ended up in this mess? Her reverie was interrupted when Jeb and Sula suddenly stood up. In the distance, the sound of hooves beat a rhythmic tattoo on the road. Heart pounding, she waited to see who was coming.

Sheriff Walls had arrived, red faced, belly swelling over the waistband of his pants. Cocky looking, despite his paunch. He spat a stream of tobacco juice to the side, hitched his pants to a more comfortable position, then glared at the gathering before him. Without any preamble he said, "Awright. Who found the body?"

Jeb shifted uncomfortably under the inscrutable gaze of the sheriff, then stepped forward. "Ah did, Suh. Ah knowed him since he wuz a little un."

The sheriff's eyes sparked with interest at the disclosure. He seemed to be taking pleasure in Jeb's discomfort. "Wahl now," he drawled. "You a *close* friend of the family, *boy*?"

Emily winced at the sheriff's tone. This was what came from associating socially with nigras. Randall had warned her to keep her distance or it would rub off on her. From the tone the sheriff was taking, he apparently had heard of the notorious Kate Randsome and was enjoying his role here immensely. She decided then to marry Randal as soon as it could be arranged. Her love for Kate warred with her fear of contaminating her own reputation any further by continuing to live in this house. She marveled now at the young woman she had been. So desperate to escape the confines of her own family that she had dared align herself with Kate. How could she have been so naive?

Foot tapping the ground impatiently, arms crossed, the sheriff waited for an answer.

Jeb, obviously aware of the sheriff's attitude, began to look nervous. "Ah knowed Miz Kate and huh boys a heap o' yeahs, suh. She been a good friend ter me an' mah wife."

Sheriff Walls sniffed in contempt. Without takin his eyes off Jeb, he spit another stream of tobacco juice to the side. Switching his chew to the other side of his mouth, he contemplated them all with a suspicious look. "Where, exactly, did you find the body?"

Jeb's eyes sparked for a moment. He replied in a sharp tone, "Ah foun' *John Wesley* on de side ob de road ter Masseyville. Ah din' know it wuz him till Ah turned him ober."

"Don't you be gittin' smart mouthed with me, *boy*. I asked you a straight question and I expect to be answered with some respect." Sheriff Walls shifted his substantial weight from foot to foot as he glared at the unrepentant Jeb.

Calmly, Jeb stared back. Looking the sheriff straight in the eye. Emily wasn't sure what would have happened next if Kate hadn't staggered out of the house. All eyes shifted to her as she stumbled down the porch steps and up to the sheriff. Emily stifled an oath. She had given her cousin enough laudanum to knock out a mule, yet here she stood confronting the sheriff.

"Sheriff! I'm so glad your here!" Kate cried. "I want you to go right over to the Spender place and arrest every man there. One of em killed my son. You just go on over there and arrest all of them to make sure you get the right one."

"Now, Miz Kate. I can see you're distraught over your boy. I cain't be going over the Spender place and arresting every man there just on your say so. Have you got any proof that one of them killed your boy?"

"I don't need the kind of proof you're talking about. John Wesly was fixin' to run off with Sally Spender and git married. Her family must have found out about it and done away with him. I'm sure it was one of them. You go on over there and arrest all of em and keep em in the jailhouse till one of em confesses to the killing. I won't rest till justice is done."

"Miz Kate, I reckon I'll be doin' everything I can to find out who kilt your boy. That's my job and I always do the best I can. I don't want you gettin any false hopes up on this. There don't appear to be no witnesses to what happened. The best I can do is to go around asking *everybody* did they see or hear anything. Unless somebody did see or hear something, I don't reckon we'll ever know who kilt your son."

"Is that what you call justice?" spat Kate. "I don't think you'll be goin to much trouble to find out who kilt the bastard son of Kate Randsome. I just ain't important enough around here for you to put yourself out. I told you who kilt him. You best be gittin over to the Spender place for one of em light out and gets away with killin my son."

"Now, you lissen here, Miz Kate. I got all the sympathy in the world for you, but I won't stand for you making accusations about how I do my job. I don't play no favorites. Who you are ain't got nothin' to do with how hard I try to find your son's killer. I got to have *facts*, ma'am. Facts that you ain't got. I'm gonna git this Nigra to take me to where he found your son. I'll start from there."

"His name is Jeb and he's my friend." Kate stated.

"Yessum, I reckon everybody knows he's your *friend*."

"That's just what I'm talkin about when I say you ain't gonna try to hard to find my son's killer. You got the same attitude that lots of folks got around here. Just cause Jeb and Sula are my friends, ya'll all think I'm not as good as the rest of you. Consorting with niggers is what they call it."

"You just stop right there, Miz Kate. I'm trying to make

allowances for you. I can see you're tore up with grief. You just go on back in the house and let me do my job. My opinion of your personal life ain't got no bearing on finding the killer."

No one had made a move to stop Kate. The sheriff observed the silent witnesses, then barked, "Cain't one of ya'll git this woman back in the house?"

Sherman glared at the sheriff as he took his mother's arm and led her away, protesting the whole time.

Sheriff Walls motioned to Jeb. "Come on, boy. Let's git this over with."

Jeb looked sullen as he mounted the mule Sherman had borrowed from the Macintosh farm. Emily and Sula watched them out of the yard. When they had disappeared from sight, the two turned and went into the house.

Sherman sat on the sofa with him arm around his mother, trying to comfort her. Emily stepped forward and took Kate by the arm. "Come on , Kate. You need to lay down again. You done more harm than good out there just now."

Kate shook off Emily's hand. Giving everyone an unforgiving look, she walked alone to her room. They heard the door slam after her.

"Lawd A Mercy!" exclaimed Sula. "Ah doan know whut done got inter her talkin ter de Sheriff lak dat."

Emily smiled grimly. "What'd got into her is grief. She's off her head. We all know that. Somebody shoulda' stopped her before she had a chance to say anything."

"Whut you tryin ter say? Ah din notice you jumpin' in to stop huh!"

"Well, you're her good friend, why didn't you do something instead of just standing there like a ninny?"

"Why din' Ah do sompin'? You is huh cousin. Why din' you stop huh?"

Sherman jumped in to stop the fight. "The fact is we all just stood there and let her carry on like that. We're all to blame, so let's stop trying to put the blame on each other. We got to pull together now. The sheriff was right. It ain't likely that he'll ever find John Wesley's killer. Who ever done it probably made sure there wasn't nobody around at the time. My brother is dead and ya'll are sitting here fussing at each other!"

The two women looked guiltily at each other and fell silent. They sat waiting for Jeb to return to the farm. When he came back, he just shook his head silently, affirming Sherman's statement that there would be no witnesses to the crime. That the crime scene had told the sheriff nothing.

Sherman and Jeb carried the new made coffin into the front room and sat it on two sawhorses. Sherman carried his brother's body from his room and laid it gently in the coffin. Everything was now ready for whoever might come to offer condolences to the family. They sat silently waiting.

The Macintosh family showed up at sundown. By then Kate had come back into the front room and sat quietly in a chair next to her son. Sarah and Eileen held her as they cried together. The cobbler Sarah brought was placed in the kitchen. After the Macintosh family left, silence again fell over the mourners. By the time the night was far advanced, they decided that no one else would be coming. Jeb and Sula went to their home. Kate, Sherman and Emily retreated to bed.

Fifty

Savannah's feet stumbled slightly as she walked nervously up the steps to Kate's front porch. She had been so shocked by the news of John Wesley's murder. Her reasons for coming here today were her own. Her guilt over her treatment of Kate over the years goaded her to come here offering solace. Would Kate be willing to let the past go? To start afresh after all that had happened? Peering through the open door, she could make out John Wesley's coffin to her right. Seated next to it was Kate, head bowed. The wooden porch creaked a warning as her weight shifted on the old boards. Kate's head snapped up and their eyes met. As her sister recognized her, Savannah suddenly felt waves of anger and rage pouring across the room. Keeping her eyes locked with Kate's, she struggled against the tidal wave of emotion to take a step across the room. Determined to do the right thing, she continued forward. She had managed to take only two steps when Kate shot to her own feet and screamed at her, "Don't you move one step closer to me!" A note of hysteria sang in Kate's voice. A frightening violence was in her eyes.

"Kate," Savannah said in a quavering voice, "I only came to tell you how sorry I am about your boy. To see if there's anything I can do to help you."

"Sorry! You're sorry!" Kate raged. "You ain't seen fit to speak to me in nigh on twenty years! You told me to get off your place and never come back when John Wesley was a baby! You show your face here now and say you're sorry and want to help me?! Git out! Git out before I throw you out with my own two hands!"

Kate's ragged breathing was the only sound in the room as they continued to stare into each other's eyes. Savanah's face was dead white, yet she refused to turn her eyes away from her sister. The deadlock was broken by Sherman running into the room.

"What's all the hollerin' about?" he demanded.

As though a spell had been broken, Savannah looked away from Kate. Reaching her hands out to her nephew, she replied, "I only came by to tell ya'll how sorry I am about John Wesley. I can see how upset your Mama is, but I though it was past time to mend old hurts. A family should pull together in times of sorrow."

"Aunt Savannah," Sherman said as he walked toward her. "I appreciate you coming by. It's been a bad shock to all of us. Mama ain't been herself since Jeb brought John Wesley home."

Just as their hands were about to make contact, Kate shouted, "Don't you touch her, Sherman! Don't you thank her for nothing either! She ain't got no business being here. I done told her to get out and she better be quick about it."

"But Mama, she's come to grieve with us in our time of trouble. She's right, family should come together in their sorrow."

"She's no kin of mine or yourn either. She gave up that right long before you was born. Ain't you ever wondered why she never come around before? Ain't you never wondered why we never talked in your whole life?"

"I know all about what happened in the past, Mama." At her startled look, he continued, "Did you think nobody would be telling me about it in all these years? Did you think the other children wouldn't use it to jeer at me? I know all about it, Mama. I say we should pull together now and let by gones be by gones."

"Son, if you knew as much as you think you know, you would turn this woman away just like I'm doing. She has no right to be coming here now when death has took your brother away from us. She's only here to salve her own guilty conscience. She ain't here out of love. She's here because she's always cared more for what other people think than about family. I speak from experience."

Doubtfully, Sherman looked from his mother to his aunt. "Is that true, Aunt Savannah? Are you only here because of what people might say iffen you didn't come?"

Savannah shifted uncomfortably under Sherman's demanding blue gaze. When she looked away, Kate crowed in triumph. Savannah looked at her sister.

"You ain't never understood me, Kate. I tried. I really, truly tried all those years ago. I just wasn't strong enough. I've been mournful over what happened for all these years. I ain't a strong woman, Kate. I ain't never been a strong woman. I love you in my own way. You done alright without me all these years."

"Done alright!" Kate spluttered. "How can you say I done alright when you know what you do? I survived, Savannah. Pure and simple. I done what I had to do to git by. I don't call that doin' alright. Iffen you cain't understand my feelings after all this time, then you ain't never gonna understand me. I reckon I don't understand you neither. Iffen we had been in each other's place, I would have stood up for you against anybody, cause that's what families do. They stick up for each other no matter what. Coming here today to tell me you're sorry about my boy ain't gonna change what's past and I ain't of a mind to let it go. Iffen you wanted to change things, you should have come to me years ago. Your kind of love ain't worth having, Savannah. You best be leaving now. There ain't nothing here for you."

"Has Sheriff Walls arrested anybody?" Savannah demanded.

Contempt written all over her face, Kate answered, "The good sheriff ain't very concerned about justice for the likes of us."

"Pride's a cold companion, Kate. I would think you would've learnt that much by now."

Kate stood silently, refusing to answer. Savannah looked helplessly at Sherman. He turned his eyes away from her. Kate pointed to the door, a hard look marring her face. Silently Savannah turned away and walked quietly out the door.

Sherman turned to his mother. "Well, Mama, I reckon you'd best be tellin' me all of it now. Reckon what I heard over the years cain't be all of it iffen you ain't willing to let your own sister mourn with us."

"Now ain't the time to be hearin' about what's past. You just take my word for it that that woman did more harm to me than a body can forgive. There ain't but one other person that done me as much harm as she did."

"Mama, how can I just take your word for something I don't know about? I'm a grown man. I deserve to know what happened that you cain't forgive."

"Don't you question me, boy! I'm your Mama. All you need is my word. You ain't grown yet by any means. When you *are* grown, I'll tell you the whole story, but you ain't grown enough to hear it yet."

Sullenly Sherman looked away.

"Now don't you sull up on me, son. We'll be burying your brother in the morning. This ain't no time for us to be fighting over the past."

Sherman stomped out of the house. Kate sat down. She was so exhausted by everything. She wanted only to be alone. To lose herself in the past, remembering John Wesley as a child. Remembering the happy years with the Stancels.

Fifty-one

Kate sat in silence throughout John Wesley's funeral. So few had come to pay their respects to such a fine young man. None of her family had come. Even Sally Spender had not shown her face. The sudden opening of the door startled her. As though conjured from her thoughts, she saw an ashen faced Sally. The girl ran to her, burying her head in Kate's lap she began weeping hysterically.

"Oh, Miz Randsome," the girl wailed. "I cain't believe he's gone. I cain't believe my Johnny's gone forever!"

Kate snapped out of her shock, roughly shoving the girl from her lap. "MURDERER!" she shouted. "Git up offen the floor. Git away from me! How can you show your face here after what you caused?!"

Crumpled on the floor, Sally looked stricken. "Muderer?" she questioned.

"Yes! Murderer! Iffen John Wesley hadn't took to courtin' you, he'd still be here today. You kilt him. You kilt him as sure as if you had been the one to bash his head in yourself! You claimed to love him, but you didn't even have the common decency to come to his funeral. What kind of love is that?"

"I *did* love him!" Sally said defiantly. "We was gonna go away together. He's the only man I ever loved. I couldn't come to the funeral, cause my Daddy locked me in the corn crib to keep me from goin'!"

"That's a fine tale to tell. Why would your Daddy lock you in the corn crib?"

"Somehow he found out about me and Johnny. I reckon him or my brothers was aspying on us when we met. I don't know how he found out, but he did. He swore no daughter of his was going to run off with a no account like John Wesley. I tried to tell him he was wrong, but he wouldn't listen to me!"

Kate stood abruptly. "I knew it!" she said. "I told the sheriff that one of your menfolk killed my son! He claimed he question all of 'em and he was sure they didn't have nothing to do with the killin', but I knew it. A mother's heart always knows. Git on back home to your family! I was right. Your love killed my son. I don't ever want to lay eyes on your face again. Iffen he had listened to me, he would never have took up with you. I told him your family would never stand for the two of you marrying up. I was right. You killed him with your love."

Tears streamed in a river down Sally's face as she begged, "Miz Randsome, don't turn on me now! I need you! I'm gonna have Johnny's baby. I cain't keep it from my family much longer. Maybe they already suspicion it. I been sick in the morning for a week now. My Mama's been giving me hard looks. You gotta take me in! When they're sure I'm gonna have a baby, I don't know what they might do to me! This is your grand baby I'm gonna have, Miz Randsome. Have some pity on me!"

Kate turned a stony gaze on the girl groveling at her feet. Her heart thudded painfully in her chest. She replied in a remote voice, "John Wesley never said nothing about you having his baby. How do I even know that it's his? You're a sneaky girl, Sally. How do I know you ain't been layin' up with men other than my son?"

The look on Sally's face cut her to the bone. Almost her heart melted as the pitiful girl wept. "Miz Randsome! You k now that I loved Johnny with all my heart. There ain't never been no other man. This is Johnny's baby."

"That's what you say," Kate answered coldly, "but I seem to remember you telling John Wesley in a round about way that your menfolk been doing things to you. I don't reckon John Wesley ever cottoned on to exactly what you mean't by that, but I surely knew what you meant."

Sally gasped at the cold voice. "I swear to you on my life that this is Johnny's baby. I thought you, of all people, would understand what's happened and help me."

"You're a right smart girl, Sally." Kate said stiffly. "But my past ain't got nothing to do with you. I didn't git nobody kilt with my love. I don't believe that you're carrying John Wesley's baby. He knew what happened to me. He was too honorable to chance putting another woman in the same position I was in all those years ago."

"He didn't know I'm carrying his baby. I was gonna tell him after we was married. We'd be married now iffen he hadn't been kilt. Everythang would have been alright."

"I don't believe that baby belongs to my son. Iffen it weren't for you, he'd still be alive today. I won't ever forgive you for that. I know your kinfolk kilt him even if it ain't ever proven that they did. I don't want to have anything to do with you. Go on home to your family and make out the best you can."

"Miz Randsome, I cain't believe you taking this view. Johnny told me about what happened to you. I thought you'd understand and take care of me and your grand baby. I don't know what my family will do when they find out."

"You were a fool to come to me. I ain't got no forgiveness in my heart. Now go on home!"

Kate watched silently as Sally got up off the floor, straightened her slender shoulders and marched stiffly out the door. Following her, Kate watched the young girl walk away, never turning her head to look back.

She felt a guilty glow of satisfaction at having vented her rage at Sally Spender. The girl had caused John Wesley's death whether she believed it or not. What did she mean coming here with that wild story about carrying her grandchild? Did she think Kate was a fool? A voice whispered in her head that the two had planned to be married in a few weeks. If there was a child it would not have been born illegitimate. She shook off the uncomfortable thought. Kate knew her son would never have put Sally in that position. Not after the treatment he had received all his life for the crime of being a bastard. No, Sally *must* be lying.

~ * ~

The next afternoon, as she was preparing their meal, Sherman came bursting through the door shouting for her. She went to the front room and found him doubled over the back of the sofa, out of breath. When his eyes caught hers, she could see he was in shock. Fearing something had happened to him, she rushed to his side. She began feeling his back and shoulders, looking for some kind of damage. He pushed her hands away and stood upright. Tears began streaming down his face. She looked at him in alarm.

"What's happened?" she questioned. "Has somebody been hurt? Have you been hurt?"

"It's Sally!" he gasped.

"Sally?"

"Oh, Mama! Sally Spender is dead! I heard the news from Angus just a little while ago. I stopped by their place to see about borrowing a mule to ride into town and he told me they found her this morning. She was hanging from a tree down by the crick where she used to meet up with John Wesley. Angus just heard about it. He was aiming to ride over here to see you, but I told him I'd tell you myself. I just cain't believe it. Why would she kill herself like that, Mama?"

He continued to weep and gasp for breath as Kate regarded him with astonishment. Sally's visit yesterday came back to her in vivid detail.

She shook Sherman by the arm, shaking him roughly. "Did Angus say that she hung herself? Is that what the sheriff thinks happened?"

"Well, Angus said that's what he heard. That she hung herself. He couldn't figure why. Unless it had to do with John Wesley being dead. Maybe she didn't want to live with him gone."

Kate's knees felt suddenly weak. Sally had pleaded with her for help. In her anger and pain she had turned the girl rudely away. Had Sally killed herself? Or had someone in her family done it for her as Sally had feared?

Sherman interrupted her self-examination. "Why, Mama? Why would she do that? Do you think it was because of John Wesley?"

"I don't know what to think, son. She always said she loved John Wesley more than anything. Maybe she did it because of him. Maybe she did it for some reason we don't know about. I don't reckon we'll ever know for sure now."

Epilogue

Was Sally really carrying my grandchild? Did she die by her own hand? Or did some member of her own family make it look like she did? Those are questions I've lived with for more years than I care to remember. In my grief and anger I turned her out of my house. She died before my feelings had cooled, so I never had the opportunity to make amends to her. I've often wondered if I had been more like Aunt Mary, would Sally be alive today? Would her child have born the look of my son? If I had reached out to her, the way Aunt Mary reached out to me, I could have changed her life. The way mine was changed. But Aunt Mary hadn't lost a son because of me. She could give free rein to her generous spirit without the grief and anger that filled me. Did I make my own Hell through my stubborn pride? These are questions I have never been able to answer for myself. I can only hope with all my heart that you will never travel that road I so blithely set my feet upon so many years ago. Good-bye, my beloved Mary Susan. May God bless and keep you.

Memories that had long ago been locked away behind iron doors in the recesses of Sherman's mind flooded his brain in a viscous tide. Old pain and shame seared him in red and black waves that caused him to crush the pages convulsively between his hands and bow his head. An untold time later he looked up to see a room unchanged by the maelstrom that had shaken his soul. The fire had burned down low. He stood with shaking knees and threw another log on the fire, stirring the embers to make it catch. The manuscript lay on his chair like a coiled snake, ready to strike. Reaching out, he picked it up and was seized by the need to destroy it, to erase the written evidence of his mother's pain and shame.

A knock sounded at the door just as he drew back his arm to fling the hateful pages into the hungry flames. He turned in surprise, letting his arm drop to his side. The knock sounded again. Opening the door, he found a stranger holding a lantern. Light spilled across shabby pants that bagged around worn boots. As the stranger lifted the lantern higher, Sherman could make out the face more clearly. A weathered face with sunken cheeks, framed by graying hair. Still he did not know the man at his front door. As he was about to ask the man why he was there, Sherman's attention was caught by the stranger's eyes. Cornflower blue they were and so familiar in some way. As he continued to hesitate, the stranger cleared his throat and spoke in a hoarse voice, "I reckon you're wondering who I am and why I'm calling here so late." The stranger scuffed his feet on the boards of the porch, looked out into the night, then looked back at Sherman.

"Fact is, I just got into town yesterday. I was aiming to talk to your Mama and hoping to set some thing to rights. I went to Savannah and Thomas first to kind of see how things were and they told me your Mama was dead, but they wouldn't' say anything else, except where to find you. I'm your Uncle George, you see. I don't reckon your Mama ever told you about me. I reckon she had some hard feelings toward me."

Suddenly, the vague sense of familiarity was answered. The eyes looking into his own were like his mother's! This was the brother who had abandoned his mother to the fate she had faced so bravely. Anger began to boil in his heart.

The man before him shifted uncomfortably, as though sensing Sherman's' feelings. Looking uncertain, he said, "I did your Mama a great wrong years ago and I came home to beg her forgiveness. It's too late now, but I wanted you to know I've regretted it deeply for a long time. I just could never get up the courage before now to come back here and face her."

Violence danced along his muscles. Sherman clenched his fists in preparation to strike the disgusting man before him. Realizing his right hand wouldn't close, he glanced down and saw that he was still holding the manuscript. His hatred for those pages mingled with his hate for the man standing before him. Thrusting the pages into the man's chest, he said, "My Mama wrote this for my daughter, but she should have written it for you! Every horror and pain and shame that she survived is written on those pages! Take them! Take them and get out of here! I don't ever want to see you or those pages again!"

His Uncle George clasped the pages reflexively against his chest and opened his mouth to speak. Before a word was uttered, Sherman slammed the door. The bolt clicked home with a resounding finality.

~ * ~

A rider passing along later glanced curiously at the stranger shuffling slowly down a lonely country road. Head hanging, arms clasping something to his chest, the stranger was quietly crying.

Dear Readers,

This book has been a dream come true for me. I've always wanted to be an author and now you hold the culmination of that dream in your hands. Thank you very much for choosing to read KATE'S PRIDE. There are so many books available on the market that I am truly thrilled that you chose this one. One more thing I'd like to offer you in return for reading this book. As a long time reader myself, I've always thought how wonderful it would be if I could actually talk to the author to ask questions or just find out more about the characters in the story. So, dear reader, I make this offer to you. If you have a book club that chooses to read this book, please email me to set up a question and answer session for your group. It will need to be in the evening or on a weekend and your group will need access to a speakerphone. If you aren't a member of a book club, but have questions feel free to contact me. All enquiries should be directed to fictionvixen@earthlink.net. Be sure to put the book title in the subject line.

Again, Thank You!!!

Sincerely,

Reneé Russell

Meet Reneé Russell

Reneé Russell has loved books since before she could read them herself. As young as the age of 2, her mother would find her with a book in hand, upside down, reciting the story from memory. As a teenager Reneé's dream was to become a published author, but the dream was put on hold while she pursued a business degree and a career in the business world. She currently works in the investment and insurance industry and freelances for The Commercial Appeal. A seventh generation West Tennessean, Reneé shares her home with her husband, Gerald and their cat, Gambit.

**VISIT OUR WEBSITE
FOR THE FULL INVENTORY
OF QUALITY BOOKS**:

http://www.wings-press.com

*Quality trade paperbacks and downloads
in multiple formats,
in genres ranging from light romantic
comedy to general fiction and horror.
Wings has something
for every reader's taste.
Visit the website, then bookmark it.
We add new titles each month!*